A DAMNED FINE WAR

★ ★ ★ ★ ★ ★ ★ ★ ★ ★ ★ **BILL YENNE**

BERKLEY BOOKS, NEW YORK

A DAMNED FINE WAR

A Berkley Book / published by arrangement with the author

PRINTING HISTORY
Berkley mass-market edition / August 2004

Copyright © 2004 by William Yenne.
Cover Photo © Joseph Sohm/Visions of America,
LLC/PictureQuest.
Cover design by Steve Ferlauto.
Interior text design by Kristin del Rosario.

Visit our website at www.penguin.com

ISBN: 0-425-18450-1

BERKLEY®
Berkley Books are published by The Berkley Publishing Group,
a division of Penguin Group (USA) Inc.,
375 Hudson Street, New York, New York 10014.
BERKLEY and the "B" design
are trademarks belonging to Penguin Group (USA) Inc.

PRINTED IN THE UNITED STATES OF AMERICA

10 9 8 7 6 5 4 3 2 1

RED SLAUGHTER

The Russians were on the street. They were on the bridge. Now they were in the boarding school. In the distance, toward the center of town, there were sounds of small-arms fire. A long burst from a Thompson sub-machine gun was interrupted by the all-too-familiar clatter of Russian small-arms fire.

Nate could see Americans on the street now. Bob Epperly, the Staff Sergeant from E Company who had saved his life at Marburg. The guys that he bunked with. The guys who had been asleep in the same room that he'd just left.

The Russians were now lining the Americans up against the side of the school. There must have been about a hundred guys. Nate couldn't look, but he did. He even put his Leica back up to his eye. It was over in a few seconds, but it seemed longer. Nate had been in some of the toughest combat faced by American soldiers in history, but he'd never seen men lined up and shot in cold blood.

PRAISE FOR

A DAMNED FINE WAR

"Bill Yenne's *A Damned Fine War* is an action-packed, Patton-size novel. Powerful and compelling, this great read captures the crucial decisions and events associated with the final days of World War II, and more importantly for history, the potential for global domination by one man and one nation. This book, a classic battle between good and evil played out on an international stage, is fast moving and entertaining. Any person interested in history will be properly moved by the what-if scenarios involving victorious armies and men of history. *A Damned Fine War* also shines as it explores the potentially catastrophic potential at the end of World War II, a titanic struggle that eventually produced a superhero with four stars on a gleaming helmet. A great read. I highly recommend it!"

—Brian Sobel, author of *The Fighting Pattons*

CONTENTS

PROLOGUE   1
   (May 21, 1945)

PART I
EIGHT DAYS IN MAY   5
   (May 22–May 29, 1945)

PART II
A DAMNED FINE WAR   109
   (June 6–July 4, 1945)

PART III
HAMMER AND SICKLE   243
   (July 4–August 6, 1945)

PART IV
THE BUCK STOPS HERE   309
   (September 3–December 7, 1945)

EPILOGUE   429
   (December 12–21, 1945)

ABOUT THE AUTHOR   435

A NOTE REGARDING
THE EVENTS
AND CHARACTERS

This book is a work of fiction that departs from historical reality on May 21, 1945. All of the attributed quotes given on the previous pages are real. The geopolitical situation that existed on May 21 is accurate, and all of the events that occurred prior to that date actually happened. The United Nations Conference in San Francisco had begun on April 25. World War II in Europe had ended two weeks earlier on May 7. The events that the author describes as having occurred on and after May 21, 1945 are fictitious. One exception concerns the references to sixteen Polish leaders arrested by the Soviet Army. This arrest did, in fact, occur in March 1945 as stated, but news of it reached the West approximately two weeks before it does in this story.

Certain historic, public figures who were alive in 1945 are used as characters in this fictitious work. In addition to General George Smith Patton, Jr., all military officers with a rank of major general or higher are real people who, in May 1945, held the posts attributed to them. So too are Adam Pragier and Father Cantillion, as well as all heads of state and cabinet members. Other characters, especially Rosemary O'Leary and Nathaniel McKinley, are entirely fictitious.

The Fourth of July segment was written eleven months before similar events actually did occur in the same city. And, yes, the *Smolnie* was really there.

VICTORY IN EUROPE, MAY 1945

The crusade on which we embarked in the early summer of 1944 has reached its glorious conclusion. It is my especial privilege, in the name of all nations represented in this theater of war, to commend each of you for the valiant performance of duty.

Full victory in Europe has been attained.

—General of the Army Dwight D. Eisenhower,
Supreme Allied Commander
(Order of the Day to the Troops.
Rheims, France. May 8, 1945.)

This is a solemn but a glorious hour. General Eisenhower informs me that the forces of Germany have surrendered to the United Nations. The flags of freedom fly over all Europe. For this victory, we join in offering our thanks to the Providence which has guided and sustained us through the dark days of adversity.

Our Armies of Liberation have restored freedom to these suffering peoples, whose spirit and will the oppressors could never enslave.

—Harry S. Truman,
President of the United States
(Radio address to the world.
Washington DC. May 8, 1945.)

On the continent of Europe we have yet to make sure that the simple and honorable purposes for which we entered the war are not brushed aside or overlooked in the months following our success, and that the words "freedom," "democracy," and "liberation" are not distorted from their true meaning as we have understood them. There would be little use in punishing the Hitlerites for their crimes if law and justice did not rule, and if totalitarian or police governments were to take the place of the German invaders.

> —Winston Spencer Churchill,
> Prime Minister of Great Britain
> (BBC radio address. London. May 13, 1945.)

One swift blow to Poland, first by the German Army and then by the Red Army, and nothing was left of this ugly offspring of the Versailles Treaty.

> —Vyacheslav Mikhailovich Skriabin Molotov,
> Foreign Commissar of the Soviet Union
> (Speaking on the defeat and dismemberment of Poland
> by the Soviet Union and Nazi Germany.
> Moscow. October 31, 1939.)

The Soviet Union has always kept its word, except in cases of "extreme necessity."

> —Josef Vissarionovich Dzhugashvili Stalin,
> Supreme Commander-in-Chief and Marshal
> of the Soviet Union
> (To United States presidential envoy Harry Hopkins.
> Moscow. May 1945.)

Words have no relation to actions, otherwise, what kind of diplomacy is it? Words are one thing, actions another. Good words are a concealment for bad deeds. Sincere diplomacy is no more possible than dry water or wooden iron.

> —Josef Vissarionovich Dzhugashvili Stalin,
> Supreme Commander-in-Chief and Marshal
> of the Soviet Union.

They have allowed us to kick the hell out of one bastard [Hitler] and at the same time forced us to establish a second one [Stalin] as evil or more evil than the first. We have won a series of battles, not a war for peace. We're headed down another long road to losing another peace. This day we have missed another date with our destiny, and this time we'll need Almighty God's constant help, if we're going to live in the same world with Stalin and his murdering cutthroats.

I wonder how the dead will speak today when they know that for the first time in centuries, we have opened Central and Western Europe to the forces of Genghis Khan. I wonder how they feel now that they know there will be no peace in our times and that Americans, some not yet born, will have to fight the Russians tomorrow, or ten, fifteen, or twenty years from tomorrow.

> —General George Smith Patton, Jr.,
> Commanding General, United States Third Army
> (Speaking to the press at Third Army Headquarters.
> Regensberg, Germany. May 8, 1945.)

PROLOGUE
★ ★

Luna County, New Mexico
Monday, May 21, 1945, 6:16 a.m.

AGAINST the vivid cobalt blue of the retreating night, the peaks of the Mogollon Mountains blazed blood-red in dawn's earliest light.

You could live here all your life and never tire of the mystical, magical beauty of the place. New Mexico highway patrolman Larry Zamora had lived here all of his life. He still loved it.

The only time he'd ever been away was between 1938 and 1942, during a stint in the Merchant Marine. He'd seen the world. He'd seen the war. He'd seen the worst of the war, crossing the icy cold North Atlantic in convoys being hunted by the German wolf packs. He'd had two freighters shot out from under him. He nearly starved to death the first time and nearly froze to death the second. Now he was back in Las Cruces with a state civil service job, and was planning never to leave again.

Larry was heading southwest on State Route 26 in his 1936 Plymouth patrol car, watching the shadows change like ghosts on the side of Cooks Peak and thinking about how glad he was that the damned war was finally over. Well, at least *half* of it was over. If Uncle Sam could beat Hitler, he could certainly whip Hirohito.

It had been more than a week since VE-Day and the celebrating had pretty much died down. The bars had closed early most places through the weekend, but now, things were getting back to what passed for normal. Everybody had slept off the festivities and was back to work.

Of course, for the folks who had family fighting in that terrible battle out on Okinawa, and Larry knew several, there really hadn't been much to celebrate. Yet.

He stopped for a cup of coffee in Deming and turned south on State Route 11 toward Columbus. It was a pretty routine day. Not many cars on the road. When the war ended and rationing stopped, that would all change, but for the time being, New Mexico highways were about as empty as they'd been back when Larry was a kid.

Off in the distance, He saw the lights of another car. It seemed to be stopped. As he approached, he saw that it was an old Ford pickup. The man standing next to it was dressed in overalls and a straw hat. He was looking off to the side of the road.

As Larry approached, he saw what the man was staring at. There was a car down in the arroyo that paralleled Route 11. The poor bastard must have gone off the road during the night.

The man in the straw hat watched as Larry pulled the patrol car to a stop and got out.

"Mornin'," Larry said.

"Mornin'," the man replied. "Looks like a car went in the ditch here."

"Yup. Looks that way," Larry said. "Didja see it happen?"

"Nope. I was just drivin' by. Seen it down there."

"Didja see anybody down there?"

"Nope."

"Well, guess I'd best have a look."

Larry didn't really relish the idea of scuffing up a new pair of Tony Lama boots going down there, but he reckoned this is what the state paid him for.

He scrambled down the steep slope, with the old man following at a respectable distance. They could see the marks on the side of the arroyo where the car had skidded after it left the road.

"Asleep at the wheel, I reckon," the old man ventured.

"I reckon," Larry agreed.

The '41 Buick was upright, but scratches on the roof indicated that it had rolled over at least once. From the distance that it had come, Larry guessed that it had probably been traveling about seventy miles per hour when it left the road. The windshield was shattered.

As he approached, Larry could see a man slumped in the front seat. He wasn't moving.

"Don't touch anything," Larry admonished as they both reached the car.

"Okey dokey," the old man replied, sheepishly putting his hands in his pockets.

After circling the car once, Larry opened the passenger's side door, and felt the pulse in the man's neck. He was dead. Probably a broken neck.

He looked into the back seat. There were sheets of paper everywhere, and at least two large black leather satchels that had apparently come open in the accident. Larry opened the rear door and started looking at the papers. Some of the pages contained long lists of numbers. At first, Larry guessed the man was probably a traveling salesman, and these were his orders or model numbers. As he searched, he found pages containing diagrams with a lot of writing that looked like the algebra he'd learned in school. He wished he remembered some of that algebra so he could read this stuff.

He noticed that one of the bags had a name stamped on it in gold: *Klaus Fuchs*. Larry guessed that this was the name of the company that made the bag. It sounded like a kraut name.

"Whatcha findin'?" The old man asked from a respectable distance away.

"Not much," Larry replied, not altogether sure what he *was* finding. "Guess he musta been a traveling salesman."

"Musta been," the old man said, not fully accepting the uncertainty of the patrolman's assessment.

As Larry leafed through the pages, a file folder slipped out and several pages fell on the ground. Larry could see they were letters. They had been typed on a typewriter using the Russian Cyrillic alphabet. He had seen the Cyrillic alphabet before, on cargo aboard ships that were headed for Russia during the war. He had never expected to see this alphabet again. Certainly not in a gully in Luna County, New Mexico.

He crammed the papers back into the bag as the old man craned his neck to read them.

"Reckon he's probably not from around here," the old man suggested.

"Reckon not," Larry agreed, wishing the old man would back off, but not wanting to raise suspicions by telling him to.

He put the bag back into the rear seat and opened the front

door again. The man was in his late twenties or early thirties, with a round, puffy face. He was well dressed and had been wearing a pair of round-lensed glasses that still hung from his left ear. Larry patted the man's jacket until he located the pocket that contained his wallet. Inside, Larry found a large number of fifty-dollar bills. There was no identification, but the wallet contained the business card of a hotel in Nuevo Casas Grandes, a town about six hours south of the border.

"Where'dya reckon he's from?" the old man asked.

"New York. The car's got New York plates."

"Long way from home. Whatcha gonna do?"

"Send a wire. Let New York figure it out . . . About all I can do."

"Yonder," the old man said, pointing back to the highway.

Larry looked up. There was now a third car parked next to the patrol car and the pickup. Two men wearing hats and dark overcoats were watching them. One of the men had a pair of binoculars.

Larry waved and started walking back toward the two men. When they saw him coming, they ran back to their car. As Larry watched in amazement, they drove off in a cloud of dust, heading south toward the Mexican border.

Though his first instinct was to give chase, Larry knew that by the time he climbed back up out of the arroyo, he would never be able to catch them. They'd be in Mexico in fifteen minutes.

"Whatcha suppose that's all about?" The old man asked, nodding in the direction of Mexico.

"I'm not sure what any of this is all about," Larry shrugged.

PART I

EIGHT DAYS
IN MAY

★ ★ ★ ★ ★

1

★ ★

Headquarters, Third United States Army
Flint Kaserne
Bad Tolz, Bavaria, Germany
Tuesday, May 22, 1945, 5:12 p.m.

A cold wind blew across the immense parade ground that had, not so long ago, echoed with the staccato *thrump thrump* of thousands of goose-stepping Nazi boots. Two entire divisions had room to drill here, and they often had in the days when this was the Junkerschule for the handpicked elite of the officer corps of Adolf Hitler's dreaded Waffen-SS.

Today, as US Army Major General Hobart Richard "Hap" Gay gazed out the window of his second-story office, there was only a single, solitary figure in all that vast expanse. Dressed in a garrison cap and military greatcoat, one man paced back and forth, lost in thought. He seemed small, and almost insignificant. However, until two weeks before, this man had been the most significant military officer of four-star rank in the entire US Army.

General George Smith Patton, Jr. was the closest thing to a warrior king in the classical sense that the US Army had seen in the European Theater of World War II. He was a charismatic tactical genius who had inherited his gift for leading troops in battle from his grandfather, Colonel George Smith Patton, the Confederate hero who was killed in action at Fredericksburg.

Because of his use of speed and mobility in combat, and his habitual insistence on always being as close to the front as possible, General George Smith Patton, Jr. was frequently compared to the legendary cavalry generals of the Civil War. John Bryson of ABC-Radio called him "the greatest military genius since Robert E. Lee and Stonewall Jackson," and "the greatest frontline general in the world."

In his sentiments, Bryson was not alone. Patton was a true media star. The press and public had found him irresistible.

Patton's record in World War II was impressive. From the time of the Normandy invasion in June 1944 until the end of the war in Europe eleven months later, Patton's Third Army had captured more enemy territory and more enemy troops than any other comparable command in American history. Some credited him as being the single Allied Commander most responsible for Germany's final defeat.

Patton's favorite maxim was his often-stated "In case of doubt, attack."

Hap Gay, Patton's chief of staff since the early days of the war, had written in his diary that "Not since 1806 has an army conquered Germany or crossed any large portion of it. I question if anyone . . . as late as last year, felt the war would end with American forces having completely overrun Germany and passed into other countries. This time the Germans know what war at home means."

A 1909 graduate of the US Military Academy at West Point, George Patton had been a member of the 1912 United States Olympic Pentathlon team and had served on General John J. "Blackjack" Pershing's staff during the 1916 Expedition into Mexico. In World War I, he led the US Army's fledgling Tank Corps into battle at St. Mihiel and had become a strong believer in the capacity of armored units to be a decisive factor in battle. As the Commanding General of the Second Armored Division during the 1941 Louisiana-Texas Maneuvers, he'd astounded the Army high command with his spectacular encirclement of the opposing forces.

After having commanded the Western Task Force during the Operation Torch invasion of North Africa in November 1942, Patton had accomplished a repeat of his Louisiana success against the Germans in Tunisia. As Commander of the Seventh Army during the campaign in Sicily, Patton established a reputation for tactical brilliance that reached all the way to Wehrmacht headquarters and Adolf Hitler's inner sanctum in Berlin.

Like his namesake, George Smith Patton, Jr. had wished that he too would die in battle, struck down, as he liked to say, "by the last bullet of the last battle of the last war." But he'd survived the war, and he'd tasted victory.

The job was done. Germany had been defeated. The three-and-a-half-million-man American Army that had helped to crush Hitler's Reich was being rapidly demobilized and sent home, or to finish the war against Japan. For a man like Patton, who had devoted his heart and his soul to achieving the victory, the victory itself was personally devastating.

"There's nothing more of interest to me in the world now that the war is over," Patton had confided in Hap Gay.

In the two weeks since the war had ended, Patton had become increasingly morose, not only because a warrior king is an anachronism in peacetime, but because he was watching the demobilization of American power in Europe, while the power of America's erstwhile ally, the Soviet Union, was increasing.

Patton had met the Soviet generals and he didn't trust them. He'd seen the greed and lust for world domination in their eyes. He'd called them bandits and had predicted that one day, perhaps sooner rather than later, the United States would be faced with having to fight them in Europe.

For their part, the Soviet leaders had found Americans eager to be cordial and accommodating. They had discovered that the American officers, like the American diplomats, were willing to compromise in order to avoid a future war.

All of the American officers, that is, except one.

San Francisco Bay
Tuesday, May 22, 1945, 9:23 a.m.

Rosemary O'Leary had awakened aboard the *City of San Francisco* as the sleek streamliner dashed through the delta of the great Sacramento River. Now Rosie was on the Oakland Pier, about to make the last leg of her transcontinental journey, across the Bay to the Golden Gate City—and home.

The familiar landmarks—the Ferry Building, the Mills Tower and the Russ Building—were all there to welcome her, silhouetted against the wispy fog bank that reached in from the Pacific to finger the grand hotels that stood atop Nob Hill.

Rosie had not been home to San Francisco for nearly five years. Through the darkest days of the war, getting train tickets for nonessential civilian travel from coast to coast had been virtually impossible. For the past year she'd been so busy with her new job with *The Washington Herald* that she couldn't afford the time. Now she was coming home.

Her homecoming was not just that of a lonely girl returning from far away at war's end, it was that of a professional journalist coming to San Francisco for the United Nations Conference at the War Memorial Opera House. The "parley" that would form the United Nations Organization was being treated as the biggest news story involving her hometown since the Gold Rush. The foreign ministers or heads of state of forty-six nations were coming, including the "Big Four" foreign ministers— Anthony Eden of Great Britain; Secretary of State Edward Stettinius; China's T.V. Soong; and the enigmatic Soviet Foreign Commissar, Vyacheslav Mikhailovich Molotov.

In what was described as a burst of bathos, the columnist Edgar Ansel Mowrer had called the United Nations Conference in San Francisco the "most important human gathering since the Last Supper," It was hardly that, but it was possibly the most important human gathering of the decade.

Not only celebrity diplomats would be coming, but celebrity journalists—from Walter Lippman to Walter Winchell—would be flocking to the Golden Gate City to cover the parley. Hedda Hopper and the *New York Post*'s Earl Wilson would be there. The celebrated Elsa Maxwell would be broadcasting live reports.

The Washington Herald was sending its own celebrity reporters—such as Seymour Stern and Richard Waldron—but *among* those on the list was Rosemary O'Leary.

She had to beg for the assignment, but then, all of the cub reporters—especially those who were female—had to beg for anything remotely like a responsible assignment. Rosie had interned at the paper during her last year at Catholic University and worked hard enough to get noticed by Rex Simmons, the cantankerous managing editor—and hard enough to get hired full time. For eight months, she had slaved at the rewrite desk, filling in with the research department whenever possible. Then, one day, she got a chance to cover a press conference at the Navy Department. They ran her story. It was only the beginning.

When the San Francisco conference was announced, she'd jumped at the chance to cover something really historic—and to go home. Rex Simmons laughed and argued. She argued back. The months in the research room paid off. When Waldron couldn't name the members of the Soviet delegation—and Rosie O'Leary *could*—Simmons's eyebrows rolled up into the wrinkles on his forehead. When she promised that she had a place to stay in San Francisco—her parents' flat on Diamond Street—and wouldn't need *The Washington Herald* to book her one of the desperately scarce hotel rooms, Simmons glanced at a glowering Waldron and told Rosie to pack her bags.

Stern and Waldron had gone out to cover the opening ceremonies on April 25, while Rosie remained in the newsroom dealing with dispatches and rumors of the end of the war in Europe, which finally came on May 7. With Hitler disposed of, Rosie headed west. The train trip was like traveling back in time to that late summer day in 1939 when a little girl from a working-class neighborhood headed out to the big Eastern college. She'd been the first of Tommy O'Leary's granddaughters to leave the state to go to college, and she'd been the first of the granddaughters to actually graduate.

On that morning in 1939 when Rosie headed east, the whole family had come down to see her off. She'd been so proud and so smug when she boarded the train, her big, new hat flapping in the stiff breeze. She'd been so proud and so smug as she waved goodbye to those who would stay behind while she went off to conquer the world. But as soon as the Golden Gate City had slipped behind the toast-colored East Bay hills, the emptiness and loneliness formed as a lump in her throat that hours of tears could not wash away.

She left San Francisco a little girl and came of age three thousand miles from home just as the nation came of age through the war. It was in the December of her junior year at Catholic University that the Japanese bombed Pearl Harbor. Bob—her first true love—went overseas that next summer. The letters gushed at first, but grew less frequent. Just as she was wondering whether he may have died a hero's death in a far-off land, she'd heard from a mutual friend that Bob had come back stateside. He'd been shacking up with a hussy down around Fort Benning for six months. He hadn't called. He'd moved on. She threw the friendship ring into the Potomac and she moved on too.

As the Ferry Building loomed larger and the familiar land-marks came into view, the lump was forming again in Rosie's throat. She'd forgotten the pale green color of the electric buses, the fragrant smell of the coffee roasting in the big Hills Brothers Building.

Mike and Bea O'Leary would be meeting their daughter at the Ferry Building. Mike was a supervisor at Hagen's Bakery now. Getting half a day off was no problem.

Rosie collected her bags and made her way down the platform, wondering for a moment whether her parents would recognize her, but not wondering for a moment whether she would recognize *them*. She looked around at the mass of swirling humanity rushing in and out of the Ferry Building and swarming toward the castles of commerce on Market Street.

Where *are* they?

Suddenly she saw them. Her mother was wearing a coat that Rosie had never seen before—not the familiar blue coat that had been her mother's trademark since the beginning of time—and her father was wearing a stylish camel-colored overcoat such as was favored by so many of the big shots in Washington DC. Rosie was struck almost immediately by how small they looked.

As she dropped her bags and ran to hug them, she could see the lines that had deepened across their faces. They were not the same people to whom she'd waved goodbye in 1939, but they *were* mom and pop. It was the first time that she'd seen her father cry.

After the tears and hugs, Mike collected Rosie's bags as she started toward the streetcar stop.

"Where you going, Rose?" Mike laughed.

"To the J-Car, Pop," Rosie said, momentarily disoriented. They lived in Noe Valley. You took the J-Car. That's how you went home from the Ferry Building.

"The daughter of Mike O'Leary comes home after bein' away for five years," he announced proudly. "She goes home in style!"

With a flourish, he reached up with his big hand and hailed a cab.

The San Francisco that Rosie saw from the cab was not the same one that she'd left five years before. Market Street reminded her of New York City. People were better dressed. Prosperity shone from the store windows despite the wartime rationing. There were men in uniform everywhere—soldiers, sailors, airmen, and, of course, Marines. Rosie realized that she was looking at the city of her birth through the eyes of an adult for the first time.

Only when they got back to Noe Valley did things seem as she remembered them. As she stepped out of the cab on Diamond Street, the cold wind still blew, but above her, the sun had broken through the clouds. She heard the peal of the bell a block away in the belfry at St. Philip's Church. Rosie O'Leary was home.

The familiar smells flooded back into Rosie's nostrils as they made their way up the stairs to the family's second floor flat. Her home was almost as she remembered it. The crucifix on the dining room wall, and the plates on the plate ledge. The dark wood breakfront that contained the set of dishes that Granny Monaghan had brought all the way from County Cork. The same rug was on the floor in the dining room, but a new, dark green rug graced the living room. The iris wallpaper in the kitchen—which she'd loved to look at when she was little and hated when she became a stylish, modern teenager—was gone, replaced by deep yellow stripes.

She walked into the living room. The school trophies were on the mantle, and next to them the pictures. Rosie's high school graduation picture, and Catherine's, a year newer. Next to them was the picture of Mike, Jr. in his uniform. Behind his picture was the flag, folded into a neat, tidy triangle.

She hadn't expected it to hit her this way. She could almost hear his voice—"Hey Sis!"—as he bounded up the stairs. Almost, but only silence. It had been on Guadalcanal during the first year of the war. She remembered her mother's tearful phone call. Rosie had not thought that this flat, once filled with the noise of "three little Irish hooligans"—as Grandma O'Leary called them—would ever seem so empty. She had never imagined how much she could miss her brother.

"I'm just gonna put these in your old room," her father said in his familiar voice.

Rosie pushed the tear off her cheek and turned to follow him. Her "old room" was not at all as she remembered it. First of all, it had never really been Rosie's room. It had been the room that she'd shared with Catherine for as long as she could remember. Catherine, who was still living at home because of the wartime housing crunch, had moved into Mike's old room—the one with the big window. Now, the old room that Catherine and Rosie had shared for so many years was empty—and *clean*. It had never, ever been *clean* when Rosie and Catherine shared it. Several of Rosie's favorite books were on the shelf. A couple of her movie star pinups were still on the wall. The room was sort of a museum of Rosie and not really Rosie's room. But after the stinging nostalgia of the living room, that was just fine.

R OSIE awoke with a start. At first, she thought she was dreaming. It took her a moment to remember where she was. She had started to unpack, but had decided to lay down— just for a minute—that was the last thing she remembered. Her eyes focused and there was a strange woman standing there smiling at her. She had short dark hair and was dressed very fashionably in a dark brown suit. Her face was vaguely familiar, like someone Rosie knew she should know. It took a split second for Rosie to realize that she hadn't even recognized her own sister.

"Cath!" Rosie said, jumping off the bed and hugging her younger sibling.

The little sister that Rosie remembered was gone, replaced by a young woman with a management job at the Fairmont Hotel on Nob Hill. While they had exchanged letters during the years that Rosie was away, there had never seemed to be any point in exchanging pictures.

"You look great, little sis," Rosie proclaimed. "You sure have grown up while I was gone."

"Well, Rosie," Catherine said mockingly. "*You* haven't changed a bit. Still falling into bed with your clothes on and sleeping in until five o'clock in the afternoon. You aren't gonna amount to a hill o' beans."

They both laughed happily at themselves.

"Oh gosh," Rosie said at last. "Is it really five o'clock? Mom is making supper. I promised to help."

"Don't worry," Catherine teased. "She's gotten along fine

without you all these years. She can get through a roast and potatoes okay on her own."

The dinner hour was upbeat, with the family obviously happy to be entertaining their guest of honor. Conversation turned initially to old family friends—including that reference to a long-ago boyfriend who was "back from the service," which received a polite "Ooooh Mom, please" from the guest of honor.

Bea O'Leary reminded her daughter that Father Cantillon would be looking forward to seeing her at Mass on Sunday. Rosie just smiled as she remembered how, as a third grader at St. Philip's School, she and Maxine Lobertini had sneaked up into the church belfry during recess and had pulled the bell rope. When Father Cantillon caught them, they recoiled in fright, but he just laughed his deep County Clare laugh and told them to get back to class or he'd tell Sister Dominica to give them a taste of her ruler. From then on, until they graduated as eighth graders in the class of 1936, he'd called them his "little bell-ringers." Rosie wondered what it would be like to see Father Cantillon again. Would he still be that intimidating presence, or would he, like her parents, seem small?

Finally, talk turned to Rosie's actual reason for being in San Francisco—the United Nations Conference.

"I think that's a really great opportunity for a girl . . . well, I guess for just about anybody . . . to be involved in a thing like this," Rosie's father said at last.

"I'm really excited to be part of it, Pop," Rosie smiled. "It's truly historic. This could really change the world for coming generations."

"Y'know, a couple of the guys down at the bakery got tickets and went down to see it a couple of weeks ago," Mike explained. "They got to see Molotov and Stettinius and all of those people. This is the biggest thing that we've had here as long as I can remember."

"Everybody's talking about that whole shipload of vodka and caviar they have anchored over by the Embarcadero," Bea added. "Some of the ladies from church said that you can drive up on Telegraph Hill and look down on it. For being communists, they live pretty high on the hog, if you ask me."

"What are you actually going to be writing about, Sis?" Catherine asked.

"I'm going to be attending some of the sessions and the press conferences," Rosie explained. "I'll write about 'em and wire dispatches back to the paper. My editor has been out here since the weekend. I'm supposed to meet him at the Palace tomorrow morning to get my first assignment. Richard Waldron is also out here, so I'll be working with him too."

"You *know* Richard Waldron?" Bea said, obviously impressed by the dropping of a famous name. "He's in the papers out *here*."

"Yeah, I know Richard," Rosie said, trying to be obviously unimpressed by a famous name that she knew from personal experience to be a boozy blowhard. "He's syndicated all over the country, but he's based in Washington. I work with him at the paper."

"So, Sis, what are you looking forward to most?" Catherine asked.

"Well," Rosie began thoughtfully, "other than getting to see Father Cantillon at Mass on Sunday . . ."

Everybody laughed except Rosie's mother, who smiled good naturedly, even though she didn't find it the least bit funny to joke about the parish priest.

"Other than that, I'm looking forward to seeing major world events *as* they happen, and getting to write about history from my own perspective . . . *as* it's happening."

"You must really be busy at your job up at the Fairmont, with the United Nations Conference in town." Rosie said, turning to her sister.

"Oh, you don't know the half of it," Catherine exclaimed. "All the biggest bigwigs and brassiest brass hats seem to be staying up there. I just did a banquet for the Argentines after they won that vote about getting seated at the conference."

"Wow!" Rosie said with a hint of jealousy. "You are right in the thick of it. That's where I want to be. Tomorrow, I *will* be."

"Yeah," Catherine said, continuing her narrative, "We even saw Molotov once."

"Oh, did you?" Rosie said, the wheels in her head were turning.

The White House, Washington DC
Wednesday, May 23, 1945, 10:56 a.m.

Henry Lewis Stimson felt the slight bump as the driver turned the big Lincoln off Pennsylvania Avenue and geared down for the short drive into the North Portico of the building that symbolized the center of power in a nation embroiled in what promised to be the crescendo of mankind's most terrible war.

This drive was all too familiar. Stimson had been coming to this house and walking through these doors on an average of several times a week for those five years that had seemed like an eternity. However, he'd been a regular visitor here for nearly half a century—longer, perhaps, than anyone who now served in the government.

The tall, scholarly Stimson had been a powerful figure in the loftiest pinnacles of political power for decades. A member of America's patrician class of professional statesmen, he'd grown up in New York City, and earned degrees from both Yale and Harvard. He'd been a trusted advisor to nearly every president since Theodore Roosevelt. He had served as President Hoover's secretary of state and as secretary of war for three presidents, beginning with Taft.

Despite his being a pillar of the Republican Party, Stimson had been Franklin Roosevelt's choice for secretary of war in 1940—and Stimson had accepted the president's call. It was, Stimson had reasoned, in the best interest of national unity at a time of severe national crisis.

Stimson had gotten along well with his boss. There had not always been full agreement, but there was always mutual respect. For five dark years, Stimson had served on Roosevelt's cabinet, part of a tightly knit and eminently qualified inner circle of military and civilian leaders who had presided over the creation of the mightiest war machine in history.

Now, just as the dawn was breaking over a Europe free of Nazi domination, Roosevelt was gone—felled by a stroke at Warm Springs, Georgia, six weeks ago. The four-term president and American icon had been succeeded by the "little haberdasher" from Kansas City.

Harry S. Truman, the feisty senator from Missouri who

headed the committee that scrutinized graft in war production, had been the Democratic Party's consensus candidate for *vice* president in 1944, but nobody, it seemed, had imagined him as *president*. Roosevelt had been president for so long that nobody could conceive of him *not* being president. Through his broadcast speeches and fireside chats he had become a father figure for two generations of Americans. During more than a dozen years in office, Roosevelt had pulled the nation out of the calamity of the Great Depression and had guided it to the threshold of victory in mankind's biggest war.

When Roosevelt died, Truman was thrust into a job for which no man can be truly prepared. But to his new job, Truman brought a sharp intuition, the political savvy of a decade in the United States Senate, and an enormous energy that Roosevelt had once possessed. Nevertheless, the presence of America's longest-serving president still loomed large within the room. At times, it almost seemed like he was just outside the door, listening to their every word. Even Truman still occasionally referred to Roosevelt as "The President."

At the age of seventy-eight, Henry Stimson could now feel the exhaustion in his own bones, but Truman had asked him pointedly to stay aboard until final victory, and he had promised he would. With the defeat of Germany, at least part of the burden had been lifted. With this, Stimson hoped, today's meeting would be easier.

Secretary of State Stettinius was back in Washington on a flying visit from San Francisco, where he was leading the American delegation. The United Nations Conference had been one of Roosevelt's highest priorities. Like Woodrow Wilson at the end of World War I, Roosevelt believed in the creation of a world organization that could serve to prevent future global conflicts. Stettinius would be making his first appearance in Washington since the Conference had begun. From the reports that the press was carrying, things were not going well.

Stimson had arrived early, but when he reached the cabinet room, Navy Secretary Jim Forrestal was already there, as was Joseph Clark Grew, the undersecretary who was serving as acting secretary of state while Stettinius was out of town.

"Good morning, gentlemen," Stimson greeted them, offering his hand.

"Good morning Mr. Secretary," Grew said in deference to the older man who had served in the cabinets of five presidents. Forrestal smiled and shook Stimson's hand.

"I guess that Secretary Stettinius's report will be at the top of the agenda today," Stimson said after he took his usual seat near the one that was reserved for the president.

"I've heard that the news in that regard is not especially good," Forrestal said.

"We'll have to see," Stimson replied. "The Russians are tough."

"And they're used to getting what they want," Grew offered.

Stimson just nodded, not wanting to get into what seemed to be an endless postmortem on what the United States and Britain should or should not have allowed Stalin to "get away with" at Yalta.

The door opened abruptly and the President came in, followed closely by the tall, white-haired Edward Stettinius, who looked as though he hadn't slept since long before his C-54 had landed at National Airport.

After a perfunctory round of handshakes and greetings, Stettinius flipped open a manila folder he'd brought with him.

"As you well know, the Conference has been going on for about a month. Our progress has been much slower than expected," he began. "Our friends from Soviet Russia have been belligerent. The Foreign Commissar, Mr. Molotov, is antagonistic. There's no other word. He's been behaving like a Hollywood gangster. To the press he's all smiles, but behind closed doors, he threatens and cajoles like a hoodlum."

The other men nodded. They'd been reading the newspaper reports—as well as Stettinius's confidential cables.

"There's going to be a real showdown on the Polish Question," Stettinius told them. "Six years ago when the Germans *and* the Russians occupied Poland, the Polish government fled to Britain . . . and we continued to recognize them as the legitimate government of Poland."

"They were legally constituted," Grew said, continuing the Secretary's thought. "They just couldn't govern while the Nazis occupied the place."

"When the Reds 'liberated' Poland," Stettinius continued, "they installed that bunch of Soviet sympathizers in Lublin as the 'Polish Provisional Government.' When I arrived in San Francisco, my friend the Foreign Commissar was insisting that the United Nations Organization recognize the Lublin Poles as the legitimate government."

"President Roosevelt and Prime Minister Churchill both rejected the Lublin government," Grew said angrily. "*We've* recognized the Polish Government in Exile in London since 1939."

"We have to keep our eye on the ball," Truman said. "As much as I sympathize with the Polish Government in Exile. We should not appear to abandon them easily, but keeping the United Nations Conference on track is the most important thing. President Roosevelt believed, and I agree, that the new world organization is of utmost importance. I don't think that upsetting that apple cart before we've even hitched it up is going to do Poland, or anyone else, any good."

"As much as I hate to say it, we've been through too much with the Russians over the past four years to pick a fight at the eleventh hour," Stimson agreed.

2

★ ★

The Palace Hotel
San Francisco
Wednesday, May 23, 1945, 8:09 a.m.

ROSEMARY O'Leary pushed her way through crowds in the lobby of the Palace Hotel. The night before, her press credentials had been impressive—the only thing of their kind ever displayed on the dining room table of her family's little flat. Here, however, nearly everybody that wasn't in some kind of uniform was armed with press credentials. The Palace Hotel was to journalism what the Opera House was to the United Nations Conference. It was a veritable United

Nations of reporters—except that nothing here was united.

There was an excitement in the air. As Rosie struggled through the multilingual mob, she heard snippets of conversations about all sorts of famous people, and she heard improbable rumors. She overheard two men talking about Adolf Hitler's daring escape to Norway, and she had to stop.

"He's dead," she told them. "The Russians found the body. I filed the story on May 16. It's over."

She turned on her heel, feeling smug and leaving the two bewildered men wondering who that girl was.

Finally Rosie found Rex Simmons. He was sitting behind a desk marked *"The Washington Herald,"* talking on the phone. She heard him say something about "the Polish Question" and promise to get right on it.

"Hiya kid," he said, "Have a nice trip?"

Rosie started to answer, but he just trampled her words and continued.

"Okay, Rose, here's the pass that'll get you into the Opera House. Do you know where that is?"

"Yes, Mr. Simmons. I grew up . . ."

"Yeah, right. I forgot. So that gets you in there. Here's a schedule for what's going on there today. Not everything that's scheduled will happen. A lot will happen that's not scheduled. We have a schedule for tomorrow, but things are changing all the time, so it's worthless."

"It seems pretty busy around here," Rosie said, grimacing as someone stepped on her toe.

"Things are heating up. A lot of the bigwigs that were in town at the beginning are starting to come back. They're smelling the finale. Things are getting interesting. Stettinius flew to Washington yesterday to see the President, but he'll be back by the end of the week. Molotov went home to see Stalin, but he just got back into town last night. There's gonna be a big showdown over the Polish Question, but nobody really knows what's going to happen."

"Where's Richard?" Rosie asked. "You look like you're all alone."

"Waldron didn't get in until two this morning," Simmons said, almost apologetically. "I don't expect to see him 'til after lunch."

Secretly, Rosie was chuckling. If her mother could only have been there to hear about the great Richard Waldron staggering in at two and sleeping 'til lunchtime.

"Don't hang around here," Simmons said in a fatherly tone. "You'll go crazy. This is where the press guys hang out to trade rumors. You can't believe anything you hear around this place. Go up there and get a feel for the place. There are briefings. The Danish Foreign Minister and the guy from Mexico are gonna explain why they don't want Spain in the Organization. That's a good one. I think it's at ten. Listen in. Take notes. File a story."

"Where can I do that?"

"Do what? Oh right. File a story. There's a Western Union telegraph center up there and a couple at the hotels." Simmons shrugged. "Find one where the line isn't too bad and cross your fingers. Someday this damned paper will get us our own hookup like the prima donnas at the *Post* have."

"Yeah, right," Rosie said as she was leaving. "Someday, we'll be able to carry telephones around in our purses and file stories from the powder room. That'll be the day."

The War Memorial Opera House was right where Rosie remembered it. She had passed it hundreds of times on her way home from school, but she'd only been inside once—on a field trip in seventh grade. The O'Learys were really not part of the opera-going set.

The Opera House was part of a group of neo-classical buildings that had been erected on the Civic Center Plaza adjacent to the imposing City Hall with its dome larger than the State Capitol in Sacramento. The Opera House had been dedicated to the soldiers who had died in World War I. Now it was being used to mark the penultimate diplomatic act of World War II.

The Civic Center was a stir of activity as Rosie had never seen it before. Men and women in expensive suits moved quickly and purposely from place to place, jumping in and out of taxis and chauffeured cars. Men in turbans and women in saris could be seen talking to military officers in uniforms of every shade of green and grey and blue. Guards checked the credentials of anyone who entered.

No sooner had she gotten inside than Rosie found herself

with her hands full. A feeding frenzy of reporters was circled around a dark-skinned man with a black mustache holding an impromptu press conference.

"Who's that?" She asked an older woman who was rapidly taking notes.

"Why, it's Abdel Pasha!" The woman repled in a condescending voice. "He's only the Foreign Minister of Egypt."

Rosie blushed, grabbed her own note pad, and filled a half-dozen pages on Mr. Pasha's opinion of the veto powers for small nations.

The press conference of "the guy from Mexico," as Simmons described him, was postponed twice, but when Rosie finally reached the low-ceilinged pressroom, it was already overcrowded with anxious reporters. Rosie squeezed into the back, thankful that she was taller than the little round man ahead of her. Next to her, a ruddy complected man with a bright blue tie greeted her.

"Here for the press conference?" he asked lamely.

"Yes, I am," she confirmed, choosing not to add the phrase "Why else would I be standing in a badly ventilated room with a hundred and twenty sweating strangers?"

"It's gonna be good," the man continued. "This is the official unofficial Latin American word on Franco. Now that all of his fascist pals are gone, Franco is pretty isolated."

"I know," she said, feigning naivete. "But could you explain 'official unofficial word?' "

"It's what they want to say, but can't really say, so instead of letting their foreign minister say it, they've got their ex-ambassador to Russia."

"Well," Rosie said thoughtfully. "Nobody expects a diplomat to be frank. The Latin Americans know that the tide's running out for fascism and they're gonna distance themselves from Spain as much as possible. They know which side of their tortilla has butter on it."

"By the way, I'm Ed Haliburton, *Denver Star-Gazette*."

"I'm Rosemary O'Leary," she said, acknowledging his awkward changing of the subject, and glad that she could banter back at his regional paper with the trappings of the national media. "I'm with *The Washington Herald*."

Suddenly there was a flurry of activity, and a man in a

dark suit approached the podium. The "guy from Mexico" turned out to be Ambassador Luis Quintanilla, who explained that he felt that the former Republican government should be seated as the United Nations Organization representative of Spain, instead of Francisco Franco's Nationalists. Someone asked why, and he said that the Nationalists wouldn't be in power if not for Hitler and Mussolini—and now that Hitler and Mussolini were gone, the Nationalists shouldn't be recognized.

Rosie had come to the Opera House to witness history in the making, but she soon realized that many of the concerns that she heard being argued in these halls—such as who should vote in which order in which committee—were as petty and self-centered as those that she'd heard being argued in the hallways of her high school—five blocks north and five terribly long years ago. She made a mental note to write a piece on that notion as she scribbled out a dispatch on the comments by the "guy from Mexico."

When Rosie reached the Western Union area, she reluctantly took her place in one of the long lines and relieved her shoulder of her heavy bag. Ahead of her, two men were whispering.

"Did you hear the latest about Hitler?" One asked the other, who shook his head eagerly.

"Well, and this is on the q.t.," the first man said proudly. "I talked to a guy who met a woman at the Palace this morning who had been with the Russians on May 16 when they found the body. She saw the body and filed the story. She confirmed that it was Hitler. He's really dead. She saw him."

Rosie couldn't believe her ears. The "woman" was she! It was all she could do to keep from breaking out in laughter at how her flippant comment had become distorted. She buried her mouth in her hands and turned.

"Hi there, O'Leary!"

It was the guy from Denver.

"Guess we're both getting our stories filed."

"I'm gonna give them the Quintanilla story," Rosie explained, "It'll be a nice break from the 'Big Four' stuff. What are you filing?"

"Polish Question," Haliburton replied. "Rumor has it that

Stettinius will back down to Molotov in order to get the Russians into the war against Japan."

"Compromise seems to be the name of the game around here," Rosie said. "Although it seems that Stettinius is doing more than his share."

"You've heard what they're saying about Stettinius? At Yalta 'the strong hand of America was used only for backslapping and waving at photographers.' "

"I did hear that Molotov got back last night," Rosie said.

"Everybody's been talking about the showdown all week," Haliburton assured her. "By the way, speaking of the Russians, have you been invited to the ship?"

"Invited to what ship?" she asked quizzically.

"The *Smolnie,* of course," he said proudly. "The ship where the Russian delegation's staying. Out in the ocean somewhere. At the Gromyko press conference on Monday they handed out the tickets to the dinner party tonight. I grabbed a couple. Didn't you get one?"

Immediately she remembered the ship that her mother had described the night before. She would do almost anything to get aboard that ship!

"Not the ocean . . . the Bay," she corrected. "Yeah, I know all about it. It's the one with all the caviar and vodka and the supposed wild parties."

"Yes, that's the one," he said. "Nobody's been allowed on board until tonight. It's not formal, but very formally informal. Aren't you going?"

"Well, I was actually planning to be at another reception tonight," she lied. "But that fell through. Since you grabbed a couple of tickets, do you mind if I tag along with you?"

"Gosh . . . um, sure," Haliburton stammered. He wasn't used to having attractive young ladies invite themselves to join him. "Yeah, sure. I'll come 'round to your hotel about six. Where are you staying? The Palace?"

"Yeah. Right. The Palace," It was Rosie's turn to stammer. She really didn't want to tell this guy that she was at her parents' house out in blue-collar Noe Valley. "Actually, I'll be coming from a meeting. I'll just meet you in the lobby at *your* hotel."

"Okay then. The St. Francis at six sharp."

What a coup. Her first night at the United Nations Conference and she'd be rubbing elbows with the Russian delegation! An invitation passed out by Andrei Gromyko, the Soviet Ambassador to the United States and the number-two Russian at the Conference after Molotov himself.

Rosie filed her story and phoned Simmons at the Palace. She left a message with her news, wondering if either he or Waldron had been invited.

Henry Lewis Stimson's Georgetown townhouse
Washington DC
Wednesday, May 23, 1945, 7:38 p.m.

The Secretary of War was looking out the window of his study, watching a robin in the branches of the old oak tree and thinking philosophically about the cycle of life. The terrible European war had torn at the fabric of civilization for nearly six years, but it was now over. Were the birds returning now to the broken trees of bombed and blasted Europe? Were there songbirds in the linden trees along Berlin's Unter den Linden? Were there still *trees* along Berlin's Unter den Linden?

Stimson glanced at the file of papers that mushroomed across his desk and wondered whether he should start plowing through the pages of troop-level assessments or leave those until tomorrow. The War and Navy Departments had just released the details of the point system by which veterans would be eligible for discharge. Now that the war in Europe was over, there was a clamor to "bring the boys home." After what they had been through, this was only natural. It was the job of the service departments to accomplish this as soon as possible. They had already brought more than a million home, but there were still more GIs in Europe. Of course, it weighed heavily on Stimson's mind to realize that many of these "boys"—at his age Stimson thought of these men as "boys"—had fought hard in Europe and would never come home from the Pacific.

Pondering such issues in the quiet of his study in the evening was a Stimson routine. He was in the office before eight o'clock a.m. and he usually left before five thirty in the evening for a round of deck tennis before he went home for dinner. The evening meal was usually just the Secretary and Mrs. Stimson, or, occasionally, two or three close friends.

Mabel White Stimson, the Secretary's wife of fifty-three years, had been patient throughout her husband's career, but he knew that she too was on a point system. While Henry had promised the new president that he would remain through the end of the war, Mabel knew that this would be their last year in Washington, a city whose climate Henry had colorfully described as "designed for the destruction of the sanity of government officials."

Soon, *they* would have enough points to go home. For the Stimsons, their real home for the past forty-two years was their estate on a Long Island ridgetop in Huntington Township, about an hour east of New York City. Dubbed "Highhold," it had been a weekend retreat when they'd lived in Manhattan. Soon it would simply be "home."

Mabel cleared the dinner dishes while her husband pondered the cycles of life. She had just turned on the radio to relax when the phone rang. He answered it in the study.

"Stimson here."

"Harry, this is Ed Stettinius, I'm sorry to bother you at home."

"No bother at all," the Secretary replied, trying to hide the fact that he *was* bothered. "I just got a call from Senator Vandenberg out at the United Nations Conference."

"Yes . . ." Stimson said. Arthur Vandenberg, the influential Michigan Republican had been serving as Stettinius's co-chairman of the American delegation. Truman felt that it lent an air of bipartisanship to the delegation, and, after all, the Senate would have to ratify the results of the parley. Having Vandenberg directly involved didn't hurt.

"Molotov has just dropped a bombshell."

"What's that."

"You know those sixteen Polish leaders who went to Warsaw in March to meet with Soviet authorities and the Lublin Provisional Government?"

"The people who were invited up there under the protection of the Red Army? The ones who disappeared? The ones that we have been trying like hell to get more information about?"

"Yes, Henry. *Those* Poles. Molotov has them."

"Molotov found the missing delegation?" Stimson asked with a sense of trepidation. "Where were they?"

"He didn't *find* them, Harry. He *has* them."

"Where?"

"In Moscow. They're under arrest and waiting to go on *trial!*"

"What?" Stimson shouted. "These people went to Warsaw to meet with the Lublin government, which they're *encouraged* to do under the Yalta agreement. They were under the protection of the Reds and the Reds *arrested* them?"

"Exactly. Molotov just said so!"

"Holy hell!" Stimson said to nobody in particular. Mabel had come to the door. She knew that something quite serious had come up. She had lived with the Secretary through two world wars and countless taxing diplomatic wranglings. She knew when things got "serious."

"I've already called the President," Stettinius replied. "We'll be meeting in his office in an hour."

The Embarcadero, San Francisco's waterfront
Wednesday, May 23, 1945, 6:45 p.m.

Rosemary O'Leary had been so preoccupied with being able to tell her mother casually that she was going to dinner aboard the mysterious *Smolnie,* that she'd forgotten to think about what she was going to *wear* to a diplomatic reception. However, a hurried modification of an old prom dress from the closet, her mother's pearls, and calming words turned young Rosemary O'Leary into a respectable attendee of the Russian soiree. How her life had changed since she'd last worn this subdued, pearl-grey dress to her late-Depression-era junior prom.

If there was any doubt about her ability to fit the bill among the other ladies attending the event, it was quickly dispelled by the nervous flicker of Ed Haliburton's Adam's apple as she came through the front door of the St. Francis. Rosie was thankful that he'd replaced his plaid sport coat and bright blue tie with an appropriate dark suit.

The drab-looking, five-thousand-ton *Smolnie* was anchored at the end of Pier 21, in the shadow of Telegraph Hill. If Rosie had been expecting a sort of glamorous ocean-going yacht like the ones she'd seen in films, she was disappointed. It was not the sort of ship that one normally associated with luxurious travel. It was sort of a combination freighter and utilitarian passenger ship. Though Soviet ships normally crossed the Pacific as neutral ships because of Russia's reluctance to declare war on Japan, it bristled with 20 mm antiaircraft guns.

The large, low-ceilinged room where the reception and dinner were to take place looked like a cafeteria. The long, L-shaped dinner table wrapped around two sides of the room and the hors d'oeuvres were displayed on a round table in the center. On the walls were numerous large pictures, some were photographs, others reproductions of what looked like paintings or heavily retouched photographs. The subject was the same in all—Josef Dzugashvili Stalin, Marshal of the Soviet Union, Commander-in-Chief of the Red Army, and the supreme leader of two hundred million Soviet citizens.

Rosie was struck by the fact that whatever the expression of his mouth in any of the various pictures, Stalin's eyes were always eerily cold.

Among the roughly forty journalists aboard, she recognized several veterans of the Washington party circuit and a girl reporter from one of the San Francisco papers—she forgot which one—whom she'd met earlier in the day at the United Nations Conference. Much to her chagrin, the woman she had met at the Egyptian minister's conference was also there, but she glided past without recognizing Rosie. Ed Haliburton ran into someone he knew, and after a cursory introduction, Rosie moved off to fend for herself.

The rumors of the mountains of caviar were untrue, but the tables were piled with copious amounts of bologna and white bread. There were platters of tomatoes and radishes that had been artfully arranged—but no caviar. She realized with a grin that the folks from the church hall out at St. Philip's who had gossiped longingly about this ship would find it more ordinary than they might have expected. She ate several of the radishes, but declined the California muscatel that was offered.

There were a number of Russians present, but most were

members of the ship's crew, standing around looking uncomfortable in their ill-fitting white uniform jackets.

"Good evening," Rosie said, smiling at a harmless-looking little fellow whom she guessed from his stripes to be probably the equivalent of a US Navy ensign.

"Hello," he replied with a nod. "I'm pleased to know you."

"It's a very lovely ship," she smiled, gesturing at the exceedingly plain, albeit well-scrubbed, interior.

"I'm pleased to know you," he replied.

Rosie nodded and smiled as she moved along. "At least they have taught them *some* English," she thought to herself, quickly realizing that she didn't know a single word of Russian.

She used her "lovely ship" line several times before she found a man who replied with a "thank you," and a quick explanation of how they were not used to hosting diplomatic dinners.

"Tell me, Lieutenant, how do you do you find America."

"Turn right at the Aleutians," he laughed. "No. I apologize. This is joke I learned from English musician I met. No. To put aside joking, I find America to be a very powerful and proud nation. I am very proud to have America as ally in struggle against fascism."

"And we're very proud to have Russia as our ally," Rosie smiled, realizing that these guys were taught to memorize more than just useful phrases. It was a pity though, he did have a sense of humor buried under all his socialist correctness.

She was about to ask about the vodka and caviar rumors when the young officer gestured behind her toward the gangplank. A group of men in suits were coming in led by a handsome man is his mid-thirties who was dressed in a slightly ostentatious uniform jacket with medals and shoulder boards of a highly decorated, higher-ranking officer. She guessed he was the ship's captain.

He introduced himself in excellent, though accented, English as Captain Georgy Petrovsky. In turn, he introduced the men in the dark suits. They looked like movie gangsters, but Petrovsky called them "information commissars." Rosie guessed they probably really *were* gangsters. She had hoped for Molotov and had half expected Gromyko, but she'd take

gangsters. At least she was part of the action. She *was* aboard the "secret Russian caviar boat," even if there was no caviar. That was good for a byline.

As the coterie of commissars fanned out to work the crowd, Rosie took a gulp of muscatel for self-confidence, pasted on a smile and moved into the fray.

The nearest commissar was chatting with Ed Haliburton's friend, but when he caught sight of an attractive young lady smiling in his direction, he quickly lost interest.

"Boris Leonov," he said, extending his hand.

"Rosemary O'Leary, *The Washington Herald*." She smiled. "I'm pleased to meet you. Thank you ever so much for inviting us aboard the *Smolnie*. I'm *so* honored."

"Oh, but it is we who are honored to entertain such a lovely lady as yourself," he flattered. "We wanted to show American press that Russians are good hosts to our comrades in the struggle against fascism."

"Well, now that two of the dictators are gone, the Americans are looking forward to your joining us in the war against fascist Japan."

Rosie couldn't believe that she'd just been so brazen with a Russian commissar. It was the muscatel. One gulp was obviously one gulp too many. Would he notice that she was suddenly turning red?

"That is important question."

Much to Rosie's surprise, Commissar Leonov was taking her seriously. He was a commissar and she was a reporter. He didn't realize that just under the surface, she was just a little girl from a working-class family that was four miles, and a long, long way from home.

"This important question is one that is, at this very moment, being discussed quite seriously at highest levels of our respective governments."

Well. She waited. Had he answered the question and had she not heard the answer? No. For heaven's sake. He was a diplomat. That *was* his answer.

She plied him with her "finding America" question, found he had no sense of humor, and worked up the courage for a second serious question. She thought about asking about why Russia got three seats in the United Nations Organization and everyone else only one, but that was a fait accompli. She already knew what he'd say, so she took a deep breath and went for it.

"A lot of people are talking about the Polish Question," she said, trying to appear casual despite the hairs on the back of her neck beginning to bristle. She felt cold beads of sweat on her forehead as she waited for what seemed like minutes for his reply.

"More than ten million Soviet citizens and soldiers fell in fight against fascism," he said, looking directly at her with his cold, icy grey eyes, all trace of affability drained from his round face. "Poles died as well. The Soviet people and the Polish people are united in the desire that they should never again be threatened by fascism. Polish people do not wish to listen to the dictates and the opinions of a small gang of counterrevolutionaries who have lived in the comfort of London while the majority of the Polish people . . . like their comrades in Russia . . . have suffered and died under the heel of fascism. There is no *question* about this, Miss O'Leary. There is no Polish Question except that being manufactured by those who sat idly by while Poland suffered. You ask about a Polish Question. There is *no* Polish Question."

Rosie felt the blood drain from her face as a cold shiver snaked its way up her spine.

To her immense relief, the tension was broken by Captain Petrovsky's jolly announcement that it was time now for his guests to be seated for dinner. When Rosie glanced back, Leonov had turned and was speaking to someone else. Clutching her purse in a trembling hand, she moved as far away as possible, deliberately seating herself between what she thought were two Americans. As it turned out, the man to her right was a British reporter who introduced himself as Richard Heathstoke.

Across the table was a large, vivacious woman with short, blonde hair who turned out to be Lidiya Vojoknia, the ship's doctor. Her cheery, almost carefree attitude was in stark contrast to that of the Commissar, but Rosie decided that she would forego more questions about Poland so long as she was a guest aboard the *Smolnie*. She decided to stick to "vodka and caviar" questions. She knew the answer to the caviar question, and the vodka question was answered immediately after the guests were seated. The crewmen brought out huge pitchers of what she initially took to be water. One whiff put that issue to rest.

"Welcome to Russia," the Englishman said with a wink.

The meal consisted of pieces of tough roast meat and boiled potatoes, leaving Rosie to wish that she'd taken more radishes when she'd had the chance. The dinner conversation that developed was principally between Dr. Vojoknia and Heathstoke, leaving Rosie to wish that she could grab her notepad out of her purse.

From the overheard conversation, she gathered that the Englishman was a staunch admirer of Stalin, whom he referred to as "the Marshal," and that he was looking forward to an end to Britain's coalition government and to Winston Churchill—whom he referred to as "the damned Tory"—being replaced as prime minister by the Labour Party leader, Clement Atlee.

"Then," Heathstoke proudly told the doctor, "both our nations will be *socialist!*"

The doctor smiled patronizingly.

As the dinner wound down, a wave of toasts were offered by Captain Petrovsky, each of which necessitated the guests slurping a small glass of vodka. Rosie responded to this particularly Russian custom by pretending to sip the vodka, smiling broadly and hoping that the other guests wouldn't notice that her glass remained full after each toast. As the fellow guests who took the toasting literally fell more under the warm seduction of the vodka, nobody seemed to care.

When Heathstoke engaged in conversation with the Russian on his right, Rosie turned to the doctor.

"I heard that Commissar Molotov is back in San Francisco," she said, catching the doctor's eye.

"Da," the woman replied, wiping a trace of vodka from her lower lip. "But we do not see Comrade Commissar here. He stays at hotel to be close to delegates."

"And Ambassador Gromyko?"

"Comrade Ambassador as well. Stays in hotel. We never see them on *Smolnie.*"

"Might I interject?" Heathstoke had overheard and had turned back to face Rosie.

"Please," Rosie smiled.

"The Foreign Commissar has taken a suite at the Fairmont. He's up there with the other chaps from the delegation. The Ambassador also has a suite I suppose. I daresay, the Commissar sort of holds court up there. It's rather hard to get an audience."

"I'm guessing that you might have been in his suite . . . on one of those rare occasions?"

"Might have been. Might be again," Heathstoke said with a wink, as he reached for his business card. "Ring me tomorrow and we'll talk further."

The White House
Washington DC
Wednesday, May 23, 1945, 8:56 p.m.

A crisis atmosphere prevailed within the cabinet room. Only Stimson and Stettinius wore neckties—Stimson because he always did, and Stettinius because he'd been on the go all day.

"I understand that the 'missing' Polish leaders are no longer missing." Truman said, looking at Stettinius.

"We've been asking the Soviets about them for a month," the Secretary replied. "They knew all the while. The Poles were led into a trap. Today, Molotov officially informed Foreign Minister Eden, and our delegation as well, that these folks are under arrest."

"What charge exactly?" The President scowled.

"Diversionist activities against the Red Army."

Forrestal shook his head and Grew squirmed angrily in his chair as Stettinius continued.

"I got word of this around three o'clock San Francisco time this afternoon. I've been in touch with Eden. We've both wired Molotov that this is really disturbing. Obviously, it's got a direct bearing on us working out the rest of the Polish problem."

"The Yalta agreement on Poland provides for consultations between representatives of the Polish factions, right?" Stimson interjected.

Stettinius nodded and continued. "Eden and I asked Molotov for a full explanation."

Do we have names of those they're holding?" the President asked.

"General Leopold Okulicki, Commander of the Polish Home Army, is included," Stettinius replied. "So's Jan Jankowski, the Deputy Prime Minister of the Polish Government in Exile. We're piecing together a complete list."

"Okulicki?" Forrestal asked. "Isn't he the general who led the underground war against the Nazis all these years?"

"Exactly," Stimson replied. "His Polish Home Army was one of the worst enemies that the Germans had in Poland."

"And of course," Grew laughed cynically, "he's exactly the kind of leader that the Reds *don't* want to have interfering with *their* Lublin *puppet* government!"

"We'll do our damnedest to get these men released as early as possible," Stettinius said.

"This is a slap in the face," Truman said, angrily breaking the lead in a pencil. "It's the Reds telling us they can do what they please in the territories they've occupied . . . the Yalta agreement be damned! It's like they're turning Poland into part of the Soviet Union."

"They're trying to call our bluff," said Grew.

"In 1939, Poland was the first country to fight Hitler's war machine," Stimson reminisced despondently.

"And the Nazis were aided and abetted by the Soviet Union in 1939," Grew interjected. "Poland has probably suffered more in relation to its size than any country in this war. If Poland can't be assured of independence within its proper frontiers . . . if a country can't be protected against a more powerful neighbor . . . then our whole elaborate attempt to create a world security organization will be seen by the world as pointless."

"I agree," Forrestal interjected. "I think Molotov . . . *and* Stalin . . . are indeed trying to call our bluff."

"Joe's right," Stimson agreed. "The whole world will judge us . . . and our postwar relationship with the Soviets by how we handle this . . . the whole Polish Question. At Munich in 1938, Chamberlain and Daladier handed Czechoslovakia to Hitler on a silver platter to avoid war, but it only encouraged Hitler to grab more. Today, it's ourselves and Mr. Churchill's government that are playing the parts of Chamberlain and Daladier, while Marshal Stalin fills in the Hitler role . . . and Poland is the victim instead of Czechoslovakia."

"The politics of the Polish Question have changed dramatically since this morning," the President said.

Regardless of their combined experience, of all the men in the room, Harry Truman, the veteran campaigner, was by far the most seasoned politician.

"This morning, it was a disagreement between two factions over who got to run a country. Now the Polish Question has a human face—sixteen human faces. These are the faces of freedom fighters. The press will be calling them 'betrayed.'"

"We need to make a strong stand on this issue," Grew insisted.

"You're darned right we do!" Truman affirmed. "I think that it's time for Uncle Joe to hear from the President!"

The War Memorial Opera House
San Francisco
Thursday, May 24, 1945, 3:10 p.m.

"Hey, Rose," Rex Simmons said, approaching Rosemary O'Leary in the crowded corridor outside the pressroom that lay beneath the great hall where the United Nations Organization was going through its difficult birthing process. "That was a helluva story. Congratulations kiddo, the paper's running it front page—thirty-six-point head reads 'THERE IS NO POLISH QUESTION!' That's great. You done good, kid."

"Well, I was lucky to get an invitation to the *Smolnie*," Rosie blushed modestly. "I really felt that I had to ask about something a little more substantial than the vodka n'caviar question."

"*That* was great too," Simmons said proudly. "Nobody had been on board that damned bucket before. Even if you didn't get the Polish story, just getting on the 'mystery ship' angle was good enough. Hey! You oughta do an 'Inside the Mystery Ship' sidebar for the Sunday paper. Yeah. That's good. 'Our Girl Reporter, who's been one of the first . . . *tells all* about Russ Mystery Ship.' Do it. I always told you that you had what it takes to be a great reporter."

"Actually, you said that I'd be a *'good'* reporter after I'd been with the paper for five years or so, and after I learned what you had to teach me," she corrected him, basking in her moment of feeling pretty good about herself.

"Oh, you know what I meant," he said, tossing off his earlier statement as an obvious understatement.

"Hey! Y'all better read this!" A man with his tie askew shouted in a Texas drawl as he handed them one of a small pile of mimeographed sheets that he was handing out. "They're passin' these out upstairs."

Simmons took the sheet as Rosie craned her neck to read along.

"What does it say?" Rosie asked, seeing that it was a press release was on US Department of State letterhead. Normally, these were pretty dry, but this seemed to be creating a bigger-than-usual stir of excitement.

Simmons skimmed through the page with an editor's eye, grabbing key words: "It's about . . . 'Polish' . . . 'sixteen' . . . 'missing.' Oh boy!"

"Wow!" Rosie squealed. "It's those people."

" 'This department has been asking the Soviet government about the Polish democratic leaders who had reportedly met for discussions with Soviet authorities during the latter part of March,' " Simmons read. "My God . . . Those people were *arrested* by the Reds . . . for 'diversionist activities against the Red Army.' Whatever the hell that means."

"Who exactly used the words 'diversionist activities?' " Rosie asked, having given up on trying to read the press release upside down in Simmons's hand.

"It was . . . our friend, Molotov."

"Oh my gosh!" Rosie exclaimed. "I forgot!"

"Forgot what?"

"Oh, I met a guy last night who was gonna introduce me to Molotov," Rosie said as she dug through her purse frantically looking for the business card of Richard Heathstoke.

"Introduce you to *who?*" Simmons gasped.

"Molotov!" Rosie said as she started running in the direction of the bank of pay phones.

"I always told you that you had what it takes to be a *great* reporter," Simmons said in amazement as she disappeared into the crowd.

In the excitement of filing her story, Rosie had forgotten all about Heathstoke's invitation. She prayed that she would catch him. His hotel number was scribbled on the back of his business card, which gave his occupation as "corresponding journalist" and listed an address on Kings Road, Chelsea, London SW10.

"Fairmont Hotel," the operator announced. So he was *also* staying at the Fairmont. How convenient—for a fellow socialist.

"Mr. Heathstoke, please."

"Please hold."

Three long rings.

"Yes."

"Mr. Heathstoke?"

"Who's ringing?"

"Rosemary O'Leary."

"Rosemary O'Leary?" he replied quizzically. "Do I know you?"

"Yes. We met last night on the *Smolnie*? You said to call you?" she said, hoping that the vodka hadn't washed away all memory of their earlier conversation.

"Rosemary . . ." He was wracking his brain.

"Rosemary!" He said with a burst of recall. "Rosemary. Jolly well! And how are you. Good to hear from you."

"I'm fine," she said, greatly relieved. "You said to call you about . . . um . . . the Foreign Commissar . . . his holding court in his suite."

"Oh yes," he said, recalling his offer. "So I did. Yes, well that might be . . . arranged. Yes. Why don't you come 'round. Yes. Come 'round at . . . say half six."

"Okay," Rosie said, trying to hide her excitement. "I'll come around at six thirty. *Where* should I come?"

"Oh yes, right. I'm in 907. See you then."

The phone went dead crisply before Rosie had a chance to reply.

She had her rendezvous, but it remained to be seen whether this Richard Heathstoke would deliver the enigmatic commissar. She also began to wonder just exactly *how* much access this English "corresponding journalist" had to the inner sanctum of the Soviet foreign minister.

With three hours on her hands, Rosie decided with a flash of inspiration that she'd pay a visit to her sister. Catherine worked at the Fairmont, so Rosie could look in on her until it was time to meet the Englishman.

It turned out to be impossible to hail a cab outside the Opera House, so Rosie walked down Market Street—relishing her first stroll along San Francisco's "main street" as an adult— and took the Powell Street cable car up the steep southern slope of Nob Hill.

As the city rushed to modernize its transportation system, the cable car lines were gradually being ripped out and re- placed by electric buses. Rosie thought that the cable cars were rather cute and quaint, but she realized that a new and more modern world was being born out of the end of the war. The passing of these curious relics of the nineteenth century would be part of San Francisco's race into its promising fu- ture. She guessed that she'd probably miss the rickety little cars.

Secretary of War Stimson's Office
The War Department, the Pentagon
Arlington, Virginia
Thursday, May 24, 1945, 6:05 p.m.

"I brought you the paper," Joseph Grew announced as he was ushered into Henry Stimson's office.

The Secretary of War stood to shake hands with the acting Secretary of State and took the copy of *The Washington Her- ald,* which Grew had folded to reveal the top of the front page.

On the left was a banner headline about the Sixth Marine Division closing in on Naha, the capital of Okinawa, but Grew directed the older man's attention to the headline on the right.

"'THERE *IS NO* POLISH QUESTION!'" Stimson read out loud. "'Information Commissar Boris Leonov asserted Wednesday that there simply *is no* Polish Question. In a con- versation with this reporter aboard the Soviet ship *Smolnie,* anchored in San Francisco Bay . . .'"

Stimson read through the first two paragraphs with obvious interest and looked up at Grew, who continued to stand, his arms folded across his chest.

"This ought to be good news for Ed Stettinius," the Secretary of War said, shaking his head. "It will certainly make his job easier when he lands in San Francisco tomorrow morning and finds out that the Polish Question has *disappeared* overnight."

"I think that the Polish Provisional Government in London will be especially amused by this," Grew said as Stimson gestured for him to take a seat. "They've just raised the Katyn Forest matter at the Conference through the Norwegian delegation."

"Katyn Forest? The Russians have been lying about that for two years. Thousands of Polish soldiers shoved in to Soviet POW camps when Hitler and Stalin divided Poland in 1939 . . ."

"And over four thousand just disappeared," Grew said, finishing Stimson's sentence.

"When the Germans found the mass grave in the Katyn Forest in 1943, they blamed the Russians," Stimson said, continuing the thought.

"But who's going to believe the Germans over our friends the Russians?" Grew shrugged. "Especially when we knew damned well that the Germans were killing Russians in droves."

"It was a case of he said, she said."

"Except that there were Russians who claimed they saw Russians doing it," Grew insisted. "And now we've got proof."

"What's that?"

"The German internal documents," Grew replied. "They documented everything. And there are photographs of the bodies as they were when the Germans dug them up. We captured the files in Germany. The Poles disappeared in January 1940. The Russians claimed that the German army had killed them after they overran the Smolensk salient in August 1941. Both German and International Red Cross investigations of the corpses in 1943 pointed to the Russians. Now we've *got* the photographs. They were wearing winter uniforms. I've never been there, but I *know* that nobody wears an overcoat in Smolensk in August."

"But Joe," Stimson cautioned cynically, "there *is no* Polish Question."

"Tell that to the folks at Katyn," Grew said.

The Fairmont Hotel
San Francisco
Thursday, May 24, 1945, 6:10 p.m.

Rosemary O'Leary made her way through the labyrinth on the lower level of the Fairmont until she found the banquet department office.

"I'm here to see Catherine O'Leary."

"Miss O'Leary's upstairs in the Tonga Room," the woman behind the desk explained. "She's getting things organized for the Venezuela party up there tonight. Are you with the florist?"

"No, I'm . . . I'm with the press," Rosie said. It sounded more professional than saying that she was looking for her little sister.

The Tonga Room was a newly redecorated banquet room done over in the south sea–island style that was just becoming popular. Rosie found her sister, dressed in one of her conservative—and terribly grown-up looking—suits, directing two boys in white jackets who were placing iced cold cuts on an elaborately decorated table.

Rosie watched from the doorway for a moment, proud of her grown-up little sister.

"They could have used you at the party I was at *last* night," Rosie said as she approached Catherine.

"Sis!" The younger woman said. "It's so good to see you. What a surprise. What are you doing here? Did mom send you to check up on me?"

"Oh no," Rosie laughed. "But you know she'd have asked me to if she knew I was coming. No, I'm here to meet someone."

"*Someone?*" Catherine asked with a smile, not knowing exactly what her sister meant, but wanting to know more.

"It's not like *that*," Rosie said, knowing what Catherine was thinking. "It's this English reporter that I met last night. He promised that he's . . . can you keep a secret?"

It was not the first time that such a question had passed between the O'Leary girls and they both giggled.

"Oh sure," Catherine said. "I'll only tell the whole school! Of course, what is it? Tell me!"

"Well," Rosie said, taking a breath and lowing her voice. "This guy, this Richard Heathstoke. He said he could get me into Molotov's suite."

"Molotov?" Catherine gasped. "He doesn't talk to *anybody*."

"We'll see in about an hour whether this Englishman is on the up and up."

This question still resonated with Rosie as she knocked on the door marked 907 at precisely six thirty. Heathstoke answered the door in his shirt sleeves and wearing a red and black speckled bow tie. His room was quite large, done in a sort of blue-green wallpaper, with a sofa and chairs to match.

"Miss O'Leary!" He smiled. "Do come in, won't you. Yes. Very good."

"Make yourself comfortable," he said, closing the door and crossing to a low table where he had a bottle of Scottish whiskey—with a long name that she couldn't take in without looking at it harder than she wanted to—and a bucket of what appeared to be very fresh ice cubes. The ice must have arrived just before she did.

"Can I pour you a drink?"

"Um . . . sure."

She usually didn't, but she did feel like a drink.

"With ice . . . please."

He handed her the drink, poured one for himself—apparently his second—and sat down in the overstuffed chair opposite hers.

"Tell me, Mr. Heathstoke," she said, crossing her legs. "How is it that a corresponding journalist such as yourself comes to be able to have the ear of the Foreign Commissar?"

"Please call me Dickie," he said. "*Everybody* does."

"Okay, Dickie," she said, repeating her question.

"Well, yes . . ." He hesitated, apparently hoping that she'd grant him the reciprocal license to use *her* first name. Which she purposely did not.

"Yes. The foreign minister. Well, you see, I was in Moscow rather quite a bit during the war. Also down in Kubyshev, where Marshal Stalin moved the government when they thought the Nazis would take Moscow. Got to know Molotov fairly well, you know. All the chaps in the sort of inner echelon, you know."

"And Stalin?" she asked, not completely sure he wasn't stretching the truth a bit.

"No," he said firmly. "The man is a mystery. Man of Steel and all. You know that 'Stalin' means 'man of steel,' right?"

Rosie nodded. "After my time on the research desk, I know a little about the kid who grew up as Josef Dzhugashvili and became Josef Vissarionovich and later called himself Stalin—which means 'man of steel.' "

She wanted to impress him as someone who was not a naive young girl, but she caught herself short of recalling the purges of the 1930s, when the "Man of Steel" murdered tens of thousands of Russians in order to stay in power. She felt that she didn't want to antagonize this man who obviously was an insider with the Soviet elite.

"I see, well, yes," he said. "I'm quite impressed. Most Yanks aren't quite so knowledgeable about . . ."

"Most *Yanks* think Stalin is a Russian, not a Georgian," she smiled, relaxing a bit, now that she'd staked herself out as a 'knowledgeable Yank.' She wanted to ask him what the Georgians thought of their native son, but she already knew from her time on the research desk that his fellow Georgians were not among Stalin's favorite Soviet ethnicities. The dislike was reciprocal.

"About Mr. Molotov, *Vyacheslav Mikhailovich* Molotov, you did say he might be 'holding court' this afternoon?" she asked awkwardly, hoping that her knowing his full name off the top of her head would be helpful.

"Yes. That's right. I did say that," he muttered. "Let me see. I'll ring."

He went to the phone across the room, dialed a four-digit number and spoke briefly to someone. Rosie strained to hear, but the only word she could make out was "yes," because he always hissed when he said it.

"About an hour. Maybe less. They'll ring," he said, cradling the receiver.

They chatted for about twenty minutes, with Rosie querying Dickie about his time in Moscow, and him pumping her for information about *The Washington Herald* and her work. As they talked, the sun was sinking behind the afternoon fog bank and the world outside began to grow darker.

"May I freshen your drink?" He asked, standing up and walking back to the table.

"No, thank you," she said nervously as he reseated himself next to her on the couch.

"Rosemary. May I call you Rosemary?"

"Okay," she said. How could she say no?

"Rosemary," he said again, seeming to relish the sound of her name, or perhaps the permission she'd granted him to use it. "Rosemary, I wanted to tell you that I very much liked the way you had your hair done last night."

"Thank you . . ." she replied. She could tell where things were going and she didn't like it.

"Has anyone ever told you that you're a very beautiful young woman?" He asked in a sultry tone with a wink that made her skin start to crawl.

"If you're asking me whether that line has been used on me before, the answer is yes," She replied cynically, crossing her arms.

"Well. Yes. I daresay that whoever said it knew what he was talking about," he said, placing his hand on her knee.

"Um . . . Maybe I *will* have that drink after all," she said, standing up abruptly. "I'll just help myself, if you don't mind."

Just as she had taken two steps and was reaching for the bottle, the phone rang, startling both of them.

He sat through the second ring, as though in a trance, and then leaped up nimbly and answered it.

"That was them," he said, putting the phone down. "It's time."

A man in a poorly cut black suit opened the door without a word when Rosie and Dickie stepped off the elevator.

Inside, they entered a large room that was thick with the haze of cigarette smoke. Only one table lamp was lit, so it was fairly dark. Rosie counted four men in dark suits seated around the periphery of the room. There was no caviar in sight—and no vodka. Two straight backed chairs positioned before a large overstuffed chair were offered, and they sat down. Rosie felt more nervous than she had the night before aboard the *Smolnie* when she was being chastised by Boris Leonov. She wanted to run, but she'd come too far for that.

After what seemed like an interminable span of time, the door to another room opened and a short, solidly built man with a close-cropped mustache and small wire-rimmed glasses came in and sat down in the chair opposite them.

"Heathstoke tells me that you want to speak with me," the number two man in the Soviet hierarchy said in clear English, albeit with a strong Russian accent.

"Yes," Rosie said. She was so nervous that her mind almost went blank. "My name is Rosemary O'Leary. I'm a reporter with . . ."

"Yes. *We know* who you are," Molotov said impatiently, lighting a short, rancid-smelling cigarette. "The substance of your article about your conversation with Comrade Leonov has been related to me."

"First off, I'd like to say that the people of the United States are aware of the great sacrifices that the Russian people made in order to defeat the Germans," Rosie said, working to get herself onto the good side of the enigmatic commissar. "Working together, our countries have accomplished a great deal. Would you say that this same cooperation bodes well for the future of the world?"

"Working *together?*" Molotov asked rhetorically. "It was the international working class led by the Soviet Union that crushed fascism. Your capitalist politicians like to claim the victory over the fascists. They want to *ignore* the role of the working class and its Communist Party leadership in victory."

"By saying that, aren't you minimizing the role of the *other* Allies?" Rosie asked. "Don't the working classes of America . . . and American GIs . . . get some of the credit?"

"Seven of every ten fascist soldiers were fighting the Red Army." Molotov replied. "Before the United States finally started fighting the fascists in 1942, the Wehrmacht had fifty divisions in Russia for every one that your English friends had to face in North Africa. The imperialist English warlords were not fighting fascism . . . they were fighting to keep their colonies. The Soviet Union fought for its *life!*"

"It seems that Britain was also fighting for its life in 1940 . . . even *before* the Soviet Union was in the war," Rosie countered, glancing at her English friend, who said nothing.

"You have a great deal of spunk, Miss O'Leary," he said, clearly relishing his command of words such as "spunk," and flicked an ash on the floor. "Hitler *never* invaded the imperialist island because it was never his intention to destroy a fellow capitalist. For three years, the Soviet Union bore the brunt of fascist onslaught . . . and the brunt of the counterattack. It was Anglo-American strategy to allow the fascists and Russian people to exhaust *one another* . . . why else would it take all those years to open a second front in the West? By then, the Red Army and the working class had nearly defeated Germany."

"There was a great deal of lend-lease coming into the Soviet Union all that time, wasn't there?" Rosie said, feeling herself being sucked into a debate. "And I don't think that Germany had already been defeated a year ago when the second front opened."

"Fighting fascism was *never* the aim of Anglo-American capitalists," Molotov said, throwing his cigarette butt on the floor and rubbing it vigorously with his shoe as he lit another. "Their aim was the same as the fascists'. Destroy the aspirations of the international workers' revolution. *Who* defeated the fascists in the recent war?

"I'll *tell you* . . . it was the tens of millions of Soviet workers and soldiers . . . and with great sacrifice," Molotov said proudly, pausing to inhale only after he had asked and answered his rhetorical question. "The only thing that could possibly motivate such sacrifice was that these workers and soldiers have lived for a quarter of a century under . . . *workers' rule*. Workers inspired by communism are invincible. *They* won the war!"

"Certainly the workers and soldiers of the Soviet Union did an admirable job fighting the Nazis . . . but a great deal has happened in the last few hours regarding the news about the sixteen Polish leaders who were arrested by the Red Army," Rosie said, abruptly steering the conversation from the commissar's lecture to the topic that was on everyone's mind at the moment.

She felt detached, as though she was in the corner watching *someone else* speak. She was so petrified that she just wasn't frightened by this ominous situation anymore. Maybe Rex Simmons was right. Maybe she did have—or soon would have—what it takes to be a great reporter. Or maybe she was just crazy.

"I think that the world would like to understand why the Red Army arrested these people."

"I appreciate your using correct word, 'understand.' People in your press are making demands and you're asking for 'understanding.' I will hope to make you *understand*. I have invited you here to help you *understand*. The American press sees this as a part of our disagreement over whether any of the revisionists and counterrevolutionaries in London should be part of the Polish Provisional Government. These gentlemen were arrested in accordance with the law. We can resolve our disagreement with Allies *only* if the Polish government is reconstructed with Poles who have present ties with Polish people and not without these people."

"How can the Red Army justify arresting Poles in Poland?" Rosie asked, still feeling as though she was watching herself from a distance.

"These men are guilty of crimes *against* Red Army," Molotov said, crushing his cigarette into the carpeting with his foot and lighting yet another. "These gentlemen are saboteurs and diversionists. Do you know the word 'diversionist?' *We* take this very seriously. Already in zones of Germany occupied by our Anglo-American 'allies,' the diversionists are creating politically incorrect environment where fascism can resurface."

"In what way is fascism resurfacing?" Rosie asked, scratching notes on her pad.

"The dark cloud of fascism has been able to resurface in Germany when your army, specifically your General Patton, allows politically incorrect persons to become civic leaders," Molotov said, a trace of impatience showing in what he was he was obviously trying to project as a relaxed demeanor. "Red Army has sacrificed millions of Soviet lives in the fight to defeat fascism. Those lives will *not be wasted*. The Red Army will not permit it. The workers of the world and Communist Party that is their beacon . . . their inspiration . . . will *not permit it*. I hope that you will convey this to your readers, Miss O'Leary. I hope you now have 'understanding.' I must conclude our conversation. Thank you for coming."

"Thank you, Commissar," Rosie blurted, taken a bit off

guard by his abruptness. Although she expected to feel relief that the tense situation was ending, she now felt disappointment.

As Molotov stood up to go back into the other room, one of the men in black silently opened the door to the corridor. As she and Heathstoke were walking toward the elevator, a door on the opposite side of the hallway opened, and another of the Russians emerged. As he was closing the door, Rosie glimpsed a number of large maps on the wall of the room, maps with large areas colored dark red. In the split second that she had to look, she couldn't tell exactly what they were maps of, but she was intrigued.

"I daresay the Foreign Commissar expressed his position rather clearly," Heathstoke said when they were back in the elevator.

"I daresay," Rosie agreed. "I appreciate your arranging for me to see him, although it seems he has already read my work. He seems to move quickly."

"As he said, they take their position rather seriously."

"Rather."

"Say now, Miss O'Leary," Heathstoke said nervously. "Care to stop back for that drink that you started to pour?"

"Oh, no, thank you," Rosie said, trying not to let her revulsion at the thought of being alone with Heathstoke show. "I think I'd better get my article written while the words are still fresh. "Maybe another time?"

"Yes," Heathstoke said hopefully. "Certainly. Another time. Which hotel are you . . . I could ring you tomorrow?"

"I'm not sure about my schedule," she replied, as the elevator stopped on the ninth floor and he waited nervously in the doorway. "I have *your* number."

The door closed. Rosie's mind raced back to the maps in the room. She *had* to get a look at those maps—but *how?* Heathstoke had outlived his usefulness, and she certainly couldn't ask the Russians.

Catherine! Rosie's sister worked here. Maybe she would know.

"A passkey," Catherine replied. Rosie had caught up to her at the Tonga Room. The Venezuela soiree was in full swing, and she was just standing back and making sure that all of the workers who reported to her were doing their job. "We use a passkey. We can get into any guest room. The hotel has keys for everything. Why do you ask?"

"I want to get into a room to take a quick look at something," Rosie said simply.

"Whose room? What is it? Why don't you just knock?"

"It's one of the rooms . . . Well, okay, it's one of the rooms that the Russians are using."

"Good Lord, Sis!" Catherine gasped. "Are you nuts? You can't just break into one of the Russians' rooms! What are you *thinking?*"

"Cath, there are maps in that room. I just had a very strange chat with Molotov. There's something very serious going on, and the key is in that room."

"Molotov? Maps?" Catherine said, shaking her head. "This is really too much. Are you telling me that you want *me* to get you a passkey to break into a Russian room? I can't do that."

"This is serious, Cath. The Russians are up to something. I know it. Can't you help me get in to that room?"

"Oh, Sis!" Catherine sighed. "No. I'm sorry. I can't. They'd fire me."

"But this is really *serious,* Cath!" Rosie pleaded. "The Russians are up to something. If something happens, I'll tell them you didn't know."

"Oh, Lord!" Catherine said, looking at the ceiling. "Rosie, I can't help you. I can't tell you that the passkeys are kept on a board on the back door of the inner room of the banquet department office downstairs. I can't tell you they're organized by floor number, with the suites on the far left. But I will tell you that I *will* check that key board before I leave the building at eleven thirty. *Every* key had better be accounted for!"

3

★ ★

The Fairmont Hotel
San Francisco
Thursday, May 24, 1945, 11:01 p.m.

THE elevator door closed behind her and Rosemary O'Leary was all alone in the corridor.

She couldn't breathe. It wasn't that she didn't want to, she just couldn't take a breath. The long hallway was completely empty, as she *hoped* it would be. The only sounds were those of the elevator as it receded to a lower floor, the pounding of her heart, and the distant sound of people talking boisterously. This, she guessed, was probably coming from Molotov's suite, far down at the end of the hallway.

Rosie couldn't believe that she was doing this. She imagined the kind of trouble that she would be in if she were to be caught. She'd been lucky so far. She had the passkey. The hall was empty. She'd half expected a Russian guard to be standing in the hallway. Did they not post a guard? Was he just going to the bathroom? Would a door suddenly open? Which one?

Knowing that she had to minimize the amount of time she was on the floor, Rosie moved quickly.

Pressing her ear to the "map room," she listened for sounds. Nothing.

That meant little.

She knocked softly, so that the knocking would not, she hoped, be heard in any adjacent room.

Nothing.

She waited. She counted to ten . . . then twenty.

With a trembling hand, she inserted the passkey and turned.

The door came open with a cacophonous "Clunk!"

She was beyond the point of no return. She knew that she was at the point where they would shoot people. These people *were* gangsters and gangsters *do* shoot people.

Rosie wondered what her parents would do if her body washed up in San Francisco Bay next week—or what they'd do if she just disappeared. That's what happened to people in Russia. They did the wrong thing and they just disappeared. She wanted to go home, but she stepped inside the darkened room and closed the door as quietly as she could.

She clicked the light switch and was immediately surrounded by more than a dozen maps. Both the bed and a large table were littered with file folders. An ashtray and two glasses on the table were filled with cigarette butts. More butts were all over the floor. These people really liked to smoke. She'd work that into an article sometime.

The maps on the opposite wall were all of Europe. Some were of the whole continent, but others appeared to be detailed maps of Germany. On the far left, she saw the images that were familiar from the maps that had appeared on the front page of every newspaper for weeks—Germany, with arrows converging on Berlin from all sides. The other maps, however, showed the red-colored arrows from the right side of the map moving toward the left, passing Berlin and converging on the familiar black line that Rosie knew represented the Rhine River—which the Americans had crossed last winter. Still other maps showed all of Germany colored red, with arrows on the left converging on Paris.

Rosie gasped. Could this be what it seemed to be? She looked more closely at the arrows and saw that each one was identified with a number and a short word or two in Cyrillic lettering. She knew from the many war maps that she'd seen that these identified military units. This was what Molotov had meant when he said he was being "very serious."

These maps were a battle plan for a Soviet attack on Western Europe!

She turned to the file folders. There were many pages of documents, most of them in the Cyrillic alphabet, which she couldn't read, but some were carbon copies on flimsy paper that were written in English. They were mostly technical descriptions of military equipment. Another listed driving times between German cities.

Should she take some of the documents? At least one? If so, *which* one? Would they miss it? She took the one with the milage numbers, just because it was in her hand at that moment and the thundering in her chest told her and her trembling hand that time was short.

As Rosie turned to leave, she noticed that there was a map of the United States on the wall next to the door. It was covered with about two dozen red stars. A large one was located near Washington DC, but another large one was located in New Mexico. What, she asked herself, did *that* mean?

She left in such a hurry that she *almost* forgot to turn out the light. Just as the elevator door closed, Rosie heard the sound of the door to another one of the rooms come open.

The War Department, the Pentagon
Arlington, Virginia
Friday, May 25, 1945, 8:56 a.m.

Henry Stimson made his way down the broad corridor of the new five-sided office building that now housed the War Department. Still shiny and spotless two years after it was completed, the "Pentagon" was the world's largest office building. He wondered what use there would be for such a vast building when the war was over.

Stimson entered the large conference room that had been set aside for meetings of all the chiefs of staff of the armed services. Before the war, the Chiefs of Staff of the Army had gone for months—or even years—without serious substantive conversations with the Chiefs of Naval Operations, but those days had ended forever on December 7, 1941. President Roosevelt had demanded cooperation, and since the beginning of the war, these formal meetings had been essential to coordinating the massive war effort.

Stimson sat in his usual place and was greeted by Jim Forrestal. He and Stimson were the only civilians present.

Silver stars glittered on the shoulders of the other men who were seated around the table. When Congress authorized the five-star rank in December 1944, only seven men had been elevated to this level of command and *four* of those men were in the room.

Seated next to Forrestal was Admiral Ernest King, the Chief of Naval Operations, who presided over the largest naval force the world had ever seen. Chatting with King was General Henry Harley "Hap" Arnold, who had transformed the prewar US Army Air Corps into the US Army Air Forces, a global force which was, like King's US Navy, the largest of its kind in the world.

Across the table from Arnold, quietly thumbing through a sheaf of papers, was the straight and stern-visaged General George Catlett Marshall, the Chief of Staff of the US Army, and the principal architect of the strategy that had helped to bring Nazi Germany to its knees. At the head of the table was Admiral William Leahy, who'd become President Roosevelt's chief of staff in 1942.

Together, these men had worked with Roosevelt to transform the United States from a marginal military power to a superpower, and to craft the strategy that was leading steadily toward a victory that had been anything but certain back in 1942.

Having called the meeting to order, Admiral Leahy explained that a fifth of the five-star officers would be arriving in Washington over the weekend for consultation with the President and with the Joint Chiefs—General Dwight D. Eisenhower, the Supreme Allied Commander in Europe.

When he joined these men in this room at their meeting the following week, the only two Americans to wear five stars that would *not* be present would be those that were guiding the war's final phase in the Pacific—General Douglas MacArthur and Admiral Chester Nimitz.

Admiral King took the floor with an update on that theater. While the war in Europe was finally over, the fighting in the Pacific was as fierce as ever. MacArthur was still battling the Japanese in the Philippines, while the campaign being waged by American soldiers and Marines on Okinawa was encountering unmatched enemy resistance.

"Our advances on Okinawa are being measured in yards,

not the hundreds of miles a day that we were enjoying in the European Theater in the final weeks," King explained. "And offshore, the Kamikaze attacks are still taking a severe toll on the Fleet. It's damned hard to defend against an enemy that is duty-bound to commit suicide!"

"In the wake of this VE-Day euphoria, it's hard for the American public to accept that we're *still* fighting a difficult battle in the Pacific," Forrestal added. "And that final victory may be another two years away. I note that General MacArthur has proposed that we move the D-Day for the Operation Olympic invasion back from 1 December to 1 November. Why is that?"

"It'll give the Japanese one month less time to reinforce that part of Japan," King replied. "And it will give *us* one month *more* time to operate before the 1946 monsoon season is upon us."

"Of course we'll need to have the manpower for Olympic in place by then," Stimson interjected. "We'll be fighting them in their home islands for the first time. We'll need a vastly larger force than we have in the Pacific now."

"The First Army is already redeploying from Europe." Marshall replied. "We're moving them *out* faster than we were moving them *in* four months ago. By summer we'll have seventy veteran combat divisions to the Pacific."

"What are your latest casualty estimates for the operations in Japan proper?" Stimson asked the Army's Chief of Staff.

"As I told the President last week," Marshall said, glancing around the room and then directly at the Secretary of War. "If the fighting in Japan matches the intensity of Iwo Jima and Okinawa . . . and we believe that it will *exceed* that intensity . . . then a *million* casualties is *not* an inconceivable number."

There was silence all around. Everybody was thinking along those same lines. All were secretly happy to let Marshall be the one to articulate the gloomy shadow that hung over any discussion of the invasion of Japan.

"Of course, we may have the weapon that will make this unnecessary," Forrestal said, alluding to the Atomic Bomb, of which all the men in the room were well aware.

At that moment, this mysterious weapon was one of the

biggest question marks of the war. Theoretically, it was a single bomb that could vaporize an entire city—but nobody knew for sure. Its development involved technology so new and so complex that not even the people who had designed it and were building it knew *whether* it would work!

"In about six weeks, we'll know if we *have* such a weapon," Stimson smiled weakly. "General Groves feels he'll be ready for a test shot in mid-July."

The Hotel St. Francis
San Francisco
Friday, May 25, 1945, 5:10 p.m.

Edward Stettinius and his entourage had arrived at the St. Francis dog tired from the all-night, cross-country flight and their exhausting round of meetings in Washington. The drive across the Golden Gate Bridge from the USAAF's Hamilton Field in Novato, north of San Francisco, had been lovely, but after his long flight from Washington, the Secretary of State was anxious for a hot shower and night in a real bed.

As he disembarked from his long black Cadillac at the hotel's Powell Street entrance, he smiled weakly and waved to the reporters who shouted questions about Molotov.

When Stettinius finally reached his suite, one of his aides handed him a copy of the *San Francisco Call* newspaper.

"Mr. Secretary, you'd better read this."

He looked at the headline.

"MOLOTOV SAYS RUSS WON'T TOLERATE FASCISTS ANYWHERE IN GERMANY."

The byline was "Rosemary O'Leary, *The Washington Herald*, Special to the *San Francisco Call*."

Dropping into an armchair, Stettinius read Rosie's story about her interview with the man who was second only to Stalin himself in the Soviet Union.

"We knew they're accusing those sixteen Poles of crimes against the Red Army," Stettinius said, shaking his head. "But it says here they'll use the Red Army to get rid of anyone they don't like in *Germany* too."

"Yes sir," the aide replied. "And he seems to be including

the zones that Britain and the United States are occupying . . ."

". . . Under the Yalta accords!" Stettinius shouted, bringing his fist down on his knee.

"Who *is* this Rosemary O'Leary?" Stettinius asked the small crescent of aides that had formed around him in the suite. "She ran that 'No Polish Question' article a couple of days ago. Now *this*. She must have some kind of special in with the Russians. Is she American? Is this a pseudonym? How is it that I've never heard the name before? Find her. Do whatever it takes. I want to speak to her."

"That won't be hard," another aide said, handing him a slip of paper. "She's looking for *you*."

"Where is this number?" Stettinius asked, unfolding the paper. "This 'Mission' prefix. I've never seen it before in San Francisco."

"It's in the central part of San Francisco, Mr. Secretary. Away from the downtown districts."

"Well, let's give Miss O'Leary a call," the Secretary of State said, reaching for the telephone.

Less than two miles from the Secretary's suite, Bea O'Leary had just reached the top of the stairs with her bag of groceries, when the old Bakelite telephone began rattling.

"Hello," she said pleasantly, expecting it to be her friend Louise, who was supposed to be calling about coffee hour after church on Sunday.

"Hello, I'm calling for Miss O'Leary," the unfamiliar voice replied.

"Well, this is *Mrs.* O'Leary."

"Mrs. *Rosemary* O'Leary."

"No, I'm *Bea*. Rosie . . . er . . . Rosemary is my daughter. Who's calling?"

"This is Secretary of State Edward Stettinius."

"Who? Well, I'm the Queen of Siam! Who is this *really?*"

"Who is it, Mom?" Rosie asked. She had come in from the living room when she had heard her name mentioned.

"Some man. Claims he's the Secretary of State."

"Oh, Mom!" Rosie shrieked, grabbing the phone.

"This is Rosemary O'Leary."

"Um . . . uh . . . This is Edward Stettinius," the Secretary said, regathering his composure. "I'm responding to a message left for me at my hotel."

"Yes, sir . . . Mr. Secretary. I'm sorry. We aren't used to getting calls . . . um . . . When I left the message, I expected to hear from one of your aides . . . not from *you*. I'm a reporter with *The Washington Herald*. I left the message because, well, I would very much like to arrange an interview with you."

"I see. Yes, Miss O'Leary. That can be done," the Secretary said. "Can you meet me at the hotel in two hours?"

"Yes sir. I'll be there."

"I do appreciate you coming on short notice, Miss O'Leary. Just so that it will be less of an inconvenience, I'll send my car."

After the arrangements had been made and Stettinius had hung up the phone, an aide asked why he'd volunteered to send a car.

"This O'Leary woman is an enigma," the Secretary replied with a smile. "The other woman just sounded like, well, like Miss O'Leary's mother. How can that be? I want you to go out to this address with the car. Find out what you can about her."

When the large black luxury car pulled up at the curb in front of the modest two-unit building on Diamond Street, there were several raised eyebrows among the O'Learys' neighbors who happened to notice, but no one was more surprised than Stephen Cuthbert, the aide that Stettinius had sent to "find out what he could."

He stepped out to open the door for Rosie, and after introductions, he asked her in a "making conversation" way, whether this was where her mother *really* lived. Rosie, replying in an "isn't it obvious?" way, explained that she'd grown up here and had gone to school two blocks away on Elizabeth Street. By the time that the Cadillac reached the St. Francis, Cuthbert had been briefed on Rosie's years at Georgetown and her short, but suddenly meteoric, career with *The Washington Herald*.

Rosie was struck by the contrast between the Secretary's well-lit suite and Molotov's dark and sinister smoke-filled room.

"Pleased to meet you, Miss O'Leary," Stettinius said affably as Cuthbert presented her to his boss. "You've become something of a celebrity in the past few days. Your articles are garnering a great deal of attention. In fact, I've just been speaking with the President about your interview with my friend, Mr. Molotov."

"I'm happy to meet you as well, Mr. Secretary," Rosie said, blushing slightly at the mention of the President, but not nearly so much as she might have a week earlier. She was realizing how far into this new world of global politics she had come in the past few days. It was almost seeming normal. "I'm flattered to have my piece being discussed by the President—*and* by you, Mr. Secretary."

Rosie felt somewhat at ease with the fatherly, white-haired Stettinius, despite his generally stern facade. The Secretary, on the other hand, was not quite sure what to make of this young woman in the conservative navy blue dress who seemed to have come out of nowhere yet apparently had inside information about the Soviet delegation. He decided that the best way to figure her out would be to let her go first.

"You said that you had some questions for me?" he asked.

"Yes, thank you. I know that your time is valuable, so I'll get right to it." Rosie said. "What I'd really like to know are *your* thoughts on the Foreign Commissar's comment to me that the Russians won't 'tolerate' a resurgence of fascism anywhere in Germany."

"Well, that is *the* question on everyone's mind, isn't it?" the Secretary replied. "First of all, he presupposes that *we* are allowing a resurgence of fascism in western Germany, which is absolute—*poppycock*! If we're using former low-level Nazis to pick up the garbage and to restring telephone wires, that's one thing, but the United States and Britain—and certainly France—have a very serious denazification program underway. Contrary to what the Foreign Commissar told you, there are absolutely no former Nazis being recruited as mayors or that sort of thing in the American occupation zone."

"Do you see this statement by Molotov as an effort to create some sort of a bargaining chip?" Rosie asked. "As something that he would back down on in order to get you to compromise on the Polish Question?"

"Despite your apparent youth, Miss O'Leary, you seem to have a very good grasp of how international diplomacy works," the Secretary smiled. "But let me reverse our roles for a moment, if I may, and ask you the same question. You met Mr. Molotov. What do *you* think he meant?"

"Well, to be truthful, I didn't get the impression that 'compromise' was on his mind," Rosie said, a bit nervous now that she was having to answer a question. "I certainly don't know Mr. Molotov as well as you do . . . I only just met him for about ten minutes . . . but I had the sense that he is serious . . . that he meant it as he *said* it. I think that he was using me to convey that message."

The Secretary thought for a moment. If this girl reporter's interpretation of Molotov's motives was correct, the situation may be getting gloomier than he'd thought.

"What do *you* think?" Rosie asked.

"The lexicon of the diplomat . . . like that of the journalist, I suppose . . . is well equipped with metaphors," Stettinius smiled. "I'll know more after I have a chance to speak with the man myself."

Rosie followed up with several less-pointed questions, but soon the white-haired man stood up and said, "I'm afraid that this is about all the time that I have. I hope that we'll meet again."

Taking the signal that the Secretary considered the interview to be concluded, Rosie stood up and politely thanked him for his time. Cuthbert and the other aide who was in the room both stood as the Secretary had, and Cuthbert opened the door to the hallway.

As she reached to shake his hand, Rosie whispered to Stettinius, "May I speak with you privately for a moment?"

The distracted smile dropped from his face. He looked directly into her eyes. There was the feel of a barely perceptible wince in his handshake.

"Why don't you go ahead and hold the elevator," the Secretary told his aides. "I'll be along in a minute. I want to ask Miss O'Leary whether she might know of a place where we could get a hot dog and a beer for dinner. I'm tired of all this rich banquet food."

They smiled as he smiled and left the room.

"Yes . . .?" he said, turning to Rosie.

"In one of the rooms near Molotov's suite," she said, taking a deep breath. "I wanted you to know. I saw maps of Western Europe. I wasn't supposed to see them. There were arrows, red arrows, and they were pointing into the Allied occupation zones. They reached all the way to Paris and were pointing across to London."

"I see." All of the color had faded from the Secretary's face. "Are you sure they *did not* want you to see this?"

"Oh yes," Rosie said emphatically, without telling him about the passkey. "I'm very, *very* sure that I wasn't supposed to see it."

The expression on Stettinius's face was briefly one of trepidation, but then he seemed to catch himself. A smile abruptly returned to his mouth, but his eyes still betrayed a sense of fear and uncertainty.

"About the hot dog place?" he said, as though nothing had happened.

"Try McKenna's Double Play on Sixteenth Street. It's across from Seals Stadium. My pop used to take us there after the ball games."

The White House
Washington DC
Friday, May 25, 1945, 6:10 p.m.

The President and his wife had just sat down for an early dinner in the White House living quarters. Unpacked boxes were still piled everywhere. After more than a month, the process of unpacking was still nowhere near being completed. While Harry Truman had been thrust into the pressure cooker of one of the world's most difficult jobs, no occupant of the White House felt more uprooted than Elizabeth Virginia Wallace Truman. The abrupt move from a modest apartment to the presidential mansion had been one thing, but the sudden move from relative obscurity to the national spotlight had been even harder.

Bess Truman had no fondness for public life. She found the lack of privacy that came with her sudden role as First Lady to be distasteful. When her husband was in the Senate,

Bess had preferred to remain in Kansas City most of the time, but now, her presence was not only expected, but demanded, in the capital. As her husband put it, she was "not especially interested" in the formalities of presidential life.

This evening, when an aide burst into the dining room as the President was passing her the gravy bowl, she felt as though she'd just about had enough.

"What do you mean, breaking in on us like this?" Bess demanded. "Can't you see that we're in the midst of having our dinner? Can't this wait?"

The President himself scowled at the young man, who quivered as he handed Truman a sheet of paper.

"I'm very sorry, ma'am," he stammered. "I didn't mean any harm. I just felt that the President should see this right away. I thought . . . well, it seemed important."

"Thank you," Truman said, adjusting his glasses to read the document. "That will be all. You may go."

When the door had closed, Bess inquired as to the contents of the memo.

"It actually *is* rather important," the President said, in a semi-apologetic tone, as though attempting to make amends for the aide's faux pas. "It's a wire from Uncle Joe in reply to mine about those sixteen Polish fellows that the Reds arrested. He says that the arrest has 'no connection with the question of reconstruction of the Polish Provisional Government.' He says that these gentlemen . . . he calls them gentlemen . . . were arrested in accordance with what he calls 'the law.' Then he calls General Okulicki a 'well-known diversionist.' I didn't know that he was well known as *that*. I thought that he was pretty well known as a soldier who fought the Germans."

"What does he say about the rest of the Polish Question?" Bess asked, responding to her husband's bitter tone.

"He says that we can resolve our present disagreement only if the Polish government is reconstituted with the people that the Reds installed. In other words, when he's had *his* way! Bess, he's telling us he won't back down on this. He's telling me to go to Hades."

"When I was growing up, those would have been what Pa would have called 'fightin' words,' " the First Lady replied.

"Well, your pa and I would have to agree on that terminology," Truman said, gazing out the window as if longing for his eye to catch some hint of a solution to the dilemma. "Unfortunately, we now live in a world where *fightin'* is a very dreadful way to resolve disputes. If the past five years have taught us anything in this world, it is that *fightin'* is not something to enter into lightly. Of all the people who *should* have learned this, I would think old Joe Stalin would be at the top of the list."

The Hotel St. Francis
San Francisco
Saturday, May 26, 1945, 5:45 a.m.

Edward Stettinius awoke suddenly. His nights and days had begun to run together. His dreams and nightmares were filled with the same endless argumentative meetings as his days at the United Nations Conference. At times, the unspooling events of the actual meetings were more convoluted and incongruous than the dreams. Now, he'd awakened to find Cuthbert standing over his bed holding an envelope.

"I'm sorry, chief," Cuthbert said as his boss suddenly snorted and sat up. "I didn't mean to . . ."

"Oh dammit, Cuthbert," Stettinius snarled. "You *did*. What is it?"

"Confidential wire, sir. Just came in to the Navy base at Treasure Island and they rushed it up here. It's from the President."

Stettinius sat on the side of the bed in his pajamas, looking terribly unkempt with his white hair tousled and a stubble on his chin. He tore open the envelope and began to read the wire as Stephen Cuthbert hovered near the door.

"What is it?" Cuthbert asked at last, knowing that he really didn't have a right to know.

"It's the end of the United Nations Organization, I'm afraid," Stettinius said without looking up. "It's a copy of Stalin's memo to Truman and the President's reply. Essentially, they're each telling the other to go to hell over the Polish Question. Stalin says he'll do what he pleases and Truman says that the Russians had better start living up to the promises they made to us at

Yalta. I'm sure that Commissar Molotov is reading the same words at this very moment. This will make today's session at the Conference very interesting."

The War Memorial Opera House
San Francisco
Saturday, May 26, 1945, 7:42 a.m.

The showdown was clearly in the wind. The press, the delegates, and most of all the general public knew that Molotov was back in town, and so was Stettinius. This created a stir of excitement on its own, but today, the biggest draw at the United Nations Conference would be Professor Adam Pragier, the minister of information for the Polish Government in Exile in London.

The stalemate of the Polish Question had meant that neither the Polish Government in Exile nor the Lublin-based Polish Provisional Government had been seated at the Conference. Because the Big Four couldn't agree, nobody from *either* Polish delegation had received an official invitation. Then, suddenly, on Thursday, Pragier had announced that *he* was coming to San Francisco. He'd demanded to speak to the General Assembly.

While Stettinius and Molotov eyed each other like circling prizefighters, Pragier had flown to Chicago—where he'd received a powerful welcome from the Windy City's large and influential Polish-American community. Congressman Alvin Okanski had come down to give a strongly worded speech in which he indicated that the jailed Polish leaders had been betrayed by the State Department and he suggested that Stettinius was "poised to sell out Poland in San Francisco, as Chamberlain had sold out the Czechs at Munich seven years ago."

Now Pragier was in San Francisco.

Stettinius didn't find out about Pragier's Chicago appearance until he read about it in the morning paper while he was eating breakfast. He gagged on a mouthful of coffee and ruined a perfectly good necktie.

Rosie O'Leary had heard the news about Pragier's arrival on Friday evening, as she was waiting in line at the Palace

Hotel telegraph room to file her story with the Stettinius interview. She and Rex Simmons had tried to find out where Pragier would be staying. They soon discovered that everybody milling around in the pressroom was asking the same question, but nobody seemed to know.

Rosie had phoned over two dozen hotels and compiled a short list of about eight whose "No" sounded like "Maybe—but we can't tell you."

"Poor devil probably figures that the Russians are going to shoot him," Simmons had finally said with a shrug.

"They can't do that . . . not *here,*" Rosie had replied before she realized how naive she was being.

They arrived at the Opera House early, but found the press boxes in the main conference chamber already filled to overflowing. Nobody wanted to miss the fireworks.

The rotating chairmanship of the main sessions had fallen on Anthony Eden, who was obviously nervous. All eyes were on Stettinius as he came in with his entourage. Rosie recognized Stephen Cuthbert.

The room hissed with audible whispers as Molotov arrived, practically invisible at the center of a knot of his men in black suits. Rosie recognized her old friend, Richard Heathstoke.

Eden called the meeting to order for a report from an agriculture subcommittee. Nobody was paying attention. All eyes were either watching Stettinius or Molotov, or scanning the room for some sign of Pragier. Since nearly none of the press people knew what he looked like, there were as many sightings as there were unidentified men lurking around the back of the room.

A half hour slipped by, and suddenly Eden announced, "The chair recognizes a guest without credentials for a brief statement . . . Professor Adam Pragier."

Eden deliberately did not mention the Polish Government in Exile, preferring to acknowledge the diplomat as a private citizen, rather than as the representative of a government. The applause was hesitant. The crowd was edgy, waiting to see whether Molotov would leap to his feet to object. He turned to his aides and was talking heatedly. The top of his nearly bald head turned red. Rosie could imagine his angry eyes steaming the insides of his little round glasses. Stettinius crossed and uncrossed his legs nervously.

"Thank you Mr. Foreign Minister," Pragier began in thinly accented English, deliberately emphasizing Eden's title.

Turning to the delegates, he added, "And thank *you*."

"Nearly six long years ago, Poland was the first to bear the brunt of Nazi aggression in World War II. And when the dust had settled, all of the Polish nation was under Hitler's vicious jackboot . . . except that which had been occupied . . . with equal disregard for Polish sovereignty by our powerful neighbor to the east . . . the Union of Soviet Socialist Republics."

At first there was a gasp—disbelief that he would dare to use such a phrase with Molotov—the second most powerful man in the Union of Soviet Socialist Republics—sitting just thirty feet away. Someone started to clap. At first it was just a single pair of hands, but then there was another. By the time that Molotov had craned his neck to look for the impertinent clapper, hundreds were applauding.

Pragier went on. He mentioned the Katyn Forest massacre and General Okulicki's wartime heroism. He used the comparison of the Anglo-Americans at Yalta to Chamberlain and Daladier. He didn't compare Stalin to Hitler. He didn't have to. He'd already implied as much.

Pragier turned to the Lublin government, finishing his remarks by saying, "Recognition of such a government, formed in violation of all laws of the Polish Republic, would be merely an attempt to justify in the eyes of the world, the imposition of a dictatorship of a foreign-sponsored Communist Party in Poland . . . This is obvious to everyone familiar with the practices and methods used by communist agents in every country of the world."

Even before Pragier wound up his speech to a standing ovation, two of Molotov's aides were at the side of the stage, talking earnestly with Eden.

When Pragier left the podium, Eden returned to the microphone.

"The Soviet Foreign Commissar, Mr. Molotov, who is scheduled to address this body in the afternoon, has asked to be recognized at this time."

As Molotov moved slowly toward the stage, the applause was polite, but nothing like that accorded Pragier.

"That this body would recognize a criminal who abandoned his country in time need is of little interest to me or to my government at this time," Molotov said, glaring at the delegates.

Rosie could see Heathstoke raise his hands to clap, but he looked around and put them back in his lap. The room was silent.

"The real issue today is the same as it has been for the past four years . . . eradication of fascism from our world . . . and the apparent unwillingness of the capitalist powers to support this goal. For four long years we fought the fascists on the soil of our Rodinya, our Mother Russia. For most of those long years, we fought them alone, begging the complacent British and Americans to open a second front. For three years, we waited for that second front. It was clear then, and it is clear now that the capitalist powers secretly longed for Russia to be bled dry by the fascists."

The room remained silent as Molotov paused to take a sip of water.

"The blood of ten million Russians was spilled so that the snake of fascism should remain forever dead. But today, even as we talk, the vicious viper of fascism is awakened in the ruins of Western Germany. We have seen that fascist snake being nurtured by the capitalists. We see Nazis returning to power throughout the British and American zones. The Russian people fought alone *before,* and will fight alone *forever* to kill the fascist snake *wherever* it comes to life."

There was a nervous murmur sweeping through the room as Molotov took a breath and brush a strand of hair away from his sweaty brow.

"As for this United Nations Organization," Molotov began again, "we came to San Francisco with high hopes that the organization we discussed with President Roosevelt in Yalta could be forged. We came to San Francisco with high hopes that the United Nations would be a force in the world to remove the fascist snake forever. I see today that we were *wrong* . . . that we were *deceived.* Marshal Stalin has informed me to tell you that further cooperation is *impossible.*"

With that, Molotov slammed shut his file folder and left the podium. The other members of the Soviet delegation and of Molotov's personal entourage stood. At first, it seemed as though they were a dozen-man standing ovation, but they simply made their way to the broad central aisle of the Opera House and followed Molotov, who walked toward the back of the room without glancing to either side.

There were a few bursts of applause, but mainly the room was filled with the sound of everyone whispering at once. In a moment, Molotov, and all the Russians, were gone.

4

★ ★

Kummersdorf, Germany
Sunday, May 27, 1945, 5:45 a.m.

STAFF Sergeant Nathaniel McKinley stared at the ceiling in the gathering yellow-grey light of dawn. It was almost the end of May, and the sunlight came early to northern Europe. He remembered the long, cold winter when the brightest time of day was, more often than not, just a gloomy *half*-light. It seemed like weeks went by without the sun being anything more than a ghostly, presence beyond the farthest hazy ridge.

Spring had come late this year, but it was now almost summer and the sun was shining almost every day. The air was filled with the sound of birds, not the hollow coughing of 50-caliber gunfire.

At the moment, though, he was being serenaded by the grating noise of a half dozen-snoring non-coms deep in the oblivion of the kind of sleep that would have been utterly impossible just a few weeks earlier. It was hard to believe that the war was finally over. After a bitter winter of unimaginable hell, it *was* finally over.

Nate McKinley sat up on his cot and groggily looked around him. A little more than a month ago, he'd been waking up in a hole in the ground, but for the last two weeks, he'd been waking up in the classroom of a former boarding school in Kummersdorf that the 27th Armored Infantry Battalion had commandeered as billets.

He glanced at his watch. An hour 'til reveille. He had just enough time. Two weeks earlier, down near Passau, he'd traded a couple of candy bars to a woman for a fairly new Leica camera and now he'd gotten his hands on a roll of film. Within a couple of weeks, he'd be going home, and he wanted to take something to show his family back in Columbia Falls, Montana.

Nate dressed quickly and pulled on his boots. He had enough time to go up to the little hill that overlooked the town and get a few pictures. Out of force of habit, he strapped on his sidearm.

He stepped onto the narrow cobblestone street and started walking toward the steel bridge that crossed the Heidenach River. He passed a couple of old women carrying their laundry toward the center of town where the locals did their washing. They stared right through him, but he smiled and nodded anyway. He could sympathize with their being inconvenienced, but, dammit, he didn't *start* the war. Anyway, these two had probably voted for Hitler back when.

Nate saluted the two MPs guarding the bridge, exchanged pleasantries about how "damned quiet" it was and walked across toward the other side. The remnants of the original German bridge still remained on the banks of the river, but most of the span was a pre-fab job rigged by XII Corps engineers when the American Third Army slashed through the German defenses around Bayreuth back at the end of the second week in April.

It seemed longer. The 27th Armored Infantry Battalion had been part of the 9th Armored Division as it spearheaded the XII Corps's drive into southern Czechoslovakia. By that time, most of the German troops had stopped shooting and had started surrendering in droves. Nate recalled one German sergeant who spoke pretty good English and who was begging the Americans to help his unit fight the Russians. The Yanks just laughed at him and sent him to the rear to join the rest of the Nazi "supermen" in the POW pen. At the time, it seemed ludicrous that Americans could possibly fight their allies from the East.

When the war finally ended in the first week of May, the 9th Armored command post was at Weiden in Bavaria, but Nate's outfit was in Czechoslovakia. A week later, they were ordered to withdraw back into Germany to set up the divisional headquarters at Bayreuth. The move back into Bavaria was a step closer to going home, and that was uppermost on everybody's mind.

If the Americans didn't care too much about the move, the locals certainly did. Nate discovered that these people, like the German soldiers, seemed to have a mortal fear of the Russians. There were all sorts of stories going around about rape and pillage in the areas to the east that the Russians had liberated, and these poor people believed them.

The official mission now was to be part of the Third Army's occupation of Bavaria, but units all over the Third Army were being deactivated or reduced in strength as people were sent home.

As far as Nate McKinley was concerned, this wasn't happening fast enough. He had come into the line in December and had caught the nightmarish final weeks of the Battle of the Bulge. For the next two months, he felt like he'd suffered a lifetime's worth of numbing cold, hunger, and sleepless nights while in a seemingly endless gun battle with desperate Germans.

Bockange. Sprimont. Soller. Zulpich. Euskirchen. Meckenheim. The places all ran together in a blur of images of stone buildings and forests, blasted apart by the rain of artillery fire from both sides.

Of course, Nate had also had his moment of glory in March when his 27th Armored Infantry Battalion and the 14th Tank Battalion captured the Ludendorff Bridge at Remagen to be the first GIs across the Rhine. After that, things were different. There were still the numbing cold, hunger, and sleepless nights, but the melting snow and ice had turned everything to mud. The desperate Germans had become more desperate.

Rheinbrehl. Rechtenbach. Grossbruchter. Hohenmolsen. Lobstadt. Weiden. Now Kummersdorf. The places all ran together in a blur of images of death, destruction, civilians with panic in their eyes, and sad old men and young kids in ill-fitting uniforms and guns they weren't very adept at using.

Now that it was finally over and redeployment was just eight days away, Nate had damned sure had enough and was ready to go home.

Across the bridge, he began making his way through the thick brush up to the hill that looked out over the town and the river as it wound its way quietly through the Bavarian landscape. The hazy sunshine that filled the scene made it almost picture-postcard beautiful.

Nate snapped a picture with his Leica and sat down to take in the view. Swallows darted over the khaki-colored water and raced beneath the steel bridge that spanned the Heidenach.

The quiet was almost unnerving. He hated the fact that he'd gotten used to the constant, distant thunder of artillery. The morning after the war had ended, he actually woke up thinking for a split second that he'd gone deaf.

Looking across the river at Kummersdorf, it was hard to believe that there had been a war. Towns that had been defended were blasted apart. Kummersdorf was too small to defend and it was more or less unscathed except for the bridge, which the Germans had blown up themselves.

As Nate watched, a deuce-and-a-half, a two and a half-ton army truck, rumbled across the loose 2×6s that formed the decking of the steel-frame bridge. The truck stopped briefly for the MPs to check their papers, and then the driver jammed the gears and the truck lurched into Kummersdorf. Nate listened as the thundering deuce-and-a-half gradually disappeared into the distance east of the town. Moments later, he heard the sound of another truck, this one coming from the east. It was a whining, high-pitched sound, like the old pickup that his uncle had back home.

The second truck came around the corner near the boarding school where Nate was billeted and rattled up to the bridge. Sure enough, it was an old Studebaker, a prewar model, and, judging from the look of it, the truck had been driven hard for a long time. It was an unfamiliar sort of pea-soup green, and there was no white star on the hood. The opposite side of the bridge was about seventy-five yards from the hill where Nate was sitting, so he couldn't make out any markings on the truck.

The MPs had stopped the truck. One of them seemed to be arguing with the driver, but Nate couldn't tell what they were saying.

For some reason, Nate put his camera up to his eye and snapped a picture of the scene. Suddenly, as Nate watched through the viewfinder, the second MP reached for his sidearm.

There was an abrupt *crack crack* and both of the MPs were lying on the deck of the bridge. Nate could see a pool of blood near one of the men. An artery had been ruptured. He'd seen this ugly sight before.

Things were happening quickly now. A man in a pea-green uniform was kneeling over one of the MPs. There were more men getting out of the truck. They were Russians. The goddam Reds had shot two American MPs! There was going to be hell to pay now!

Before Nate could decide what to do next, the truck had driven across the bridge and there were more trucks. Two crossed the bridge and three others had parked near the boarding school. There were Russians everywhere, all carrying assault rifles or submachine guns.

The Russians were on the street. They were on the bridge. Now they were in the boarding school. In the distance, toward the center of town, there were sounds of small-arms fire. A long burst from a Thompson submachine gun was interrupted by the all-too-familiar clatter of Russian small-arms fire.

Nate could see Americans on the street now. Bob Epperly, the Staff Sergeant from E Company that had saved his life at Marburg. Steve Steinberg, that Brooklyn kid from C Company that was with him at Remagen. The guys that he bunked with. The guys who had been asleep in the same room that he'd just left. They were all being pushed and shoved by the Russians.

There were four shots in rapid succession. Two Russians were down. Maybe a third. The others were looking and pointing. There was a GI in a third-floor window with a Garand rifle. Nate couldn't tell who it was. Some guy with dark hair.

There was a hail of gunfire—clouds of dust rose as bullets pocked the stucco around the window frame, chips of wood and broken glass flew from the frame.

The Garand tumbled to the ground and it was all over.

The Russians scooped up their two men that had gone down and went back to pushing, and even kicking, the other GIs.

Nate realized that he could have been down there. If he hadn't gotten up early and gone for this walk, he *would* be there. He'd be standing helplessly on that street. He racked his brain for what to do. He had a .45 in his holster, but at this range, he would be lucky to hit anything, and he'd seen what had happened to the guy on the third floor.

The Russians were now lining the Americans up against the side of the school. There must have been about a hundred guys. Jesus Christ. Nate couldn't look, but he did. He even put his Leica back up to his eye. It was over in a few seconds, but it seemed longer. Nate had been in some of the toughest combat faced by American soldiers in history, but he'd never seen men lined up and shot in cold blood. It stunned him.

He fought the urge to run down the hill and empty his clip into the nearest Russian, but he just gritted his teeth and watched. There was no effort made to pick up the crumpled forms that had once been the soldiers of the 27th Armored Infantry.

The Russians just climbed back into their trucks. As these started moving across the Heidenach bridge, others started coming through the town. There were not just trucks, but armored personnel carriers. Nate counted five T34 tanks. He guessed that this was a reinforced infantry battalion or maybe even a full division. Most of the vehicles were unmarked, but some had large red stars, or handpainted lettering in that indecipherable Russian alphabet. He took a couple of pictures of these.

The Soviet Army convoy rumbled beneath the hill where Nate was hiding. Through the thick brush, he could see the faces of the Russian troops, barely thirty yards below. If they had known where to look, they would have seen him too. Realizing this, he crouched down as low as he could.

Finally, the convoy had passed, rolling west in the direction of Bayreuth.

Just wait 'til the 9th Armored gets hold of you, you bastards!

Nate McKinley tried to comprehend what he'd just seen. A bunch of America's Russian allies—at least a battalion of them—had just driven through an American position in force and had massacred over a hundred GIs. There were probably a lot more than that, but there were at least a hundred that he'd seen.

Why?

Nate had heard of some incidents over the past few weeks where Russians and Americans had traded shots, but those were isolated, and mostly accidental screwups. This was not that. *These* guys weren't just off on a shooting spree. This was a deliberate, well-organized military action.

Maybe the United States and Russia were at war and nobody had told the 27th Armored Infantry? There had been that big blowup between our diplomats and theirs at the San Francisco conference, but Nate couldn't imagine this coming to war. After everything that he'd seen, Nate couldn't imagine *anybody* wanting to jump into another war this soon after the other one, but maybe the politicians still had the stomach for it.

It sure looked like war.

Seething with anger, Nate realized that he had to figure out what to do next. Waking up early had saved his life. He wasn't religious, but he decided there had to be some reason that he'd survived and all the other guys were lying there on the cobblestones across the river.

He wondered about going back into town, but he could see that there were still a handful of Russians left over there, probably to watch the bridge and pick off any stragglers—such as Nate—who might show up.

The best thing that he could do would be to get back to American lines—wherever they were. The last he knew, the Russian and American line was at least fifty miles to the east, but that was then. The Russian lines now included Kummersdorf.

He wondered how widespread this invasion could be. Was this an isolated action, or were the Russians coming through American lines elsewhere?

There was no way of knowing what was going on. Nate

had no radio, and no way to get in touch with the 9th Armored's command post. He'd just have to walk, just keep his head down and walk *west*. Luckily, he was on the right side of the river. This was a lucky break—one fewer obstacle to surmount.

He decided to follow the road toward Bayreuth and hope for the best. He knew that it ran through a shallow valley, so he figured he could keep to the ridge line with the road in sight and make pretty good progress without being seen. The trees along the ridge line would screen him from view from below, and he could see if any more troops came along.

Just as he was about to strike out through the brush toward the ridge, Nate caught a movement out of the corner of his eye. There was a Russian about twenty-five yards away at the bottom of the hill near the edge of the road. He hadn't noticed that they had posted guards at the west end of the bridge. Better to notice now than never.

Nate could see the guy clearly. He was puffing on a cigarette and looking at the ground along the road. Nate fingered his sidearm. At this range, the .45 slug would take the bastard's head off like kicking a ripe melon. Of course, this would certainly be Nate's last act as well. Killing the Russian would blow his cover and make his escape impossible.

Finally, the Russian finished his cigarette, took a leak and ambled back across the bridge.

Nate breathed a sigh of relief, hung his camera strap around his neck, and carefully made his way through the underbrush away from the bridge.

The tangle of bushes in the river bottom made the going tough, but by the time that Nate reached the slope of the ridge, it thinned out to meadow grass about twenty inches high. He looked back to be sure that he wasn't being followed. He couldn't see the bridge because of the trees down along the river, so he knew that the troops at the bridge wouldn't see him.

In the haze of fires that were burning within the town, he could barely make out the buildings of Kummersdorf in the distance. The Russians must have decided to burn the evidence. Maybe they were punishing the Germans. Maybe this was rape and pillage time.

This notion was confirmed a few minutes later when Nate

rounded a bend and could see the road clearly again. He saw two of the handcarts that he'd seen the German civilians using. They *had been* horse carts, but most of the horses had been eaten to get the people through the winter, so the horse carts had become handcarts.

Strewn around these handcarts were what looked at first like piles of old clothes. Then, Nate made out that they were people. The Russians had just gunned them down.

As he looked down at the scene, Nate tried to imagine what anger the Russians must harbor to make them kill defenseless women and children. At the end of the scattered remnants, Nate could see a cluster of naked bodies. They were smaller than the rest. Before they killed these people, they had stripped and raped the kids.

As Nate reached the trees at the top of the ridge, he heard the sound of airplane engines coming from the east. A pair of dark green airplanes flashed by at low level, headed west. They were marked with red stars, and they carried racks of bombs under their wings. There was no question about what this meant.

An invasion was on.

St. Philip's Church
San Francisco
Sunday, May 27, 1945, 9:54 a.m.

"*Deo gratias*," Father John Cantillon announced from the altar, closing his enormous missal as the choir began the recessional hymn.

"There," Rosie O'Leary thought, glancing at her mother. "Mom wanted me at Mass, and I was."

Actually, after Molotov's sinister words the previous day, going to Mass had seemed like a reassuring thing to do.

Rosie had spent the rest of Saturday discovering how serious things had become. When the Soviet delegation walked out of the Opera House, everyone had seemed to expect that Molotov would be going back to Nob Hill to sulk. When the word spread that he left town, it really began to sink in that the United Nations Conference was effectively—*over*.

Father Cantillon had spoken of the Polish Question in his homily this morning, suggesting that communism was just as much an impediment to religious freedom in Poland as was Nazism. He also added that he was "deeply troubled" by the news that was now coming out about the Nazi persecution of Jews in Poland. Pope Pius XII may have been ambivalent about the Nazi treatment of the Jews, but many Catholics remembered that Pius XI had not held *his* tongue on the issue.

As Rosie and her family were filing out, Bea grabbed the priest by the arm.

"You remember my daughter, don't you, Father," she said proudly.

"Rosemary," he smiled. "My little bell-ringer, who is now a famous journalist with bylines in papers throughout the land. How are you, Rosemary?"

"I'm very well, Father Cantillon. I'm trying to stay on top of events. It has been a busy few days for people in my line of work."

"That it has. It seems that the peace may be as hard to win as this long and terrible war has been."

Suddenly, out of the corner of her eye, Rosie saw Stephen Cuthbert coming up the church steps.

"They said you'd be here," he announced officiously. "Can I speak with you?"

"This is Mr. Cuthbert," Rosie said, introducing him to her mother and to Father Cantillon. "He works for Secretary Stettinius."

Cuthbert smiled and shook hands cordially.

"What is it?" Rosie asked, when they had stepped to one side.

"All hell . . . pardon me for saying *that* in front of your church . . . has broken loose in Germany," he replied. "Haven't you heard?"

"No. What happened?"

"Actually, the news is just coming in. We're not really clear. The Russian forces are moving across the demarcation lines. The information is still sketchy, but it seems they've crossed out of *their* zone and are taking up positions in the other Allied zones."

"What does this have to do with me?" Rosie asked, her head

spinning as she tried to imagine what might be happening.

"On Friday, you told Secretary Stettinius something about some maps," Cuthbert said. "He wants to talk to you about what you saw."

In the Sunday morning traffic, the government car managed to reach the Secretary's hotel in about 15 minutes. Stettinius was standing over a map that he'd pulled from a newspaper.

"Miss O'Leary," he smiled weakly. "So nice of you to come. Cuthbert, offer the lady some coffee. On Friday, you said you saw maps?"

"I thought you should know," Rosie replied. "I didn't see them very well, so anything that I could say would be speculation. This is why I couldn't and didn't write about them. I could only speculate and guess. I would have needed more facts to do a story, so I didn't, but I wanted *you* to know they *existed*. It's not the job of a reporter to relate unpublished material, but in *this* case, I decided that it was important to tell you."

"In light of what's *now* happening, the existence of those maps is quite pertinent," Stettinius replied.

"Exactly *what is* happening?" Rosie asked.

"Well . . ."

"I gave *you* information that I didn't *have* to," Rosie prodded.

"The Russians are entering our zone," Stettinius said. "It's a very serious crisis. The biggest that we've had in Europe since the war ended."

"How *far?* Weren't the Americans *supposed* to pull back?" Rosie asked. "Wasn't that in the Yalta agreement? Didn't they draw the lines at Yalta before they knew where the troops would end up?"

"That's right, but we'd *already* completed our withdrawal a week ago," Stettinius confirmed. "When the war ended, the Third Army was all the way up to Pilsen. We weren't supposed to be in Czechoslovakia at all, because it was in the Russian zone, so we agreed to pull back, and we *did*. In the north, the First Army met the Russians on the Elbe, but that was in their zone, so we pulled back. We captured Leipzig, but that was in their zone, so we pulled out there too, and let them occupy it."

"Maybe they're just moving into areas they think are actually in their zone?" Rosie offered. "Maybe it's all just a big snafu?"

"Come now, Miss O'Leary, that's *not* what it looked like on those maps that you wanted to tell me about, was it?" Stettinius asked, folding his arms across his chest.

"No," Rosie replied with a shrug. "It wasn't."

"In the interest of national security, would you please tell me exactly what you *did* see?" Stettinius insisted.

Rosie felt a sense of power that she could not have even imagined a week earlier. She had learned a lot in a few days, and she decided to use it.

"I'll tell you what I know," she said slowly. "If you'll give me a first crack at information about this thing before you release it to the press."

"You want an exclusive, then," Cuthbert interjected.

"Something like that."

"Okay," Stettinius said impatiently. "Give us your card and I'll see that you get called first whenever I can."

"I saw about a dozen maps of Europe, including some that were just of Germany. As I said on Friday, there were red arrows that were pointing into the Allied zones. Some of them went all the way to Paris. Some were pointing to London."

"What did you think they meant?"

"I didn't know. I can't read the Russian writing. I guess in the *worst* case, they were invasion plans, but I didn't want to jump to that conclusion."

"Did you tell anyone?" Stettinius asked

"I told you."

"Anyone else."

"I told my sister. She works at the Fairmont. I saw her immediately after I saw them."

"Why didn't you tell the authorities?"

"*What* authorities? *Really.* The police couldn't do anything. I knew that I was going to be trying to see you the next day . . . and you're almost the highest authority there is in this country."

"Yesterday, I just couldn't imagine such a thing," Stettinius said, shaking his head. "Until today, such a thing was unfathomable. Can you tell us any more?"

"There was also a map of the United States," Rosie said, as Stettinius's eyes grew wide. "It was covered with red stars. There was a big one on Washington, and another big one on New Mexico. Do you have any idea what this meant?"

"No. None at all," he lied, realizing that the most important thing in New Mexico was the most secret bomb factory in the world. Quite possibly, it was *not* now a secret from the Russians.

"Is there any chance that you were seeing something that they *wanted* you to see?" Cuthbert asked.

"Absolutely not," Rosie said emphatically. "I told Mr. Stettinius this on Friday. I was not where they wanted me to be at all."

"You're certain."

"Oh yes!" Rosie smiled. "But . . . since I'm already in trouble for looking where I wasn't supposed to, I'll also admit to having had *this* stick to my fingers."

"This was among some pages that I could decipher," she said, opening her purse to pulled out the flimsy sheet of paper that she had taken. "It's got names of German cities, with what looks like distances in kilometers."

"I see," Stettinius said, studying the page. "I see Leipzig opposite Nurnberg with 295. Berlin and Hannover, 283. Lubeck and Hamburg, just 53. Here's Pilsen and Munich at 229 kilometers. And Dresden to Koln, that's Cologne in English, at 642 kilometers. This is amazing. This must have been in the works for months. This is a bombshell. Cuthbert, make copies. We're leaving for Washington immediately."

"Mr. Secretary," Rosie smiled sweetly. "I know that sometimes you allow members of the press corps to travel on your plane . . ."

"I hope you can pack quickly," Stettinius said, shaking his head.

On a ridge, west of Kummersdorf, Germany
Sunday, May 27, 1945, 12:18 p.m.

Nathaniel McKinley felt as though he was making good progress. Kummersdorf was long out of sight and he could see another town in the distance ahead. He had seen no vehicles moving on the road below. He had passed several farmhouses, but had circled around, giving them wide berth. He wasn't in the mood for having to deal with any German civilians today.

He had realized that he hadn't eaten, but he really wasn't too hungry yet. He had gone without eating for most of a day frequently when he was in the line, and he knew that he could get by. He had grabbed a few small, slightly underripe apples from a tree that he'd passed and shoved them in his pockets for later.

He had no idea what he was going to do, other than to walk west until he found an American unit—wherever or whenever that happened. He had no idea whether this would take hours or days, or whether he still might be overtaken by the Russians.

By mid-afternoon, it was actually starting to get hot. Nate sat down to rest and to take a look around. In the distance, in the direction of Bayreuth, he could see two or three columns of smoke rising into some low clouds that hung over the Main River valley. He wished that he knew what was going on and whether the main body of the 9th Armored Division had been caught off guard.

He bit into one of the apples and was stretching to get up when he heard, from behind him, the unmistakable click of a round being chambered in a bolt-action rifle. He raised his hands and turned slowly toward the origin of the sound.

About thirty feet away, uphill among the pine trees, was a man in the feldgrau uniform of a Wehrmacht infantry soldier. He was about thirty, wearing a cap rather than a helmet, and he was pointing his Mauser directly and unflinchingly at Nate.

A sense of sickening irony swept over Nate. He had survived the Battle of the Bulge, the Remagen Bridgehead fight, and the drive across Germany only to get killed three weeks after the war ended and eight days before he was supposed to go home.

"Sie sehen jetzt, warum wir den Bolsheviki hassen . . . You see now why we hate the Bolsheviki, ja?" the man said in heavily accented English.

"I have seen that side of the Russians, yes," Nate affirmed grimly. "Am I your prisoner, or are you going to shoot me?"

"Not my prisoner," the German said, moving closer, but keeping the rifle trained on Nate. "We are not now at war. My generals surrendered to your generals, but today, we have a new war."

"So I'm the first Allied soldier that you get to kill in *this* war," Nate said, clasping his hands behind his head and hoping that the bullet, when it came, would hit something vital so that he didn't have to bleed to death on this hillside.

"I saw what happened in Kummersdorf," he said with a half grin. "It is your Red friends who are shooting you now, Yankee. We *knew* this would happen. We did not know that it would happen so *soon*."

"So, what are you gonna do with me?" Nate asked.

"We hunt the bear together," the German said, as though this option was the only obvious one.

Nate thought for a minute. On one level, it was a case of doing anything to get the Mauser barrel out of his face. On another level, the fellow had the right idea. In the past few hours, Nate had seen Russians killing Americans and Russians killing Germans.

"The enemy of my enemy is my friend," Nate said at last, slowly extending his right hand. "I'm Nate McKinley, 27th Armored Infantry, US Army."

Gripping the rifle firmly with his left hand, the German grasped Nate's hand with his right.

"Gunther Hass, 110th Panzer Grenadier Regiment, 11th Panzer Division . . . retired."

The new friends eyed one another warily as Hass lowered his weapon.

"So, you saw what happened in Kummersdorf? Were you following me?"

"Nein. Not from Kummersdorf. I follow you for one hour. I was on the road when I heard the shots. I hid, and then went back to look. I had the same thought as you. Follow this ridge and walk west."

"Where's your unit?" Nate asked, scanning the trees above them on the slope.

"Kaput," Hass shrugged. "All gone. No more Panzer Grenadier Regiment. Everybody is trying to go home. Me? I will go to Bremen. See what's left. I thought maybe I would be captured by the Americans, but no. They don't seem to care about a small fish like me. They want the big Nazis. Where is your unit?"

"Back in Kummersdorf," Nate gestured. "You saw 'em. The main force is up in Bayreuth. I guess that's where the fighting is now. I'm trying to find somebody I can link up with."

"And you found me," Hass laughed.

Suddenly, a half-dozen Soviet Sturmoviks screamed overhead at low level. The two men flattened themselves on the hillside, but the big green birds were gone in a moment. They had bigger fish to fry.

Neither of the two former enemies had a plan, so they continued walking west, watching the smoke billow up from the direction of Bayreuth. As they walked, the setting sun gradually colored the smoky sky the deep red of blood—the same deep red as the Soviet flag.

By dusk, they had reached a point where they could see that the east-west road that they had been following was intersected by a north-south road they assumed was one of those that angled toward Nurnberg, and a major American troop concentration. Throughout the day, they had seen more Soviet mechanized units on the east-west road, but as they scanned the scene, the narrower north-south road appeared quiet. At the crossroads, however, there were several—at least five— T34s dug in to hold the area in the case of a counterattack.

Cautiously, they made their way down the hill toward the Nurnberg road in the gathering darkness. They had made good time walking through the grassy slopes and among the pines on the ridge, but the brambles that clustered in the valley— encouraged by the runoff of an especially wet winter—were a struggle to get through in the near darkness. Not only that, but getting through the brush was noisy. Each man imagined a Russian patrol lurking and listening to the clamor and crunching of breaking twigs and branches.

Finally, after what seemed like an interminable hour, they reached the road, exhausted. Sitting down, the German offered his canteen to the American, who sipped a bit of water and handed it back.

"I wish we had something to eat," Nate said, more rhetorically than actually proposing a food-gathering expedition.

"Ja," Hass agreed. "But I am happy still to be hunting the bear and not to be like my former comrades who have been taken away to be guests of the bear."

"We haven't had much of a chance to do any bear hunting yet," Nate observed. "And I'm happy to keep it that way as long as the odds are not on our side."

"The odds, you say!" Hass laughed. "*This* is an experience that I have had for three years!"

"I still can't believe this," Nate said, shaking his head. "This has to be a mistake. I can't believe that we're at war with the Russians already."

"Seeing ist believing, my friend," Hass said, offering him the canteen again. "I'm surprised that it took a month for the Russians to continue to march to the West."

"Let's continue *our* march to the south," Nate said, crossing the road.

Instinctively, the two soldiers took opposite sides and walked as far from the road as the tangled underbrush would permit. They couldn't see the moon, but there was enough ambient light to see the road fairly easily.

The idle conversation continued. At first, they talked a little bit about combat actions they'd been in, but gradually the discussion turned to home. Gunther Hass had taught mathematics at a "gymnasium" in a Bremen suburb, which seemed strange to Nate until he learned that a gymnasium was actually a high school. As for Nate, he explained that he had been out of high school for a few years when the war started and he'd joined the army.

They both wondered what going home would be like. For Hass, he was trying to imagine going home to a city that didn't exist anymore.

"I don't know what to expect," he said philosophically. "I have heard stories about the bombing and the devastation, but there were no pictures published of Bremen that I saw. With my eyes, I saw Dresden after the bombing, and I can imagine, but I don't want to. Hitler told us that we were winning. Just a few months and we will have secret weapons to push the Allies into the Atlantic. He said that all winter, but the bombers kept coming. I don't know whether my home is there. I don't know whether my family is alive."

"When did you last hear?"

"Last letter from Gretl . . . meine frau . . . in January. Last letter from meine mutter at Weinachten . . . at Christmas. They were holding on bravely. Not much news. Nothing since."

"I hope the Russians don't get *that* far," Nate mused, wishing he hadn't almost as soon as he said it.

"And you, you have a frau, a fraulein?" Gunther asked, choosing not to dwell on the thought of Russians swarming into Bremen. Everyone had heard the dreadful stories about the Red Army unleashing its pent-up hatred of Germans on the civilians. There was no need for either of them to discuss what Gunther feared for Gretl if the Russians got as far as Bremen.

"Sort of." Nate nodded. "There *is* a fraulein. But I don't know if she's still *meine* fraulein. We almost got married before I shipped out two years ago. Until last winter, her letters were dripping with this mushy 'can't wait' stuff, but since then, I think there's somebody else. I heard that from a friend who's back there now. A lot of the older guys that went to war in '42 are back now. They're all grown up and dripping with medals. I heard that she's got herself one of those. He's an officer. I guess Maggie remembers me as just a kid that's all wet behind the ears."

"Wet behind the ears?" Hass asked, trying to imagine the origin of what he saw as a bizarre euphemism.

Nate laughed and started to explain, when suddenly Gunther hushed him.

"Motor!"

Just then a vehicle rounded a bend about a hundred yards back up the road toward the north. It was coming toward them at about thirty miles per hour with just its blackout lights illuminated.

Nate tried to dive into the brush, but it was too thick, so he just pushed himself into it as best he could.

As it drew closer, Nate could make out the familiar contours and the white star of an American Willys jeep. He relaxed slightly just as the jeep slowed.

They'd seen him, but, as he quickly saw, they *weren't Americans*.

He reached for his Colt, but with the flap over the holster, he knew that he wouldn't be able to execute his Montana quick draw fast enough.

Two Soviet soldiers were out of the jeep now and shouting at him in Russian. One had a Tokarev automatic rifle and the other had a pistol that appeared, in the darkness, to be a captured American .45 automatic.

He counted four Russians. Two had remained in the jeep. Nate turned toward the one with the pistol because he looked older and had something on his epaulets that made him look like an officer. Nate had just started to ask whether he spoke any English, when he felt the horrendous pain of the butt of the Tokarev slamming into his left shoulder blade.

As Nate crumpled to the ground, he heard the ear-shattering *crack* of the pistol and felt the shock wave of the slug as it nearly missed his ear. He knew that the second one wouldn't miss.

What a damned screwed-up way to die!

The War Department, The Pentagon.
Arlington, Virginia
Sunday, May 27, 1945, 8:38 p.m.

The last time that Henry Stimson had been in the room where all the European battle maps were displayed had been three weeks ago. The German forces had just surrendered, and the circumstance was a briefing on the final disposition of various units. It had been a happy occasion at which champagne had been suggested and cigars offered. Now, the situation was quite somber, made that much worse by the fact that no one really knew what the situation *was*.

"General Marshall and General Arnold phoned to say they'd be joining us late," Leahy said when Forrestal, King, and Stimson had taken their seats. "The situation in Europe seems to be very fluid at the moment. Russian mechanized units have moved into a number of areas in the British and American zones that were not physically occupied by Allied troops, mainly using back roads and open fields in areas where we have checkpoints on the main roads. As you know, our troops have been under orders since the first of the month to *avoid* any kind of confrontation with the Russians. They've withdrawn from legitimate positions in order to refrain from any kind of altercation, but there have been reports of shots being fired."

"Are there any reports of casualties?" Forrestal asked.

"I have not seen any confirmed reports," Leahy answered. "But there is a rumor that an armored infantry battalion somewhere east of Bayreuth was attacked. The division headquarters has lost contact."

"This is an obvious provocation," Forrestal said. "Do we have any idea how much of the front is affected?"

"The reports that we have are from mainly in the North, the Ninth Army and First Army area," Leahy replied, looking at a sheet of paper. "There's only a couple in the Third Army area down in Bavaria."

"That's my friend George Patton," Stimson smiled, noting the commander of the Third Army. "Nobody wants to provoke George."

"I haven't been around long enough to know him, but his reputation certainly speaks for itself," Forrestal said.

"And it speaks loudly," Stimson answered. "I've known him since he was stationed at Fort Myer in 1912, when I was in President Taft's cabinet."

"That's going back a ways," Leahy interjected.

"George is an impetuous man with an ill temper and a profane tongue," Stimson continued. "But it's hard to find a better combat leader. What his Third Army has accomplished in the past year is legendary."

"So far, almost all of the incidents with the Russians are reported north of Third Army country," Leahy continued. "But, as I said, things are still in a pretty confused state. It's been dark in Europe for some hours. We'll probably have to wait for first light to get a true picture of what's going on . . . Until we can get some recon airplanes up."

"I phoned the President from my office fifteen minutes ago," Forrestal added. "He sent a wire to Stalin asking what the hell's going on, but he hasn't had an answer. Maybe not until morning."

"I don't understand that," Stimson mused. "The Marshal

usually doesn't go to bed until the wee hours. Has anyone tried to contact the Russian generals in Germany?"

"As you know, there was supposed to be an Allied high command authority for the occupation in place by now," Leahy reminded the group. "But the Russians have been dragging their feet and there's no mechanism for communicating with them, like we have with the Brits."

"How are the Brits taking this?" Forrestal asked.

"They're getting some incidents up in their Second Army area," Leahy said. "But they're just as much in the dark as we are."

At that moment, the door opened, and both George Marshall and Hap Arnold came in. Leahy started to refer Forrestal's question about the British to Marshall, but stopped in mid-sentence when he saw a look of total horror on the General's ashen face.

"What's wrong . . . ?" Stimson started to ask.

"It's General Eisenhower," Marshall replied. "Ike's plane's been *lost* over Greenland."

"What happened?" King gasped. The thought of losing the Supreme Allied Commander three weeks after VE-Day was somehow incomprehensible. It was, in many ways, more inconceivable than the death of President Roosevelt five weeks earlier. Ike was at the peak of his form and at the peak of his career, whereas Roosevelt was, admittedly, a tired old man.

"There was a storm over the North Atlantic between Iceland and Labrador," Arnold explained. "Ike's pilot decided to try to go north around the edge, but they got caught in it. The P-61 night fighters that were flying escort lost visual on them. It was your usual 'thick as pea soup' stuff. They had Ike's C-54 on radar for awhile, but then there was a 'Mayday' and the C-54 just vanished. The P-61s got under the cover to look for them, but the snow was coming down too thick. They searched until they were too low on fuel and went back to Iceland. The C-54 never arrived in Labrador."

"My God," Stimson said. "Is there any chance?"

"Maybe, if they were over land," Arnold replied. "Not if they're in the water. It's too dark to keep searching tonight, but we'll have everything we got in the air at dawn."

"What can we do?" Leahy asked.

"Aside from getting every ship and plane in the area into a search, about all we can do is pray," Marshall said.

There was silence in the room, as everyone present dipped his head.

On the road
Somewhere south of Bayreuth, Germany
Monday, May 28, 1945, 2:01 a.m.

Nate McKinley lay helpless in the ditch of a Bavarian back road, a numbing pain burning in his left shoulder. At least two automatic weapons were being aimed at him from close range. It was an ordeal that few men have ever described from personal experience.

What a damned screwed-up way to die!

He heard one shot and then another.

Time slowed. It seemed like forever and he still had not yet felt the impact from the bullet. He had been hit before—only a minor flesh wound during the Remagen fight—but he knew what it felt like, so he waited.

Was this what being shot to death was like? Time was moving so slowly. It seemed like it was taking minutes for the bullet to travel from the muzzle to his flesh. Maybe he was already dead. Maybe this is what *death* was like?

There were more shots. Then screams. Then pain. It was his shoulder again, but not a gunshot wound.

Something fell near him, something large, heavy, and unbelievably foul smelling.

Nate suddenly snapped out of his near-death reverie. He realized what had happened. Gunther was shooting at the Russians. One was down. No, two were down.

Adrenaline surged. Endorphins rushed. Oblivious to the pain in his left shoulder, Nate rolled up into a crouching position and grabbed his Colt. He realized that he hadn't even felt the holster flap.

Nate could barely see the profile of one of the Russians crouching behind the spare tire of the Willys, his head weaving slightly as he tried to make out where the German was hiding across the road. As he was taking aim, so did Nate. Without hesitation, Nate squeezed off a shot at a distance of barely twelve feet.

The low-velocity slug did what it did best, hitting its target with the blunt power of a jack hammer. The Russian's head jerked abruptly and unnaturally, and simply tipped over.

Silence flooded over the scene. The only sounds that Nate heard were the ringing in his ears and the pounding of his heart. His nostrils filled with the familiar smell of burnt powder.

There were two down around him and another behind the jeep. That left one more.

Still crouching and still holding his pistol ahead of him, Nate carefully circled the jeep, which appeared, in the darkness, to be empty.

Suddenly, Nate's ears exploded with the *Whack! Whack!* of two shots being fired by a Tokarev automatic rifle at close range. Out of the corner of his eye, he could see the reflection of the muzzle flash. The damned Russian was under the jeep. No wonder it had looked empty!

He could hear the scraping sound of metal on pavement as the Russian squirmed to reposition himself for another shot. Nate leaped for the only safe place in this microcosmic battlefield—the jeep itself.

Without thinking twice, Nate shoved the muzzle of his Colt against the floorboard of the jeep ahead of where the gas tank was, and fired two rounds. If he would have thought longer, he would have reasoned that many US Army jeeps had armor in the floorboards as a safeguard against exploding mines. Fortunately for him at this moment, this jeep was an exception.

There was a sound beneath the jeep like the cry of a wounded animal, that was followed by the scuffling sound of the Russian writhing in pain. It was impossible for him to return fire from beneath the jeep with a rifle, but Nate hoped that he didn't have a side arm. He knew that he had to finish this guy off quickly, and he began to calculate where in the floorboard to place his last three shots.

Nate knew that if he was under the jeep, and he was thinking clearly—which is a big "if" when you're badly wounded—he would try to wriggle under the rear axle so that another shot would be deflected by the steel casing of the axle or the differential. With this in mind, he placed the Colt's muzzle directly above the place that he calculated to be just forward of the axle on the side of the jeep where the Russian's head would be.

Just as Nate prepared to pull the trigger, a volley of shots rang out, ricocheting off the road beneath the jeep.

"Gunther!" He shouted.

In the struggle to concentrate on the Russian, Nate had forgotten about his German friend. He looked up to see Gunther moving haltingly from the shadows on the other side of the road.

Leaning down over the side of the jeep, Nate made a quick glance under the chassis to see whether the Russian was still active. Even in the darkness, it was clear that the last fusillade from Gunther's Mauser had put the Russian out of his earlier misery.

"That's four," Nate said confidently as the German approached.

"Yesterday, we're enemies," Gunther replied. "Today, we hunt the bear together."

From the gasping sound of his voice, Nate could tell that the German was hurt.

"Are you all right?" Nate asked. "Where are you hit?"

"For three years at the front, I'm never shot," the German said without answering Nate's question. "Now I'm shot in a war between two of my enemies. Dieses ist eine grosse *Ironie!*"

Nate could understand the gross irony even more easily than he could see the dark stain that spread across the left side of the German's tunic.

Nate pulled off the jacket and Gunther's shirt. He used this to push into the wound, which was just below the rib cage and bleeding heavily.

"We've got to get you to an aid station. We've got to get to American lines. Here, let me help you into the jeep."

"You and I aren't going far in this car," Gunther wheezed as he leaned against the jeep. "It hast ein reifenpanne . . . a flat tire!"

He was right. In his effort to kill the last Russian, one of Gunther's shots had pierced the left rear tire.

Quickly, Nate circled the Willys, kicking the others, including the spare that was mounted on the rear of the jeep. Thank God. Only the one was hit. He rummaged around, looking for a jack and lug wrench. Just as his heart began to sink, he found them, crammed under a pile of old chains under the driver's seat.

Despite the darkness, never in his life had Nate changed a tire so fast. Not even the time in the winter of his junior year of high school when he'd had Molly Perkins out past her curfew. In the back of his mind, he found himself comparing the relative lethality of the Red Army to that of Molly Perkins's dad. He breathed a sigh of relief that it was merely the Red Army on his tail.

It wasn't until he was nearly finished with the tire that Nate thought to smell for a ruptured gas tank. Even if the jeep had not exploded, one of the Mauser's slugs could easily have had punctured the tank, draining it faster than Nate could change the tire.

Just as Nate threw the first turn on the last bolt, his ears caught the sound of a motor in the distance. For a moment, he froze. Another vehicle was approaching, and it was coming from the direction of the Russian lines.

"Oh shit!" Nate cursed. He knew that if he didn't finish quickly, they'd have to take to the woods and hope that the Russians would not be able to find them in the darkness. He hoped that if it came to that, he'd be able to make it deep enough into the jungle of willow saplings before he would have to stop because of the noise that it would make.

Finally the last bolt squeaked tight. Nate threw the wrench aside, dropped the jack and began dragging Gunther into the jeep. Together they pushed the dead Russian from the rear seat. As the man tumbled out, Nate noticed a PPSh-1941 submachine gun with a large disc-shaped drum magazine that had fallen onto the road. He instinctively reached for it. Now half sitting, half slouching across the back seat, Gunther grabbed the gun out of Nate's hand.

"I can still *shoot*," he smiled, nodding toward the growing noise of the oncoming vehicle. "I hope you can *drive*."

Without comment, Nate swung into the driver's seat, rammed in the clutch and turned the key. After a few heart-stopping sputters the engine turned over and began to whir.

Just as Nate glanced in his mirror, the blackout lights of the other vehicle came around a corner about a hundred yards back up the road. There was at least two more behind it.

The Russians were coming!

Somewhere over the American Midwest
Sunday, May 27, 1945, 11:19 a.m.

Rosie O'Leary couldn't sleep. Outside the window, an occasional flicker of lightning shown through her eyelids every time she closed them. The bumping and jerking of the C-54 as it bounced across the tops of the day's dying thunderheads was unnerving for someone taking her first airplane ride. If she survived—and she was praying she *would*—Rosie would be in Washington in just a matter of hours instead of the four days that it had taken her to cross the continent by train. Someday, she thought, they'll have airplanes that can fly above these clouds.

Nine rows ahead, she could see Edward Stettinius's white hair buried in a pillow. The Secretary of State was fast asleep. Most of the other members of the Secretary's entourage were either asleep, or, like Rosie, wishing they were. Stephen Cuthbert, on the other hand, had been up and down. She guessed that he was probably seasick, or, as they call it in airplanes, airsick. He had disappeared into the forward part of the aircraft. She supposed that he was talking to the pilots.

As she watched, he suddenly came through the curtain at the front of the plane and woke up the Secretary. Several of the others joined in and there was a sort of agitated conference going on. Rosie's curiosity got the best of her and she moved up toward the front of the plane to eavesdrop.

"He said *that!*" Stettinius could be heard to say. "I can't believe that Stalin said *that!*"

"But he did," Cuthbert insisted. "He gave the President twenty-four hours."

"I beg your pardon," Rosie interrupted. "Stalin gave *who* twenty-four hours?"

"The President," Cuthbert explained. "Truman complained to Stalin about the troop movements and Stalin gave him twenty-four hours to begin a complete pullout of American troops from Germany. He says the Red Army is going to crush fascism where they find it. They're taking over *all* of Germany."

"But Yalta?" Stettinius said desperately. "Stalin signed. He agreed. He can't do this."

"He did what he wanted in Poland," Rosie interjected. "Nobody stopped him *there.*"

Suddenly the copilot emerged from the flight deck, a ghastly expression on his face.

"Is the plane all right?" Stettinius asked, responding to his appearance. "Is something wrong with the plane?"

"No the plane is fine," he said reassuringly in that partially condescending tone that pilots of transports use with nervous passengers. "It's not that. It's . . . We just got the word. Sir, they wanted you to know right away. Sir, General Eisenhower is dead. He was killed in a plane crash."

At that moment, the C-54 bucked abruptly from the turbulence and Rosie felt her hands go numb as she clinched the armrests and closed her eyes.

On the road
Somewhere south of Bayreuth, Germany
Monday, May 28, 1945, 3:23 a.m.

Nate McKinley glanced from the rearview mirror of the jeep to dark road ahead, and back again. The lead vehicle of what was almost certainly a Red Army convoy had come around the corner less than a hundred yards away. Fortunately, the faint blackout lights were not powerful enough to catch the jeep in their glare, but Nate knew it would be just a matter of seconds before they shone on four deceased Soviet soldiers lying in pools of blood that spread across the roadway.

Nate did not wait to watch. Slamming the Willys into third gear, he was traveling as fast as he could in the darkness. Without his own lights, which he dared not use, Nate's perception of the road was that of a very dark gray ribbon winding through the blackness of the forest, a reflection of the grey wedge of sky above the tops of the trees.

Until he rounded the first corner and put a few trees between him and the headlights behind, Nate did not even dare breathe.

In his mind, he estimated that the Russians would stop for no more than a minute when they found the bodies. This would buy him the chance to put some space behind him, but not much. When they saw the bodies and the bloody tracks of the jeep, would the Reds move more slowly, not knowing how many of their enemies were present? Or would they speed up to catch the jeep?

There was a strong urge on Nate's part to just floor it and drive as fast as he could until he made contact with friendly forces. How far were the American lines? He was assuming that there *were* American lines.

What if this captured American jeep that he and Gunther Hass had ambushed was not the *first* Russian-manned vehicle on the road?

What if he was racing away from the Russians behind him, only to come around a corner and find another Russian convoy *ahead?*

There was nothing to do but drive. He watched the radium dial of his wristwatch as it ticked off two hours, then four. Thankfully, the drive was entirely uneventful. He had felt tired earlier, but now he was beyond exhaustion. Gunther, he noticed, had dozed off and was snoring uncomfortably.

For the first time since the shootout, Nate realized that he still had the old Leica camera around his neck. For a moment, he thought about pulling it off and tossing it, but as he was weighing the pros and cons, he glimpsed a cluster of road signs that indicated that the jeep was approaching a town.

Gunther awoke as Nate slowed abruptly.

"Wo bin ich? Was passt?" He muttered, his eyes half opening.

"We're coming to a town. We've gotta be careful."

Gunther struggled to sit up and he grasped the Russian submachine gun, ready to use it if necessary.

As they emerged from the darkness of the woods into the clearing where the village was situated, they could see the first weak pinkish hue of the approaching dawn spreading across the sky.

It was, as far as Nate could see, a typical small Bavarian

village, filled with wood and stone buildings that began abruptly at the edge of town and crowded close on either side of the road. In a town like this back home, houses would have at least a quarter acre around them.

There was no sign of life. No lights were visible in any of the windows. The only vehicle was an American deuce-and-a-half truck parked at the edge of the road. Nate approached carefully, but the hood was up and he guessed that it had had engine trouble and was abandoned. There was no sign of it having been shot at. Nate sensed that this meant they were ahead of the Russian vanguard. Apparently there had been American forces in town, but they had withdrawn without having been attacked.

On the south side of the town, the road forked. A signpost between the forks had been reduced to a raw stump. Whoever had been here last had taken it away as a keepsake, or to help confuse whomever came later. Nate *was* confused, but Gunther gestured weakly toward the right fork.

Just as he was turning, Nate heard the ripping sound of a large truck backfiring as it slowed on the narrow main street behind them. As Nate looked back, Gunther jerked himself from the grogginess of his painful stupor and raised the broad snout of the PPSh-1941. An American truck came around the corner, just fifty feet behind them. Nate could see the pea-green uniforms of three Russians in the cab. They saw the jeep and one of them reacted quickly, raising his side arm to fire.

Gunther, however, reacted quicker. He sprayed the cab from left to right, the jagging down into the grille, shredding the radiator of the big GMC.

As the truck jerked sideways in a cloud of white steam, striking the wall of a stone building at about forty miles per hour, Nate put the jeep into second gear and pushed the pedal to the metal. For nearly an hour, he'd paced himself carefully through the forest, but now it was time to say "Hang on!"

With its small engine and low gear ratio, the jeep was never intended for high speeds, but Nate decided to wring every mph possible out of those four cylinders.

By causing the truck to crash on the narrow street, Gunther had bought them more precious time. Any other vehicles behind it would be backed up trying to get ahead of the wreck. This would give the jeep more of a chance to get away.

What they had not counted on, however, was for three of the vehicles behind the truck to be motorcycles.

The jeep screamed from the strain of the rpms as the thundering motorcycles gained ground. Despite Nate's best efforts, the Willys was no match for the captured German BMWs. In his mirror, he could see the Russian on the lead motorcycle draw a pistol. Wincing in the sixty-five-mile-an-hour slipstream because he was not wearing goggles, the Russian struggled to take aim.

Gunther waited until the motorcycle was within easy range and squeezed off a very short burst.

Nate did not see the 7.62 mm slugs strike their target, but in the mirror, he saw the BMW suddenly upend and bounce high into the air. The rider became separated from the machine as it spiralled back down onto the road. They struck the pavement and bounced again. The motorcycle bounced higher than the body of the Russian.

The other two motorcycles made no attempt to stop, but slowed to maintain a respectable distance from the jeep. Gunther Hass waited a moment for them to close, but they held their separation. Sensing what the German was trying to do, Nate let up slightly on the accelerator and the two BMWs quickly slid into range.

Gunther took aim and pulled the trigger.

Nate heard two pops as two shots pierced the air, followed by the whirring sound of a hammer hitting an empty chamber. The 71-round drum magazine was empty.

Pushing the accelerator back down, Nate grabbed desperately for the speed that he knew the straining Willys could not provide. He heard the thunder of one of the motorcycles coming up on his left barely a few feet behind.

Now the BMW was abreast of the jeep.

He could see the angry face of the Russian. He was cursing, but the words were inaudible over the roar of the engines.

Ahead, Nate could see a hairpin turn to the right. Instinctively, he thought to brake going into the turn, but instead, he allowed the Willys to slide into the adjacent side of the road, using the centrifugal velocity of the turn to slam the BMW.

Nate felt the jolt of the impact as he cranked the wheel to the right.

For a moment, the Russian's face was barely two feet from his own.

The angry leer turned to wide-eyed fright as the motorcycle began to skid.

The face turned away and began to sink as the BMW turned toward its side. It slipped to a forty-five degree angle, then slumped quickly.

Nate heard no sound as it hit the pavement and started to skid. In his mirror, Nate saw the dust cloud as the mass of wreckage tumbled into a low stone retaining wall.

Suddenly, the windshield of the jeep exploded in a hailstorm of broken safety glass. To his right, the last motorcycle rider was pointing his pistol directly at Nate.

Because of the grinding right turn, the centrifugal force was pulling the jeep away from the motorcycle. The rider knew this, and knew that he was safe, at least for the moment, from the fate of his comrade.

As the Russian took aim for another shot, many thoughts raced through Nate's head, not the least of which was the many hours that Nate and his brother had practiced their quick draws with their handguns back home in Montana. Almost instinctively, he reached for his Colt. In an instant, it was out of its holster.

The look of surprise on the Russian's face quickly disappeared as his head jerked to the side in a puff of pink froth.

Jerking his head back to the road ahead, Nate saw no longer a deserted rural highway, but crowds of people scurrying to get out of the way of the careening Willys and dozens of other vehicles—other jeeps, deuce-and-a-halfs, and even tanks.

Nate was surrounded, but not by figures in the pea-colored Red Army uniform nor in the feldgrau of the Wehrmacht, but by dozens of men in the khaki and olive drab of the US Army.

He slammed on the brakes, squealing to a stop in a cloud of burning rubber.

Cautiously, a man with captain's bars on his helmet approached the jeep, accompanied by two who had M14 rifles trained on Nate. He just put his hands on the top of the steering wheel and took a deep breath.

"Nate McKinley, Staff Sergeant, 27th Armored Infantry

Battalion . . ." he said before the captain could say anything.
"The war's not over anymore. The *Russians* are coming."

"Who's this?" The captain asked, pointing to the silent,
blood-spattered form crumpled into the rear seat of the jeep.

Nate glanced back at the German whom he had not known
twelve hours ago, but who had saved his life at least twice
since. He looked into the half-opened eyes and could tell they
would never again see Bremen—or Gretl.

"This is . . . was . . . Gunther Hass. He and I used to hunt
bear together."

At that moment, the morning sun broke over the mountains
to the east. Nate looked up as a crowd of GIs closed in on the
jeep to look it over. Suddenly, the crowd turned to look toward
something that was ahead of the jeep.

Through the blasted-out windshield frame, Nate beheld a
sight that he would never forget.

The crowd of GIs parted like the waters of the Red Sea as
a tall, powerful man strode through the crowd to stand before
the jeep, bathed in the first rays of the sunrise.

From the toes of his riding boots to the top of his steel helmet, which glistened with four silver stars, the man was the
epitome of spit and polish. His powerful shoulders and stern
jaw radiated an awesome sense of power and strength. His presence commanded such an aura of total authority that Nate could
think to do nothing short of scrambling from the jeep and
standing at attention before this man.

Nate straightened himself as best he could, and executed
his smartest salute since boot camp.

General George Smith Patton, Jr. stared at Nate for a split
second with his glacial blue eyes, then transferred his binoculars to his left hand and crisply returned Nate's salute.

To be in such close proximity to the great Patton for the
first time was not something that one took lightly. Nate had
seen him once before, at a distance, soon after the Battle of
the Bulge, but his presence was a constant fact of life throughout the European Theater. To most of the men who had fought
under him—and against him—through the bitter months between the breakout from Normandy in August 1944 and the final victory on May 7, 1945, he was the greatest American
combat leader in Europe. Even those who hated and feared

him still respected him and were dazzled by his tactical skill.

"At ease, son," Patton said in his incongruously high-pitched voice.

"Yes, sir."

That was all that Nate could think of to say.

"What's your name sergeant?" Patton asked, glancing at Nate's stripes.

"Nate McKinley, sir."

"Well, Sergeant McKinley, I watched you out there just now, and *damn it,* I like the way you drive. I need a driver like you. My driver, Sergeant Mims. He's been with me since before D-Day. Gone home. Had enough points, dammit. I need driver, and son, you've got a new assignment."

"Thank you, sir," Nate gulped.

"What unit are you with, son?" Patton asked.

"I'm with the 27th Armored Infantry Battalion, sir."

"Oh my God, you were with the outfit that was . . . that was massacred by those bastards."

"Yes, sir," Nate said, reaching for his camera. "And I have the *pictures.*"

5

★ ★

The White House
Washington DC
Tuesday, May 29, 1945, 9:16 a.m.

WITHIN an hour of Nate McKinley's roll of film coming out of the developer at the Third Army photographic lab, eight-by-ten enlargements were on their way to Washington. By the end of the day, another set of prints had found its way to one of the eager journalists that hovered around Third Army headquarters.

As he now sat in his office, staring silently at the images of the line of GIs being gunned down in cold blood, Harry Truman was numb. He had fought in World War I and he'd seen men die. As a senator, and as president, he'd seen horrible photographs of death and destruction. As with all Americans, the sudden shock of Pearl Harbor was a memory that was still fresh in his mind. Yet these pictures represented something even worse. This was an unambiguous act of war perpetrated by a nation with which the United States was technically still allied. It had occurred against the backdrop of widespread illegal incursions against territory occupied by American and British forces.

The news of Eisenhower's death had been quickly overshadowed by events of yet greater magnitude. The President hadn't slept a wink since the wee hours of Monday morning when he had replied to Stalin's ultimatum with one sentence: "The United States adamantly refuses to accede to your demands."

He had thought about just saying "nuts," as General McAuliffe had to the Germans at Bastogne in December, but decided on a little more verbosity. Now, with these pictures in hand, he could think of several words that he wished he'd used and which would have been even stronger than "nuts." Of course, the newspapers wouldn't have been able to quote him— but this was not necessarily such a bad thing.

There had been no further word from Stalin. Ed Stettinius had not been able to reach Molotov. Both Truman and Prime Minister Churchill had issued statements insisting that the Soviet forces withdraw immediately—but this had been midday on Monday, before the Kummersdorf pictures cast an entirely more sinister light on the situation.

If Truman and his cabinet had heard nothing from the Soviet government, the President and his administration had heard plenty from the government in Washington, especially from Capitol Hill. Last night, Truman had been one of a handful of people in America who had seen the pictures. This morning, they were on every front page in the land. The President had gotten his first phone call from Capitol Hill before he'd brushed his teeth. Until he asked his secretary to hold all his calls, the phone had been ringing off the hook.

Congressman Alvin Okanski, the outspoken supporter of the Polish Government in Exile, had echoed most of the editorial pages by calling on the President to consider a declaration of war. Both Senate Majority Leader Alben Barkley of Kentucky and Senate Minority Leader Wallace White had called to say that their constituents and their colleagues would now support a declaration of war.

Speaker of the House Sam Rayburn, the most powerful man on the Hill, and a longtime supporter of Franklin Roosevelt, had called Truman to discuss *when,* not *whether,* a declaration of war should be introduced in Congress. Truman invited Rayburn to bring a delegation to the White House to discuss just that and they settled on noon, because, as Truman explained, he would be meeting with Stimson, Stettinius, and Forrestal in a few minutes, and a half hour later, they'd be joined by the military brass.

Stettinius was the first to arrive, and he came bearing a copy of the morning paper.

Headlines were already using the phrase "Kummersdorf Massacre," and editorial writers were using the phrase in the same sentence with "Pearl Harbor." Truman saw that the names of the men of the 27th Infantry Battalion who died at Kummersdorf were listed in a large, black-edged box.

"The papers are calling it a war," the Secretary observed as he sat down opposite the President's desk.

"Sam Rayburn is coming down from the Hill in a couple of hours," Truman said soberly. "Until Kummersdorf, Stalin could have weaseled his way out, but not now. Rayburn says that the calls that he's getting are running strongly in favor of war."

"I would have thought that the American people would have little stomach for another war in Europe less than a month after VE-Day," Stettinius suggested.

"Stalin's gone too damned far with this," Truman insisted. "Look at the pictures. These are more graphic than anything from Pearl Harbor. As you and I both know, this is not a random attack. It's very premeditated. Uncle Joe went too far. It seems that he's been planning for some time to go much further. Tell me about this reporter you met who had seen what she thought were battle plans."

"She claims to have seen maps in Molotov's suite in San Francisco that had the Russians going all the way to Paris and London," Stettinius said. "She was *not* making this up. In fact, she first told me about it on Friday. *Before* the attacks."

Henry Stimson and Jim Forrestal both arrived as Stettinius was describing the maps. Forrestal commented that what was shown on the maps seemed to parallel what the Russians were actually doing.

"Except that the maps allegedly showed London and Paris," Stimson pointed out. "And Stalin's ultimatum referred only to Germany."

"I think the time has come," Truman said emphatically. "To stop wallowing in the fiction of Uncle Joe actually meaning what he says."

"Agreed," Stimson said. "What these maps apparently showed, and subsequent events have *certainly* shown, is that Stalin intends to extend his empire as deeply into Europe as Hitler did. Poland was just the dress rehearsal."

The four civilians were joined by the military chiefs who had come bearing maps of their own. The first map told a story that no one in the room wanted to hear. It was, Stettinius imagined, not unlike those that Rosie O'Leary had described. Red arrows pointed west. There was little doubt where things were headed.

"I'd like to point out that our friends in Congress are talking about a declaration of war," Truman began. "So we'd better get to the point of thinking of this as the first planning session for World War III . . . or, I should say, the first planning session on *this* side."

"We managed to get some photo-recon missions off on Monday," Hap Arnold added. "We got some pictures of the area about fifty miles deep into their zone. Our guys were challenged by Red fighters, so they backed off. They didn't want to get into a tangle until we knew what was going on. We're going back today with tactical bombers . . . and fighter escort."

"What did those pictures show?" Truman asked.

"Tank columns. Most of the crossings on Sunday and Monday were by light mechanized outfits, but they're moving a lot of armor up to the demarcation line . . . I suppose I should call it the 'front.' "

"According to the reports we're getting this morning, there were more than a few shots being fired," Marshall said, pointing to his map. "There's a very big push in the north in the British Second Army salient. It looks like they're aiming for Hamburg. We captured the Elbe bridgeheads in April, but because of Yalta, we had to turn them over to the Reds. Now they're pouring across."

"Which gave them a jump start on the invasion," Admiral King added.

"So, to be specific about the tactical situation," Marshall said, returning to the map with a typewritten list from his briefcase. "We've got Zhukov's 1st Byelorussian Front opposite the 12th Army Group sector, and the 2nd Byelorussian Front under Rokossovski already moving to encircle Hamburg."

"What are the British doing?" Truman asked.

"They're monitoring the situation and getting ready to defend themselves. Up until now, they've been avoiding the Russians as much as we have, but that could change any minute if . . ."

A knock at the door interrupted the Army's Chief of Staff in mid-sentence.

"Who is it?" Truman barked. Who could possibly deign to interrupt the President of the United States in a war conference with his highest-ranking cabinet members and military officers?

"Sir?" It was his secretary.

"Yes. What is it? Why are we being interrupted?"

"It's the phone. It's Prime Minister Churchill."

"Well, I suppose that warrants an interruption," Truman sighed.

"Mr. Prime Minister," Truman said, picking up the receiver from the phone on the side table behind his chair. "Good of you to call. We were just discussing this situation."

"More than a goddam situation, Mr. President," Churchill shouted. "The bastards are shelling my people. There's an artillery barrage falling on Hamburg. It's World War III! I'm going to Parliament in an hour to ask for a declaration."

"Have you been able to reach Stalin?" Truman asked.

"Why? What would that lying blackguard say that his howitzers have not said already?"

Capitol Hill
Washington DC
Tuesday, May 29, 1945, 2:06 p.m.

Rosie O'Leary had squeezed into the last available seat in the press box, high in the rafters of the House Chamber at the Capitol. When the rumors had started to come in, the other reporters from *The Washington Herald* had scooted over to the White House to try to get a comment from one of the long line of military and political dignitaries that were reported to be arriving there to confer with the President. Rosie, on the other hand, had taken one look at the Kummersdorf Massacre photos and the wire reports from around the country and had headed for the Capitol. If it was to come to World War III, there was only one room in Washington where it would be declared.

In the Capitol, the hallways were already teeming with journalists. At the podium, workmen were already installing the radio network microphones.

"Where were you the last time this happened?" The woman next to Rosie asked in a polite British accent. She was very well dressed in a nicely tailored suit, and she had an obviously sophisticated air about her.

"I was . . . I was in San Francisco," Rosie said, not wanting to admit to the thirtyish woman that she'd still been in high school on December 8, 1941 when Franklin Roosevelt delivered his "Day of Infamy" speech in this room. "Where were you?"

"In a pub off the Strand," the English woman replied. "I was with the *Mirror* at the time. Just a copyreader. We were jolly glad to hear that the Yanks were finally coming to help us get rid of Hitler. By the way, my name is Fiona Wells, I'm a Washington correspondent with the *Standard* now."

"Rosemary O'Leary, *The Washington Herald*."

"O'Leary? Are you the girl who did that piece on Molotov saying there was no Polish Question?"

"That was me," Rosie said, trying not to blush.

"Smashing. That issue seems to have been a bit superseded by other events. What's your take on the mood here in the States on what seems to be happening here, here in this room this afternoon?"

"Americans are really tired of war. But I don't think anyone wants to see us win one war and lose a second war a month later. Everyone seems to be comparing what happened at Kummersdorf to what happened at Pearl Harbor. I think that really says it all. What's the mood in Britain?"

"I've been here since Kummersdorf happened, so I haven't talked to the man and woman in the street, but it seems to be more or less the same. If anything, I think we're a bit *more* upset with the 'Man of Steel' than you Yanks. You know what I mean by 'Man of . . .'"

"Stalin, of course. Means 'man of steel.'" Rosie said impatiently. "What exactly do you mean, though, by *more* upset?"

"Well, what I meant was, Prime Minister Churchill has been more outspoken on the Polish Question and the shameful behavior of the Red Army in Eastern Europe than anyone in your government. Mr. Stettinius, for example. Seems rather much too conciliatory. Don't you think?"

"I had a chance to spend some time with Stettinius on several occasions in San Francisco last week," Rosie said, carefully name dropping. "Until Sunday, I think he was of a mind that the United Nations Organization was the chief goal of American foreign policy."

"So you spent some time with the Secretary?" Miss Wells said, evincing a genuine interest.

"Yes, and I also had a chance to talk with one of your fellow countrymen . . . who seemed to be fairly well connected with the Russian delegation. In fact, it was he who introduced me to Commissar Molotov. He was rather outspoken in his antagonism toward Churchill."

"After five years of coalition government with a Tory Prime Minister, Labour is very anxious to get into power on its own."

"The British people would never vote Churchill out of office, would they?" Rosie asked, prodding the British woman, who was obviously a Churchill devotee. "Not after what he has done for your country."

"We were expecting him to call for new elections next month, but now it looks as though the coalition is going to be around for awhile."

By this time, most of the Senators and Congressmen were in place, although most were still standing and talking. Speaker Sam Rayburn entered from the side of the room, and, as he made his way to the podium, the hiss of conversation abruptly tapered off, and there was a round of applause.

The big Texas Congressman and kingmaker, veteran of sixteen terms in the House of Representatives, rapped the gavel and announced in a booming voice, "Ladies and Gentlemen, the President of the Yoo-nited States!"

The applause was tremendous, with nearly everyone remembering where they were on that terrible Monday morning in 1941 when Franklin Roosevelt, his legs clamped in steel braces, stood in this room to ask for a declaration of war. Indeed, many of the people now in this room to cast their votes today had cast their votes then.

Truman walked briskly up the aisle like a man with a purpose. He mounted the podium, as Rayburn and Senate President Pro-tempore Kenneth McKellar of Tennessee took their places behind him.

"Just twenty-one days ago, I spoke to the world of a solemn but glorious hour in which the flags of freedom flew over all of Europe. I spoke of the terrible price we'd paid to rid the world of Hitler and his evil band. I told you that the Western world had been freed of the evil forces who had imprisoned the bodies and broken the lives of millions upon millions of free-born men.

"In the three weeks that have passed since that glorious day when victory seemed won, we have watched a wartime ally manifest himself as a tyrant and bully of the same stripe as Hitler. We watched with disbelief as Poland, the first nation to be crushed by Hitler's jackboot, was enslaved by one who came wearing the cloak of a liberator.

"We have worked hard through the past year to build a United Nations Organization as a means to circumvent distrust and greed and all of the root causes of war. While we imagined a noble purpose for the United Nations, Soviet Russia saw it only as a means to its own ends.

"Almost forty-two months ago, President Roosevelt stood in this room and spoke of a Sunday morning that will live forever in infamy. Today, I speak to you of another Sunday morning that will live in infamy."

A standing ovation shook the chamber for nearly four minutes. Everyone seemed to have expected him to use the word "infamy," and they used it as a cue to break the tension.

"Though the two Sunday mornings are half a world and forty-two months apart, they're linked by the greed of those who are incapable of feeling secure without enslaving others, and by the deaths of Americans whose sacrifice will *never* be forgotten."

The second standing ovation lasted for a shorter period of time, not so much out of lack of enthusiasm, but out of an apparent excitement to hear what else the President had to say.

"Today, we're *still* locked in the deadly struggle to defeat the same foe that was responsible for the infamy of that Sunday morning forty-two months ago, but the Empire of Japan is all but staggering and soon will fall. Today, just three weeks after our grand victory over Nazi Germany, we have found that our job is not yet finished in that theater. The American people are tired of war. *I'm* tired of this war . . . but just as we accepted the challenge of fighting a global war in 1941, we must do so today.

"Along with our British allies, who went to war in 1939 to fight the forces of tyranny and who are voting today on a similar resolution to that before you, we must take up the sword in Europe again.

"We must complete the task which our late General Eisenhower described as a Crusade in Europe. I ask you, and I ask the American people, to stand with me and to shoulder the sacrifice necessary to see the job done, once and for all, so that the beacon of freedom will be visible in all the corners of the Earth.

"We must not rest until we have driven the forces of Soviet aggression from Germany, and from all of the countries of Europe where they imposed their tyranny through force of arms. Just as it was with the tyranny of Nazi aggression, so too must the nations subjected to Soviet tyranny be allowed to choose their governments freely and to chart the course of their own affairs. The beacon of freedom must be visible in all the corners of the Earth.

"I ask you to vote 'aye' on the resolution before you, calling for the declaration of a state of war between the United States and the Soviet Union."

The President left the room to a third ovation, but the House members turned quickly to the matter at hand and the senators retired to their own chamber. A roll call vote allowed those in favor to posture a bit, and weeded out those who might be inclined to waffle. When it was all over, there were just a half-dozen abstentions and three "nay" votes from strongly pro-leftist congressmen.

"How do you suppose the vote went in Parliament?" Rosie asked Miss Wells as they were leaving the House Chamber.

"Rather much the same, I'd say, although I'd reckon there will be a larger number of nays. The Labour MPs are die-hards."

"I thought you said they were *more* upset with the 'Man of Steel' than we Yanks?" Rosie smiled.

"But we have the Labour hooligans," the older woman admitted. "Here, I see a colleague of mine, maybe he's heard."

The two woman approached the British journalist and posed the question.

"Oh, Churchill *won*," he replied. "By just a single vote."

The smile faded from Fiona Wells's face.

PART II

A DAMNED
FINE WAR

★ ★ ★ ★ ★

6

★ ★

Henry Lewis Stimson's Georgetown townhouse
Washington DC
Wednesday, June 6, 1945, 1:28 a.m.

THE Secretary of War opened the front door as quietly as he could. Mabel would be sleeping and Henry Stimson knew that one of them awake at this hour was one too many. He tiptoed to his study, heaved his briefcase onto his desk and pulled the chain on his lamp. Before him, his desk calendar reminded him of the irony of this day.

Who could have imagined a year ago that Americans would be fighting *two* world wars today?

Exactly one year had passed since the Anglo-American Allies had fought their way ashore at Normandy to begin Eisenhower's noble crusade against Hitler and Nazi tyranny.

Irony lay in the fact that the Normandy Invasion had been undertaken against the backdrop of Stalin's demands for a second front in Europe to take the pressure off his Red Army, which was fighting against the bulk of German might on the Eastern Front. Now, it was the Red Army that was on the offensive, with a stated goal of pushing the Anglo-Americans back into the Normandy surf.

This time though, Eisenhower was dead and Stalin was unmasked as the enemy.

The Soviets had spent the three weeks following VE-Day regrouping and preparing for the *next* offensive, while the Allies, as the Anglo-Americans still called themselves, had spent those weeks doing exactly the opposite—demobilizing, dismantling, and moving as fast as possible to get their manpower *away* from the front for redeployment to the Pacific or home.

When the war had begun on May 27, the Red Army was

rested and ready. The Allies were in disarray. The 2nd Byelorussian Front under Marshal Konstantin Rokossovsky, who had devastated von Kluge's Wehrmacht forces at Kursk in 1943, now captured Hamburg in a brutal thrust. Rokossovsky had then cut off the land route into Denmark and had surrounded Bremen, leaving it the only major German port in Allied hands.

Meanwhile, the 1st Byelorussian Front, which was under the direct command of Marshal Georgi Zhukov, the Red Army's supreme commander, had used the access to the Elbe River bridges to move armored and machinized forces up to the demarcation line in large numbers.

On May 27, they had started slipping through the line, and on May 29, covered by a massive artillery barrage such as Zhukov had used during his Berlin offensive a month earlier, the 1st Byelorussian Front, backed by the troops of Ivan Koniev's 1st Ukrainian Front, had burst through in overwhelming force. These two army groups, which had battered their way through determined German resistance from Warsaw and Krakow into Berlin, now faced pitifully little in the way of organized American opposition.

On VE-Day, the American 12th Army Group, including the First and Ninth Armies, had been present in this area in force. Three weeks later, the entire First had been pulled out to regroup for movement to the Pacific, leaving behind only mountains of supplies, which were earmarked for later shipment, and which were quickly captured by the advancing Soviet troops. Remnants of the Ninth Army that were still billeted in the area had been on alert for forty-eight hours when the 1st Byelorussian Front hit them, but they had not had time to dig in or to construct defensive positions.

The rout had been complete, with thousands of Americans captured.

General William Hood Simpson, who had commanded the Ninth through VE-Day, had been reassigned back home in the largely ceremonial post of commander of the Second Army. He was in Paris en route home when the Soviets attacked, and had raced back to take charge. Given the status of his former command, there was little that he could do but try to consolidate the units that he had and organize a defense of the Rhineland.

Against two army groups, Simpson's Ninth faced an impossible task.

Meanwhile, in southern Germany, Alexander "Sandy" Patch's Seventh Army was almost fully demobilized. George Patton's Third Army remained in Bavaria, the only counterweight to a possible move by one or more of the three Soviet army groups in Austria and Czechoslovakia.

In Italy, General Lucian Truscott's US Fifth Army had been officially demobilized, although many of the troops and a great deal of their materiel still remained.

Formidable as they were, the forces that Stalin had committed to action thus far represented fewer than half of his frontline troops. Regrouping in East Prussia, Vasilievsky's 3rd Byelorussian Front and Bagramyan's 2nd Baltic Front represented a strategic reserve for Zhukov, Rokossovsky, and Koniev. Meanwhile, to the south, three Soviet army groups waited, poised for action. The 4th Ukrainian Front, under Stalingrad hero Marshal Andrei Yeremenko was in Erfurt, southwest of Leipzig—a salient liberated by the United States First Army in May, but turned over to the Soviets under the Yalta agreement.

Meanwhile, Marshal Fyodor Tolbukhin's 3rd Ukrainian Front was in Czechoslovakia, in and around Prague, and Marshal Rodion Malinovsky's 2nd Ukrainian Front was waiting in Vienna.

Waiting for *what?*

This was Stimson's last conscious thought as he nodded off, resting his left cheek on the papers spread across his desk.

"Lucky Forward," The Third Army Forward Command Post
Kummersdorf, Germany
Wednesday, June 6, 1945, 5:40 a.m.

"Dammit Hap, I hate waiting around here like this," General George Smith Patton, Jr. said to his Chief of Staff, Major General Hobart R. Gay. "Those poor devils up there in 12th Army Group are getting the shit kicked out of them by the damnable Reds, and here we sit, waiting for goddam orders. In the very least, we could go up and relieve Frankfurt like we did last winter at Bastogne. If Ike was still in charge, he'd have ordered it."

Patton turned his back to the window in the Kummers-dorf stadthalle tower that he'd been using as an observation point from which to scan the surrounding countryside, and from which he'd been watching the dawn begin to break on the eastern horizon. Nate McKinley watched the big man pace the room like a caged Bengal tiger, the four highly polished silver stars on his lapels flickering like fire in the light of the gas lamp.

He had known Patton personally for just a few days, but he had already come to be fond of the very complex man within this pacing tiger. Nate had particularly appreciated Patton's insistence on using a recaptured Kummersdorf as his forward command post.

In the week that he'd been Patton's driver, Nate had rarely left the General's side. During this time, Patton became the hub of frantic activity, as his division and corps commanders repositioned and reoriented their troops for the inevitable. It would often be just the two of them. On more than one occasion, Patton had recalled the time during the Battle of the Bulge, when Sergeant Mims had said that the Third Army didn't need a staff because Patton and Mims had managed to run the entire operation with just the two of them, a jeep and a two-way radio. Patton absolutely loved this idea of commanding his troops from a mobile command post, just like a Civil War general would have done from the back of a good cavalry horse.

George Smith Patton, Jr. was, for all his faults, a soldier's general. He made a point of being with his frontline combat troops as much as he possibly could. Unlike many other high-ranking officers who'd spent the recently completed war in secure command posts safely removed from flying bullets and artillery rounds, Patton had earned the respect, if not the admiration of his troops by being *with* them.

His short postwar sojourn as military governor of Bavaria had been a monumental letdown. After the thrill of battle—and Patton indeed savored the thrill—he found his new role as an administrator downright boring.

Suddenly, however, there was a *new* war, a high-stakes war

with an adversary more powerful on the ground than any the US Army had ever faced. It was a war that seemed tailor-made for Patton, the tactical genius with the unrelenting will to win.

The day after the war began, Patton had personally led units of the 9th Armored and 97th Infantry Divisions in a swift counterattack against the Soviet forces that had earlier wiped out Nate's buddies in the 27th Armored Infantry Battalion. Giving no quarter, the 9th Armored Division's Sherman tanks had made quick work of the Soviet mechanized forces. They had reclaimed the territory lost to the Soviets in the new war's first days, but Patton had been ordered to halt and wait.

For Patton, this order stung like a personal insult. His long-time nemesis, General Omar Nelson Bradley, the commander of the 12th Army Group, had been named as acting commander of Allied forces in Europe, while the politicians in London and Washington had bickered over whether to name Bradley or Britain's Field Marshall Bernard Law Montgomery as Eisenhower's replacement as the permanent Supreme Allied Commander in Europe.

The bespectacled Bradley was everything that Patton was not. His unassuming and even timid appearance masked a calculating, politically adept organizer, who left little to chance. Where Patton spoke his mind, regardless of whether it was a position with which Eisenhower would agree, Bradley had carefully and methodically cultivated a close working relationship with the Supreme Commander. Now, with Ike gone, Bradley had found himself in the right place at the right time. Unfortunately, the forces under his command were taking a severe beating—while Patton had been ordered to *wait*.

"Well, here we are!" Patton said, turning his back on the window and pacing across the floor. "In nine months, the Third Army took half again more ground than the rest of his whole damned 12th Army *Group,* and we're guarding Bradley's right flank! Hell, Zhukov's moved so far in the last week that Brad doesn't even *have* a right flank any more. First those damned Mongols kicked his ass, then they chewed off his flank. If we don't get into this fight pretty damned soon, those bastards will be dancing a jig in Paris just like 'der Fuhrer' did when he whipped the French back in 1940."

"Well, sir," General Gay suggested meekly, "the Russians

do have *three* whole army groups sitting there opposite us. If we weren't here, Zhukov could put *them* into the line."

"Those bastards know that the American fighting man is worth a dozen of their people," Patton said, glancing at Gay and looking directly at Nate. "And a *Third Army* fighting man is worth twenty! Do you know what my worst fear is?"

"No, sir," Nate replied.

"His worst fear," Gay answered, "is that the politicians in Washington are going to strike a negotiated settlement of some kind with Stalin before Third Army has a chance to prove what we can do."

The War Department, The Pentagon
Arlington, Virginia
Wednesday, June 6, 1945, 7:47 a.m.

Henry Stimson stifled a yawn as he sat among America's top military leaders at the big mahogany table in the Pentagon war room. He had not slept well. He had dozed for nearly four hours in the chair in his study, but when he shed his suit and went to bed, his mind would not let his body go back to sleep. He lay awake, thinking about the meeting this morning of the joint chiefs. He had thought again about the irony of this day being the first anniversary. He prayed that the success that had followed *that* nail-biter might prevail again.

As the sky lightened and he knew that sleep would not rescue him, his thoughts turned to Highhold. Just two weeks before, he had dared to dream that soon he'd be able to retire to his ridgetop. As things stood now, Stimson wondered when he'd even *see* Highhold again.

As the car was driving him to the Pentagon, the Secretary of War had observed the change of mood that had settled upon the capital. The springtime euphoria of early May was gone, replaced by a somberness that reminded him of 1942. People were walking with their heads down again.

At the Pentagon, the guards were edgy. The mood in the Joint Chiefs' conference room was bleak. One after another, briefers came into the room with maps and charts to explain what was going wrong—and why.

"American forces have not been in a retreat on this scale since the Civil War," a young colonel explained soberly. "Meanwhile, the Red Army has been gaining ground faster against us than they did against the Germans at any time since their Operation Bagration offensive in Byelorussia in July last year."

"How bad is it?" James Forrestal asked.

"We've been beaten badly so far," Marshall summarized. "We've taken roughly nine thousand casualties in a week, about the same as a year ago during the six weeks following the invasion. The really horrible news is that we've had as many as thirty thousand of our people captured. We're not sure of the exact numbers because of the confusion. In the first forty-eight hours, we had whole units captured because they'd been told to avoid confronting the Russians. They thought it was just a massive snafu between allies that would be sorted out soon."

"Now these poor guys are on their way to Siberia," Hap Arnold said disgustedly.

"What can be done?" Stimson asked. "What is the strategic plan?"

"Our first line of defense is the Rhine. Bradley's plan is to hold Frankfurt and to stop the Red Army advance at the Rhine," Marshall said. "If we can hold them until we're able to get reinforcements flowing back into the line, then we can prepare to mount a counteroffensive."

"When will that be?" Stimson asked.

"I'm hoping that we will be able to do so by the first of September."

"Why so long?" Stimson said, shaking his head. "I seem to recall that eight weeks ago, we had the biggest force in American history deployed to this very ground."

"Frankly, our strength has been declining rapidly since then. When we saw the end of the war against Germany, we started to ship entire units to the Pacific."

"It also cut into the organization," the young colonel added. "There are regiments missing entire battalions; divisions are missing entire regiments. What remained was disorganized and understrength . . . and without much equipment. It was stockpiled in Germany. The Russians have it now."

"Now we have to undo the demobilization and try to re-build what we once had," Marshall said. "It will be August be-fore we'll be able to turn things around. It'll take longer to get more materiel into the pipeline. Factories that were turning out tanks a year ago had been given the green light to start building passenger cars for the 1945 model year."

"Fortunately the new M26 tanks will be available now," an-other one of the briefers added. "It's heavier than the Sherman. It's about the equivalent of a German Panther, and it's got a 90 mm gun compared to the 76 mm on the M4A3 Sherman and the 88 on the big Kraut tanks. A few of them got overseas last winter, but we should be able to start putting a lot of them into the line before September."

"What about the Air Force?" Stimson asked, turning to Hap Arnold.

"We're hampered by the same thing as the guys on the ground," Arnold admitted. "When this thing started, we were understrength in Europe and not at all ready to fight another war. Wings were missing squadrons, and squadrons were miss-ing their best aircrews. All of these guys had enough points for a ticket home. The Eighth Air Force, which smashed Germany, is gone. We've got over 2,400 bombers scattered at fields from Iceland to California on their way to Okinawa to fight Japan. They're everywhere but England. There's only one group that's combat capable in England at this moment, so we'll have them making a U-turn and heading back to their former bases. We expect the Eighth to be fully operational by July. The Fifteenth Air Force in Italy has pretty much folded its tents to go home, but it has more intact groups than the Eighth. It was supposed to be demobilized, rather than redeployed, so all the equipment and a lot of aircrews are still in the the-ater."

"I assume that you'll be sending B-29s to Europe now," Stimson said, referring to the massive Boeing superbomber, which Arnold had deliberately earmarked for use only against Japan.

"Yes, we will," Arnold said. "We concentrated them in the Pacific, because by the time they were ready . . . which was only a year ago . . . the B-17s and B-24s were more than adequate for the job in Europe. We needed the B-29's extremely long range in the Pacific, where we didn't have bases close to Japan. Now, we need all the firepower we can concentrate in Europe. We're going to relocate Curt LeMay's entire XXI Bomber Command from the Pacific to England. He has five wings out there now. If we step up B-29 production, we can add three more by September. Since the first of the year, LeMay has essentially made Japan a country without cities. That's the kind of firepower we need. We also need the range, because the Russians moved all their heavy industry across the Urals to get it away from the Germans. We can't reach that far with B-17s or B-24s."

"What about tactical operations in Europe?" Stimson queried Arnold.

"The Ninth Air Force still had fighter bombers and A-26s at bases in Germany and France and Belgium," Arnold said. "We lost quite a few to the Red Air Force Il-2s during the first forty-eight hours because they weren't ready for operations, but our maintenance guys did a helluva job and we're getting a respectable number of sorties off. The problem is that the roads are all flooded with refugees and it's hard to attack the Russians when refugees are mixed in.

"We're also going to start activating jet fighter squadrons in both Eighth Air Force and Ninth Air Force with the new Lockheed P-80s. This is a high priority, essential to achieve air superiority over the battlefield."

"I'm hearing a great deal about *September*," Stimson said. "Is there nothing that we can do in the meantime except hope that we can stop the Red Army at the Rhine?"

"It's that, and hope that Patton's presence in Bavaria will keep the Reds from doing anything on the South German Front," Marshall replied. "They know that we can't release him to help us in the North as long as he has those three army groups opposite his Third Army, but they know they'll have to take out the Third Army in order to support Zhukov with those three army groups. The threat of Patton's Third Army will have to be enough to hold them from committing those forces."

"I'm sure that will give them pause," Stimson nodded. "I imagine they have learned to be as wary of Patton as the Germans were. After the way that he outmaneuvered them in Tunisia and Sicily, he had a reputation they took seriously. After the success of the Third Army this past winter, our friends the Russians also take Patton quite seriously. Perhaps he would be more useful in a more active role."

"What are you suggesting?" Leahy asked.

"I'm suggesting that perhaps *we* should start taking Patton as seriously as the enemy does," Stimson said succinctly.

"He's a loose cannon," Leahy countered. "Not to mention those *pistols*. Isn't it a bit of puffery for a general to be strutting around with a pair of pearl-handled revolvers?"

"Ivory, not pearl," Stimson corrected. "One of which he actually used in combat when he was down in Mexico with Pershing in 1916 chasing Pancho Villa and Jose Cardenas . . . after their gang killed those civilians in New Mexico. Patton was riding with the 6th Cavalry down around San Miguelito. They cornered about a dozen of the banditos in a hacienda . . . shot them in an Old West-style shootout. One of them was Cardenas himself. He was killed with one of those guns that is still on Patton's hip."

Military men sitting around tables frequently disparage their subordinates, but they're almost never highly critical of bravery in situations of one-on-one combat, so Leahy was relieved when the awkward silence was broken by a young sailor being granted entrance to the room with an urgent teletype for the Admiral.

Leahy scanned it quickly, and looked up anxiously.

"The question of a more active role for General Patton is now moot," Leahy said. "Yeremenko's 4th Ukrainian Front had just attacked his Third Army position *in force*."

"Lucky Forward," The Third Army Forward Command Post
Kummersdorf, Germany
Wednesday, June 6, 1945, 6:07 a.m.

"Sounds like we're in for some rain," General Gay mentioned casually to Nate when Patton had left the tower to go downstairs to the war room that he'd set up in the main hall of Kummersdorf's city hall. "It seems a bit early in the day for the thunderstorms to be moving in, though."

"That's not thunder, sir," Nate replied, listening carefully to the distant rumbling sound. "When I was in the line, and we started hearing that sound, we'd find the nearest foxhole and pull the hole in behind us."

Suddenly, the faint sound of the distant artillery was drowned out by a clamor in the General's war room.

"Time to go to work," Gay said, grabbing his helmet and heading for the stairs.

They found Patton leaning over the table in the middle of the room, surrounded by about a dozen men, including his G2, Colonel Oscar Koch, and Brigadier General Halley Maddox, his operations officer.

"It's Yeremenko," Koch explained, showing his boss a set of aerial photographs still reeking of fixative. "He's throwing his main attack on our left flank . . . through the Thuringerwald against Schweinfurt."

"He's picked a helluva day to jump off. You know damned well he knows that it's the anniversary. It's probably Stalin's idea," Patton said with a laugh. "And he's made the worst mistake of his career. He seems to be operating under the illusion that all our forces are spread across central Bavaria."

"If we were, it would be a powerful stroke," Maddox said, watching Patton trace a counterclockwise quarter-circle between Erfurt and Schweinfurt on the map. "He'd be cutting us in half."

"It could be that their idea is to widen Koniev's front to the south," Koch suggested. "Or it could be a preemptive move to keep us from being able to relieve Frankfurt."

"In either case, they're sticking their necks out," Patton asserted. "What's their latest position?"

"Recon shows that Kurochkin's 60th Army is coming through at Meiningen, heading toward Schweinfurt," Maddox explained. "It's the same pattern that we saw up north; they're probing the line with armor and mechanized forces, looking for a soft spot. Then they'll come across with lots of infantry, preceded by an artillery barrage."

"Which we're hearing in the distance this morning?" Patton asked Koch.

"They were shelling the line up around Hof. That would be in a direct sequence with their 18th Army, which is still up around Jena. They don't seem to be going anywhere yet, so that artillery was probably a diversion."

"Okay, we'll give them something to divert around," Patton said, studying the map. "We've got Leroy Irwin's XII Corps down at Amberg. Let's get them moving up toward Hof. Including the forces assigned to Third Army directly, how many divisions does that give us on the right flank?"

"That would be nine, sir," Maddox replied. "The 9th, 4th and 11th Armored Divisions, plus five infantry divisions. One of those is the 1st Division. The 'Big Red 1' is at full strength."

"On the left flank, what do we have? Walker's XX Corps in Wurzburg and Koenigshin with two armored and three infantry," Patton asked and then answered. He had repositioned General Walton Walker's troops himself, and had a mental picture of his left flank that was probably clearer than the maps on the table. He also knew that the legendary Big Red 1—so named for its insignia, a big red numeral—was at full strength, because he'd deliberately kept it that way.

"In the center, we've got Van Fleet's III Corps and Huebner's V Corps, which is very understrength at the moment," Hap Gay interjected.

"Well, V Corps has the 16th Armored," Patton shrugged. "I wish that Troy Middleton's VIII Corps hadn't gone over to First Army. We could use 'em. What do the Russians have in the center?"

"Their center is between Erfurt and Jena, up here in the German state of Thuringia," Koch said, referring to the map. "They have Moskalenko's 38th Army and Grechko's First Guards Army, which is the cream of Yeremenko's 4th Ukrainian Front."

"How are we doing in the air?" Patton asked, turning to Colonel Ira Kranebaum, an Army Air Force officer who was liaison with the XIX Tactical Air Command. Patton was a firm believer in coordinated air-ground operations, and had said more than once that Third Army's spectacular dash across France in August–September 1944 would have not been possible without Major General Otto Weyland's XIX Tactical Air Command fighter-bombers to cover his flanks.

"Our P-51 Mustang wing, the 100th, is down from twelve squadrons to six since VE-Day, and our P-47 "Jug" wing is down from nine to six, but we still have our four recon squadrons. Like you, we're short of men, but the scuttlebutt is that Ninth Air Force is going to be rebuilding fast. We may get back a lot of what we lost when they started stripping us for the Pacific. This morning, our P-51s have been flying sorties over at Schweinfurt."

"What exactly has the Red Air Force been trying to do over there?" Patton queried.

"So far, it's just been small numbers of Sturmovik fighter-bombers in tight formations doing recon and looking for targets of opportunity," Kranebaum replied. "The Mustangs chased them off. Killed a few. They're hard to shoot down because the have so much armor in the top of the fuselage, but we debriefed some Kraut pilots who say they're easy to nail from below. Our guys will be working this one out."

"What about Red fighters?" Patton asked.

"Our recon guys got jumped by a couple of Yaks up around Erfurt this morning, but we haven't seen much yet. I imagine things are going to be getting pretty lively when they start with massed attacks by Sturmoviks supported by fighters."

"Where are they based?" Patton asked.

"Some at Jena, more around Leipzig. They're using the old Luftwaffe fields that we mauled pretty bad in the last war. That sounds funny, doesn't it? The last war? Seems like yesterday. Anyway, their engineers have been a lot slower in getting these fields back in operation than we've been."

"I think Weyland's first priority with his Jugs ought to be to take out as many of those planes on the ground as possible," Gay suggested.

"And the same with those airfields," Patton added. "The Russians have got lots of planes, but it won't do them a damned bit of good if they don't have airfields where they need them. I'd suggest that he put his Jugs on the airfields today, because I'm going to have tanks for him to bust tomorrow. How are *we* on airfields?"

"As you know, sir, General Weyland has been dispersing our squadrons for the past week to get them away from Reim at Munich in case of an attack. The engineers are working overtime."

"Hap, how are we doing on numeric strength, overall?" Patton asked his Chief of Staff.

"We're outnumbered about two to three," Gay said. "On

paper, one of our corps is nearly equivalent to one of their armies, but we're not at full strength. On the other hand, up north, the Allies were hit by surprise and down here, we're ready."

"Being outnumbered overall doesn't matter, as long as you have a larger force than the other guy at the point of *contact*," Patton said with a grin. "That's a quote from Napoleon, and he didn't have half the mobility that we've got."

Turning to his staff, Patton issued his orders of the day.

"Tell Walker to let the 60th Army stick its neck out as far as he sees fit, then to chop it off. Tell him to coordinate with air command for support. Get Irwin's XII Corps rolling on up to Hof. They're going to hit us on our left flank, so we'll hit them on *theirs*."

Patton stood back from the table slightly, so that everyone could see what he envisioned.

"Yeremenko is expecting me to meet his attack with my full force, or at least most of it. But instead, the 60th Army will be chasing Walker practically to Wurzburg until they get themselves ambushed. Yeremenko doesn't expect a counterattack until *after* we've had our first battle. He'll expect us to be coming from the south, which is where we are in relation to him. So we'll do what he *doesn't* expect. We'll go around to the east of Jena, and hit him from the north and east. We'll use Huebner's V Corps to lead the attack through Schleiz. Transfer Leonard's 9th Armored from Third Army to his command for this operation. The 9th has M26 tanks and I want those 90 mm guns in the van. We can use the autobahn, but they'll probably have strong points up there, so the M26s will be important to punch through. We'll jump off at 0445 tomorrow. Irwin's XII Corps and Van Fleet's III Corps should be in position in time to get some rest. Gentlemen, it's time to *go to war!*"

7

★ ★

The Capitol Coffee Shop
17th and M Streets, NW
Washington DC
Wednesday, June 6, 1945, 12:43 p.m.

"Who had the poached eggs on toast?" the waitress asked, juggling an armload of plates filled with steaming food through the crowded diner.

"That would be me," Fiona Wells said primly.

"I'm the BLT on wheat," Rosie O'Leary added, as the waitress slammed the plate down, jiggling the pickle onto the Formica tabletop.

Having met at the historic declaration of war a week earlier, the two women had become friends. Being part of a small, albeit growing, coterie of women journalists in Washington, they had a camaraderie, but also a symbiotic relationship. Rosie found the older woman well connected in the social and diplomatic circles that represented the centers of power, and Rosie was able to give Fiona an insight into "the peculiar ways of thinking of the average Yank," a mystery that the upper-class English woman found nearly incomprehensible.

"Have you seen the front page of *The Washington Herald* this morning?" Fiona asked.

"Yes, I *wrote* part of it last night," Rosie answered.

"Well, of course. But the headline! 'STALIN DECLARES WAR ON WORLD.' The Man of Steel has really outdone himself this time."

"He's put his cards on the table," Rosie said. "That's what we Americans would say. All the excuses are gone. He's saying what he means. I suppose he means what he says."

"Oh, yes, I agree," Fiona said, excitedly. "I'm delighted that you Yanks have finally seen the old bear for what he is."

"When he comes out with a statement that *we're* out to enslave the world, and it's the duty of the Red Army to stop *us,* that's pretty unambiguous."

"It's the old Comintern," Fiona said emphatically with a wave of her hand. "It's nothing new. In the thirties, Stalin said he wanted to overthrow every government in the world. When Hitler attacked *him,* he had to cozy up to Uncle Sam. With Hitler gone, Uncle *Joe* is back to his old tricks."

"Except that now he's got an army of ten million to help him do overthrow the world," Rosie added.

"He's cutting across Europe like a hot knife through butter. I fear that there's nothing left to stop him." Fiona said. "Why do you suppose your General Patton is not involved?"

"I don't mean to butt in on your conversation, ladies," the man at the adjacent table said, obviously interested in getting into a conversation with a pair of attractive women. "But I just heard it on the radio. Patton's been *attacked*. I don't remember exactly, but I think they said he was outnumbered three to one or something. He's not going to make it this time."

"What exactly did you hear?" Rosie asked urgently, trampling on Fiona, who opened her mouth a split second too late to ask the same question.

"It was a bulletin. I heard it on the radio at the newsstand on my way over here to have lunch. He was attacked by a huge Russian army."

"At least he had a week to get ready," Rosie reflected.

"When you're attacked and put on the run by somebody who outnumbers you, it's bad," the man said. "I was with the 99th Division in the Bulge last December. I saw what can happen when you're hit with those kinds of odds. If it hadn't been for the weather and the Germans running out of gas, I don't know what would have happened. The Russians don't have that problem here. We had Patton coming to our rescue. This time, he's on his own and outnumbered. It doesn't look good."

As the man spoke of having been with the 99th in the Bulge, Rosie noticed that the empty left sleeve of his jacket was pinned neatly to his shoulder.

Somewhere south of Schleiz, Germany
Thursday, June 7, 1945, 9:14 a.m.

"Keep 'em moving!" Patton demanded, shouting from the jeep. "Keep the bastards moving to the rear!"

It was the first time since that morning in Kummersdorf that Nate McKinley had seen large numbers of Red Army troops in daylight. Their pea-green uniforms were threadbare, with the tattered appearance of having been in the field for a really long time. Nevertheless, the men appeared to be well fed and their boots were in good shape.

The 16th Armored Division had rapidly overrun the Soviet artillery positions, which were associated with the 18th Army on Yeremenko's left. Meanwhile, the 9th Armored—the Division to which Nate's decimated 27th Armored Infantry had belonged—and elements of the Big Red 1 had caught the Soviet infantrymen who were supposed to be protecting the artillery by surprise. Most had surrendered without putting up much of a fight.

Patton, who was following just behind the V Corps vanguard, was obviously pleased. Nate could sense the wheels turning in his head as he compared his map to the terrain features that opened up before him.

This rolling version of Lucky Forward consisted of a line of jeeps moving up the autobahn, each armed with a .50 caliber machine gun. Nate drove Patton's, with the General in the front seat and the radio operator in the back. They were second in line behind a jeep carrying three men armed with Thompson submachine guns, and followed by jeeps carrying several of the Third Army staff officers, each in their own jeep with a driver and another man riding shotgun with a Thompson.

Several of the jeeps literally carried a shotgun in a scabbard adjacent to the right side of the windshield. In a close-range shootout, a shotgun was as effective a weapon as a submachine gun. The British had discovered this during the trench warfare of World War I. They referred to shotguns as "trench cleaners."

General Gay would have been among the staff officers, but

Patton had detailed him to return to Munich to fill in as military governor and to badger SHAEF in Paris to badger the Pentagon for more supplies—especially more fuel. Lack of fuel had halted Patton's advance the previous autumn, and he was anxious not to face a similar crisis again.

After many months of being at the periphery of battle, Nate found it interesting to be going into battle with the man who had the "Big Picture" literally in the palm of his hand.

Nate had seen numerous aircraft thundering overhead, all of them marked with white stars. According to the predawn briefing that was held before the General headed north this morning, the XIX Tactical Air Command had severely damaged the airfields near Leipzig and Nate had seen or heard of no air attacks on American troops—yet.

"Sir, it's General Leonard," the radio man said, handing Patton a handset.

"So the bastards are trying to hold you up? Artillery . . . Good. Air support? Good. How many? How many T34s? Good. Okay. Good. Keep me posted. Over."

"Leonard ran into a Red armored division up in Schleiz," Patton reported. "He's got his artillery on them. He's going to outflank 'em with his M26s. Dammit, I wish we'd had those last winter. He says the Reds are really short of T34s, but he's got a prisoner who insists that it's an armored *division* . . . Get me Walker!"

Patton's XX Corps operation was going as planned. General Kurochkin's 60th Army had begun probing Walton Walker's XX Corps in force late on the afternoon of June 6, and had made steady progress in their drive on Schweinfurt. As they moved south, Walker had used his 80th Infantry Division as bait for his trap. He'd used two battalions to engage the advance guard of the 60th Army with the determined resistance of well-prepared defensive positions. They'd skirmished with the Russians briefly during the afternoon and evening, and at daybreak on June 7, they retreated quickly down the road toward Schweinfurt. The Soviets, sensing that they had routed the Americans, gave chase.

Because of the terrain in the Thuringerwald, Kurochkin kept mainly to the road. As his pursuit of the "routed" 80th Infantry

Division unfolded over the course of two hours, his units became more and more dispersed, until they were strung out over many miles.

Suddenly, Walker sprang the ambush. The tanks of Major General William H. H. Morris's 10th Armored Division, along with most of Major General Harry Maloney's 94th Infantry Division, lay hidden and out of sight as the Soviet forces passed and became thinned out. Then, like an Apache ambush in nineteenth-century Arizona, they jumped a twenty-mile section of the 60th Army and cut them to ribbons.

Major General Roderick Allen's 12th Armored Division then hit the bulk of the 60th Army's armor in several well coordinated strikes. They soon discovered that the T34s were actually less suited to the steep, wooded terrain of the Thuringerwald than were the smaller American M4A3s. The Shermans could maneuver better on the hillsides and in the narrow, twisting side roads than the T34s, which had been at their best on the open steppes.

As Walker attacked the thinly spaced Soviets with concentrations of tanks and artillery, Weyland's P-47 Jugs struck from above. Most of the enemy vehicles were destroyed by late morning, and XX Corps moved north. Yeremenko was still under the impression that Kurochkin and his 60th Army were fighting their way south.

As had been the case with the V Corps's push north from Hof at dawn, XX Corps found itself processing larger-than-expected numbers of prisoners.

The Pentagon
Arlington, Virginia
Thursday, June 7, 1945, 10:24 a.m.

"It is hoped that the Royal Navy will have them all evacuated by 1800 hours on Friday if the weather holds," the young ensign replied in response to a question from Navy Secretary Jim Forrestal. "They've got sixty-two landing craft and twenty-four liberty ships at work now and more merchantmen en route."

"And they're still refusing our help?" Forrestal asked.

"Actually, sir, they're reporting they have adequate forces available for the task at hand."

"It's their goddam pride," Admiral King interjected. "They don't want to have to say later that *we* saved their butts at the second Dunkirk."

"Actually sir, the comparisons that the newspapers are making between the evacuation from Dunkirk in 1940 and the evacuation from Den Helder this week are erroneous. For one thing, Den Helder is more than two hundred miles from the port at Dover. Dunkirk is less than fifty. This time, the Royal Navy has landing craft, whereas the June 1940 Dunkirk evacuation depended on civilian small craft. Furthermore, Den Helder represents only about thirty percent of the total British ground troops in northern Europe. Dunkirk was closer to a hundred percent."

Secretary of War Henry Stimson didn't know which he despised more, the news that the young ensign was presenting in his briefing, or the crisp, almost automatic, way in which he delivered it. The essential fact was that one year and one day after His Majesty's Army landed at Normandy, it was being evacuated under fire from an equally barren strip of salt-soaked sand in the Netherlands. The technical details didn't matter. The newspapers compared it to the British Army's brave, but humiliating, escape from continental Europe in 1940. After everything was said and done, it really *was* the same.

The headlines in the June 6 evening papers told of little else than the fall of Amsterdam to Zhukov's armies and the irony of this coming on the first anniversary. For several days, the political cartoonists had pictured Britain's great Field Marshal Bernard Law Montgomery as the little boy with his finger in the dike as he tried his best to protect the Netherlands. Now, his Second Army was sitting in the dunes at Den Helder, hoping that it could escape before Soviet tanks pushed it into the North Sea.

On the North German Front, Montgomery and Bradley had desperately tried to reconfigure their wartime 12th and 21st Army Groups to staunch what the newspapers had started to call the "Red Tide." But the Red Tide had swept them out of Northern Germany in a week. Hamburg had been captured.

Bremen had been captured. Not an inch of German North Sea coastline remained in Allied hands. And now, Amsterdam had fallen as well.

As Rokossovsky's 2nd Byelorussian Front battered the cornered British Second Army, Zhukov's own 1st Byelorussian Front was surrounding the great port cities of Antwerp and Rotterdam. Koniev's 1st Ukrainian Front, meanwhile, was encircling the Ruhr, Germany's industrial heartland.

The Red Tide was unstoppable.

"General Bradley does not feel that Zhukov's present drive against the ports can be stopped, but he's still confident that he can hold Koniev at the Ruhr."

It was now a young Army captain with a new set of charts and maps.

"Speaking of General Bradley, have any decisions or recommendations been made on confirming him as successor to General Eisenhower as head of SHAEF?"

The question came from one of Admiral King's aides.

"The President's been in discussions with Prime Minister Churchill," Stimson answered. "As you know, the Prime Minister suggested Montgomery and we suggested Bradley. The Prime Minister feels that it's Britain's turn."

"But three out of four Allied soldiers in Europe are American," Forrestal said. "And after Montgomery's getting pushed into the sea in Holland, I don't imagine that the Prime Minister will be pushing quite so hard. Of course, Brad's tactical withdrawals around the ports are not especially inspirational."

"Neither of these officers have had what they needed to achieve the kinds of successes that we all got used to during the spring," Marshall added. "But I trust that Truman and Churchill will make an inspired choice. What is the current situation on the South German Front?"

"On the South German Front, General Patton in under attack from two sides," the young captain continued. "Reports have his XX Corps in retreat between the former zonal boundary and the city of Schweinfurt. Our information is sketchy, but apparently some of his units, such as the 10th Armored Division and the 94th Infantry Division are entirely unaccounted for. We can only assume that they've been destroyed."

"What about the rest of his command?" Stimson asked hopefully, mindful that at the earlier briefings, he'd been Patton's staunchist advocate.

"We know there's heavy fighting in the area of the zonal boundary north of the Thuringian city of Hof, and that Third Army is committing a large number of its units to this action. Our available forces are outnumbered. We hope they'll hold."

"I guess that Patton has finally met his Waterloo," Admiral King said grimly with a nod toward Stimson. "Don't feel too bad. I'm sure that he's making a gallant effort."

"Modern communications are wonderful. Once it took days, if not weeks, but now we get the bad news from a third of the way around the world in less than a day," Forrestal groused, trying to change the subject.

"As hard as this will seem to accept, I believe that it's time for us to direct the Joint War Plans Division to work up an emergency evacuation plan," Admiral Leahy said.

"An evacuation from all of Germany?" Stimson asked.

"No. An evacuation from all of *Europe*."

In the forest west of Zeitz, Germany
Friday, June 8, 1945, 4:30 a.m.

It was the smell of bacon, not the noise of the engines and grinding gears that woke Nate McKinley. Months of combat had dulled him to the noise, but the experience of waking up in a combat zone to the smell of *sizzling bacon* was entirely new. Even if he *was* still sleeping like a badger, curled up in a ball inside a foxhole, travelling with a general staff certainly had its perks.

Nate had bedded down late after making sure that the General's jeep was gassed and ready. As an extra precaution, he'd spent the night twelve feet from its rear bumper.

Through the strange patterns in the camouflage netting, he could see the dark blue sky. It would soon be growing lighter, but it was now still hung with stars. Another clear day. It would be good for the flyboys. Nate hoped it would be better for the *Yank* flyboys, but he feared that the Red flyboys would be making up for their lack of action yesterday. Nate had gone into the line after the Luftwaffe's ground attack capability had been seriously degraded, so he had only a handful of experiences with "fire from above," but he'd seen what Allied aircraft had done to the Germans. Being on the receiving end was not pretty.

As he filled his mess kit, Nate spotted Patton, already clean shaven, and already dressed in a virtually spotless uniform with necktie and polished boots. He was with General Leonard of the 9th Armored Division, General Pierce of the 16th Armored, and some staff officers that Nate recognized as being part of Van Fleet's III Corps staff. They were eating their breakfast standing in front of the command tent that had been set up under the camouflage netting at the edge of some tall pines. Everyone was in a pretty jovial mood.

"Ready to roll, Sergeant?" Nate turned to see Colonel Koch, the G2, who was arriving with a bundle of paperwork and maps.

"Yessir," Nate replied, attempting to come to attention as best he could with his hands full.

"At ease," Koch grinned. "I think that the General is planning to have you put a lot of miles on that jeep today."

"Well, sir," Nate replied. "The jeep's ready and so am I."

The previous day's advance had gone much more rapidly than expected, and Nate had actually found himself worrying about whether they would be able to gas up the jeep for today. He shouldn't have worried. After nearly running dry during the advance into Lorraine the previous autumn, Patton had put a very high priority on fuel.

After taking down the Soviet 18th Army strong points in Schleitz and Dittersdorf, III Corps and V Corps had moved quickly on the autobahn. Their advance had taken them nearly eighty kilometers into enemy territory, and now put them slightly northeast of Jena. Patton's idea of outflanking Yeremenko on his left had already been accomplished. Of course, the hardest part was still to come.

Inside the command tent, Koch spread out the maps and quickly began his briefing for the General and the division commanders. On the large map of the Thuringia area, Nate could see the three dark blue, arrow-headed lines pointing north, and a large number of red symbols located on the line between Jena, Weimar, and Erfurt. He could see Zeitz and the hook on the center blue line that circled deep into the enemy's left flank.

"We're here with V Corps in Zeitz, and III Corps is ahead of us at Naumberg," Koch affirmed, pointing to the menacing-looking hook. "We came north from Hof on the autobahn and intersected the Elster River north of Gera. Meanwhile, XII Corps paralleled us on our right. They followed the Elster valley through Gera. They expected more of the Red 18th Army in Plauen, but the Reds chose to dig in at Gera. XII Corps has had some hard going here, but we've got airpower on the enemy this morning. The 1st Division, who followed our advance yesterday as far as the Jena-Gera autobahn, will hit Gera from the west today. General Irwin thinks that with the Big Red 1 squeezing them from the other side, he'll be able to wrap up Gera today."

"Don't let the bastards escape to the north," Patton said in an almost rhetorical tone.

"If they do, they'll be on the road exposing themselves to us," said Kranebaum, the liaison man from XIX Tactical Air Command.

"So we're secure in the Saale River valley north and south of Jena?" Patton asked, looking around the room.

"We secured the ridge between the Elster and the Saale valleys last night. Now we're downriver from the Reds at Jena," the man from III Corps offered.

"And Walker's XX Corps is just a few miles to the south of Jena," Koch continued. "They had a tough fight yesterday, but between them and the Air Force, the Red 60th Army is out of action."

"Dammit," Patton said. "That's music to my ears."

"But we still have the 1st Guards Army. They're supposed to be tough sons of bitches," Koch cautioned. "And they're in here with the Red 38th Army."

"Third Army is a bunch of *tougher* sons of bitches!" Patton laughed. "What sort of resistance did you run into last night getting into Naumberg?" he asked the man from III Corps.

"None," he shrugged. "The town was deserted. Even the civilians had hightailed it out of there. The Krauts are scared to death of the Russians."

"I still expect that we'll run into elements of the 18th Army, but Naumberg was deserted of Reds because Yeremenko has his main force in the Jena-Erfurt area of Thuringia. His supply line back through Leipzig runs *through* Zeitz and we're here *in* Zeitz," Koch explained.

"Good," Patton laughed. "III Corps made a helluva lot of progress yesterday. Getting around to the east and repositioned north of Jena was superb. You've earned a rest. Make sure that you've got your flanks covered and get a patrol down to Auerstadt. That's just about a dozen kilometers. If you run into any 18th Army Reds, or anybody else, avoid letting them get a sense that we've got a whole *corps* on that side of the ridge. Other than that, just tell Van Fleet to let the men rest up and be ready to attack south through Auerstadt at dawn Saturday."

"You're thinking that Saturday will be the day, then?" Pierce asked, studying the map.

"That'll give XII Corps time to clear Gera," Patton nodded. "Both III Corps and XX Corps had a big day yesterday. They put more miles and more Red casualties behind them than anyone expected, so this will give them a day for their supply trains to catch up. XII Corps and the Big Red 1 are having a big day *today,* so the main part of the work on Saturday will be III Corps and XX Corps. XII Corps will fill in on the middle. It's only about twenty kilometers from Gera to Jena. They won't have far to go."

"Yeremenko's well aware of XX Corps south of Jena. He'll be concentrating his 1st Guards Army and most of his 38th . . . but he's barely aware that he has III Corps to the north," Koch mused.

"You're reading my mind, Colonel," Patton chuckled. "He'll expect the main attack from XX Corps and we'll give him a helluva show of artillery from XX Corps. But the main attraction will be III Corps coming south from Auerstadt and hitting his rear west of Jena. Meantime, V Corps, with all the rest of us, will deploy to Dornburg, north of Jena."

Nate could see that the General had earmarked the column with which he was traveling for the longest drive of the day. They had at least thirty kilometers of mountain roads through a ridgeline that had not been cleared of any enemy that might be deployed there to guard Jena's northern approaches.

As had been the case on Thursday, Leonard's 9th Armored Division—Nate's former division—would lead the way. Patton and Leonard huddled with V Corps commander, Lieutenant General Ralph Huebner, on a plan that put the various elements on different roads, with tanks and armored infantry leading the way and the six armored field artillery battalions bringing up the rear. The 9th Armored Division's 89th Cavalry, with its fast M8 Greyhound armored cars, would lead the main branch of the advance through Wetzdorf. Patton's mobile headquarters would follow them.

As they climbed into the mountains out of the Elster River valley, Nate was reminded of the mountains back home in northwestern Montana, where he'd climbed and hunted since he was a kid. Thick pine forests covered the slopes, but unlike the valley floor, the hillsides were relatively free of underbrush. It was just a rust-colored mat of pine needles stretching off among the thick brown trunks, punctuated here and there by an outcropping of granite bedrock.

If he hadn't known that they were just hours away from a life or death struggle with a Soviet army group, this would have been a lovely drive in the woods. It was a sunny summer day, with skies that would remain blue and cloudless until early afternoon, when the afternoon thunderheads started to form over the higher mountains. It was actually getting to be quite warm. Nate shed his jacket at about nine in the morning and wished that he could do the same with his helmet.

Patton seemed relatively relaxed as he spent his time checking in with General Irwin, whose XII Corps was battling the Soviet 18th Army at Gera. Nate gathered that things were going well. Some Soviet fighter bombers had managed to slip through the XIX Tactical Air Command's air defense screen, causing a great deal of mischief until some 358th Fighter Group P-51 Mustangs managed to take them out.

High overhead, Nate could hear the distinctive drone of the Mustangs' Merlin engines as they patrolled the skies above the Third Army's advance. Aside from that, and Patton's occasional outburst on the radio, everything was pretty quiet.

The column was moving at about forty-five miles per hour, which was an easy pace for Greyhounds, jeeps, and deuce-and-a-half trucks. The columns with the Shermans and M26s would be moving more slowly, and had taken one of the shorter routes to Dornburg. Nate maintained a distance of about twenty yards between the General's jeep and the jeep ahead. On the open highway, they would let the distance be greater, but on these winding roads through the wooded mountains, it was harder to keep the other vehicles in sight.

Suddenly, just as Nate was lulling himself in to a sense of security, there was a series pops from the uphill slope. Patton heard it too and craned his neck to see what it was, as Nate tapped the brake and pushed in the clutch.

"There!" Patton pointed. "There was a muzzle flash up there behind that rock in those trees."

Nate looked but couldn't see it. The gunner on the jeep ahead was scanning the hillside with the sights of his .50 caliber. Two of the infantrymen with Thompsons were already starting to work their way up the hillside.

"We better take cover, General," Nate said, gesturing to the downhill slope, which was on Patton's side of the jeep.

"Other side," Patton corrected. "If they're going to also hit us from below, we're better off at the base of the uphill slope. The bastards up there will have a hard time hitting us if we get close to the hillside. It's a damned near impossible shot."

After his years of hunting in woods exactly like these, Nate knew that the General was right.

A group of GIs from the trailing jeep quickly surrounded Nate and Patton, determined to protect their general with their own lives. Such was the devotion to this man among the people of the Third Army. Of course, *nobody* wanted to suffer the consequences of being the man who let Patton get hit.

There were more pops, and the jeep gunner poured a stream of .50 caliber fire into the trees. There were shouts and the crashing of brush as the other men rushed the snipers.

Nate heard the cackle of tommy gun fire. There were more shouts, more sounds of running and more gunfire. The sounds grew more distant, and Nate could see the man with the .50 caliber relax.

"What happened?" Patton demanded. "How many were there?"

"I saw three," the gunner said, not taking his eyes off the hillside. "I got one at least. Maybe two. Two ran off. I think they got 'em."

"Looks like just a small patrol." By this time, the radio

operator was in touch with the head of the column, which had stopped. "Nobody else was hit. They must have just waited for the jeeps. Easier pickings than the M8s."

Within ten minutes, the GIs who had chased the snipers came crashing back down the hillside carrying various pieces of gear and insignia which they dropped into a pile at Patton's feet like a cat displaying a dead mouse. Koch dived into the pile like a uniformed Sherlock Holmes, inspecting each piece for clues.

"It's an 18th Army patrol," Koch said at last. "All part of the same infantry battalion. They're enlisted men. Not even noncoms. Lightly armed. These are just standard-issue 7.62 mm carbines. Did you guys see any submachine guns?"

"No sir, and if they'd had 'em, we'd have damned sure known it."

"How many were there?"

"Just four. Gunny got one right up there. We chased two up the hill and there was a fourth one hiding farther up. We fanned out and looked for more. We were almost to the top of the ridge. We went all the way and searched the other side. Didn't see any sign of another road. We listened. If anybody ran, we'd have heard 'em. If they were waiting, they would've had plenty of chances to take a shot at one of us."

"What do you think Colonel?" Patton asked.

"Isolated patrol. Remnants of some 18th Army unit. The worst case is that there's significantly more of the 18th Army than what's fighting down at Gera, and they're somewhere around here. The good news is that they aren't part of 1st Guards or 38th Army, which means that those guys are still concentrated over in the Jena-Erfurt salient like we thought."

"Eyes and ears open," Patton said, striding back toward the jeep. "Let's move out and get the hell across this ridge."

The White House
Washington DC
Friday, June 8, 1945, 8:43 a.m.

"The time has come for the long awaited global revolution to spread to all corners of the Earth," President Truman read aloud from the newspaper as he stood in front of his desk. "We call upon the people of France, Italy, and England to rise up . . . and to stand in solidarity with the victorious Red Army . . . and to throw the American capitalists and the British imperialists into the sea. Let the ruling classes tremble at the Communist revolution. The proletariats have nothing to lose but their chains."

All of Washington was astir with the most recent statement issued by the supreme leader of the Soviet Union. In 1941 Stalin had toned down the Comintern, the Communist International, in order to cooperate with the other enemies of Hitler. With the Red Tide of Soviet forces sweeping across Europe, he'd officially resurrected his 1928 master plan for the Soviet Union to conquer the world.

"I'd like to ask the Russian proletarians where their 'friend' was when they were being shoved into labor camps by the millions before the war," Forrestal quipped.

"I can't believe that this is the same man whom we met at Yalta," Stettinius said, shaking his head. "Certainly, his main interest then was victory over Hitler, but he *seemed* committed to a peaceful postwar world."

"He was committed to *his* kind of peace," Stimson said. "The United Nations Organization was just a means to his end. His vision of a 'peaceful' postwar world was of a world controlled by *him*."

"He's calling for sabotage behind our lines," Truman said, looking up from the paper that he'd been reading. "He wants the workers of France to sabotage the war effort and to fight *us* . . . just like the resistance fought the Germans during the war."

"I wouldn't minimize this situation," Stimson said. "I spoke to some people who were in Paris ten days ago. There are red banners everywhere."

"We need to support de Gaulle in every way possible," Truman said, laying his paper down.

"We have," Stettinius replied. "Since before Normandy . . . *and* we gave his people a seat on the United Nations Security Council."

"*And* we're going to have to make sure that General Charles de Gaulle knows that we think that he walks on water," Truman said. "I don't want him waffling in his support for us. I can see exactly what Stalin's doing. He's got Northern Germany . . . and he's in the Netherlands and Belgium. France is next. Like Hitler in 1940, like Bismarck in 1870, and as the Kaiser *tried* to do in 1914. Hitler never got Russia and neither did Napoleon, but Stalin might get *all three*. What better way to cut our legs out from under us than to convince the French that it's a holy war to deliver *them*. If he can get the French Reds to launch a revolt, his job is half done."

"Would they actually buy that?" Forrestal asked rhetorically.

"Why not? There were Frenchmen who bought Hitler," Stimson replied. "The Vichy government was just another French faction. The French just blow with the wind."

"The Red Army's momentum can only strengthen the case of the French communists," Stimson said, "and lower the morale of those who support us. If the Red Army looks like a winner, then support will swing *Stalin's* way."

"Tactically, nothing stands between Stalin and conquering France." Marshall said. "Unless something happens to buy us some time. We have the bulk of our forces there, along with half the British Army and the entire Free French Army. If we suffer sabotage and a lack of popular support by the French people, it would be bad. If Rokossovsky and Zhukov move quickly, I can't see what could stop them."

"Well," said Stimson thoughtfully. "It may take a miracle."

"Lucky Forward"
Landgraftenberg
Immediately north of Jena, Germany
Friday, June 8, 1945, 7:46 p.m.

"Where's my goddam artillery?" Patton demanded rhetorically. Since midday, when the 9th Armored Division spearhead that he'd been traveling with had come across a large number of civilians massacred at Wetzdorf, the General had displayed the angry determination of a man obsessed. His obsession was Marshal Yeremenko and the remainder of his 4th Ukrainian Front.

Nate McKinley was glad that it wasn't he whom General Patton ordered to photograph the atrocities at Wetzdorf, but he realized that, like the Nazi death camps, this was an image that the world would have to see to believe. It would obviously be with Patton for some time.

Shortly after Wetzdorf, Patton had gotten the word from XIX Tactical Air Command intelligence that Yeremenko was preparing to mount a massive attack against Walker's XX Corps from Jena. General Grechko's elite 1st Guards Army, as well as most of the 38th Army, was now concentrated there. Yeremenko's idea was to deal a powerful blow, send the Americans reeling, then drive south into Bavaria.

Walker's corps alone was vastly outnumbered, but Yeremenko seemed oblivious to the fact—or at least to the *importance* of the fact—that Patton and the bulk of Third Army had outflanked him.

As he made his rendezvous with Huebner and the rest of V Corps at Dornberg, Patton got word that III Corps was in Auerstadt. Shortly after, he was informed that, with the help of the Big Red 1, XII Corps had taken down the bulk of the Soviet 18th Army at Gera. Supported by three additional divisions from the Third Army reserve, they were now just fifteen kilometers from Jena.

With all this in mind, Patton had made the command decision to cross the Saale River at Dornberg and continue his advance to the Landgraftenberg, an open, rocky plateau immediately north of Jena. The Landgraftenberg was a huge flat arrowhead with its point at Jena, and its sides defined by the Saale on the east and the road to Weimar and Erfurt on the west.

"Too many battles have been lost by commanders who chose to halt on the wrong side of a river," Patton said as he looked at the lights of Jena in the distance.

Most of V Corps had been in position in time for an early supper, but the armored artillery battalions were still a no-show, when Patton said, "C'mon Sergeant, we need to find my damned artillery."

Just before nightfall, Nate drove Patton back down the road from which they'd come that afternoon. About two kilometers from the bivouac area that Patton had picked for his latest

Lucky Forward, they passed a deuce-and-a-half coming toward them up the road.

"Have you seen any artillery?" Nate called, slowing the jeep and winking the lights, which were shrouded with blackout hoods. The driver stiffened noticeably as he recognized Nate's passenger.

"Yessir," the driver replied. "Back thataway, but they're stuck."

"Stuck?"

"Yessir, stuck plumb solid, sir. But they're a'workin' on it."

"How far back?"

"Less'n a mile, sir."

"Thank you soldier, carry on."

The narrow road that led to the Landgraftenberg from the Saale River valley floor had been, in many cases, cut as a groove in the rocky cliffs. Originally carved in the eighteenth century, it had never been widened for large modern vehicles. There had been no perceived need, as the main road—which Patton could not take for obvious reasons—led through the valley and through Jena.

The road up the Landgraftenberg cliffs should have been adequate for trucks pulling artillery, but the twists and bends in the road were complicated and difficult. A truck pulling a 155 mm gun had jackknifed on the road after the gun carriage was wedged between the black granite cliff faces on either side of the road. Nothing could pass.

It was a scene of chaos as dozens of men climbed over the trapped vehicles like ants devouring a piece of a Hershey bar. Beyond these vehicles, a line of ammunition trucks and artillery pieces that stretched as far as the eye could see in the near twilight had ground to a halt. It took little imagination to realize what could happen here if this line of trucks was attacked by the Red Air Force.

Grabbing a flashlight from beneath the dashboard of the jeep, Patton leapt into action.

"Sergeant, back the jeep up and let these people through," the General shouted. He then ordered all of the trucks that had stopped on the uphill side of the incident to move out.

Nate backed up to the first wide spot in the road as the General waded into the chaos below.

"Who's in charge? Where's your regimental commander?"

Nobody seemed to know, so Patton took charge. The man who had apparently been driving the truck was white as a sheet as Patton began poking around.

Using the flashlight, the Third Army commander inspected the hitch that connected the deuce-and-a-half to the gun carriage. It had obviously been too badly bent when the truck turned over to be detached. It appeared as though numerous attempts had been made to pry it apart. Even if the truck was detached, the gun would remain wedged in place.

Barking orders like a drill sergeant, Patton ordered one group of men to get jacks under the downhill side of the truck, so that it wouldn't roll when and if the carriage was unhitched. He then ordered Nate to radio his command post for a tank recovery vehicle and an acetylene cutting torch be sent back down the road.

That done, he explained his plan.

"We'll make one attempt to break these sons of bitches apart using jacks," he told the small group of men who had emerged as being the most helpful and knowledgeable—the types of men who frequently received battlefield promotions. "If that doesn't work, we'll cut 'em apart when the torch gets here. We'll lower the truck and drive it the hell out of here. Then we'll pray that the TRV can get this howitzer out."

After an agonizing hour of working and carefully cutting the twisted metal, the two were finally separated and the truck rattled up the hill into the darkness. All the while, Nate compared the hooded headlights and the religiously enforced blackouts to the blinding flash of the cutting torch. Patton had ordered the tarps to be removed from two deuce-and-a-half trucks and placed around the scene, but still, Nate imagined that the light would be bright enough to be visible in Moscow. At least Jena and Yeremenko's armies were on the opposite side of the Landgraftenberg.

The M32 TRV, a heavy-duty wrecker on a Sherman tank chassis, crawled forward and began working the 155 mm howitzer. Finally, it jerked free and a cheer went up from the men who'd been watching the scene.

"Pull that sonuvabitch out of the way and let my ammo trucks get through," Patton ordered the M32 driver.

Within minutes, the convoy was moving again. The sight of the man with the highly polished helmet and star en-crusted lapels that was directing traffic with the flashlight was an obvious boost to the men's morale. Patton's own spir-its were clearly buoyed by the occasional cheers.

"This is one of the rewards of leading troops in battle," Patton mused to Nate as they were driving back to the crest of the Landgraftenberg.

When they reached Lucky Forward, Patton asked Nate to stop short of their parking area. "I'd like to walk from here," he said, looking up at the star-encrusted June sky. "Did you know that Napoleon bivouacked on this very hill on the eve of his battle of Jena in October 1806?"

"No, sir, I didn't," Nate admitted.

"Most of the Prussian Army was in roughly the same posi-tions as Yeremenko."

"How did Napoleon do?" Nate asked.

"He kicked their butts," Patton laughed. "But then, he was only fighting the King of Prussia . . . not Marshal Andrei Yeremenko, the great hero of Stalingrad, who decimated the entire 6th German Army."

The White House
Washington DC
Saturday, June 9, 1945, 7:13 a.m.

By coincidence or synchronicity, Henry Stimson had re-ceived an unexpected phone call just as he was leaving his of-fice Friday evening. It was Major General Leslie Groves, the head of the Manhattan Project. He'd just arrived in Washington, and he was anxious to have Stimson arrange an urgent meeting with the President. Normally, secretaries of war do not field calls from major generals wanting to see the president, but the man who headed America's dash into the unknown of nuclear weaponry was the exception among exceptions.

After a week of gloomy, overcast skies to accompany the gloomy mood that hung over the nation's capital, Saturday had dawned bright and sunny. Stimson's Lincoln rolled into the north portico of the White House just as the stocky, ruddy-faced Groves was stepping from a War Department motor pool Chevy. The two greeted one another with small talk and made their way to the receptionist, who hurried them quickly into Truman's office.

Stimson, as always, was wearing a suit and tie, while Groves was in his khakis. The President wore his customary bowtie, but no jacket.

"General, are we still on schedule for a test in the middle of July?" Truman asked.

"That's why I'm here," Groves said sheepishly. "When the new war in Europe began, I considered it critical to finish our work ahead of schedule if we could, so I ordered extra shifts . . . but that's when we started running into some problems . . . technical and otherwise."

"What sort of technical problems?"

"Well, let me explain the process. Detonation of the bomb requires a technique called 'implosion.' In order to detonate the bomb and create the atomic *ex*plosion, we need to *im*plode fissionable material. We'd create a symmetrical shock wave within the case of the bomb using an array of TNT charges around the inside of the steel bomb case, which is a sphere. This compresses a subcritical mass of fissionable material . . . uranium or plutonium . . . into a critical mass. When it reaches critical mass, it will release energy . . . more energy than has ever been released in one time and place on this Earth since Creation."

After a pause, the President leaned forward with a very serious expression on his face.

"This *im*plosion is very violent, but it's also extremely delicate and requires absolute precision," the General continued. "*That's* where the problem comes in. Our scientists have figured out how to set the thing off, and we've processed the uranium and the plutonium, but we haven't perfected the implosion trigger."

"Can you resolve this by July?" Truman asked.

"I hope so." Groves said. "Fortunately . . . if there's fortune to be found . . . by trying to push ahead of schedule, we got to the point of testing the triggers this week instead of at the end of the month. We found the problem sooner. If all goes well, we can make the schedule. If not . . ."

"A moment ago . . . you alluded to problems other than technical." Stimson recalled.

"It's a personnel problem . . . a potentially dangerous personnel problem." Groves began. "As you know, we're depending almost entirely on civilian scientists. They're your typical academic types . . . Left-leaning politically, if you know what I mean."

Stimson nodded as Groves continued.

"Well, the academic types were always dead-set anti-Hitler and it was easy to get them to work on this gadget when it was a matter of getting the bomb before Hitler got it. When Hitler was gone, the enthusiasm started to wane. Now that Stalin is the potential enemy . . . Well, these folks are sort of idealistic about their left-wing sympathies."

"Certainly, you can't be suggesting that your scientists allow politics to interfere with their duties as Americans in the service of their country during *wartime*," Truman snarled. "I supported the New Deal at a time when people on Wall Street saw it as a Red conspiracy, but when it comes to patriotism in wartime, there's no room for partisan bickering."

"Not all of our scientists are American," Groves said succinctly. "And one of these has come up missing."

"Missing?" Stimson asked incredulously.

"About two weeks ago . . . the weekend before last, this German-born Brit named Klaus Fuchs turned up missing. He was one of our best men, a theoretical physicist. He was brilliant. He once got us back on track when we were *very* far off the mark. Trouble is, he's not just a leftist college-professor type, he's a hard-core Marxist."

"What happened?"

"We've been grilling everyone. Nobody inside has any idea. Outside the fence, we have to be really hush-hush, but we've talked discretely with the sheriffs in Santa Fe and Albuquerque. Nothing."

"If he left on his own or got kidnapped, he's farther away than that," Truman said.

"When we went through his stuff, we found the address of

a hotel down in Mexico." Groves said. "I sent a couple of Spanish-speaking MPs down there in civvies to ask around discreetly. Nobody recognized his picture."

"My biggest fear . . ." Stimson began.

"Is that he went over to the Russians?" Groves interrupted.

Stimson nodded silently and glanced at the President. For once, the feisty man from Missouri was speechless.

Lucky Forward
Landgraftenberg, Immediately north of Jena, Germany
Saturday, June 9, 1945, 5:48 a.m.

"The natives are getting restless," Colonel Oscar Koch reported.

"I don't see how the natives can see a damn thing in this crap," Patton sneered. During the night, a dense fog had settled across the landscape, drastically reducing visibility.

"Yeremenko is using the fog as cover to probe Walker's defenses on the south of town," Koch said, looking at the General's map. "He's still convinced that XX Corps is our main force. But he can still wheel the 1st Guards around and hit us on our right flank."

"I guess we'll see if what they say about holding the high ground is true," Patton smiled.

The General had been up for two hours, fine-tuning his plan and visiting the troops that were preparing for what promised to be a decisive battle. Yeremenko was facing Walton Walker's XX Corps with two entire Soviet armies, but XII Corps and the First Infantry Division were on Yeremenko's left flank and Patton was on his rear with more than two corps—of whose strength the Soviet Marshal was blissfully unaware.

At exactly 0600, the silent, foggy morning was shattered by a massive American artillery barrage exploding across Jena from three sides. The Third Army's timed precision barrages had become a thing of legend, and one of the Wehrmacht's greatest fears during the last year of World War II.

The 9th and 16th Armored Divisions had jumped off moments earlier, tasked with clearing the towns of Cospeda and

Closewitz, which lay on the Third Army's right flank. Patton planned to use them to anchor his right in the battle that he presumed would take place when Yeremenko maneuvered the 1st Guards Army clockwise to strike the Third Army from the west.

The muzzle flashes and exploding shells appeared as patches of yellow orange, strangely refracted by the thick fog. As the dawn began to break across the scene, it seemed as though heaven and earth were on fire. Tanks, trucks, and other vehicles were everywhere, moving like thunderous shadows in the mist.

In was nearly 0800 when Patton ordered his command caravan to move out. Pierce's 16th Division, backed by units of the 97th Infantry Division, had reported Closewitz secure, and the General wanted to see his new right flank.

As they drove into the town, evidence of a vicious firefight was evident on all sides. Images flickered in and out of view like frames of an old movie. Nate saw Russian prisoners kneeling on the damp ground with their hands clasped behind their heads as GIs searched them for weapons. There was an American aid station with men lying on stretchers. One man, naked from the waist up, with a large white bandage around his chest was trying with obvious difficulty to smoke a cigarette. The chassis of a Russian tank, its turret blown off, was still burning furiously. In the firelight, Nate could see the red star and a slogan in Cyrillic letters painted across the side.

From Closewitz, Patton ordered his motorcade south toward Cospeda, where the scene was much the same as in the first town. It was here that the fog began to lift. The abrupt change was almost uncanny. Nate had noticed that visibility on the narrow road was better, and then shafts of morning light broke through. The booming sound of the artillery grew less muffled. The air was filled with the snarl of aircraft engines.

A half-dozen Sturmoviks raced in to hit a cluster of M4A3s. There was a series of explosions near the tanks and the Russian planes vanished behind a cloud of smoke and dust. The Shermans maneuvered and kept moving. One was stopped, but Nate couldn't tell whether it had been hit. There was a roar of Merlin engines and two P-51 Mustangs flashed past, chasing the Sturmoviks.

Patton pointed to a wooded rise of ground about fifty yards away and they left the road. The oaks provided good screening for the jeeps, and the rise gave the General an excellent overview of the battlefield. Nate imagined that this was what it probably would have been like to ride with one of the great field generals of the past—like Sherman or Stonewall Jackson, or even Bonaparte himself. The nature of warfare had changed considerably in a century. In 1945, a general's command post was usually far to the rear, with banks of telephones, well-lighted map rooms, and bevies of staff assistants—but not Patton's.

As the fog burned off in warm sunshine, the scene was breathtaking. North, across the open plain that formed the western shoulder of the Landgraftenberg, Nate could see the spires of Isserstadt. The mobile units of Van Fleet's III Corps, which had broken camp at Auerstadt three hours before, were merging with the V Corps armored divisions, forming a broad front.

Meanwhile, billowing clouds of dust to the southwest indicated that Yeremenko was now turning the 1st Guards away from Walker's XX Corps to the south, and wheeling them north—just as Patton had predicted.

Word was starting to come in by radio from the observers that the deadly accurate fire control of the American artillery—the same guns that Patton himself had squeezed onto the Landgraftenberg last night—had taken a severe toll on Yeremenko's forces in Jena. The Soviet Marshal had massed his own artillery on his south against XX Corps when he thought it was the main American force. When he realized what had happened, it was too late to reorient the guns 180 degrees, so he was launching his attack to the north using his mobile forces without artillery. He was hoping to make up for this shortcoming with airpower. Sturmoviks were coming in at low level from all directions, but Weyland's P-51s managed to break up most of the attacks.

Soviet forces in Isserstadt skirmished with the 16th Armored Division as the tanks of General Grechko's 1st Guards arrived. After a brief firefight and heavy casualties, the Americans withdrew. Yeremenko apparently intended to use the town to anchor his new line.

The T34s, too many to count, were fanning out across the plain before Isserstadt, backed by enormous numbers of foot soldiers. Estimates ranged to twenty thousand. In the foreground, the M26s began to pick at the enemy tanks. With superior range and accuracy, their 90 mm guns were able to make a difference, but the battle would be fierce.

As the morning wore on and the sun shone brightly, a haze of smoke and dust settled across the battlefield. As in the early morning fog, visibility was greatly compromised, so Patton was forced to trade his binoculars for a radio headset. He and Koch spread a map on the ground and began to update it with the myriad reports that were coming in.

As the 1st Guards had surged out of Jena to their northwest, V Corps artillery rotated fifteen degrees to follow them. Then, XII Corps began to advance into the edge of the city—and into Yeremenko's right flank—from the east.

By noon, the optimism of the morning began to fade. Patton received the disconcerting news that III Corps was being pushed back. The Soviet 38th Army had joined the fray, coming through Isserstadt from the west to reinforce the left flank of Grechko's 1st Guards offensive.

Patton studied the map and barked orders. Walker's XX Corps, which had pulled back under the withering Red Army artillery fire at dawn, was advancing again. The probing attacks that Yeremenko had launched under cover of his earlier barrage had been blunted and turned. Major General Rod Allen's 12th Armored Division had outflanked the artillery on the XX Corps front and had cut it to bits. Major General Harry Maloney's 94th Infantry Division was moving into Jena from the south.

Meanwhile, the Big Red 1 entered the city from the east. After his winter at Stalingrad, Yeremenko understood house-to-house fighting, but the Big Red 1 had cut its urban warfare teeth in October 1944, when it took down Aachen, the first German city captured by the Allies.

Overhead, Weyland's P-47s were swarming like flies, braving Soviet antiaircraft fire to unleash sheets of fiery rockets from their wing racks. Occasionally, a Jug would be hit and could be seen cartwheeling out of the sky in a streak of black smoke. Nate saw a pilot try to bail out of one as its starboard wing crumpled. There was a wisp of white parachute silk, but he was too low. Nate didn't see him land.

"Here we go!" Oscar Koch shouted. He was looking into the sky about thirty degrees west of where Nate had seen the P-47 go down. It was a ragged line of twin-engined aircraft coming almost directly at them at treetop level.

"They're ours!" Koch said. "They're A-26s from Ninth Air Force. General Vandenberg wrangled permission to redeploy two wings from the North German front. They weren't supposed to be available until next week. Somebody must've pulled some strings!"

The A-26 Invaders, which had reached the USAAF a year before, just in time for the Normandy battles, were potent machines with the speed of a fighter-bomber—but with twice the range and payload. Two waves of about a dozen Invaders each had hit the heart of Yeremenko's mechanized units with lines of five-hundred pound bombs. Nate could see them banking as they made a wide arc over the city. Flying low, they disappeared into the haze in the distance, but suddenly they were back, flying wingtip to wingtip across the two-mile wide front on their strafing run. They flew at barely fifty feet, too low for the Russian gunners to lead them or line up a shot. Although the sky was filled with tracers, most of the fire filled the sky behind the A-26s. None appeared to be hit.

Both waves of the air attack had consumed less than eight minutes, but the Soviet forces were now in disarray. Through a break in the swirling dust, Nate could see burning vehicles, including at least one tank. Even the undamaged ones had stopped. Troops had gathered in clusters and had halted their advance.

After about fifteen minutes, the 1st Guards troops got themselves reorganized and the advance resumed. They moved slowly at first, but soon picked up speed. Suddenly, there were explosions. An armored personnel carrier took a direct hit. The Russian troops were diving for cover. Several had been hit. More explosions bracketed the line of advance. The dust that had been stirred up by a great many moving vehicles had cleared slightly. Nate could see many vehicles on fire or wrecked.

He saw two T34s reversing and going into a defensive posture behind a small ridge. Next he saw a number of troops in Soviet pea-green withdrawing to the cover of the same ridge. Other troops that had taken cover farther back moved up, but most of the Russians stayed where they were.

There was a round of explosions about forty yards behind the small ridge. In the respite that followed the last explosion, the entrenched soldiers opened fire on the far woods that were barely visible in the smoky haze. The T34s fired as fast as their gunners could reload.

The next round of explosions bracketed the defensive line. It was apparent that the Russians took a large number of casualties in that last salvo, but the T34s continued to fire. Finally, one stopped firing, backed up, and began maneuvering to one side. The second tank took a near miss and stopped firing. Farther back, the Soviet troops were preoccupied with their wounded or digging slit trenches. The 1st Guards attack seemed to have ground to a halt.

There was a series of extremely loud explosions from the direction of Isserstadt and suddenly the sky was again filled with the sleek A-26s. Huge columns of black smoke boiled up from the town.

When Nate glanced back at the battlefield, American tanks, mostly M4A3 Shermans, were everywhere—hitting the 1st Guards from the right. Clusters of Russian troops fought back feverishly. One Sherman stopped abruptly, its tread apparently damaged by a Russian antitank weapon, but the others continued to move forward, mowing down the Russian defensive positions with methodical precision.

"They've linked up."

Nate turned. It was one of Colonel Koch's staffers, taking a cigarette break from the frantic staff meeting that had been going on all day.

"Who is that, sir?" Nate asked. "Who's linked up?"

"Fifth Corps and the 1st Infantry Division. They've linked up inside Jena on the east side of the river. Fifth Corps is chasing 1st Guards back into Jena, but XX Corps is already there. Between XX Corps and the Big Red 1, we now have control of the south side of the city on both sides of the river. And III Corps broke through the 38th Army on the other side of Isserstadt. The Reds are in a vice. Things are starting to get interesting."

"Sergeant, let's go visit III Corps," Patton said confidently.

Nate was happy to be on the move again after standing around with nothing to do until well after noon. With three 16th Armored Division Greyhounds as an escort, they moved out across the battlefield that had been visible for most of the day. It was littered with great piles of the detritus of war, from scraps of uniforms and small arms, to entire blackened tanks that still entombed crews of once living, once breathing human beings—human beings who had felt the cold dampness of the fog this morning, who had felt the fear of anxiety about the impending battle, who had felt the unimaginable heat of being burned alive—and who would feel nothing ever again.

They passed about a quarter of a mile south of Isserstadt, where small-arms fire still snapped and cackled as M4A3s blasted the buildings that contained the remnants of the Russian 38th Army defenders. Nate was struck by the scale of the battle that had just taken place. Even after what he'd been through since the Bulge, driving across an area where tens of thousands of men had fought was sobering. Most of the battles that he'd been in previously had been division-size fights, or, like the Battle of the Bulge, they had taken place in irregular terrain, where there were few vast, open fields of battle.

As they drove in search of the III Corps command post, Nate saw larger and larger numbers of prisoners. Whereas Grechko's 1st Guards had managed to withdraw generally intact, Moskalenko's 38th Army had been enveloped faster and their escape cut off.

At last, they reached a circle of jeeps clustered around a farmhouse that was being utilized as the General James Van Fleet's field headquarters. When Patton strode in, the stars on his lapel blazing, everyone present snapped to attention. There was a quick exchange of salutes, an "At ease" from Patton, and a jovial round of congratulations.

Van Fleet pointed out the direction that III Corps was taking in the operation designed to cut off any possible Soviet escape from Jena. Patton nodded as Koch explained XX Corps's position and that of the 1st Division relative to the XII Corps push into the city from the east.

"I want two corps on the road to Weimar and Erfurt tomorrow morning . . . early," Patton explained. "G2 tells us that Yeremenko put all his chips on Jena, but I want to be *sure*. I want an American flag flying in Erfurt. If SHAEF decides on a counterattack in the north, they're going to want to hold the line between here and Frankfurt, and I want to make sure that Thuringia, and this side of the front, is anchored."

"Shall we turn III Corps west now?" Van Fleet asked.

"I think we need to get someone from XX Corps up here so we can have a little powwow," Patton said.

"Sergeant, I'd like you to take a little run over to Walker's command post," Patton said, looking at Nate. "Tell him that I'd like to have him send somebody here with you so we can work this out."

"Yessir," Nate replied, hoping that someone in the III Corps command post could tell him *where,* in the middle of chaos below, to find Walton Walker.

One of Van Fleet's operations people took Nate aside and spread out a map of the city. Based on a prewar tourist map, it had been prepared only days earlier when Patton had ordered the counterattack into Thuringia.

"Sorry about the map. It's the most detailed we have. Jena's built along a bend in the Saale River. We're up here on the northwest side. Fifth Corps holds the northeast tip. Twentieth Corps and the 1st Division have the bottom, with XX Corps on the west side of the river. The enemy still has the northwest side of the city, where we, I mean us in III Corps, are about to attack."

"So, where do you think the command post is?"

"It's probably been a half-dozen places since sunup," the operations man shrugged. "Your best bet is to get to XX Corps and start asking. I'd suggest that you go through V Corps and take the east side of the river. We got control of pretty much the whole works over there. When you get into 1st Division country, you oughta be able to just cross back into XX Corps and ask anybody."

"Thanks," Nate said apprehensively, tracing a route on the map with his finger.

"You can't miss it!" The man laughed. "Good luck."

Nate made good time driving through the V Corps sector until he reached the river. He had to fight the flow of traffic converging on the only bridge north of the heart of the city, but he finally got across. Nobody he asked could tell him how far 1st Division was, so he just drove south, following the river as closely as possible and dodging the flow of men and materiel that was moving toward the fighting.

He imagined that in its prewar days the riverfront area of Jena had been rather picturesque, but now, most of the sandstone-colored, eighteenth-century buildings were little more than hulks blasted by wartime bombing or artillery. The oak trees were broken and splintered, although occasionally Nate would see one that was intact. Abandoned or damaged Russian equipment was everywhere. In some places, the Americans had made an attempt to push it into the river to get it out of the way.

As he reached the bend in the river, he could see evidence of intense fighting earlier in the day, and he could hear the sounds of gunfire across the Saale to the west. He spotted a group of men standing near a pair of Sherman tanks and noticed the big red numerals on their shoulder patches.

"I'm from Third Army headquarters," he told a captain who seemed to be in charge. "I've got orders to find the XX Corps command post. I was told they're across the river. Where's it safe to cross."

"It ain't." A young corporal grinned. "Ain't safe to cross this damned river, *nowhere*."

"Well, yeah," the captain drawled in a thick Texas accent. "He's just about right. Damned Reds are makin' it difficult. Every once in a while, they'll cut loose a barrage on the bridges."

"What would you suggest?"

"Well, lemme see your map," the captain said, gesturing toward the map that Nate had shoved into his shirt pocket.

"Okay. Now you're right here on the bend in the river. The next bridge ahead is the one you can see from here. If it's still standing when you get to it, take it across to this street called Steinweg that leads to the center of town . . . this area called Eichplatz. I heard that XX Corps was up in there, but I dunno where'n the hell the command post would be. You'll just hafta go over'n ask around. Good luck."

Nate had an eerie feeling as he turned onto the bridge. Unlike the previous bridge that he'd crossed, it was completely deserted. He recalled what the captain had said about the barrages that the Russians were dropping on the bridges. He hoped that one of these was not imminent.

Though it was still standing, the bridge showed evidence of a difficult recent history. Originally built of stone, it had fallen to Allied bombing only to be carefully rebuilt by the Germans with wooden timbers at least twice. The rubble and splintered wood on the eastern approach showed that somebody's artillery had a near miss within the last few hours. In several places, Nate could look down and see the churning brown waters of the Salle through cracks in the planking as he carefully maneuvered the jeep.

When he was nearly across, Nate heard the high-pitched whistle of an incoming artillery round. His infantryman's instinct was to dive for cover, but there was no cover to dive for. An instant later, the shell hit the river about twenty feet downstream—so close that Nate could feel the splash of water on his hands and face.

Another whine. Another splash. Another whine. No splash. The shell exploded behind him. The bridge shook violently. Nate floored the accelerator. To hell with being careful. He'd trade the possibility of *falling* in the river for the probability of getting *blasted* into the river any day.

As irony would have it, only that one shell actually hit the bridge. The barrage, which was evidently being launched without a forward observer, continued to move upstream away from the bridge. Somebody was firing blind, but Nate had no idea whether it was the Russians or the Americans.

He was well into the city before he slowed down to take a look around. He was evidently on the street called Steinweg, although he could see no signs to confirm it. The Germans had pulled down most of their street signs as the Allies had approached in March, and most European street signs were hard to see anyway.

The city ahead of him was as deserted as the bridge had

been. There was plenty of gunfire to be heard, but it seemed blocks away, and the continuous *crumping* sound of the artillery was farther still.

The captain had been sure that XX Corps had reached this open city square called Eichplatz, but Nate knew that XX Corps was coming from the south, so he decided that he'd circle around and approach from the south. He turned left and made a right at the next main street, which abruptly opened onto a square that the map called the Marktplatz. Across this square was an imposing, low, fortress-like building.

The plaza was too empty. It was too quiet. Something in his GI instinct told him that this was not a good place to be. He could almost smell a Russian gunner eying him.

Deciding to make for a smaller street that he could see off to his right, he turned the wheel sharply as he floored the accelerator.

A machine gun clattered and rounds spattered across the cobblestones. The gunner had fired wide, but he compensated on his second burst.

Suddenly the jeep slowed and ground to a halt. The tires!

Nate didn't pause to check the damage. He just grabbed the 12-gauge shotgun from the scabbard on the jeep and catapulted out. He crouched behind the jeep, wishing that he'd substituted a carbine for the shotgun when he'd started on this expedition.

More rounds slammed into the jeep. Nate decided that he'd better put some space between himself and the jeep.

"Hey you, soldier! This way!"

The voice seemed to come out of nowhere. Nate glanced around.

"Here. On your left."

Nate looked left and saw another GI peering though an open window in one of the big stone buildings that fronted the square. He needed no coaxing. A mad, nine-second dash that seemed like twenty minutes had Nate diving through the open window just as a fusillade of slugs poured through after him.

"What in the hell are you doing here, soldier?"

It was a lieutenant with the blue "battle-axe" shoulder patch of the 65th Infantry Division that Nate knew was part of

XX Corps. In the dim light, Nate could see four other men with the same insignia. One was badly wounded.

"I'm from Third Army headquarters. I'm trying to find the XX Corps command post."

"Hate to tell you," a big man with master's sergeant's stripes said, "but you have *really* come to the wrong place."

"At least I came to the right corps area," Nate said, trying to appear nonchalant. "Over at 1st Division, they seem to think that XX Corps is in control of this place called Eichplatz, which is on the other side of that place where the Russians are."

"The Eichplatz is still no-man's land," the lieutenant, whose name was Timmons, explained. "The Russians have gunners everywhere in these buildings, especially the big solid ones like that . . . it's the city hall, I think."

"Where's the rest of your outfit?"

"Damned if we know," the sergeant said. "Just around the corner? Half a mile away? Could be anywhere and it wouldn't matter. It's hard to keep track in this damned city fighting. Can't see a fuckin' thing. Russians are everywhere."

"These are the guys who beat the Germans at Stalingrad," another man said. "This house-to-house stuff is in their blood."

"Our radio was hit," Timmons added. "We took cover in here. It had to be the only place on this damned square without a back door. We're trapped!"

"You got a radio?" The sergeant asked Nate.

"In the jeep."

"Wanna go get it?"

"Okay," Nate said without thinking. "Cover me."

He reached the jeep before the Russian gunner saw him and was running back to the open window with the walkie-talkie when the bullets started to fly.

The lieutenant adjusted the frequency on the radio and began attempting to reach his battalion. As often happens in the midst of a battle, the communications channels were so clogged with chatter that communication was impossible.

With growing impatience, Timmons tried again and again to reach his headquarters. Finally, he shrugged and set the radio down on the floor.

"I've got an idea." Nate said.

"What's that?"

"When I went out there just now, it took them awhile to start shooting. I could go do it again, use the jeep for cover and draw their fire until they hit one of the jeep cans. The smoke and fire would shield us long enough to get out of here."

"Where would we go?"

"Around the corner? Next door? I dunno." Nate shrugged. "Somewhere with a back door."

"How do we know that next door *has* a back door?"

"There's a fifty-fifty chance there," Nate calculated. "And zero chance here."

"Let's try calling for help one more time," Timmons said, picking up the walkie-talkie.

"We really should get Davy to an aid station pretty quick," one of the men attending the wounded soldier said after Timmons spent a frustrating five minutes trying to break through the wall of static.

Davy, the wounded man, was in pitiful shape. He was awake, but obviously in shock from a serious abdominal wound. He was bandaged, and the bleeding had been stopped, but Davy really *did* need to get to an aid station.

"You said the Russians were everywhere," Nate said, peeking out the window. "But the only ones *I've* seen are those in that building with the steeple. Are there any others that you know about?"

"We took some fire from that side street down there to the left," Timmons said. "But maybe they can't see us over here where we are now?"

"They probably set this up so they've got separate gunners with fields of fire that cover all the streets around here individually," Nate said. "Probably something they learned in Stalingrad."

"Let's get ready, so that we know what to do and go quick," Nate said. "I saw an opening about twenty feet from the window. It's a sorta covered alleyway. I don't know how far it goes, but I'm guessing it'll go through this block of buildings farther than another storefront like this."

"Okay, the main thing is to move Davy as fast as we can," Timmons began to explain. "As soon we get our smoke, I'll go out first. Two of you guys hand Davy to me shoulders first.

Soon as he's out, one of you guys help me carry him. Sarge, cover us from in here with the BAR, and come last."

"When we start to run, I'll take point," Nate offered. "If we run into any bad guys in that alley, this shotgun will come in handy."

Nate was right about the readiness of the Russian gunners. He was able to get to the cover of the jeep again before they started to fire. As he lay on the ground counting the seconds, the *pung* sound of the 7.62 mm slugs hitting the side of the jeep was deafening. He expected that at any moment, one would rip through the vehicle and crash into his helmet.

After what seemed like the better part of an hour, but what was actually less than twenty seconds, one of the tracers that was mixed in with the other ammo impacted a jeep can. There was a deafening *whump* as it exploded, followed by a second mar as the first can's companion caught fire.

Nate could feel the flames singe the hairs on the backs of his hands, which he'd instinctively clasped over the back of his head as he lay face down on the ground. The huge black cloud billowed up from the jeep. The gunfire ceased. The Russian gunners were probably congratulating themselves and didn't know that this destruction of US government property was literally a smokescreen for the escape of their quarry.

The GIs knew they'd have to move quickly before the initial cloud of smoke subsided. Indeed, they had Davy mostly out the window before Nate was on his feet. Knowing they should all move together to minimize the amount of time they were exposed between the jeep and the archway that led to the alley, he paused until Sarge was out, then sprinted for the opening.

Crouching and holding the shotgun at the ready, Nate entered the alley and moved quickly. It was damp and musty, but it did lead beneath the building and intersect with another passage under another building.

Davy was out of harm's way before the Russian gunner opened up again, but Sarge was not so lucky.

"Oh shit!" he said, gritting his teeth in obvious pain.

As he came into the alley, Nate looked back to see him silhouetted in the arched entryway. His left shoulder was already soaked with blood.

"It's okay," he said through gritted teeth. "I can still move, but somebody else is going to have to take the BAR."

Setting the twenty-two-pound Browning Automatic Rifle aside, Timmons got him into a seated position, tore off part of his own shirt and shoved it into the wound.

"Okay, that's two for the aid station. Let's move out."

Nate and the man who picked up the BAR to cover their rear were now the only men neither wounded nor carrying someone who was. Nate didn't like the odds. He hoped they'd reach American lines sooner rather than later.

They had a vague idea of which direction to go, but for the moment, they just went where the alley took them.

At the first junction, one direction led to a huge, imposing wooden door, and the other to a bend, around which they could see a hint of reflected daylight. Someone muttered something about "the light at the end of the tunnel," and they headed in that direction.

As they reached the bend, they heard the sound of people walking. Nate crouched and peaked around the corner. What he saw made his thumping heart leap into his throat. A large number of Russian soldiers were walking quickly toward them.

"Red patrol," he whispered, as he ducked back.

They were outnumbered four to one with no place to go. Even without the need to carry Davy, there was probably no way they could escape.

The corporal who was carrying the BAR dropped his pack and braced himself in firing position. Timmons and the other man carrying Davy set him down gently and unslung their carbines. Nate checked the shotgun and unfastened the flap of his sidearm holster. Sarge took out his Colt automatic.

As the Russian patrol reached the bend from the other side, Nate expected them to slacken their pace out of apprehension about what might be waiting for them, but they did not. Maybe the thought didn't occur to them. Maybe they were in a hurry.

Two of the Russians turned the corner. One was an officer in a garrison cap, while the other wore a helmet and carried a PPD submachine gun.

For Nate, everything seemed to go by in slow motion. He had the feeling that he had time to study the expressions on their faces, as determined detachment turned to shock and surprise. The soldier with the submachine gun froze, the officer fumbled for his pistol. Nate fired the shotgun and the officer's expression disappeared along with the face that held it. The soldier's face exploded with the next squeeze of the trigger.

Nate drew his pistol and started aiming for the Russians that were in the tunnel around the corner. The corporal with the BAR was next to him, lying prone and squeezing the trigger.

The noise of gunfire in a confined space was deafening, but after awhile, all that Nate heard was the ringing in his ears.

Nate tried to aim as carefully as he could, but he didn't know what he was hitting. All he saw was a tumbling mass of flesh, metal, pea-green cloth, and blood—gushing, splattering blood.

At last it was over. The tumbling mass of flesh, metal, pea-green cloth, and blood no longer tumbled. A dense blue cloud hung in the tunnel; the stench of burnt powder overwhelmed the damp mustiness.

Nate was gripping his .45 with both hands. His hands ached. There was an empty cartridge clip laying nearby. He must have reloaded without thinking. He looked right. The young corporal was staring at him. The whites of his eyes stood in sharp contrast to the powder-blackened skin of his face.

"Are you all right?" Nate asked him. That was all that he could think of to say.

"B'lieve so," the kid said after a long pause.

As the two of them started to stand up, Nate saw that the kid's knuckles were torn and bleeding. As Nate knew from personal experience, one of the BAR's inherent flaws was the bottom-mounted magazine, which was hard to change when the gunner was lying prone, and lying prone was necessary for accuracy with the big weapon. Of course, its 20 mm rounds were a good deal *more* inconvenient for the enemy.

Behind them, Nate saw Timmons wiping his forehead and staring at the man who had been helping him carry Davy. The poor guy had taken at least four really bad hits while he was still standing. He'd probably been dead within the first five seconds. Nate realized that he didn't even know the guy's name.

Timmons was bending over Davy now.

"How is he?" Nate asked.

"I'll be damned," Timmons said. "Poor guy's still got a pulse."

Without any further conversation, Nate helped Timmons pick Davy up and start to carry him toward the daylight. The corporal with the BAR took the point, moving ahead about twenty feet.

As they picked their way through the mass of Russian bodies, Nate lost count at twenty-three. They had really massacred the Russian patrol, but they had been aided by the fact that this tunnel-like alley was so narrow that no more than two or three of the Russian could get a clear shot at a time. Indeed, some of these guys had probably shot each other in the shooting frenzy.

Nate was starting to smell the tantalizing sweetness of the fresh outside air when he heard the corporal suddenly exclaim "Don't shoot!"

Nate, who was walking backward carrying Davy's shoulders, craned his neck to look. The corporal was silhouetted in the arched doorway with his hands raised over his head.

"Oh nooo," Timmons said, a look of despair coming over his face.

For a moment, they just stood there. Reflections on death and the misery of a Soviet prison had not yet started to crowd Nate's mind when he was suddenly surrounded by many men.

Much to his relief, their uniform color was olive drab, not pea-green, and the shoulder patches had blue and white battle-axes, not hammers and sickles.

They quickly carried Davy to the entrance, where two medical corpsmen took over.

Timmons saluted a major whom he apparently knew and who explained that they had been in pursuit of the Russian patrol, and had lost them. The Reds had ducked into the alley and were on the verge of escaping. In his turn, Timmons explained that his patrol had been ambushed, pinned down, and ultimately "rescued" by this quick-thinking sergeant. Nate realized that Timmons was talking about *him*.

Nate shrugged off what he felt was an exaggerated accolade and explained to the major who he was and that he'd been trying to reach the XX Corps command post. As soon as Nate mentioned the word "Patton," the major called for a jeep and ordered an armed escort to take him to General Walker.

This time, Nate's drive through the winding streets of Jena was a great deal less eventful. As they reached a broad street called Westbahnhofstrasse, American forces were everywhere. The sounds of artillery were much more distant now. There was a prevailing sense that the Americans were now in control.

Finally, they reached the XX Corps nerve center, which had been set up in a narrow city park near what seemed to be a main road leading westward out of town. The shadows were growing long now, and it seemed that the battle was winding down.

"Major Lutz said you were looking for me," General Walker smiled as he returned Nate's salute. "At ease soldier. I heard that you were quite a hero this afternoon over at the Marktplatz."

"We got through, sir, but we lost a man."

"The way I heard it, it was *your* quick thinking that saved everybody else . . . Twice."

"Thank you, sir," Nate said weakly. If a three-star general wanted to think that he was a hero, then the three-star general could think he was a hero.

Nate explained to Walker that Patton was at the III Corps command post and that he wanted to have someone from XX Corps who knew the status of things in the XX Corps sector to come to meet with him. After a bit of discussion with his staff, Walker picked a Lieutenant Colonel named Wade, assigned a jeep to escort them and sent them on their way.

They returned to the Landgraftenberg by a different route, through territory west of Jena that XX Corps had cleared during the three hours that Nate had been delayed.

As they reached III Corps, the sun was sinking low toward the mountains of the distant Thuringerwald. Patton was where

Nate had left him, pouring over maps with Van Fleet and their staffs.

"Sir, this is Colonel Wade of XX Corps," Nate said as soon as he caught the General's eye.

"Soldier, where the hell have you been all afternoon?" Patton thundered.

Nate stiffened as he stood at attention. He could feel his hands start to tremble. He was more frightened now than he'd been on the Marktplatz. Of course, there, he hadn't really had the time to stop and think about being afraid.

"And I heard that you lost one of my damned jeeps!"

Suddenly a grin spread across Patton's face.

"There's a major named Lutz who recommended you for a Bronze Star for what you did. Damned good work."

With the great clouds of smoke that hung in the air and still billowed from places west of the city, the sunset was spectacular. All around him, just as in the city, Nate saw men and equipment moving steadily and purposefully into the valley. Wrecked Russian gear was everywhere.

If the Third Army had won today, and there was every reason to believe they had, it would the first victory in a war against an enemy that had lost many battles only to win war after war after war. Napoleon had defeated the Russians only to stagger home beaten and shamed. The Wehrmacht had destroyed half of the Soviet military establishment in six weeks, but it was Hitler who lost the war.

Just as the sun dipped behind the horizon, men began emerging from the command post and climbing into jeeps. Oscar Koch walked over to where Nate was.

"The Soviet 4th Ukrainian Front is through," Koch said, surveying the sprawling, burning landscape before them. "Third Army won a big one here today. There are still some pockets out there, but Yeremenko's been defeated. Tomorrow, III and XII Corps'll reach Weimar, but there's only a skeleton force of Reds left. Yeremenko gambled everything on Jena and lost."

"Gentlemen, nearly 139 years ago, Napoleon fought one of the most important battles of his career on these fields." It was Patton. He had come out to join them on the bluff to survey the scene. "He beat a force twice his size. He whipped the

Duke of Brunswick and the King of Prussia. Within two weeks, he beat the whole damned Prussian Army and was marching into Berlin. He changed the course of history here at Jena.

"I hope that history will say the same for us. The dedication and skill of every soldier in this Third Army has given us a helluva first victory. What a *damned fine war!*"

8

★ ★

The White House
Washington DC
Monday, June 11, 1945, 8:31 a.m.

"IT's like waking up from a nightmare," the President of the United States exclaimed, holding up a copy of *The Washington Herald*. "On Thursday, we were told that Patton was on the verge of total defeat."

He dropped the paper on the table so that Secretary of War Henry Stimson and the two five-star officers could see the headline which read, "PATTON CRUSHES RED ARMY."

"At the time, we knew that two Third Army corps were heavily engaged," General George Marshall explained. "But we didn't know the details of Patton's tactical plan."

"Whatever it was, it seems to have worked," Truman beamed.

"Yes, Mr. President," Marshall agreed. "It worked splendidly. It worked even better than the newspapers have suggested."

"What exactly happened?" Truman asked, relishing the details.

"Patton used his XX Corps to feign a defense against the main Russian attack on his left flank, while he simultaneously counterattacked on his right," Marshall explained. "XX Corps then feigned a retreat, only to counterattack when the Soviet forces were too disorganized to defend."

"And then . . ." Truman urged, like a small child engrossed in a bedtime story.

"Patton managed to get his main force into Yeremenko's rear without him realizing that it was *really* Patton's main force. Patton outflanked them and attacked from three sides. Two days later, the entire 4th Ukrainian has been destroyed. Every single tank and artillery piece in the entire army group was destroyed or captured. Third Army has decimated a much larger force. They've taken more than twenty thousand prisoners since Thursday. We don't even have an exact count yet. Toward the end of the day on Saturday, there was attempt to flee with two intact divisions, but Yeremenko escaped with only about two hundred troops."

"Ninth Air Force put a stop to that," General Hap Arnold smiled. The USAAF chief was smiling like a Cheshire cat. He was as pleased as the President that two weeks of continual disaster had culminated in a resounding victory, but he was especially pleased with the role that his A-26s had played in turning a Russian retreat into a highway from hell.

"I can't tell you what this has done for morale in this country," Truman beamed. "This morning, the telegrams are pouring in. People are ecstatic. It's a complete turnabout from the blue mood last week."

"The papers love Patton," Stimson smiled. "He's their colorful, incorrigible hero, and he hasn't lost his ability to command the inches of copy. The British papers seem to like him, too. A week ago, they were complaining that the situation was hopeless. The Den Helder disaster put them in the depths. But now, old George Patton is seen as having gotten them some measure of revenge."

"And it *was* a decisive victory," Truman added, relishing the moment.

"It clearly was," Marshall said, speaking in a tone more sober than his colleagues.

"We needed a hero," Truman said emphatically. "And this country needed a solid victory."

"If he can only keep it up," Marshall said. "He still has

Marshal Tolbukhin's 3rd Ukrainian Front on his right, and Malinovsky's 2nd Ukrainian Front at his rear in Austria. Marshal Koniev's successfully occupied everything east of the Rhine and north of Frankfurt, but XIII Corps and XIX Corps and other Ninth Army outfits are holding fast. Koniev has his hands full in the Rhineland, but he could turn south and east against Patton. Koniev's solidly preoccupied with holding his side of the Rhine, but we've got reports that Tolbukhin is preparing to attack Third Army. His 3rd Ukrainian Front is twice the size of the 4th Ukrainian Front *and* it includes three of their elite Guards armies. Patton will need more men and materiel, and he needs Seventh Army rebuilt and put back into southern Germany. Hopefully, Fifth Army in Italy can be put back into shape, too."

"Give him what he needs," Truman insisted. "If he can win one like this, he deserves everything that we can give him."

"What is the logistics situation at the moment, General?" Stimson asked.

"We've gotten a supply pipeline running through southern France and the Alsace into Bavaria. This will benefit Patton immensely. We're also working to build Seventh Army back up to full strength in order to support Third Army. First Army should be up to strength to support Bradley in the north ahead of schedule. We lost a great deal of the Ninth Army during the Red offensive in May, but Bradley still has the Fifteenth Army. The Eighth Army is already under way from the Pacific. Sixth Army will follow in about sixty days. The new Twelfth Army should be ready by the end of the year."

"Patton's asked for more air support," Arnold said. "Specifically, he's asking for help from Fifteenth Air Force in Italy. They're partially demobilized, but General Twining has been working night and day to get some of his key groups back into shape. I've suggested that Twining fly up to Germany and work things out with Patton directly."

"That's great," Truman smiled, obviously caught up in the mood of the moment.

"But the Fifteenth is not a ground support force, it's a strategic bombing outfit?" Marshall said to Arnold quizzically. "With heavy bombers."

"That's correct, sir," Hap Arnold smiled. "I reckon that General Patton may have some heavy bombing in mind."

Reim Airport
Near Munich, Germany
Tuesday, June 12, 1945, 1:45 p.m.

"It was only *one* damned battle," Patton was reminding people. "We still have a *war* to fight, and we're still outnumbered four to one."

With three days to digest the fruits of the Jena victory, and with the Western press comparing it to Napoleon's victory, the mood within the Third Army was decidedly upbeat. Nevertheless, Patton was pushing them hard, admonishing them to keep their attention focused on the job still left to be done.

The B-17 that was bringing the commander of the USAAF Fifteenth Air Force from his headquarters at Bari in Italy made one low pass over the former Luftwaffe fighter base before the pilot lined up for a landing. Patton was there with a Third Army honor guard and the Third Army band. Even in wartime, the General relished the role of showman and that of gracious host. The Third Army staff was out in its spit and polish, which for Nate McKinley included a little piece of red, white, and blue ribbon of his bronze star that was pinned over his pocket above the ribbon of his World War II Victory Medal. He wondered what the World War III Victory Medal would look like, and whether he'd ever see it.

Major General Nathan Twining was the first man out of the Flying Fortress, followed by a half-dozen staff officers. Like Patton, he liked keeping his staff compact when he was in the field.

The tall, square-jawed Twining saluted Patton and the two men shook hands as the band played a Sousa march. Nate thought it ironic that the work of a Marine Corps composer was being played as a backdrop to a meeting between an old-school Army man and an air officer who was part of that coterie that wanted to see the USAAF as a separate US Air Force.

Rather than driving Twining into Munich, Patton had arranged for the meeting to take place in a conference room at the old Luftwaffe headquarters building at Reim. Patton, who was still the military governor of Bavaria, put on a great show of Bavarian hospitality, with a lavish spread of Bavarian cheeses and sausages for Twining, who admitted that he and his staff had not had lunch yet. At several points during the small talk that accompanied the informal meal, Patton had joked with the airmen, introducing a particular tray as "This is some of *our* great Bavarian . . ."

When the meeting was officially convened, the General ordered a large map displayed, which showed all of Austria and southern Germany, as well as most of Czechoslovakia.

"If I'd been in Stalin's boots, I would have used Tolbukhin's 3rd Ukrainian Front to back Yeremenko's 4th Ukrainian in the battles last week," Patton began. "On paper, the 3rd Ukrainian is twice as big, and it's got three Guards Armies. Between Yeremenko and Tolbukhin, they'd have made it a lot harder for the good old US Third Army. But Stalin did not do this, and who am I to question the wisdom of the great Joe Stalin?"

There was a brief ripple of laughter.

"My G2 tells me that one reason Tolbukhin didn't join the fight was that he was still licking his wounds from his tussle with Schorner's Kraut Army Group Center, which, as you will recall, was going on in Czechoslovakia until a month ago. Whatever the reason that he didn't *last* week, Tolbukhin is on the move *this* week."

Patton took a drink of water and picked up a pointer, which he held like a riding crop as he spoke.

"One of the fleeting benefits of Third Army's victory over the weekend is that it has caused the Russians to think for the moment of shoring up their own defenses. As you can see, a week ago, they had Thuringia, and Yeremenko was holding Leipzig. This week, Third Army owns Thuringia, and Leipzig is virtually undefended. An important part of their north-south strategy between the Elbe and Oder hinges on the line that runs from Berlin to Leipzig to Prague. If you were them and you were going to predict old George Patton's next move, what would you say?"

Several voices said "Leipzig," knowing that this was what Patton expected them to say, but knowing full well by his tone of voice that he had something else up his sleeve.

"Undefended Leipzig?" Patton smiled. "An *undefended* key city, just sixty kilometers from where the main body of our forces are? That's what they'd think, and I've gone so far as to mention to some British newspaper people that Third Army plans to take Leipzig are the key to our strategy. I'm doing so before the end of the month. I've also ordered our various units to be supplied with this in mind. I've had a big commercial printer here in Munich start putting together Leipzig city maps."

The General grinned devilishly and took another sip of water.

"Old Fyodor Tolbukhin is already beating old Georgie Patton to the punch. He's activated his forces and he's moving north out of the heavily wooded and highly defensible terrain around Prague. He's moving up to the open terrain around Leipzig. My G2 says that he's even borrowing tanks from other outfits. Remember how Third Army will be moving into 'undefended' Leipzig 'by the *end* of the month?' That'll give the Russians plenty of time to dig in. When poor old Third Army tries to move across these flats southwest of Leipzig, it'll run straight into Fyodor Tolbukhin, who chased the Krauts out of the Crimea last spring and out of Belgrade last fall. In February, it was his 3rd Ukrainian, along with Malinovsky's 2nd Ukrainian, that smashed the last German panzer force at Budapest. These outfits included the Third SS 'Death's Head' Panzer Division that escaped after Kursk."

"Was Tolbukhin at Kursk?" someone asked, referring to the summer of 1943 battle on steppes north of Kharkov that was the largest tank battle of the war, and the last great German panzer offensive.

"No, Tolbukhin wasn't, but Malinovsky commanded the Southwest Front at Kursk. Word has it that Tolbukhin was always jealous that he missed it. He always wanted *his* big tank battle. He got one at Budapest, but had to share it with his old rival, Malinovsky. Now, he's looking forward to fighting his big tank battle with the Third Army. He's got the chance to dig in and set us up, just like the Reds did with the Krauts at

Kursk. Tolbukhin fancies *this* as a repeat of one of the Red Army's greatest triumphs in World War II. *But* the *Third* Army won't be coming."

Patton paused to take a sip of water while that notion sank in.

"Gentlemen, throughout history, great campaigns have been lost by armies that fought the kind of battle that the other guy was expecting," Patton continued. "*If* Third Army did what Tolbukhin expects, and what is most logical for us to do, we'd face a force twice the size of what we faced in the 4th Ukrainian, and we'd leave our right flank, the salient between Munich and Vienna, wide open to be exploited by Malinovsky."

Watching from the back of the room, Nate was amused by the way Patton was playing the crowd. He had shown them how easy and obvious a move into Leipzig would be. Now he was tearing apart his original thesis by showing all the flaws. Nate could imagine Tolbukhin, convinced that Patton was headed for Leipzig, gloating as he also discovered the same flaws.

"The reason that I've invited my friends from Fifteenth Air Force to join us here today is a little scheme that General Weyland and I cooked up involving the use of airpower," Patton continued. "You Air Force boys have been crowing about airpower for a long time. I will admit, those of us on the ground-hugging side of the service took some convincing, but Weyland and his XIX Tactical convinced me. Now we're going to take airpower a step further. In the coming battle, I intend to use Fifteenth Air Force as I would another land army. Until this moment, nobody other than General Weyland and General Twining have seen this plan."

There was a murmur of voices reacting to this bold statement as Patton and a staff officer flipped to a new map on the easel.

"Tolbukhin's preparing to fight a land battle, but we're *denying* his expectations," Patton said, looking at the Fifteenth Air Force men. "When he's chosen his positions, and our aerial recon boys have carefully mapped these positions, Fifteenth Air Force will hit him from high altitude with the biggest precision aerial bombardment ever launched against an army in the field. Operating this deep into Europe, we have the advantage of more accurate weather forecasting, so we can pick a time when the visibility is good, and the visibility in June is generally good. The enemy's antiaircraft units will be ready, but ready for tactical air power at *low* altitude."

"How many days will we need to run these missions?" one of the Fifteenth Air Force officers asked.

"With maximum bomb loads and experienced bombardiers, General Weyland estimates that four hundred bombers could eliminate the fighting effectiveness of the 3rd Ukrainian Front in less than a week, if they're concentrated as we expect them to be."

"Does Fifteenth Air Force have that capability?" Asked a Third Army officer.

Patton deferred to Twining who walked to the front of the room to explain. "When General Weyland and General Patton discussed this with me this morning, I said that current levels of available resources could sustain a maximum level of operations for only four days, but we've got a lot of ordnance and fuel in the pipeline that will start arriving by next week."

"What about the distance?" Asked another Fifteenth Air Force man. "Leipzig is really at the outer limit of our effective combat radius."

"That was one of my first questions when General Patton first suggested the plan," Twining admitted. "But we won't have to fly out of the usual bases in Italy. When this war started, General Weyland ordered his XIX Tactical Air Command dispersed to ancillary fields, and the Third Army engineers have got these operational now. This means that the old Luftwaffe bases with the long runways, such as here at Munich and up at Nurnberg, can be made available. We'll need less fuel and we'll carry more bombs. Because the missions will be shorter than those we've flown out of Italy for the past two years, the crews will get more rest and have a higher level of availability."

"What do we expect in the way of fighter opposition?" The same Fifteenth Air Force officer asked.

"The Luftwaffe never had a high altitude heavy bomber capability, or at least not that was much used on the Eastern Front," Twining replied. "So the Red Air Force doesn't have the interceptor experience that the Luftwaffe gained fighting us.

They'll be more inept, but are not to be discounted. We'll have our usual fighter escorts, but they'll have more time on target because they can share airfield space with XIX Air Command."

"And the fields that we captured in Thuringia last week, which are just a few minutes' air time from Leipzig, can be used by the fighters exclusively," Patton added. "General Weyland's people will be conducting raids on the Red air bases around Dresden and Prague. These will be timed to co-incide with your attack on Tolbukhin."

"The Royal Air Force has been conducting raids against the Reds in Berlin recently, and I'm planning to coordinate our operation with them, so that the Red Air Force fighters in Berlin will be spread thin," Twining explained.

"Where will Third Army be while this operation is going on?" asked one of Patton's own operations staffers. "I'm sure that we won't be just sitting back watching the planes go over-head."

"No, I'm afraid not," Patton replied. "Since Marshal Tol-bukhin is expecting us in Leipzig, he's pulling most of his peo-ple out of Prague. We'll be going to Prague. I recognize several faces here in this room who were with XII Corps and V Corps when they went into Czechoslovakia two months ago and were prevented from going on to Prague by the politicians. Well, next week you're going back . . . and dammit, you're going *all the way*."

The Capitol Coffee Shop
17th and M Streets, NW
Washington DC
Wednesday, June 19, 1945, 2:56 p.m.

"Have you heard the excitement about your General Pat-ton?" Fiona Wells asked her friend Rosemary O'Leary as she arrived at the cramped booth at the popular Washington diner where the two friends often met to exchange rumors.

"I heard that the Russians seem to be taking their loss at Jena very seriously."

"I just got a wire from London," Fiona smiled smugly. She relished flaunting her connection to a city where news from continental Europe had been gathered and processed for half a day before the Yanks were awake. "He's moving into Leipzig. It's *undefended*. The Allies will be just 185 kilometers from Berlin!"

"Don't you think he's spreading himself kinda thin?" Rosie asked. "Aren't there a lot of Russians over in Czecho-slovakia and Austria?"

"I suppose," Fiona said thoughtfully. "But I rather imagine that he knows what he's doing."

"Everybody rather thinks that," Rosie said, looking away to order a club sandwich from the harried waitress.

"You don't sound so enthusiastic about General Patton." Fiona said quizzically after she'd ordered the soup du jour, no crackers. "I'd sort of thought all you Yanks would be wild about Georgie."

"Actually, I'm kind of intrigued by this Sergeant McKin-ley, Patton's driver," Rosie said, scrutinizing the article in *The Washington Herald* about Nate's Bronze Star exploits. "He's the man who took the famous massacre pictures at Kummers-dorf. He ended up escaping from the Russians, then Patton hired him as a driver. Now he's gotten a Bronze Star for res-cuing some other GIs."

"Let me see," Fiona insisted, craning her neck to look at the small picture accompanying the article. "Oooh, as you Yanks say, he's rather easy on the eyes."

"That's *not* what I meant!" Rosie said, feeling herself blush slightly. "I think there's a interesting story here. It says that he's a cowboy from Montana."

"*Whoopie ti yi yo!*" Fiona teased. "He's a classic Ameri-can hero. He's a cowboy turned war hero, and handsome to boot."

"Well, as you said, they're making Patton out as the real hero," Rosie said, changing the subject.

"This battle was tremendous," Fiona enthused. "More than a million men fighting in exactly the same place where Napoleon defeated the Prussians and changed the course of history. It was the same ground!"

"Are you excited about this battle changing history or about a place where there were a million men working up a sweat?" Rosie smiled.

"Oh, Rosemary, that was a blow below the belt," Fiona scolded. "You sound rather cynical about the Napoleonic scale of Patton's triumph?"

"Just cautious, I suppose," Rosie said. "He has a great record and all, but I don't know how much of him is just bluster. It's great if he doesn't let it go to his head and make a stupid mistake. Bonaparte won at Jena, but it was *Leipzig* that was almost as big a 'Waterloo' for him as *Waterloo* was a year later."

"But Patton's changed everything," Fiona insisted. "The morale at home is way up. You know, the Labour Party even sent a telegram of congratulations. There's no more talk of Churchill having to call elections. There's no more 'Stalin this' and 'Stalin that,' even among the leftists. Patton's changed *everything*."

"What do you hear about the leftists in France?"

"I've heard that Patton's rather the hero in France this week," Fiona replied. "That whole thing about calling for a workers' revolt over there seems to have fizzled. As I heard it, there were posters everywhere in Paris. The French communists were coming on pretty strong. This week, Uncle Joe doesn't seem to be the cat's nightshirt anymore."

"Cat's *pajamas*."

"What?"

"The idiom is 'cat's pajamas.' "

"Oh yes, rather. Where does that come from?"

"Don't know. It's just there."

"You Yanks are a strange lot."

"But we *do* have generals that win battles," Rosie smiled. "You said so yourself."

"For the time being," Fiona smiled. "*You* said that."

Leipzig, Germany
Tuesday, June 20, 1945, 5:15 a.m.

Marshal Fyodor Ivanovich Tolbukhin's intelligence reports had been encouraging. After Patton's victory in Thuringia, there had been a great deal of gnashing of teeth in Moscow. Stalin had thrown a tantrum. Marshal Yeremenko, who had managed to escape into Marshal Koniev's sector through Erfurt with two hundred men, was in Moscow—under arrest. Knowing what Stalin had in store for him, it was plain that having died with his troops in Jena would have been the best choice.

Tolbukhin *wouldn't* have to make that choice. After all the concern about the great Patton, the Third Army seemed to have lost steam. Tolbukhin's intelligence showed that Patton's XX Corps, which was still in Jena, was combat-ready and prepared to attack Leipzig, but other units were still refitting. Apparently V Corps and XII Corps had been pulled back to Regensberg for reorganization. XX Corps might attack at any moment, but Tolbukhin had virtually his entire 3rd Ukrainian Front drawn up around Leipzig. They would make quick work of one corps. Despite this, he hoped that XX Corps would not attack. Tolbukhin simply wanted to be attacked by the *entire* Third Army, so that he could *destroy* the entire Third Army and dash this General Patton myth once and for all.

The Red Army defense of Leipzig was similar to that used to trap the Germans when they launched their Operation Citadel at Kursk nearly two years earlier. Tolbukhin had constructed three concentric semicircles of fixed defensive lines, and had positioned a mobile reserve behind them. When Patton attacked, he would be gradually slowed as he tried to battle through the layers of lines. Then, Red Army divisions would grind him into cattle fodder. If he divided his forces into a pincer—as the Germans had done at Kursk—the mobile reserve could attack the weaker half of the pincer while the other was sucked into the quagmire of the defensive lines.

Tolbukhin glanced up. High above the future battlefield and high above the breaking cloud cover, he saw the contrails of many aircraft. Most Red Army troops had never seen this phenomenon, because, on the Eastern Front, aircraft usually had not been flying so high. The Russian officers knew that these were probably the Fifteenth Air Force bombers that were reported to have been deployed to Munich for raids on Soviet forces in Berlin.

At first, he thought the explosions were XX Corps artillery. The Americans were about sixty kilometers away, but most of the Russian troops figured that somehow they had moved some of their guns forward to harass the Soviet forces. After all, this was something that the Red Army itself had often done.

The explosions continued. They were well timed and concentrated. The Russians were confused. Could it be that the American bombers were bombing *them* instead of going north to Berlin?

The first wave consisted of the nearly a hundred B-24 Liberator bombers of the 98th and 376th Bomb Groups. The masses of five-hundred pound bombs that dropped from their sagging bays tumbled onto the tank parks where Tolbukhin had positioned his strategic reserves.

After an interminable and concentrated pounding, the attack finally ceased and Soviet commanders were faced with trying to assess the damage. Even as they were doing this, there were contrails crossing in an opposite direction and a new attack began. These bombers, B-24s from eight squadrons of the 464th and 465th Bomb Groups, began methodically working over the defensive rings.

Four waves of bombers came and went in less than ninety minutes. The damage was considerable. Tolbukhin was incensed. He had lost more than a hundred tanks and an unknown number of artillery pieces. More details of bad news were still coming in. Attempts had been made to shoot at the high-flying bombers, but none of the antiaircraft weapons had the range. Tolbukhin ordered the captured German 88 mm antiaircraft guns stockpiled in Leipzig to be made ready for use. He made an urgent call to Berlin for more.

Of course, none of this was in place when two Nurnberg-based B-17 Groups began their bomb runs at high noon. In the interest of maintenance and logistics, Twining had chosen to concentrate his B-24 fleet in and around Munich, and his B-17s at Nurnberg. Ironically, these same aircraft had been used to bomb these same cities just a few months earlier. The German civilians who had once feared these bombers, were now glad to see them. Their fear of the Red Army ran high.

The first two waves of B-17s hit sections of the 3rd Ukrainian Front entrenchment that had been untouched during the morning, while the next two waves concentrated on the already damaged strategic reserves. Accompanying each wave of bombers, reconnaissance aircraft exposed the film that would produce many sheets of aerial photographs. These would be used both in measuring the work done in previous raids and to monitor the way that Tolbukhin was repositioning his surviving assets.

For five days the raids would continue—and for five nights as well. The Norden bombsight was ineffective in night raids, but many of the bombers were now equipped with the new radar bombsights. Even without these, the reconnaissance people had mapped the Soviet positions so well that the aircraft could drop their bombs with reasonable accuracy using just a compass and the locations of fires left burning from the daylight raids.

Massive incendiary attacks came on the last two days, as Twining's aircrews went to work on Tolbukhin's fuel dumps. The plan had been to attack the most portable elements—such as the mobile reserves—first, and the least movable—such as piles of supplies—last.

Though his antiaircraft defenses slowly improved as the week dragged on, Tolbukhin's inexperienced gunners claimed few of the American heavy bombers. The Fifteenth Air Force took its heaviest losses from the Red Air Force, but the Yak-9s and Lavochkin La-7s had just a limited window of operation. The air bases near Leipzig were rendered unusable, so the fighters had to fly in from Dresden and Berlin. Meanwhile the Mustangs protecting the bombers were minutes away. The American pilots developed a strategy of jumping Soviet fighters that were trying to get home and were too low on fuel to get into a dogfight. It was a trick that the Luftwaffe had used against many of these same Americans during the earlier war.

By the end of the five days, estimating his situation to be untenable, Tolbukhin made a tactical withdrawal from Leipzig, abandoning a city that the American V Corps had captured from the Germans on May 18, only to hand it over to the Red Army three weeks later.

When XX Corps entered Leipzig on June 27, the scene was dramatically different than that observed the last time that Americans entered the city two months earlier. In many German cities, the GIs had seen the results of Allied strategic air power on an urban landscape. Here they saw the effects of a concentration of that same air power on an army in defensive positions in the field.

About twelve kilometers from the edge of Leipzig, XX Corps passed through Tolbukhin's first line of defense. The going was difficult, not because of a wall of defensive fire, nor even the rows of barbed wire, but because the road simply disappeared in a mass of bomb craters. Rather than using tanks or infantry to lead his advance, General Walton Walker sent his engineers. Though the battlefield was silent except for the gunning of engines and the scraping of bulldozer blades, it took XX Corps most of the day to advance those twelve kilometers.

Everywhere were the artifacts of Tolbukhin's rehash of the Kursk defenses. There were hulks of tanks and an occasional artillery piece, but for the most part, the approaches to Leipzig were filled with endless strands of barbed wire, trash heaps of broken or unidentifiable pieces of equipment, and oceans of mud.

In the city itself, Walker reached Napoleonplatz, the center of the city, with his 12th Armored Division at about dusk. The Battle of Nations Monument, the Volkerschlachtsdenkmal, which commemorated Napoleon's defeat by the Prussians at Leipzig in 1814, was still standing. The irony of this battle having been the Prussian revenge for Napoleon's win at Jena was not lost on Walton Walker.

As had been the modus operandi of the Red Army during its earlier "tactical withdrawals" on the Eastern Front, Tolbukhin had adhered to a "scorched earth" policy. Little of value remained in the center of the city, although large outlying areas seemed reasonably intact.

Small groups of shell-shocked civilians were on the street as XX Corps secured the main thoroughfares. They were certainly happy that the Russians were gone, even if another recent enemy was occupying their city. Beyond ideology, they were just hoping to rely on the legendary generosity of the Yanks—they wanted something to eat.

As for the discredited Tolbukhin, he was making the best of things, fearing the summons from Stalin to return to Moscow, and digging in at Dresden. He had hoped to go back to beautiful Prague, with its tree-lined streets, its lovely river and its famous beer.

However, that choice was unavailable—George Patton was already there!

The White House
Washington DC
Monday, June 25, 1945, 4:01 p.m.

It was raining in Washington, but the mood in President Harry Truman's office could not have been sunnier. The unstoppable Red Tide of Rokossovsky's 2nd Byelorussian Front and Zhukov's 1st Byelorussian Front had swept across all of northern Germany and had swallowed all of the Netherlands, but then, they had sputtered to a stop after their string of incredible victories. They had run out of gas and had to wait for their supply trains to catch up.

In the south, Tolbukhin and Yeremenko might have coordinated their attacks against General George Patton's Third Army, but they did not. Patton was able to take them out in an amazing one-two punch.

"With a million-man force at Zhukov's disposal, anything more than guarded optimism is premature," Stimson cautioned.

"We have some breathing space," Truman reminded the military and civilian leaders that were gathered around the cabinet room table. "And I believe it essential to use this to come up with a concrete plan of action in this war."

"We've been just fighting for our lives over the past four weeks," Marshall said defensively. "It's been a bit premature for thinking about an endgame, but I agree, now is the time."

"With all due respect, all I've seen so far from the Joint War Plans people has been the plan to evacuate Europe," Truman said.

"That was essential at the time," Marshall explained. "With the force levels that we had, and the momentum that Zhukov had, we could've easily been forced into a situation where such a plan would've been the only alternative to disaster."

"I understand," Truman said crisply. "But now's the time to

move forward. I've had several wires from Churchill where he's urging me to start discussing a replacement for General Eisenhower as Supreme Commander. Someone needs to be selected so that a concrete war plan can be developed. Churchill is suggesting that I get together with him for a 'Big Two' conference, maybe in Labrador or Scotland."

"Who's the Prime Minister proposing for SACEUR?" Marshall asked. "Field Marshal Montgomery, I'd suspect."

"He definitely believes that the Supreme Commander should be British this time."

"Even though we have three times as many men under arms and will have five times as many airplanes overhead?" Stimson asked rhetorically.

"That would be my argument," Truman said. "But if I get into a discussion with him, I need to have an American proposal. Who would you suggest?"

"General Bradley, of course," Marshall replied quickly. "He's got staff experience. He worked closely with Ike in planning Overlord, as well as the drive across France and Germany. He commanded 12th Army Group, the largest single command in the US Army."

"He's already the senior man in the theater," Forrestal offered.

"I vote for *Patton*," Stimson said, watching for an incredulous look from Marshall.

"In our last meeting here at the White House, Mr. President, you said that we needed a hero," Stimson said. "I submit to you that what we need as Supreme Commander is a Themistocles, a man who can win decisive battles using bold and innovative tactics, and who can earn the respect of both his own people and those of the enemy."

"We seem to be at an impasse, gentlemen," Truman said abruptly. "But we've got to be absolutely certain that we pick a man who can *win* a war. How soon do you suppose that you'll be able to name our man?"

"Immediately after our fact-finding trip to France," Stimson answered. "By the weekend, General Marshall and I will have met with both General Bradley *and* General Patton."

"Gentlemen, I've given your trip some thought. I've decided to accompany you," Truman said. "I think that it's time for the Commander-in-Chief to meet his generals. Everything they know about me and everything that I know about them is second hand. I'm from Missouri. I like to size a man up by looking him in the eye."

"Isn't that a bit dangerous?" Stettinius said. "There's a war going on over there. Maybe we should have the Generals fly to Washington."

"No," Truman said emphatically. "They've got a war to fight. I think that a president should visit his troops in the field, or close to the field, at least. Lincoln did it. President Roosevelt did it in North Africa. Besides, it'll help me understand the way things are in Europe better if I can see them for myself."

"I'm really opposed to the idea," Stettinius said. "What if you were killed?"

"Then you'd be president," Truman smiled. "Without a vice president, the secretary of state is next in line if something happens to me. Back before 1886, it would have been the president pro-tem of the senate. Frankly, I'm going to propose to Congress that we use the Speaker of the House. But if something happens to me on this trip, *you'll* have my job."

"I know," Stettinius said. "That's why I *especially* don't want you to go! I have enough of an appreciation for your job to know that I don't *want* it."

"Well you don't have a choice," Truman said. "If it's any consolation, I'll go secretly. We'll let the press think that Secretary Stimson and General Marshall are going alone. I'll just ride along. I won't make any public appearances. I'll just meet with our field commanders in private. In and out in forty-eight hours. Nobody'll know that I was there until I'm back."

9

* *

Karluv Most (Charles Bridge), Vltava River
Prague, Czechoslovakia
Wednesday, June 27, 1945, 1:44 p.m.

WITH birds singing, people strolling, and the city virtually undamaged by a war that had mauled most of Europe, Prague was an almost dreamlike place. There was even a
man with a cart selling ice cream.

It was a new experience for Nate McKinley. Except for a
few barely inhabited villages in Belgium, his entire combat
career had taken place within the borders of the former German Reich. Through the winter and spring, and now the summer, he'd ridden or marched into dozens of cities that had
been conquered or occupied by a victorious Third Army. In
each place, the civilian cousins of the German soldiers whom
he'd just helped to defeat, had greeted the Yanks with sullen
and often hostile expressions. This week, the Yanks were suddenly no longer conquerors—they were liberators.

The progress of the Shermans and Greyhounds was
blocked not by tank traps and defensive positions, but by curious children, women in colorful summer dresses holding ba-
bies, and old men waving American flags. A similar reception
had welcomed III Corps and V Corps in April, but this time
the greeting was even more enthusiastic, because it was an unexpected second chance.

Two months earlier, the people had welcomed their liberators after six hard years of Nazi tyranny only to discover
that the Yalta agreement had condemned them to occupation
by the Red Army. Now the Yanks were back. As Patton had
announced on the steps of the city hall at Pilsen on June 22:

"No paper signed at Yalta is going to keep me out of Prague *this* time!"

The Third Army's advance into Czechoslovakia had been timed to begin at dawn on June 20, simultaneously with the Fifteenth Air Force assault on Marshal Tolbukhin's 3rd Ukrainian Front in Leipzig. Patton had planned the advance to Prague to take four days—one short of planned duration of the air assault on Leipzig—but he was within sight of the famous city on the morning of the third day.

With a sense of déjà vu, V Corps followed the route that it had taken two months before between Nurnberg and Pilsen, the second largest city in western Czechoslovakia. XII Corps followed its previous route up the Vltava River through Pisek.

Red Army resistance at the border was determined, although not fierce. Both corps managed to punch through the line after about four hours on the first day. Tolbukhin had withdrawn to Leipzig for his "Second Battle of Kursk" without a plan for the possible defense of western Czechoslovakia. The troops that faced the GIs were little more than well-armed sentries. Pilsen was undefended, and resistance on the outskirts of Prague was overcome during the afternoon of June 21. Inside the city, the remaining elements of Tolbukhin's command barricaded themselves in a former police headquarters, which was quickly surrounded by units of troops of the 26th Infantry Division.

In the month that Tolbukhin had garrisoned his troops in Prague, he'd made few friends among the locals. He'd given free rein to the Soviet secret police, the dreaded Narodny Kommisariat Vnutrennikh Del (NKVD), or People's Commissariat for Internal Affairs. The NKVD thugs carried on with a brutality that exceeded that of the Gestapo. When the last of the Red Army defenders finally surrendered to the 26th Infantry Division on June 24, they *begged* not be turned over to Czech civilians.

The Americans, meanwhile, were *overwhelmed* by civilians. The lead tank battalion of General Pierce's 16th Armored Division was actually trapped at the foot of Wenceslas Square for nearly three hours by an enormous crowd wanting to bury their tanks in flowers. Hundreds of men climbed on the tanks wanting to share beer and war stories with the Yanks, while dozens of young women simply wanted to share themselves. One GI bragged that he'd been kissed by over a hundred Czech girls before he lost count.

Three days later, things had quieted down considerably, but there was still a sense of euphoria in the air. President Edvard Benes, the country's still-popular, prewar leader, who had maintained a government in exile in London during the war, had announced his plan to return on June 30. He'd already sent a congratulatory telegram to Patton inviting him to use Hradcany Castle as his interim headquarters.

On a hill immediately west of the Vltava River, the castle dominated the city skyline from nearly every vantage point. Dating back to the tenth century, it had been used by kings of Bohemia, Holy Roman Emperors, and the Hapsburgs. For two decades, until the Germans came, it had been the residence of the president of the Republic of Czechoslovakia. Now, with the Germans gone, and the brief stay by the Red Army abruptly terminated, its medieval cellars and opulent Baroque halls were General George Patton's latest Lucky Forward.

For Patton, who recalled intimate details of the military history of the families who had lived here, the castle was an exciting temporary home.

For Nate McKinley, Hradcany Castle was the fanciest building he'd ever spent the night in—just as Prague was the first European city that he'd seen where the civilians were cheerful.

With the General not presently in need of being driven anywhere, Nate had asked the afternoon off to reconnoiter the city. It was the first time that he'd had to himself since that morning in Kummersdorf nearly a month ago. He had walked down to the river and was making his way toward the old part of town, across the Karluv Most, the bridge built in the fourteenth century by the Czech King Karluv IV.

At mid-span, he stopped to idly contemplate the river and the contrast between this leisurely stroll and his drive across the Saale in Jena. Although dark clouds had started to gather in the west and it felt a little like rain, it was a warm summer day.

"Excuse me, Sergeant," a voice said in heavily accented English.

Nate turned with a start. A rather stern-looking man with a round face and a shabby overcoat was standing six feet behind him.

"Yeah? What can I do for you?" Nate replied warily, taking him for one of the characters that lurked about European cities looking for handouts from the "wealthy" Americans. "I don't have any cigarettes."

"I don't want cigarettes," the man said. "I want to speak with your boss."

"My boss?"

"Yes. I know that you are the driver of General Patton."

"Whoa!" Nate gasped. He must have really screwed up. Here was a civilian who knew that about him. If the guy wanted to, he could have just shot Nate in the back. "Where'd you get *that* idea?"

"General Patton made a public entry to the city yesterday. You were driving. This is no secret. I have a message of urgent importance to give to General Patton."

"Why me? Why don't you just go up to the Castle and . . ."

"Imagine what would happen to me if I did that," the man explained patiently, nodding at the castle, which was clearly visible past the end of the bridge. "I'm a civilian without papers. A sentry would arrest me. But to meet you here, where I can have your attention and make you listen . . ."

"What do you want to talk to him about?"

"I cannot say to you. Only to him. I have my orders."

"What orders? Who are you with?"

"I have said too much already," the man said at last, reaching toward the opening of his overcoat. "Just give . . ."

"Wait a minute, buster, keep your hands where I can see them," Nate said as he tried to reach inside his coat.

"Of course."

The man carefully pulled back the lapel, so that Nate could see the inside pocket.

"I have, in my pocket, a small package of brown paper. It contains something that I wish to have you give to General Patton."

Nate nodded, and the man carefully removed the small packet, which was roughly the size of a pack of cigarettes.

"Please give it to General Patton and tell him that if he wants more, he should meet with me. I will be in this place again at 1800 this evening."

With that, the man turned and walked away, melting into a crowd of civilians.

Thirty minutes later, Nate was in the large office suite at the castle that Patton had appropriated for his own use.

"What the hell is it?" Patton said as he sat at the ornate desk studying the package that Nate had delivered.

"Why don't you open it?" Oscar Koch said.

"It might be a bomb," Hap Gay cautioned.

"It's too light to be a bomb," Patton said thoughtfully. "I think."

"So you think that this guy was a Russian?" Koch asked Nate.

"That was what I thought, but I'm not sure. He might've been Czech. I can tell French from German, but these Eastern Europeans all sound alike to me."

"Screw it," Patton said at last, gently unwrapping the package. Koch leaned in for a better look, while Hap Gay instinctively took a step toward the door.

The package came open and a piece of cloth fell out.

"It's a damned uniform patch," Patton exclaimed, sounding half disappointed. "It's definitely Russian. Whadya make of it, Oscar?"

"Wow!" Koch said. "It's a marshall's insignia. It's got a numeral '2' here on this part."

"There aren't many of these around," Patton said. "2nd Ukrainian Front?"

"That's the only 'second' anything in this part of the world that would be commanded by a marshal," Koch confirmed.

"This guy works for Rodion Malinovsky?" Gay said incredulously.

"He's taking a helluva chance walking around Prague!" Patton said, studying the patch. "This must be pretty goddam important to him."

"It *may* be pretty goddam important to us too," Koch said.

"Okay, sergeant, go down there to the bridge and meet this guy at 1800 hours," Patton said finally. "When you meet him, make damned sure that he's alone, and when you get him back up here, see that the MPs search him good."

The Offices of *The Washington Herald*
Washington DC
Wednesday, June 27, 1945, 5:27 p.m.

"To Paris?" Rosie O'Leary asked, hardly believing her ears. "I've never even been outside the United States before!"

"Well, it's your lucky day," Rex Simmons said, leaning across his desk, which was piled high with chaotic stacks of papers, some of which dated back to 1943. "I got the word that Assistant Secretary of State Grew is going on Stimson's trip to France. You're in like Flynn with all those people over at the State Department. It wouldn't hurt to have you go over."

Simmons explained that Stimson was going on a fact-finding trip to Paris and that Grew was going to meet with some of the leading political people, possibly including General de Gaulle.

"Thanks," Rosie said, trying not to show her excitement. Imagine, little Rosie O'Leary from Noe Valley, going to the City of Lights! Even after four years of Nazi occupation and a year of political chaos, Paris had the magic allure of its pre-war years, of the excitement of the smoky jazz clubs, of the avant-garde, and of that element of romance that tugged at the imaginations of young women the world over.

"Besides, I can't spare a *man* to go on such short notice," Simmons said, lighting a cigar. It was a game that he played with her. Since she'd become one of his inner circle of favorite reporters—the only *woman* in that circle—he'd never failed to give her the same opportunities as any male reporter at *The Washington Herald*. Nevertheless, he was constantly teasing her about being a woman in what was largely a man's game. Of course, she'd played her role equally well, scolding him for being a bully and for his detestable cigars.

"Gee, thanks, Mr. Simmons!" she said, feigning anger. "I'm sure that the State Department will think that they're being snubbed when they find out that *The Washington Herald* is just sending a *girl* to do a man's job!"

"Better hurry or you'll miss the flight," he smiled as she turned on her heel and walked out of his office.

Rex Simmons caught himself watching her as she walked away, down the open aisle between the dozens of desks filled with hammering typewriters. He caught himself watching the sway of her hips inside that summer dress, and the shape of her legs. He noticed for the first time that she was wearing nylons. All through the war, the girls had made do with drawing mascara-pencil lines down the backs of their legs to simulate stocking seams. For a brief few weeks, nylon had been plentiful. Now, with another war on, the girls were complaining again. With little Rosemary O'Leary, it was not so much the stockings or not, but remembering that when she had first come to *The Washington Herald* as an intern, she'd been wearing bobbie socks. She'd been just a schoolgirl. Over the past year, indeed over the past few weeks, she'd grown up before his eyes. He hadn't really noticed—until now.

Across the room, the big brass elevator doors opened and he caught a glimpse of her glaring at him, her bright red lips in a pout. Just as the doors closed, he thought he caught a wink. His eyes drifted back to the mass of papers on his desk, the detestable cigar, smoldering amid the deceased stumps of fellow members of its species—and the backs of his aging, leathery hands.

Hradcany Castle
Prague, Czechoslovakia
Wednesday, June 27, 1945, 6:24 p.m.

The unidentified man stood before Patton.

Outside it was dark and windy. Rain splattered the old leaded glass windows. A log snapped and popped on the hearth, the orange light flickering against the ornately carved mantle of the fireplace.

Hap Gay and Oscar Koch were standing by in the fireplace as Nate McKinley brought the man in to see the General.

"I'm sorry if my people roughed you up any when you were being searched," Patton said perfunctorily, as he stood and walked around to the front of the desk. "You obviously know who I am, but I don't believe I know *your* name."

"Borysuk, I am Colonel Ivan Borysuk," he said, stiffening to attention.

"And you're with Marshal Malinovsky's 2nd Ukrainian

Front, I take it?" Patton said, nodding at the patch that still lay on his desk.

"Yes, General."

"And you have a message for me from the Marshal?" Patton asked in a rhetorical tone, more a statement than a question. "If he's come to ask for my surrender, he already knows where he can shove *that!*"

"No, sir. Marshal Malinovsky would like to meet with you to discuss allying his forces with yours."

Even Patton was stunned by this one.

"*Allying* his forces with mine?" Patton asked after a long pause. "Let me get this straight? He doesn't want to kill me. He wants to be my *ally?*"

"That is correct, sir."

"Well, Colonel, may I remind you that the United States is currently at war with the Soviet Union," Patton said, folding his arms across his large bemedaled chest. "Field commanders in wartime *defeat* enemy armies and get defeated by enemy armies. They surrender and they accept surrenders, but they *do not* become allied with the enemy."

"May I explain, sir?"

"Please."

"Your nation has declared war on the Soviet Union," Borysuk began, still standing ramrod strait. "My nation has been occupied by the Russian Empire or the Soviet Union for three centuries."

"*Your* nation?"

"Ukraine. I am Ukrainian. Marshal Malinovsky is Ukrainian. Our army is mostly Ukrainian. The vast majority of Ukrainians feel that now is time for Ukraine to be free of Russians."

"But Malinovsky wears a Russian uniform," Patton reminded him.

"*Soviet* uniform. But, so did your General Washington once wear the uniform of King George," Borysuk shot back. "There were tens of millions who wore the uniform of the Soviet Army that fought to throw Hitler out. Equally, there are tens of millions who have no heart for Stalin's war now that Hitler is gone. Ukrainians do not wish to die to help Stalin conquer France, or England, or America."

"So you're suggesting that Ukrainians are prepared to fight Russians?" Patton asked, still groping to understand this fissure in what he had previously seen as a monolithic Red Army. He knew the history of the Ukraine, but not firsthand. Like most Westerners, he naturally assumed that after its long relationship with Russia, the two walked in step.

"Ukrainians are prepared to fight *Stalin*. When the German armies entered Ukraine in 1941, they were welcomed as liberators. For that moment, Germany could have had an ally to fight Stalin. A powerful ally to *defeat* Stalin. But the Germans treated Ukrainians like a defeated enemy. They came with their arrogance and pushed our face into mud with their boots. They became a bigger devil than Stalin, but Stalin is no less a devil than before."

"He's right," Koch interjected. "There were a great many Ukrainian volunteers that joined up with the Krauts. Many of these guys were captured along with the German troops . . . and they're still in American prison camps in Bavaria."

"Now that you mention it, I remember that uprising in the Ukraine after the First World War," Gay added.

"In 1917, Ukraine did not want to become free of the Russian Empire only to become part of Bolshevik Empire," Borysuk smiled, sensing that the Americans were starting to understand.

"So, Malinovsky wants to offer me the same deal that the Ukrainians offered the Krauts in 1941?" Patton asked.

"Exactly," Borysuk said. "We will fight *with* you to defeat Stalin, if Ukraine is fully independent nation when Stalin is gone. As you know, we're *already* members of United Nations Organization. Our representatives are puppets of Stalin, but Ukraine flag flies. We want it flying *free*."

"And you're prepared to turn and fight Stalin *now?*"

"We are prepared to fight Stalin," Borysuk smiled. "You will find that many *Russians* are ready to fight Stalin also."

"That's what our intelligence shows," Koch confirmed. "There were a lot of Russian defectors to the Krauts all through the war."

"How do we know that everything that you're saying about Malinovsky's intentions is on the up and up?" Gay asked.

"The orders that 2nd Ukrainian Front has at this moment

are to attack Third Army," Borysuk said, turning to Gay and then back to Patton. "Stalin has ordered Marshal Malinovsky at once to take the pressure off Marshal Tolbukhin. You are a master strategist. You know that this is the strategically correct move. Marshal Malinovsky could attack *now,* even yesterday. He gave excuses . . . Stalled for time . . . Sent me here instead."

"When did he tell Stalin that he would attack me?" Patton asked, taking the attack personally.

"As soon as possible," Borysuk said succinctly. "You Americans have the saying about 'rock and hard place.' Marshal Malinovsky is in such a hard place. He's taking a very big risk to defy Stalin. He must attack soon."

"We're ready for him." Patton cautioned.

"We have no stomach to fight Americans for Bavaria. You may win, or we may win. But eventually, if we meet again in Ukraine as *enemies,* you will *not* win. If we meet as friends it will be the end of Stalin. You must decide."

"This is a question for the politicians," Patton said after a long pause. "I'm in the Army. Our job is to catch the fish. The politicians get to decide how to cook them."

"I'm not sure that I understand," Borysuk said.

"What General Patton means is that soldiers do the fighting, and that alliances and agreements are up to our respective governments," General Gay interjected in an effort to calm things down. "The US Army cannot enter into an alliance with your army or with the Ukraine without the agreement of our own government."

"Tell Malinovsky, that I'm *interested* in his proposal," Patton said at last. "Tell him that I'll run it past my politicians. Tell him I'll get a politician down here to talk about it. Tell him to send me a couple of people who speak for him . . . including a *politician* . . . a Ukrainian politician."

"I think I can arrange this," Borysuk said.

"Well, be sure you can and be sure that you do," Patton said. "I don't want to pussyfoot around with this. If Malinovsky's serious, have him send me some people who are serious. Be here Friday. We'll have our guy come in for the weekend and we'll all fly over to Munich and have a meeting."

"Munich?" Borysuk asked nervously.

"That's my headquarters. If we have a meeting, it will be there. Sergeant McKinley will meet you at 0800 wherever it is down there that he's been meeting you. Any questions?"

"No, sir."

Patton returned the man's salute even though he was out of uniform, and Nate escorted him out. When they had gone, Koch's aide asked about the Munich flight.

"I don't think that the General actually means to take them to Munich," Koch replied.

"That's right," Patton said. "We're not really going to Munich, but I'm damned sure not going to tell this character where we're *really* going. His timing is good though."

"What the General means is that we have another trip planned for this weekend," Koch hinted. "It's very hush-hush, and not known outside of this room. But you would have been briefed tomorrow anyway, so we'll tell you. We're actually flying to Paris."

"And the politician . . .?" Gay asked.

"Harry Truman." Patton replied.

Chateau Rambuteau
Moisselles, France
Friday, June 29, 1945, 9:07 a.m.

Just two months on the job, and the new president was holding his own with a man who had been a hailed as one of the titans of the century. Both had a complex and ironic sense of humor, both had a good understanding of their own nation's role in the unfolding events of history, and they shared that unique camaraderie of fellow soldiers thrown together against the harsh demands of war. Winston Churchill even had an acquiescent proposal for Harry Truman.

"I'm convinced that it should be Patton," the Prime Minister said, looking across the breakfast table at Truman and Secretary of War Henry Stimson.

The President had not come to his first Big Two conference expecting to have the British Prime Minister nominate an American general over a British field marshal as Supreme Allied Commander for Europe.

"I'd have thought that you would have proposed Field Marshal Montgomery," Truman told the Prime Minister.

"I have . . . *publicly,*" Churchill smiled. "Politically, he's the choice that a prime minister must advance, but privately, I'm suggesting that I will *'allow myself to be convinced'* by you to choose Patton. For obvious sentimental reasons, the British people favor Montgomery as Supreme Commander. Until Den Helder, there was no other choice. After Jena, there's no choice but Patton. We can debate Monty's culpability for Den Helder ad nauseam. He was obviously not at fault, but it happened on his watch. The Yanks would never accept him. Our nation is fond of Patton. After Jena, they *will* support *him.*"

"Not that it's the choice of the people to pick generals like they pick us politicians," Truman added.

"No, but a Supreme Commander chosen under *these* circumstances must be. He must be a man who can inspire, lead, and command respect among the troops that he leads and the people they defend," Churchill replied. "And he must inspire the *enemy* with a level of fear . . . and both sides with a sense that he knows how to win. Patton is the *only* choice."

Truman nodded noncommitally.

"And I'm not alone in proposing General Patton," Churchill added.

"No?"

"No. Field Marshal Montgomery also agrees. I had a long discussion with Monty after Den Helder. He feels that we need . . . especially for the men in the field . . . a strong rallying point . . . someone who can inspire as well as lead."

"I'm flattered that both of you would back an American," Truman smiled.

"And you? I detect a certain reticence about choosing Patton as Supreme Commander," Churchill said, leaning back from the table and lighting a long Cohiba. "You were thinking of General Bradley?"

"There are two points of view in my government," Truman admitted. "General Marshall supports General Bradley. He was General Eisenhower's protegé, and he has higher-level command experience."

Churchill nodded thoughtfully.

"Secretary Stimson supports General Patton," Truman continued. "They've known one another for years."

"I believe that we politicians should make the *political* decisions," Stimson added. "But I agree with the Prime Minister. A general who wins battles should be the general who makes the *military* decisions."

"And you?" Churchill asked. "Who does the Commander-in-Chief support?"

"Bradley is a devoted, hard-working commander. Patton is an arrogant prima donna who speaks without thinking. The highest levels of command in the US Army have confidence in General Bradley. The same levels of command worry constantly about what Patton will do or say next to embarrass them. However, the GIs who actually do the fighting seem to have a great deal of faith in Patton. He inspires enthusiasm and loyalty. Bradley merely inspires respect. In the last war, Patton captured more ground than any other army commander. In this war, he has destroyed two enemy army groups while Brad has lost ground at every turn. I want to win this war. I want to pick the man best suited for the job."

"The ability to inspire is crucial," Churchill replied. "Even in desperate times . . . *especially* in desperate times, such leaders can make all the difference in the world. I have no doubt that if your Continental Congress had withdrawn its support for General Washington, as it nearly did on several occasions, you and I would still be saluting the same flag."

"But the troops, or the majority of them, never lost their faith in Washington's ability to lead," Stimson added.

"He was an audacious man, especially at Brooklyn Heights and Trenton," Churchill mused. "There were times when he *should* have lost, but he triumphed. He reminds me of Patton."

"Let me show you something," Truman said, reaching into his pocket and handing Churchill a small leather-covered box about the size of a pack of cigarettes. "Open it and take a look."

Inside, Churchill saw two circular clusters, each containing five gleaming silver stars.

"General of the Army stars," Churchill exclaimed. "Who is the lucky fellow, or can I guess?"

"I came to this parley trying to maintain an open mind," Truman said, placing the box containing the stars back in his pocket. "I came here to promote one of my four-star generals. Regardless of a choice of Supreme Commander, I need to promote *one* American to five-star rank in this theater. I came here deciding to ask each to give me his assessment of how he would resolve the present situation and win this war."

Churchill nodded approvingly. He liked Truman's style.

"I came looking for a leader who can convince me that he has what it takes to lead the American armies to victory. General Bradley is here now. General Patton will be here this evening. I'll speak to him tomorrow. Then, we'll make that announcement. Uncle Joe won't mind waiting another day."

With that, the three men made their way to the vast Baroque dining room where General Bradley stood at attention, along with nine members of the SHAEF staff, waiting to make his presentation to the President. General Marshall and members of his staff were also in the room.

As the President reached out to shake the General's hand, he nodded to Churchill. "You know the Prime Minister."

"Yes, sir. It's a pleasure to see you again, Mr. Prime Minister."

"Carry on, I'm anxious to hear what you have," the President said, nodding to the four-star general who was General Eisenhower's heir apparent, and on whose shoulders now lay the responsibility of defending most of northern Europe.

Omar Nelson Bradley was a man whose subdued appearance, pursed lips, and round wire-rimmed glasses made him look more like a college math professor than the commander of an army group.

He'd planned to be giving this presentation to the President, but the presence of the Prime Minister was disconcerting. Bradley was anxious to succeed Eisenhower as SACEUR, and he saw Montgomery as his chief rival. He wanted to impress Truman and secure his blessing without having to face Churchill. He had no idea that Churchill had already rejected Montgomery. He certainly had no inkling of Churchill's preference for Patton.

"I'm pleased to report that the situation in Belgium has

stabilized during the last ten days," Bradley said after a long explanation of where his forces and those of Montgomery were digging in. "Zhukov's 1st Byelorussian Front is occupying a line running roughly between Brussels and Ostend. Rokossovsky has occupied all of the Netherlands. Koniev continues to besiege the Ruhr. He's made no attempt to cross the Rhine south of Cologne and we're continuing to hold Frankfurt with XIII Corps and XIX Corps. Frankfurt *is* under siege, but, so far, Koniev has made no move to try to move in. We expect no major movements from the Reds on the Northern Front while Zhukov prepares for the coming action against France."

"And what about the South German Front?" Churchill asked. "Where General Patton has been counterattacking."

"General Patton's *diversionary* attacks have been useful," Bradley explained, deliberately emphasizing the word *diversionary*. "And I'm certain that Zhukov is aware that Koniev has some competent Allied forces on his left flank."

After presenting a series of charts that tacitly supported a strategy of digging in to a siege line in northern France, Bradley worked around to asking the President whether he had any questions.

"As you've pointed out, Zhukov has apparently decided to interrupt his offensive in order to regroup," the President said slowly and deliberately. "While this seems to have certainly given us some welcome breathing space, it's clearly the calm before the storm. *In your opinion,* General Bradley, what should a theater commander adopt as a strategy for the next several months . . . say, from now through December?"

Bradley was excited. He could almost feel his fifth star. The President of the United States had asked him for his opinion about what the SACEUR should do. He could almost feel the weight of rank—equivalent to that of a field marshal—on his shoulders.

"In the immediate term, our paramount responsibility is the defense of northern France," Bradley began. "For that reason, we've devoted a great deal of our energy and resources to building the capability for a defense in depth from the Sambre River in Belgium to the Marne, here in France."

Truman winced instinctively at the mention of the word

"Marne," and he noticed Churchill's jaw drop slightly. Both men knew only too well that the Marne River had been the last line of French defenses in 1914. It had stopped the Germans, but *barely*. Halting the Germans on the Marne had left them so deep into France that it took four years and the blood of millions upon millions of Frenchmen, Englishmen, and Americans to push them back.

"If Zhukov launches his offensive before September, we'll be ready," Bradley said confidently. "If he waits until October, we should have a sufficient level of force present to launch a major counterattack in Belgium with the object of retaking Antwerp. By spring, we'll be ready to break out of our enclaves along the Rhine and begin the task of pushing the Soviet forces out of Germany."

"You would conduct such an operation in the spring?" Stimson asked.

"Yes, sir," Bradley replied. "As we discovered last winter in the Ardennes, operations under winter conditions are difficult, and the Soviets are masters of winter warfare. If we begin an overall offensive in early March, as we did this year, we'd avoid having to fight under conditions that favor the enemy. It would also allow us more time to build up our forces. With any kind of luck, we would repeat our offensive of this year and be back to Berlin by May of 1946."

"Which is where we should have been in May of *1945!*" Churchill snarled. "If we hadn't allowed ourselves to be cozened by Uncle Joe at Yalta."

"What role would General Patton play in this operation?" Stimson asked.

"Patton will be useful in holding our southern flank as long as he's able," Bradley said, taking a deep breath as though rankled by the mention of the Third Army commander's name. He was also using the word "our" as though he already held the SACEUR title.

"In light of his recent successes, wouldn't it serve the overall objective to use Patton a bit more aggressively?" Churchill asked.

"General Patton is an excellent soldier," Bradley said, in a tone that matched his lecturing professor appearance. "But he's a capricious man who often attacks when he should be more prudent. You may recall his assault on the Hammelburg POW camp last March. He launched an attack on impulse that was too ambitious for the force involved, and he paid the price. Of course, we all now know that his son-in-law was in the camp."

Truman bristled slightly at Bradley's resorting to a personal attack, but Churchill spared him the need for a follow-up comment by leaping into the lurch.

"I also recall that you ordered him not to *impulsively* try to capture Trier with two divisions," the Prime Minister reminded Bradley with a wry grin. "And when he got your message *after* he had taken it with two divisions, he asked whether to give it *back*."

It was now Bradley's turn to bristle, and his sallow cheeks reddened slightly.

"Just for the record, General, and we know that you've faced enormous difficulties, what would you say to the criticism we're reading in all the papers back home that Patton has successfully defeated two Red army groups, while you've been pushed back?" Stimson asked, trying to at least sound conciliatory.

"There is no comparison," Bradley said decisively. "Field Marshal Montgomery and I have been facing the forces of Marshals Rokossovsky, Zhukov, and Koniev. This is the cream of the Red Army. This is obviously the principal thrust of their offensive. The press sees General Patton's victories out of context. There is no comparison between the *war* that we're fighting and the *battles* that he has won. Furthermore, he *still* has Marshal Malinovsky's 2nd Ukrainian Front to contend with."

Chateau Rambuteau
Moisselles, France
Friday, June 29, 1945, 5:01 p.m.

Nate McKinley had spent six of the roughest months of his life walking or riding across Europe. Now he had flown back across those same bloody miles in less than six hours.

True to the plan, Colonel Ivan Borysuk had turned up on schedule with Marshal Malinovsky's "delegation." The Colonel himself would be part of the group, as would a dark-haired man who was introduced as Major General Aleksandr Krupko, and a plain-looking woman named Svetlana Taramova, who Borysuk said had been a minister in the short-lived Ukrainian National-ist government proclaimed in 1941. Unlike many of her col-leagues, she'd managed to elude arrest when the Germans decided to put this Ukrainian government out of business. Nate guessed that if she was for real, she was now probably on Stalin's "wanted list."

Two hours into the flight, when General Gay had broken the news that they were *not* going to Munich, the trio had pan-icked, but they relaxed somewhat when he told them where they were really going.

When Patton's C-47 set down in a light rain at Le Bourget field east of the French capital, they were met not by jeeps and deuce-and-a-half trucks, but by a line of passenger cars that were assigned for their use by SHAEF headquarters. Instead of an open-topped Willys, Nate found himself at the wheel of a 1940 Lincoln Zephyr four-door with an especially plush in-terior. It felt strange to be driving a real car again. He had trouble adjusting to the first traffic lights that he'd seen since leaving the United States a lifetime before.

With a SHAEF car in the lead and the car carrying Colonel Koch and the Ukrainians following, Nate drove General Pat-ton and his chief of staff to a walled compound near a small town north of the city. For security reasons, the President would be meeting them here, rather than in the heart of Paris.

The chateau at the center of the compound was modest by comparison to Hradcany Castle, but far more lavish than most other places that Nate had seen on this war-torn continent. The great entry hall alone was large enough to park a pair of deuce-and-a-halfs side by side and another two on top. A dozen gigantic tapestries with pictures of people hunting deer on horseback were well illuminated by the blaze of the biggest chandelier that Nate had ever seen. Outside, GIs in rain slick-ers manned checkpoints, while inside, well-dressed civilians and people in well-pressed uniforms were scurrying about.

As Patton and Gay strode through the massive doorway, preceded by the three SHAEF colonels who had met them at Le Bourget, the commotion of an obviously busy and active facility sputtered to a halt. From the stairways, balconies and adjacent rooms, all eyes turned to Patton. Men in uniform immediately stiffened to attention and saluted. It was, Nate thought, as though Julius Caesar and Napoleon Bonaparte had been rolled into one and brought back to life.

With his glittering stars and his ivory-handled pistols, Patton seemed to live up to every inch of the warrior king that the press had portrayed. Nate also realized that he, Gay, and the General were the only people in the room with helmets and sidearms, underscoring the effect of their being *combat* soldiers returning to civilization from the arduous, if glorious, world of armed conflict.

Patton himself was obviously enjoying the theatrics of the scene. Without smiling, he strode forward, returning the salutes of the soldiers and nodding to the civilians, who were also standing at attention. Even though he knew that he was there merely as an ornament to the General's showmanship, Nate too, felt important. They moved through the great hall, following the three SHAEF colonels toward a set of large, heavily carved doors that obviously led to someplace important. Just as the General was walking through this doorway, the entire entrance hall erupted with spontaneous applause.

They walked down a long hallway and though another doorway. Placing their helmets on a table that was provided, they entered a huge sitting room, with magnificent floor-to-ceiling paintings on every wall. Four men who were seated around a blazing fire stood up and came toward the Third Army men.

It was now Patton's turn to snap to attention and salute. Nate was already as stiff as a corpse as he recognized the men in the room: Secretary of War Henry Stimson, Army Chief of Staff General George Marshall, President Truman, and Prime Minister Winston Churchill—four of the half-dozen highest-ranking individuals in the Western World.

"At ease, men," Marshall said, returning the salutes of the Third Army men.

"I'm pleased to meet you, General," the President said, extending his hand. "Your reputation has preceded you and I have to say, we're happy with your work."

"The pleasure is entirely mine, sir," Patton replied, firmly grasping the President's hand.

"You know Mr. Churchill," the President continued, presenting the Prime Minister, who smiled broadly as he extended his hand.

"A great deal of water has flowed under the Rhine bridges since we met in England two winters ago before Overlord," Churchill said with a wink, obviously referring to the fact that the two of them were the highest-ranking members of the Allied forces to have publicly urinated into Germany's signature river.

"Hello, sir," Patton smiled as he shook Churchill's hand.

The General introduced Hap Gay, and then turned to Nate.

"Gentlemen, I'd like you to meet my driver, Sergeant McKinley."

Nate felt himself turning red as Truman shook his hand.

"Sergeant," the President smiled. "I want you to know that you're my favorite photographer."

"And a combat hero to boot," Churchill added as he shook Nate's hand. "General Patton has always had a knack for picking the best."

As Patton was invited to join the men in the semicircle of chairs before the fireplace, the General ordered Nate to find Colonel Koch.

"Tell him to have our friends be ready to join us."

"General, we're planning for a formal presentation from you tomorrow morning, but, informally, what is your assessment of the situation?" Truman said after a short round of small talk about Patton's flight from Bavaria.

"On my part of the front, or the whole front, sir?"

"The *whole* front."

"Zhukov and Rokossovsky are waiting to allow their supply trains to catch up. Within ten days, they'll launch an attack in the north to cut off the ports in northern France. Both Zhukov and Koniev will bypass the Ruhr and Koniev will attempt to cross the Rhine between Coblenz and Mainz."

"George, what makes you think that Koniev would bypass the Ruhr?" Stimson asked. "We've been led to believe that Germany's industrial heartland is one of Stalin's key objectives."

"Long term, yes. Short term, no," Patton said confidently. "In the long term, those factories would be very important to him. In the short term, they're worthless. They've been crip-pled by three years of Allied bombs. It'll take a year to get them up and running. Stalin is not fighting this war in the long run, he's fighting it *this month*. And this month, the Ruhr is a bunch of blasted cities bloated with refugees from all over Germany and defended by an American force that doesn't have the strength to counterattack. The Ruhr is not a prize, it's a lia-bility. If I was Stalin or Zhukov or Koniev, I'd let the Ameri-cans stay there and worry about feeding all those refugees. Why tie up forces that are better used elsewhere? The Ruhr garrison is no threat to the Red Army. Koniev figures he'll leave 'em for the time being, and finish 'em off later."

"What about the strategy on the Northern Front?" Marshall asked. "Why do you assume that Zhukov would want to reach out to the French ports rather than capturing Paris?"

"It's a difference in style," Patton explained. "We assume that Paris is the objective because it was in 1870, 1914, and 1940, but that was the Germans. Paris is a political objective, not a military one. The Germans and the French have a politi-cal rivalry. Hitler was obsessed with that and he wanted Paris. Stalin had the same kind of obsession with Berlin, so he ex-pended huge resources to capture it. But, except for *that*, the Russian style since Stalingrad is to leave the cities alone."

"Stalin did spend a lot of energy capturing Berlin," Tru-man observed.

"Yes, but *that* was personal," Patton replied. "He wanted to deliver a coup de grace to Hitler, and he wanted the Red Army, and not the Allies, to go down in history for capturing it. Elsewhere, he avoided cities when he could. He surrounded Warsaw, Breslau, and Danzig and let them die on the vine. He waited until the war was over to take Prague, and he let *us* take Leipzig for him. Budapest was one of only a couple of excep-tions. Paris is like the Ruhr. If he cuts it off, it's just a big in-defensible city full of refugees."

"Fighting in a city is notoriously difficult," Marshall added. "I shiver when I remember our own fight in Aachen last winter."

"Cities make poor battlefields. They use up troops that can better be used to fight *armies*," Patton said. "Remember

Grant's reply when Lincoln asked him whether he was going to attack the Confederate capital at Richmond."

"Robert E. Lee's army, and *not* Richmond, is my objective," Marshall said, quoting General Ulysses S. Grant.

"A week ago, I could have attacked Tolbukhin in Dresden," Patton pointed out. "But why? We had already destroyed his army as a fighting force. We flattened most of his equipment, all of his artillery, and virtually all of his supplies at Leipzig. We killed or captured most of his troops. As XX Corps moved through the city, we had situations where a hundred and fifty Russians were trying to surrender to a single tank. Zhukov has seen what happened and he wants to strike while the iron is hot and while he's got momentum."

"And you expect this to come soon?" Churchill asked.

"Yes. Every intelligence report that I've seen . . . and my G2 has a knack for coming up with intelligence reports . . . shows that he's massing for an attack . . . probably around the end of July. Our own estimates are that we won't be ready to fight back until mid-August or so. He knows that."

"Facing these kinds of overwhelming odds, what would *you* do?" Truman asked. Stimson glanced at Marshall. They knew what the President was leading up to. Churchill just leaned back in his chair as though waiting to be entertained. In a sense, he was.

"I'd do the *last* thing that Zhukov would expect me to do," Patton said quickly, betraying the fact that he'd obviously given this question a great deal of thought. "I'd attack."

"Attack?" Truman asked with a furrow in his brow. "You'd attack against such ponderous odds? The Allies are at a complete disadvantage here in northern France. Zhukov vastly outnumbers the forces that we have at our disposal. His force is not just sleeping over there, they've got the taste for blood and they're lined up to strike *us!* It would be another 'meat grinder' on the Somme."

"I wouldn't attack Zhukov on the Somme, or *anywhere* in northern France," Patton smiled, slowly reaching into his shirt pocket for his map. "I wouldn't even attack Zhukov, or at least not frontally. I'd attack Berlin."

"Berlin?" Truman asked incredulously.

"Yes, *Berlin*," Patton said with a Cheshire cat grin as he unfolded the small map. "When you're outnumbered overall, you attack on the part of the front where they're *not*."

He placed the map so that the President could see the map and both Marshall and Stimson moved closer to watch him outline his strategy. Only Churchill, with his photographic memory for European geographical detail, remained as he was. The Prime Minister nodded to General Gay, who was sitting off to the side, listening and smiling comfortably.

"As we know, Zhukov directly or indirectly controls three army groups arrayed between the Ruhr and the North Sea, not to mention Koniev's force holding the Rhineland," Patton explained. "As menacing as this force looks, I've watched Stalin show two signs of weakness."

"Weakness?" Truman asked, showing more curiosity than incredulity this time.

"Two things show me that Stalin isn't as confident in what Zhukov can do as *we* seem to be. First, he slowed Zhukov and called for a revolt behind Allied lines. That tells me that he isn't a hundred percent sure of his drive into France. When the call for a revolt here in France fizzled, he brought up his reserve . . . Vasilievsky's 3rd Byelorussian Front. It had been here, in and around Berlin. He added it to Zhukov's force. By doing this, Stalin shifted his center of gravity to the west, exposing his flank."

"So you'd hit his rear, while he's facing the other way?" Marshall nodded, starting to show some interest.

"I know that the Allied buildup is ahead of schedule," Patton said. "By the end of July, First Army and Seventh Army will be ready to fight . . . Probably Fifth Army as well. I know that you're moving Eighth Army from the Pacific. First Army would reinforce the line here in northern France, while *we* attack from the south. We'd take Berlin with Third Army like we did Leipzig. I'd use Seventh Army and Fifteenth Air Force to hit Koniev's gang down here at Frankfurt. The Reds in Berlin would be caught with their pants down. When you're outnumbered overall, you attack on the part of the front where they're *not*."

"And *then* you'd attack Zhukov with the First and Fifteenth?" Stimson asked, noticing that, by now, there were two generals and a cabinet secretary on their hands and knees in front of the President's chair like little boys playing with model soldiers.

"Not yet," Patton smiled. "If we attack him *frontally,* he'll fight back in the place where he has superior numbers. No, we've attacked his rear, so he'll do what comes natural, he'll counterattack. This will mean that he'll have to go through all the trouble of turning a huge army that was facing west and face them east. Also notice that the maneuvering ground that he's got between the Ardennes and the swamps and rivers south of Antwerp is fairly narrow."

By now, even Churchill had begun to lean closer.

"Does anyone remember the Battle of Salamis?" Patton asked. "Where the Greeks whipped the Persians?"

"I'm not old enough to remember the actual battle," Churchill laughed. "But Lady Astor was there . . . I think she was the figurehead on a trireme."

"Remember how old Themistocles played the numbers against Xerxes," Patton said excitedly. "First, he attacked them where they were weakest. He made damned sure of it by forcing them into that narrow neck of water at Salamis, where they just didn't have room to put all their boats. He could just pick them off one by one. Xerxes couldn't get his whole force into the right place if he'd wanted to. The same thing happens here. Zhukov will want to get some of his best divisions from the farthest west to the farthest east. It will be chaos and confusion. All movement will be at a crawl. Tanks and mechanized units will be on the same roads at the same time going in all directions. It will be like midtown Manhattan at five in the afternoon."

"And *then* you'd attack Zhukov with the First and Fifteenth?" Stimson asked, noticing that, by now, the people in the room who had previously expressed skepticism were smiling.

"No, not yet," Patton grinned. "Having taken Berlin, Third Army will continue north to retake Hamburg, which is also lightly defended. The Red supply lines to the east will then be cut. They'll be isolated. At that point, Zhukov, Koniev, and the cream of the Red Army will be surrounded in a pocket that is within easy range of both Eighth Air Force and Fifteenth Air Force."

"Won't that reach to Hamburg be spreading Third Army rather thin?" Marshall cautioned.

"Not when *Eighth* Army lands at the newly recaptured port of Hamburg," Patton explained with a wink. "You were planning to bring them in through France. This way, we'd bring them in *behind* Zhukov. We'll outflank the old bastard. Then, when the North German pocket is reduced, we'll be ready to take the war all the way to Stalin."

"To Stalin?" Marshall asked.

"Do you think that it is prudent and possible to take the war to Stalin?" Truman asked. "To *invade Russia?*"

"We demanded that Hitler surrender without condition. Ditto for Hirohito!" Patton replied, raising his eyebrows. "Unless we take the war *to him,* how in the hell else are we going to make that miscreant surrender without condition?"

"Hear, hear," Churchill said, making a clapping motion with his hands. "This is a man after my own heart."

"George, as you know, the unconditional surrender doctrine was not adopted until more than a year after we entered World War II," Stimson reminded his old friend. "We've been in this war for just a little more than a month, and we've been on the defensive . . . at least here in northern Europe . . . for the whole time. Defense . . . and stopping Stalin's offensive . . . have been our focus. Discussions of the ultimate Allied objectives have not been formalized."

"Stalin knows what *he* wants," Patton replied, leaning forward. "World domination. Am I not right? We can't fight a war not knowing what *we* want when Stalin does. We'll get less than nothing as a result. If we have to fight him, we should fight him with all the force and strength and determination we have. This is the only language that he speaks . . . and it's the only language that he understands and respects. Stalin is fighting for keeps. Those American boys of Third Army who I saw with their legs shot off and their heads caved in at Jena were fighting Stalin for keeps. Anything short of victory is not victory."

"General Patton is absolutely correct," Churchill said soberly. "From what I've seen of our Russian friends during the recent war, I'm convinced that there's nothing they admire so much as strength. There's nothing for which they have less respect than weakness . . . especially military weakness."

"As with Hitler," General Marshall nodded.

"What I sense in General Patton's remarks a moment ago is a challenge laid before President Truman and myself as the leaders of respective nations, to define and articulate the overall strategic concept of that which the press calls World War III. What should that be?" the Prime Minister continued. "I suggest that what's at stake here is nothing less than the safety and welfare, the freedom and progress, of all the homes and families of all the men and women in all of Europe. Similar words were the theme of President Truman's recent speech to Congress and mine to Commons. To give security to the countless homes on this continent and beyond, they must be shielded from both war and tyranny. This truly is another *world* war.

"A shadow has fallen upon the scenes so lately lighted by the Allied victory. Having been stabbed in the back from Kummersdorf to Den Helder, we now know what Soviet Russia and its communist international organization intends to do. From Antwerp on the North Sea to Trieste in the Adriatic, an iron curtain has descended across Europe. Behind that line lie all the capitals of the ancient states of Central and Eastern Europe: Warsaw, Berlin, Vienna, Budapest . . . as well as now Amsterdam and Brussels. Will Paris, Rome, and London come next? What about Ottawa and Washington? We saw Poland being turned into a Soviet police state against her will. To borrow a popular phrase from President Truman, I believe that the buck must stop *here*. With us, in this room, now."

"General Marshall, what are your thoughts?" Truman asked.

"Taking the war into Russia is a military adventure not to be entered into lightly," Marshall observed. "Napoleon and Hitler tried . . . and failed."

"Many battles have been lost because of an army stopping on the wrong side of a river," Patton replied. "And the same is true, I suppose, of wars. A soldier should never let fear of failure guide his actions. In this case, I believe that the failure to cross the river would guarantee a failure to win the war. I have boundless faith in the ability of our fighting men and in the ability of our industry and our people at home to supply them.

Give me three more field armies, constant air support, an unlimited supply of fuel and M26 Pershing tanks, and I'll give
you Joe Stalin's head on a goddam plate."

"It is a very long way to Moscow," Marshall replied. "Not
to mention the millions . . . tens of millions . . . of Russians
who stand in the way . . . ready to die for Stalin and for their
'Rodinya,' their Motherland . . . their Mother Russia."

"The trick is to estrange Uncle Joe from Mother Russia,"
Patton observed. "Actually, he's not really a Russian, is he?"

"Georgian," Churchill replied. "Napoleon was Corsican . . .
and Hitler was Austrian. Nothing is as it appears."

"As far as the idea of separating Stalin from the Motherland
goes, I'd say this is easier said than done," Truman added.

"But not entirely impossible," Patton smiled.

"On what is possibly a related topic, another point that
worries me is getting your plan off the ground," General Marshall said thoughtfully. "In your offensive against Berlin—
which is necessarily the first step to Moscow . . . you seem to
have ignored Marshal Malinovsky, who's lurking in Austria.
His 2nd Ukrainian Front could do a great deal of damage to
Third Army's right flank before you even get to Berlin."

"Malinovsky may have been eliminated as a problem,"
Patton smiled. "And he may have given us the key to the trick
of separating Stalin from the Rodinya."

"How?" Marshall asked, obviously intrigued by Patton's
smugness on this thorny issue. "I don't understand. Malinovsky's forces are still intact . . . Aren't they?"

"Yes they are," Patton nodded. "But I've been approached
by a fellow from Malinovsky's staff who says that the Marshal
is ready to switch sides. I guess you could say that the old boy
would rather fight *with* Georgie Patton than *against* him."

"Switch sides?" Truman said, unable to believe what he
was hearing. "How is that possible?"

"I could start to explain, but, if you'll excuse me, I think
that it's time to invite my G2, Colonel Koch, and several of
our traveling companions to join us."

As Patton walked away from the group, Truman glanced at
Stimson.

"What do you think?" he asked Henry Stimson under his
breath.

"I've heard General Bradley suggest going on the defensive and into winter quarters with an eye toward reaching Berlin next May," the Secretary of War answered. "And I've heard what appears to be a viable plan to go on the offensive and be in Berlin in about six weeks. What do you think, General?"

"If you want boldness and initiative, you've got it," George Marshall replied. "But I'm anxious to see what sort of tricks Malinovsky has up his sleeve."

Patton returned to their circle accompanied by Colonel Koch. The three civilians were ringed by a half-dozen heavily armed Third Army MPs and three SHAEF staff officers.

"I lied to these people," Patton announced. "They wanted to talk politics and I told them that I don't talk politics. I promised that I'd take them over to Third Army headquarters to talk to a civilian from our government. I didn't tell them that we were going to Paris and I didn't tell them who the civilian was."

Patton nodded to Koch, who turned to introduce Colonel Borysuk, General Krupko, and Svetlana Taramova. He explained that the men were Soviet officers who happened to be Ukrainians, and that Taramova had been a minister in the Ukrainian government.

"In the Ukrainian government?" Truman asked. "What Ukrainian government? The *Soviet* government?"

"No, sir," she said in clear, albeit accented English. "The independent, free *Ukrainian* government. On 30th June in 1941, when the Bolsheviks were on the run, leaving Ukraine, Stepan Bandera, head of Organization of Ukrainian Nationalists, proclaimed a government . . . free of Bolsheviks, free of Russians. It is a free and independent government, answers only to the Ukrainian people. I was minister of finance."

The President of the United States was dumbfounded. Here was a group of people claiming to represent the government of what he understood only as one of the "Socialist Republics" of the Union of Soviet Socialist Republics.

"We heard of this government at the time," Churchill interjected. "They declared their independence of Russia when they thought the Germans were there to *liberate* them from the communists. Your prime minister was . . ."

"Yaroslav Stetsko," Taramova interrupted. "Was arrested by Gestapo after one week. Sent to prison with Bandera and many others. Now they're in a Russian jail. Maybe dead. Some of us got away. I was in France, then Switzerland . . . made contact with General Krupko . . . come to see General Patton . . . now you."

"What is it that you want from us?" the President asked, amazed by what he was hearing.

"Free Ukraine," Taramova replied in a an exasperated tone such as one would use with someone who hadn't been paying attention. "A *free Ukraine*. Nothing more."

"I think they want us to help free the Soviet Ukraine from Stalin," Churchill interpreted.

"My understanding, if I'm interpreting what Colonel Borysuk said correctly, is that they have something to trade," Patton interjected. "Colonel, could you tell the President and the Prime Minister exactly what you knocked me over with the other night in Prague?"

All eyes turned to Borysuk. The poor man had dressed in shabby clothes, gone out on a bridge in a strange city, and made himself a traitor to the Red Army. He had hoped to find a way to tell his story to a Western ear with a modicum of authority. Now he was standing in a palace in France, where he had the ears of both the President of the United States and the Prime Minister of Great Britain.

"For four years, almost all Europe has been united for one goal," the Colonel began. "When Hitler was gone, Stalin became Hitler. He uses the Red Army to conquer the world. The people of Poland fought to be free of Hitler. Now they want to be free of Stalin. Same with people of Lithuania, Latvia, and Estonia. Same with people of Ukraine. We want no part of Stalin's plan to rule the world for Bolshevism. Marshal Malinovsky is Ukrainian. Our army is mostly Ukrainian, especially officers. Ukrainians feel that now is time for Ukraine to be free of Russians. My nation has been occupied by the Russian Empire or the Soviet Union for three centuries. Now Ukrainians are prepared to fight Stalin."

"Wouldn't this constitute treason?" General Marshall asked. "As an officer in the Soviet Army, he's sworn his allegiance to Stalin."

"General Patton asked me such a question," Borysuk smiled. "I remind him that your George Washington was in the English Army of King George. He led an insurrection against tyranny to free his nation."

"That's correct," Truman said, glancing at Churchill. "We were just talking about that over breakfast."

"Marshal Malinovsky has *already* committed treason," Borysuk said. "One week ago, he was ordered to attack your armies. He did not . . . he sent me to talk to General Patton. He has already disobeyed orders. There is no going back. We must go *forward* . . . together!"

10

★ ★

Boulevard Barbes
Paris, France
Saturday, June 30, 1945, 10:14 a.m.

"*EST-CE que votre premier voyage à Paris, mademoiselle?*" the cab driver asked.

"*Mais oui,*" Rosemary O'Leary explained, trying her best to remember her high school French.

She did remember that Sister Jacqueline, who actually was French, had once lived in Paris. She attempted to imagine this nun as a young girl in this strange place. She heard the peal of a church bell above the roar of the motorcycles that were buzzing about everywhere in little moving clouds of black smoke. The bells made her think of the church bells of her youth and of the woman who had taught her the rudiments of the language she was now seeing written on the signs that raced past the taxi window. It was almost as if Sister Jacqueline was here, or had come here to arrange these signs suddenly, like flashcards, for a quiz as she often had in class so long ago. Now, here Rosie was,

on the same streets that had been walked by Sister Jacqueline—
who was then "Jacqueline" with a real last name.

The boulangeries and patisseries were everywhere, with
their windows well stocked with bread and pastries, but many of
the bijouteries and boutiques did not appear to have been open
for months. Posters were everywhere, announcing entertainment—from cinemas to jazz clubs. Occasionally she saw the
remnants of a fading red political poster, usually peeking out
from behind a poster for a dance hall or an aperitif. Rosie had
heard that Paris had been awash in Communist Party banners
during early June, but apparently the Parisians would rather
eat, drink, and be merry than vote for Stalin—at least for the
moment.

There were fewer cars on the streets than in Washington or
San Francisco, but the sidewalks were crowded with people
who seemed to be enjoying themselves—either walking, or sitting at cafes. The crowds were a mix of Parisians and soldiers in
uniform, mostly American. Here and there, Rosie saw groups
of forlorn looking people whom she guessed were probably
refugees from Belgium and the Netherlands, who had fled here
to stay ahead of the Soviet onslaught.

Rosie had entered the city under a cold, wet sky that spat
angrily at the cab, but just as they reached the banks of the
River Seine, the morning sun burst through, painting the chalk-
colored buildings a brilliant gold. In the distance, on the bank
of the river, she saw a painter with an easel. The sky in the
painting was bright blue. In a moment, he disappeared from
sight as the cab raced toward her hotel.

"C'est l'hotel George V. Le tarif est 40 francs, s'il vous
plait. Deux francs par kilomètre."

"Mais oui," Rosemary O'Leary replied. "Voici. Merci
beaucoup. Je prendrai mes bagages sur le bord."

It was only when the cab had raced away, leaving her alone
on the sidewalk, that Rosie realized how exhausted she was after the long flight across the Atlantic in the military transport.
Still, the discomfort of sleeping on an airplane was worth the
effort if it avoided the week that it would have taken to get here
by boat. The government was willing to extend the courtesy of
space-available air travel to correspondents to help satisfy the

American public's insatiable demand for war news. After four years, the USAAF Air Transport Command's North Atlantic service was the busiest "airline" route in the world.

Rosie picked up her bags and made her way toward the entrance of the once-grand hotel. She imagined another time and place when uniformed porters would have raced out to relieve her of her luggage and open the doors for her. Of course, in her romantic image of Paris, the air would be filled with the aroma of roasting chestnuts and the sounds of Gypsy accordions instead of the stench of diesel exhaust and the Big Band sounds of "Swing'n'Sway with Sammy Kaye" that wafted from the hotel lobby.

Much of the American press corps was billeted in the Hotel George V, which had previously hosted much of the Wehrmacht elite, and before that the swank set of the thirties. The press corps came because the George V was also favored by the military brass. Eisenhower had stayed here, and many of the brass hats from SHAEF were still here. The reporters naturally gravitated to a place where they could buttonhole a colonel or a major general for a juicy tidbit over croissants and coffee in the morning, and have the morsel on the wire before the Washington and New York newsrooms had opened for business.

"Rosemary! Dear girl, so good to see you in Paree!"

Rosie whirled around at the sound of her name. It was Richard Waldron, tottering from the bar with a drink in his hand, his half-frame glasses perched near the tip of his round, ruddy nose. She hadn't seen him since he left *The Washington Herald* about a month ago to take a job with one of the wire services. It didn't surprise her to see him here in Paris, although it was uncanny to have the second person she spoke with in Paris be a familiar voice.

"Hello, Richard. What are you doing this close to the front? I'll bet you're on the trail of a really good story. I know that I must've come to the right place."

"Any place that you are is always right, my dear. I'm here to cover the great Patton. Rumor has it that he's in town. Nobody knows exactly where. My guess is that he'll be staying here."

"Here?"

"Yes, *here*. This is where Goering stayed when he came to

Paris to loot paintings from the Louvre for his private collection at Karinhall. Look at all the Third Army shoulder patches. What brings you to the City of Lights?"

"The Secretary of War came over on a fact-finding trip," Rosie explained. "Rex wanted me to come over and find out what sorts of facts he's finding."

"Well, I can give you the scoop," Waldron said in a hushed tone, leaning close to Rosie. "This Russian, Marshal Malinovsky, is preparing to attack Patton. It's Zhukov's plan. Knock Patton out of the war. Then Zhukov's army comes heading this way. Rumor has it that Zhukov has already made reservations here at the George V."

"Here?"

"Yes. He's reserved the Goering Suite."

"Really?"

"That's what my sources say. Can I buy you a drink? You look tired. You could use some refreshment."

"Thanks, Richard. Rain check. I've only just arrived. I need to find my room and get a shower."

"Ask for the Goering Suite," Waldron said with a wink as he turned back toward the bar.

"Thanks, Richard."

Chateau Rambuteau
Moisselles, France
Saturday, June 30, 1945, 10:14 a.m.

Omar Bradley eyed George Patton suspiciously as the Third Army Commander entered the room. Despite the fact that they each wore the uniform of the US Army—and each uniform was marked by quartets of silver stars—the two men could not have been more different. They were different in style, in approach, and in substance. It could probably be said that they detested one another. In private, Bradley would describe Patton as an uncontrollable madman, while Patton thought of Bradley as a dithering buffoon.

Both men were career officers at the apogee of their respective careers. Patton had graduated from West Point in 1909. Bradley graduated six years later, a classmate of Dwight

Eisenhower, in 1915. Patton had been Bradley's boss in the North African campaign, but Bradley, sporting a fourth star a year earlier than Patton, had leapfrogged ahead of him by the time of the Normandy Invasion. During the final year of the war, Patton became bitterly jealous of Bradley's command, which was an army group more than quadruple the size of Patton's Third Army. Meanwhile Bradley was bitterly jealous of Patton's battlefield triumphs.

When World War II ended, Bradley looked forward to going home to a desk, while Patton had become morose over having no more battles to fight.

Bradley and his staff were clustered at the foot of the long table in the room where they had made their presentation to President Truman the day before. Patton, flanked only by Major General Hobart Gay and Colonel Oscar Koch, took his place at the middle of one side. Opposite Patton was an unusually subdued Field Marshal Bernard Law Montgomery, and his staff, who had flown in overnight for what promised to be the most important meeting of this war.

Britain's senior field commander sensed that a theater commander would be chosen at this meeting. Just as certainly, he knew that it would *not* be him. As commander of Britain's Eighth Army, Montgomery had broken the German offensive in North Africa in 1942, and he'd gone on to command the British 21st Army Group from Normandy through VE-Day. He was a serious professional rival of both—but he was also respected by both to a much larger measure than they respected one another.

The three clusters of military officers did not have to small talk long before the President and Prime Minister Churchill entered the room, accompanied by General George Marshall and Secretary of War Henry Stimson. Everyone in the room stood at attention for the usual round of salutes, but the President quickly invited them to be seated. Only the three civilians among all the military men were fully relaxed. Truman, in a checked sport jacket and a navy blue bow tie, was the least formally dressed. Both Churchill and Stimson wore dark grey pinstripes.

"Gentlemen, we have very little time, and we have a war to win," Truman began. "We must move quickly or we'll be looking at a war being won by somebody else. What became apparent to the Prime Minister and me last night was that it's

our responsibility to clarify our thinking on the overall strategic concept of the present war."

"That concept, if I may be so bold as to interrupt the President," Churchill said, accepting Truman's nod to him as a cue,
"that concept is what was articulated by the President himself
in his speech to Congress on 29 May. He said that we must not
rest until we have driven the forces of Soviet aggression from
Germany, and from all of the countries of Europe where they
have imposed their tyranny through force of arms. What was
unsaid, but implicit, in the phrase 'all of the countries of Europe,' is that those countries include not just Poland and Holland,
but Estonia, Latvia, Lithuania, the Ukraine, and even Russia itself."

"To put it succinctly, the goal of our military operations in
World War III will be the same with regard to Stalin as our
goal in World War II was with regard to Hitler," Truman said.
"Total victory and unconditional surrender."

Nobody at the table flinched. It was a previously unarticu-
lated goal that they all expected and would have all proposed.
There was unanimity and determination regarding the ends,
even if there was a great deal of potential for disagreement
about the means.

"Having said all this, the next item of business for us this
morning is to tell you who we have chosen to lead our armies
as Supreme Allied Commander," Truman explained. "This is a
subject to which both Mr. Churchill and myself have given a
great deal of thought over the past weeks, and one which we
have discussed for many hours over the past two days."

Truman reached into his pocket and withdrew the leather
box, which he placed conspicuously on the table ahead of him.

"When I told Secretary Stimson that I would be joining
him secretly on this fact-finding trip to Europe, I told him that
I wanted to meet with my two senior field commanders and
meet them face to face . . . and to promote one of them to five-
star rank as Supreme Allied Commander."

As the President opened the box, every military man in the
room stared. For a soldier's career, no honor that can be be-
stowed can equal what was represented by the matched pair of
glittering five-star insignia.

"I'd like to present these . . ."

The president picked up the box and rose to his feet.

". . . to General of the Army, George S. Patton."

For a split second, the room was in absolute silence. Everyone looked at Patton. His eyes were on the box in the President's hand. Broad grins rose on the faces of Hap Gay and Oscar Koch—and Winston Churchill. Bradley's grim, usually expressionless face trembled and twitched slightly.

Patton rose, snapped to attention, and faced the President.

Handing Patton the box with his left hand, he extended his right for a handshake.

"Congratulations, General," Truman said. "I know that you won't let us down."

At the foot of the table, Omar Bradley suddenly rose to his feet and eyes now turned to him.

"Mr. President. General Patton," he said.

"Yes, General," Truman said.

"Please allow me to be the second to offer my congratulations to a fine American soldier."

With that, Bradley stepped forward and grasped Patton's hand.

Patton, thoroughly impressed by the magnanimity of his bitter rival, gave Bradley a bear hug.

After a round of congratulations, the President turned the floor over to his new "field marshal."

"As the President has said, this war stops when and where Stalin stops, and not short of total victory," Patton began, gesturing for the maps that were on easels near the edge of the room to be brought forward. "To paraphrase Mr. Truman, the 'buck' stops in Moscow. Even more than Hitler, Stalin is in this war to conquer the whole damned world. He's playing for keeps and we're going to have to play twice as hard. We have a helluva job ahead of us, but this war *can* be won and we *will* win it."

With that, Patton began to outline the battle plan that he'd sketched the night before, only this time he went into meticulous detail. He impressed the officers with his ability to pull most of the data out of his head, but occasionally he asked Koch or Gay for figures they had in the sheafs of papers they'd brought with them.

As the presentation went on, Truman was impressed by Patton's cordiality toward Bradley and Montgomery, often asking them for suggestions and seeming to go out of his way to discuss the roles that would be played by their respective 12th and 21st Army Groups in the coming counteroffensive.

At one point Patton announced that he would postpone publicly pinning on his new stars until after the initial phase of the operation.

"I know that I've got somewhat of a reputation as a prima donna," Patton said with a smile to a thin ripple of chuckles. "I don't know *where* the hell that came from . . . but, despite this reputation, I'm gonna put off pinning on these stars until we've played our first hand against Zhukov. Reason being, I want to achieve some measure of surprise on the Southern Front. The idea is to attack him where he *doesn't* expect it. He thinks the big battle is between here and Belgium. If he knows that he's got a damned five-star on his flank, he'll think twice. If he does any thinking, I want it to be after we've given this bastard something to think about. So I'm going to get my ass back down to the South German Front . . . and we're going to get this show on the road."

It was then, almost as though on cue, that one of Bradley's staff officers asked the question that General Marshall had asked the night before.

"Sir, what about Marshal Malinovsky's 2nd Ukrainian Front, which is on your . . . Third Army's . . . left flank down in Austria?"

"The key word there is 'Ukrainian.' " Patton smiled, slipping the leather box into his pocket and ordering the maps to be turned to face the wall. "Colonel Koch, could you please invite our friends to join us?"

Ivan Borysuk had succeeded beyond his dreams. He'd felt that his mission to Patton was madness. He had expected to be shot—and he almost was—but he managed to slip through the lines in his tattered civilian clothes. He had imagined that he'd be taken prisoner. He had imagined that he would never actually see Patton, but he'd not only seen Patton, he'd met with Truman and Churchill. Now, he and Krupko were in the innermost sanctum of Allied power.

The two men proceeded to outline the plan by which Malinovsky would proceed to realign his entire 2nd Ukrainian

Front—as well as tens of thousands of resistance fighters in Ukraine—to the Allied side.

"This is almost impossible to imagine," Montgomery smiled. "You have an intact army group that is fully prepared to turn and fight Stalin?"

"Yes."

"And you will operate under the command of the Supreme Allied Commander?"

"We operate under blue and gold flag of Ukraine, but we operate in coordination with American and British units with full cooperation," Borysuk said, asserting the independence of his forces, but trying to be cooperative. "Many Ukrainian soldiers captured by General Patton will also join us."

"We've confirmed this at least partially," Koch interrupted. "When these officers first told us this story, I had some of my people who were interrogating the prisoners ask some leading questions . . ."

"And it's no secret that we had a helluva lot of surrenders in the Thuringia campaign," Patton added. "And a lot of these poor devils were real happy to give up."

"*Nobody* wants to live in same house with NKVD!" Borysuk laughed nervously.

"What about the non-Ukrainians in 2nd Ukrainian Front?" Bradley asked.

"Estonian, Latvian, and Lithuanian troops . . . *Nobody* wants to live in same house with NKVD!"

"What about the Russians?" Bradley repeated. "There must be lots of Russians in Malinovsky's command."

"This is another matter that we're only just coming to grips with," Koch replied. "Apparently, there are large numbers of Russians who are also ready to change sides. When the war ended, we liberated . . . and I know that other British and American units also liberated large numbers of Red Army troops that had been captured by the Krauts. Most of them refused to be turned back over to the Reds."

"Nobody wants to live in same house with NKVD!" Borysuk repeated. "Where is General Vlasov? The Russians will fight for *him* before they go back to Red Army."

"Who's General Vlasov?" Bradley asked.

"Russian mystery man," Koch explained. "He was the former commander of the 37th and 20th Soviet Armies, and later a deputy commander on the Volkhov Front. Became a hero in the defense of Moscow in December '41. He was captured in '42 and was later used by the Germans to start a phantom anti-Soviet Russian Army. He managed to get about a million Red troops to defect. He was a legend among the rank-and-file Red Army troops. I don't know what ever happened to him. Colonel Borysuk? Can you fill in any of the details?"

"Yes, as you say," Borysuk replied, "all is true, but he was used by Germans only so much. He caused a lot of trouble for Red Army because he was a big hero and he told the Russians to turn on Stalin. Thousands defected. Risked death on both sides to join Vlasov to fight Stalin. He had thousands of supporters."

"Wasn't he the one who headed the Committee for the Liberation of the Peoples of Russia?" Churchill asked. "Who issued that Smolensk Manifesto, that said all Russian nationalities should have the right of self-determination?"

"Yes," Borysuk said. "He had support in Ukraine. He had support with many Uzbeks, Tatars, Azerbaijanis. All nationalities, especially Cossacks."

"Does anyone know where this mysterious General Vlasov is now?" Truman asked, looking first at Patton and then glancing around the room. "I think we'd better find him, and find him quite soon."

"Sir, I don't think that will be necessary," Koch replied. "I can practically guarantee that as soon as it becomes known that Marshal Malinovsky has switched sides . . . Vlasov will go out of his way to find *us*."

Hotel George V
Paris, France
Sunday, July 1, 1945, 10:13 a.m.

"I can't hear you if you're all talking at once," Captain Tim Cunningham said, deliberately not raising his voice to a shout. He then mouthed the words and the din gradually subsided. The news of Patton's presence in France had broken officially. It had been announced that he would be holding a press conference at the George V before returning to the Front.

"That's better," Cunningham smiled, as nearly a hundred reporters that were crammed into the hotel lobby stopped talking to listen to the words of this Third Army press officer who was their link to the hottest newsmaker in Paris.

"The General has been conferring with Secretary Stimson at another location since Friday. He will be available for a press conference here at this hotel at 1700 hours today. That's five o'clock local time. We'll be using the banquet room over there."

"What time is the General actually arriving?"

"Around 1400 hours."

"Is it true that he'll be driving through the Arc du Triomphe?"

"I don't know. I imagine that he'll be coming from that direction."

"Why is he coming into Paris at all tonight?"

"He's been invited to have dinner with General de Gaulle."

"Is General Bradley also coming to dinner?"

"I don't know. de Gaulle had dinner with Bradley a week ago and Patton wasn't there, so maybe Bradley won't be there tonight."

"How can I schedule a one-on-one interview with the General?"

"As I tried to say earlier, there's too many of you and the General has too many other commitments for any individual interviews," Cunningham said, resorting to raising his voice. "You can ask anything you want at the press conference."

Rosie O'Leary stood on the far side of the room watching the feeding frenzy and calculating the best strategy for getting into the front row at the General's press conference.

She had awakened before sunup, not knowing what time it was, but thinking for a moment that she was in Washington and that it was late in the afternoon. She was experiencing that strange disorientation phenomena that people talked about having when they traveled long distances by air. A generation earlier, most people had never traveled so far so fast, but now it was becoming commonplace for people in Rosie's line of work.

She had decided to go for another walk and was drawn back

toward the Left Bank by the sounds of the church bells. The streets were nearly empty. She had expected to see the all-night girls, but she saw almost nobody. The Pont de l'Alma seemed strangely empty and forlorn. The bells led her further on and she found herself on a narrow street passing a church called St. Severin, where people were bustling in for services. She almost never went to Mass anymore, but somehow, the feeling of having Sister Jacqueline just over her shoulder spurred her on.

Rosie understood the Latin as well as she had back in San Francisco at St. Philip's, but she lost track of the French in the priest's homily. Her thoughts just began to drift.

She thought about how far she was from home. She thought of her brother Mike. How he must have felt, being so far from home in the South Pacific. She wondered what he must have thought when he landed in this forlorn place so far, far away at a time when the war seemed lost. For the first time since she saw the folded flag on the mantle at Diamond Street, she thought about how she would never, ever get a chance to talk to him about that. Most of the time, it had just felt like he was away and she was away, but that some day they'd both come home. When the Mass had ended, she had lit a candle for Mike.

As she walked back to the George V, Rosie had watched the city coming to life. People were washing sidewalks, carrying crates of produce to the cafes, beginning the hurried pace that would not abate until past midnight. Now, at the hotel, the crowd of reporters was breaking up, as the men—and a tiny handful of women—moved off in small jabbering clusters toward the dining room or out the big revolving door into the city.

As she returned to figuring her strategy for getting into the front row at the General's press conference, Rosie had a brainstorm.

As the turmoil began to abate, she squeezed through the crowd and approached Captain Cunningham, who was packing up his gear and preparing to leave.

"Captain, I'm Rosemary O'Leary . . . *The Washington Herald,*" she said, extending her hand. "I know that you said there'd be no one-on-one . . ."

"That's correct ma'am. And don't ask me to make an exception for you."

"No. That's not it. I don't want to interview General Patton," she said. "Well, actually I *do,* but what I wanted to ask was whether I could have an interview with his driver . . . Sergeant . . ."

"Sergeant McKinley. Nate McKinley. Nobody's asked to interview *him.*"

"Well, he *is* a sort of colorful character in his own right," Rosie said. "He'd be good human interest. A war hero who became the General's driver. People would like to read about him."

"I guess," Cunningham said, thinking over Rosie's request. "Okay. I'll see what I can do. Be right here in this area around 1700 hours, and if it's gonna happen, I'll come get you."

Place de l'Etoile
Paris, France
Sunday, July 1, 1945, 2:12 p.m.

"See that up ahead?" Patton asked Nate, pointing to a large grey arch that seemed to straddle the boulevard ahead of their Jeep. "That's the biggest triumphal arch in the world. Bigger than anything that the Romans ever had. Napoleon designed it. This morning, you and I are going to have a privilege that Bonaparte himself never had. He planned his arch after he beat the Russians at Austerlitz in 1806, but it wasn't finished for another thirty years, so he never got to use it."

The Arc du Triomphe, sitting in an ocean of cobblestones that seemed to Nate to be about five acres in size, was draped with French and American flags. Military vehicles and military brass were everywhere. Rather than entering Paris quietly in the Lincoln Zephyr they'd used when they'd arrived, Patton decided that he wanted use a Willys—and not go quietly. As he told Nate, they were going to want to see him, and they'd expect to see a soldier. Nate was getting used to the General's flair for the dramatic.

As they reached the arch, the General pointed toward the vast opening in the arch, beneath which a group of French and American officers were clustered around a flame that was burning on the ground.

"That's their tomb of the unknown French soldier from

World War I," Patton told him. "They put the poor devil here in 1920 and they have this perpetual flame. We're here to pay respects."

As Nate brought the jeep to a halt, a group of officers, who'd already come to attention, saluted Patton, who returned their salute promptly. Nate could hear the sound of a band playing somewhere, but since he was standing at attention, he knew he shouldn't be gawking around. Patton walked back to one of the jeeps in the column and returned carrying a wreath of flowers. This he placed on the plaque next to the flame.

There were more salutes and Patton spoke with the men under the arch for about five minutes. Nate could see him gesturing with his arms and pointing up to the top of the massive arch. Knowing him, he probably knew more about all the carvings and statues than many of the French officers. At last there was a round of salutes and Patton returned to the jeep.

"Let's go."

If the crowds had been large on the other side of the arch, they were gargantuan over here. The broad boulevard sloped downhill for a great distance. There were people massing everywhere. They all wanted to see America's great warrior king. Nearby were dozens of photographers recording them.

They headed down the Champs Elysees. As they passed, the crowd started to cheer. There were people hanging out of windows and hanging on lampposts.

Patton was grinning ear to ear and waving to the people on both sides of the street. Nate thought that for somebody who didn't like politicians, Patton was certainly working the crowd like one.

Place de l'Etoile
Paris, France
Sunday, July 1, 1945, 2:12 p.m.

"Pourquoi êtes-vous ainsi impressionné par Patton?" Rosie O'Leary asked a woman about her mother's age who was standing on the street corner waving a small paper tricolore. She was amazed by how enthusiastic the French were about this American general.

"Il est notre Napoléon du vingtième siècle!" the woman replied with a smile and an emphasis on the phrase describing Patton as *our* Napoleon. "Il représente l'honneur et la gloire qui est manquante."

"De Gaulle n'est-il pas dotée honneur et gloire?" Rosie asked, wondering whether this woman would compare France's own to Bonaparte. "Il est un citoyen français."

"Mais le Général Patton est un héros de conquête," the woman said with a little shrug. "Qui ceci indique toute!"

"That says it all," Rosie repeated in English. Everybody loves conquering hero. Everybody loves a winner.

Rosie had decided to walk up to the Place de l'Etoile, the vast circular plaza surrounding the Arc du Triomphe, for Patton's grand entrance. She soon discovered that the enthusiasm surrounding Patton's arrival was infectious. The closer she got, the bigger and more animated the crowds became. This morning, she'd seen the streets virtually deserted. Now there were more people than she'd seen on any street since VE-Day in Washington.

Above, she saw someone unfurl a handmade American flag—actually just a bedsheet with some red stripes and blue stars on it—from a window. She elbowed her way through the crowd to the edge of the plaza. There, she could see the Arc du Triomphe, draped with the red, white, and blue of the French and American flags, with a British one mixed among them.

There was also a large number of Dutch and Belgian refugees in the crowd, but they had left home too quickly to pack their flags.

Rosie had glimpsed the Arc at a distance before, but only now did she realize how huge it was, especially compared to how tiny the people and vehicles were that were clustered around the base.

A band struck up a march and there was a buzz of excitement. Patton must be getting close.

Above the murmur of the crowd and the noise of the band, she heard a hissing sound that grew into a deafening shriek. Suddenly, seven shiny grey airplanes whisked overhead at tremendous speed, traveling in the direction of the Champs Elysees. They had short wings with rounded tips and no propellers. Rosie guessed they must be those new American jet fighters that she'd heard about. They were certainly fast. She saw them for a split second, and then they were gone.

Rosie looked down as a jeep came past the arch sporting a red placard with four silver stars. Inside, a powerful-looking, barrel-chested man with a gleaming green helmet was waving at the crowd.

"Vive Patton! Vive Patton!"

A roar went up from the multitude. Rosie even felt a little tinge of goose flesh on her own back.

Rosie strained to see the driver, but in a moment, the jeep was gone, swallowed by the crowd. The loud explosion of cheers moved away slowly as well, like the noise of the jets.

As Rosie reached the hotel, people were chattering and looking out the windows. Patton entered the lobby at the head of an entourage of smartly dressed officers, moving with a sense of power and assuredness. He was a tall man, but the charisma that he radiated made him seem larger than life. Four stars shone from his helmet, four more from each shoulder, and four from each of his lapels. Above his breast pocket was the largest garden of ribbons and decorations that she'd ever seen. The ivory-handled pistols on his hips seemed to underscore the image of a warrior king.

Flash bulbs popped, and people—including not a few of the reporters—applauded. Patton removed his helmet, returned the salutes that he was offered with a gloved hand, and walked quickly to the elevator. As with his appearance at the Place de l'Etoile, he was gone in less than a minute.

"So this is the great Patton."

Rosie looked around. It was Richard Waldron.

"Hello, Richard." She smiled. "Did you enjoy the parade?"

"Behold the conquering hero," Waldron said. "No, I didn't actually go out to the street and watch his entrance. I heard it was quite impressive at that."

"The people love him," Rosie shrugged.

"He's their Napoleon and their Caesar," Waldron pontificated. "He's their conquering hero. You saw how he took command of this room without saying a word. He inspired a great deal of confidence. With the situation at hand, stirring the soul is the first step to shaping up the troops. These people here in

France don't want to see their nation overrun twice in half a decade."

"What is it about a man like this that inspires people?" Rosie asked rhetorically.

"The nature of heroism is a mystery that becomes a legend and a myth," Waldron said. "Look at the East Indian Vedas. Look at the Greek tragedies. To paraphrase William James, mankind's common instinct for reality has always held the world to be essentially a theater for heroism. In heroism, we feel, life's supreme mystery is hidden. No matter what a man's frailties otherwise may be, if he be willing to risk death, and still more. If he suffer it heroically, in the service he has chosen, the fact consecrates him forever."

PATTON strode heroically into the banquet room to meet the press at precisely 1700 hours.

"I can't talk to you for long," he announced as he reached the podium. "The brass thinks I'm prone to stepping on my tongue when I talk to you folks. Don't know how they got that idea."

There was a ripple of laughter. Patton's reputation for speaking his mind too candidly was notorious.

"Do you believe that Marshal Zhukov will resume his offensive against Paris, now that Stalin's call for a popular uprising seems to have failed?"

"Stalin sent Zhukov to do the job. I expect that he'll *try* to do it."

"When you say 'try,' does that mean that you expect Zhukov to fail?"

"He's up against the best-trained, best-equipped, and best-manned army in the history of the world."

"That hasn't seemed to stop him so far."

"Well, he didn't have old Georgie Patton raising hell on his left flank until he'd raced all the way across northern Germany."

"When do you expect Zhukov to resume the attack?"

"If I could read minds, I'd quit the Army and become a fortune teller."

"What will the Allied strategy be, if he does?"

"The Northern Front is not my theater of operations, but if it was, I wouldn't answer that question in public. I *can* tell you that this *is* the principal theater of this war. The war will be won or lost in Northern Europe."

Patton worried for a moment—but just a moment—that he might have gone a bit too far in his ruse to spread the word that the Allies were placing all their bets on the coming battle with Zhukov, and the defense of France.

"Could you summarize the overall Allied strategy in general terms?"

"Yes. It'll be the same as it was against the Krauts. Kill more of them than they do of us, and keep it up 'til they stop."

"Is there any truth to the rumor that you've been named as the new Supreme Commander?"

"Where'n the hell did you hear a rumor like that?" Patton replied, wondering indeed where such a rumor may have originated. "If that was true, you'd damn sure be seeing me wearing my fifth star!"

"After the Battle of Jena, you were being compared to Napoleon. Would you care to comment on any similarities between yourself and him?"

"His men damned near starved to death during their Moscow campaign. Mine are a helluva lot better fed!"

"Does this mean that you're actually planning a Moscow campaign?"

"My boss, the Commander-in-Chief, said that Stalin has to be put out of business. If he surrendered to me tomorrow, it would save us all a helluva lot of trouble, but, barring that, I guess you'd have to say that the buck stops in Moscow."

With that, the General waved to the reporters and left the podium. Rosie moved back, trying to avoid the great tide of journalistic humanity that surged after Patton shouting like harpies with their myriad of "one last" questions.

As she was watching the tempest move out of the banquet room like a fast-moving thunderstorm over the ocean, she felt a tap on her shoulder.

She turned. It was Captain Cunningham—and another man.

"Here he is, Miss, this is Sergeant McKinley."

"How do you do, Sergeant McKinley," she said, turning

away from Waldron. "Thank you so much for taking the time to speak with me."

When Rosie turned, she'd not known what to expect. She had seen so many thousands of GIs in Washington, Paris, and San Francisco. There were short ones, fat ones, and silly looking ones. There were tall ones, dark ones, and handsome ones. This man was somehow strangely unlike the others. He was much taller than she'd expected from having seen him in a newspaper photograph. His face was so different. It seemed so chiseled and angular that it made the faces of everyone else in the room seem puffy and out of focus. His blue eyes were riveting. They were powerful and piercing. At the same time there was a sense of infinite kindness. If Patton exuded the charisma of the warrior king, this man exuded the aura of the knight errant, the solitary rider.

She smiled and extended her hand.

His handshake was firm but gentle, evoking a sense of tremendous, yet restrained power. His grip seemed to tremble with an infinite strength.

As the reporter turned and looked up at him, Nate experienced a blinding flash like a phosphorus shell exploding against the armor of a tank turret. Looking into her face was like looking into the sun. It was true that he hadn't talked to many women for the past seven or eight months, but he'd never experienced anything like this. Miss O'Leary was small and unassuming, but his first impression was of almost supernatural beauty and presence. Her smile radiated a kind of magic that he'd never seen in a woman before.

Nate could see an innocent, yet playful sparkle in those eyes that seemed to flow from somewhere deep within her, as though she was the daughter of a mystical race of sirens that possessed infinite powers of enchantment. She was so dazzling that nothing else in the room seemed to have color. As Nate shook her hand, he felt like he'd just put his hand in a light socket. He felt his hand start to tremble slightly, so he made the handshake as quick as possible.

"Excuse me. I'm a little out of breath," she said as she flipped open her notebook and tried to regain her composure. "It's been a rather busy day around here."

"That's fine, ma'am. I've been kinda busy myself."

"One of the things that struck me about General Patton's grand entrance here today is how the people seem to have welcomed him almost as a savior," she said.

"Yes ma'am," he replied. "I was really surprised myself today. We got a pretty nice welcome from the folks over in Prague, but this was a real parade. I don't know whether I'd use a word like 'savior.' I'd just say that they see somebody who's on their side and has proved that he can deliver. I think that it's also the flag that we're flying. It doesn't say 'we're out to conquer the world.' I think that the people over here know the United States came here to kick the bad guys out and go home. We're not here to build an empire like the Reds."

"I like that idea of the flag 'saying' that the United States is not out to build an empire," Rosie said, now imagining this man as being in the mold of the great warriors of Greek mythology, who could turn a phrase as easily as they could wield a sword.

"Thanks."

"Without betraying any military secrets, do you men in the Third Army have the confidence that General Patton will succeed in helping win this war as he did the last one?" she asked.

"I've been with Third Army since the Battle of the Bulge last winter," Nate replied. "And the one thing I understood from the beginning . . . even before I met the man . . . is that whether you love him or hate him, almost nobody has ever doubted that he'll figure out a way to get the job done. I watched him up on the Landgraftenberg the night before our big fight down at Jena. There was a 155 mm howitzer and a jackknifed truck blocking the road. The old man just waded in, told 'em all what to do and where to go. He was right in there getting his hands dirty. Then, when they did what he told 'em and got it cleared, Patton stood there directing traffic for half an hour. The GIs were shoutin' and cheerin' him as they drove by. That's the kind of leader he is."

"I suppose that this makes for pretty strong morale."

"Yes, ma'am." Nate nodded. "It doesn't matter whether an officer is a mean son of a . . . I mean a mean *fellow* . . . It only matters that he knows what he's doing. If he knows what he's doing, whether it's at the battalion level, or if he's running the whole damned . . . darn army . . . the men will follow him to hell and back. I'm sorry about the language ma'am. Been overseas too long."

"That's okay, Sergeant McKinley," Rosie smiled, blushing slightly. "I've heard most of the words that you've heard."

Rosie was struck again by this amazing man. Not only was he a compassionate warrior poet, he was an almost bashful man.

"Let's talk about *you* for a minute," Rosie said, wishing that she could talk about him all night. "When exactly did you come overseas?"

"I landed up in Le Havre just after the Battle of the Bulge started. I went into the line as a replacement with the 27th Armored Infantry Battalion in the 9th Armored Division on the day before Christmas. My Christmas dinner was a can of crackers. Saw quite a bit of action from there on. Across the Rhine. All the way across Germany. I was in the same outfit until VE-Day."

"And you were in Kummersdorf on that morning . . ." Rosie started to ask, realizing immediately how painful this must be for such a compassionate man.

"Yeah, that story is pretty well known, I guess," he said grimly. "Through all of last winter, I watched a lot of guys get killed. Well, not a lot, I suppose, but many. And this was different. They were just rounded up by people who were supposed to be on our side and shot. Point blank. Just shot. This guy, Bob Epperly, from E Company. He saved my life at Marburg. I watched him get shot in cold blood. In *cold blood*. Steve Steinberg, this wise-cracking Jewish kid from Brooklyn. We crossed at Remagen together. They just shot him while he was standing there. I watched it. It's one of those things that just changes you."

"I realize that it must be a sobering experience to see death and to face it yourself," she said, feeling self-conscious about leading him.

"War is a killing business," he replied, fighting unsuccessfully to restrain himself from sharing his innermost feelings with this goddess. "As General Patton puts it, you have to spill *their* blood or they'll spill *yours*. War is direct, simple, and ruthless. We didn't start it, but we're here to finish it. It's not my first choice of a thing to be doing with my life, but it's my job. It's a duty to a lot of other guys my age . . . your age, too . . . as it is to our country. I can't let another guy down. I won't let down all the guys at Kummersdorf. I can't let down those guys . . . our age . . . all over the world that I don't even know."

Nate watched her pause. A little furrow appeared in her gentle brow.

"I was just thinking," Rosie said thoughtfully, "you're the first person that I've interviewed that's my age, the first guy who talks about our generation. I've spoken with a lot of big-wigs who shape policy and send people like you into this bat-tle or that. And now I've been speaking with someone who has actually lived through a battle. I can never know what it must be like . . . But it's personal for *me,* too."

"Do you . . . Did you . . . have someone . . . ?" Nate asked, feeling a fire building in him to avenge the guy who may have once held the love of this wonderful woman.

"Yes," Rosie said, feeling tears welling up in her eyes, and wishing she could will them to stop. This was so damned unprofessional.

"Yes," she repeated, quickly and as discreetly as possible wiping her eyes. "My brother, Mike. Guadalcanal. Almost three years ago. Broke my . . . Pop's . . . heart. Mine too."

"Oh God, I'm so sorry," Nate said, secretly relieved that she hadn't lost a lover. Of course, the odds of a clod like Nate McKinley having a chance with this goddess were between slim and none, but he could dream. "I don't know what to say."

"You already have," she told him softly. "You do. You un-derstand. Better than me. I don't have the memories of the bat-tle. I was away at school. It didn't really hit me until I went home a couple of months ago. It was so quiet. Just the sound of the old clock ticking. And next to the clock . . . you know . . . the folded flag."

"I'm sorry," he said.

"It's okay," she lied, instinctively jerking back as he moved imperceptibly closer. "*No,* it's *not* okay. My brother's death was not okay. Kummersdorf was not okay. I guess that's why the world needs people like you, and like General Patton, who will root out and finish the Hitlers and the Hirohitos and the Stalins who think it *is* okay."

"That's what makes us different," he said thoughtfully after a moment. "It's that thing about what the flag says. What makes us Americans different from all those other guys is that we just want to get it over with . . . *really* over with . . . and go home."

"Where *is* home for you, Sergeant?" she asked, knowing his home state, but wanting to hear him talk more about it. "What will you do when you go home?"

"Montana," he shrugged, displaying that sense of inferiority that people from remote rural states often have when talking to people they perceive as being more cosmopolitan. "I'm from Montana, up on the North Fork of the Flathead River. My dad runs about fifty head of horses on a place up there. I guess I'll go back and do the same . . . place of my own some day . . . maybe have some cattle. Just a dream."

"What a beautiful dream," Rosie said, imagining herself riding the plains with this great man under cobalt blue skies and towering mountains.

"Well, it isn't much, but it sure beats living in a foxhole," Nate replied with a nervous grin, feeling like a hick, talking about horses and ranching to a woman who was probably raised on champagne and caviar.

"Oh, I really think it's great," Rosie said weakly, knowing that Sister Jacqueline would be reaching for her heavy, eighteen-inch ironwood ruler if she could see the impure thoughts that Rosie was having at this moment.

"So, where are you from? What's your family into?" Nate asked. The interview had turned into a conversation. Nate had been too busy looking into her face to notice that she'd stopped taking notes.

"Well, nothing as exciting as you," she smiled, comparing her own mundane life as a little Catholic schoolgirl chasing the Market Street trolley car as being pathetically drab compared to growing up astride a magnificent steed on the crown of the continent. "I grew up in a flat in San Francisco. My pop's a baker. My sister works at a hotel. My mom does an awful lot of work for the church."

"San Francisco? Did you ever go to see the Seals . . . in person?" Nate asked, his mind suddenly filled with visions of San Francisco's Pacific Coast League baseball team. Growing up in

a professional sports void, the young boys of the Mountain
time zone had been compelled to live vicariously through the
exploits of the nearest pro teams, even if they were two thousand miles away. "Did you ever see Joe DiMaggio before he
went to the Yankees?"

"Sure," Rosie replied, recalling all those cold nights at Sixteenth and Bryant as a kid. "My pop used to take Mike and me
out to Seals Stadium all the time. Not my sister, though. She
didn't like baseball. I liked it. Pop used to always buy us hot
dogs in the fourth inning. No matter who was up next or who
was ahead. Hot dogs at the top of the fourth. Yeah . . . we saw
Joe DiMaggio . . . and both his brothers . . . that was before he
was famous."

Nate was incredulous. He couldn't picture this radiant
creature sitting in the bleachers eating a hot dog. He wished
that he could've been there.

Rosie was completely lost. The mention of the Seals had
brought a disarming smile to the face of this powerful man
with the serious face.

"Guess they don't have baseball over here," Nate said, trying to fill the awkward silence.

"All they've got are sidewalk cafes," Rosie said, wishing
they were at a sidewalk cafe on Boulevard St. Germain with
the damned war a distant memory.

"Miss O'Leary . . . I'm going to have to steal the sergeant
away from you." It was Captain Cunningham. "The General's
ready to roll . . . and he's asking for his driver."

Nate stood up quickly and instinctively.

"Thank you for taking the time to speak with me,
Sergeant," Rosie said, shaking his hand and tying to smile
cheerfully.

"Thank you, ma'am. I hope to read your article," Nate said
as he turned and left the room.

Rosie looked around dizzily, feeling as though the lights
had gone out. She knew that Patton was leaving Paris in the
morning and that she would probably never see Sergeant
McKinley again. She wanted to run after him and tell that
she'd wait for him until the war was over.

"How'd it go with the press?" Cunningham asked.

"Okay, I guess," Nate shrugged. "Can't really remember too

much of what I said. Did you know that she's a baseball fan?"

"Really?" the press officer asked suspiciously. "Yeah, that's a line they like to use to get you to relax. Broads don't care about baseball. She wasn't too hard on you was she? I mean with her questions?"

"Well," Nate said thoughtfully. "Yes and no."

USAAF Station 106
Grafton Underwood
Northants, England
Tuesday, July 3, 1945, 9:40 p.m.

Henry Stimson gazed though the rain-spattered window at the rolling green hills, the country lanes, and thatched cottages of rural Northamptonshire as they moved beneath the wing of the big airplane.

He realized that Ike's last view of land on Earth would have been of these hills. It was in a C-54 very much like this one, on a flight very much like that which Stimson would make later today, that General Eisenhower had gone down in darkness, somewhere over the North Atlantic. They'd stopped searching for the wreckage. Nobody could have survived. Stimson wondered what hell it must be to swirl down into the blackness and to die beneath the icy waves.

The *Sacred Cow,* the same C-54 that had carried him and President Roosevelt on their fateful rendezvous with Josef Stalin at Yalta, had now carried Roosevelt's successor to an equally important rendezvous with destiny in France. Now, it was carrying them home again. One fast stop in England, and the President would be back on the White House balcony for the Fourth of July celebration—America's fourth consecutive Independence Day at war.

As the *Sacred Cow* dropped lower, Stimson saw dozens of silver airplanes on the ground, huge silver airplanes with the stars of the USAAF on their wings and black triangles framing the letter "P" on their tails. He marvelled at these great killing machines and hoped that their power would ultimately be adequate to stop the killing once and for all. The Secretary of War eyed these brutal-looking Flying Fortresses as the C-54 landed

and began to taxi across the tarmac. Their fuselages bristled
with guns from the tip of their tails to the twin-gun turret hanging from the upturned chin of each aircraft. These, General
Marshall had told him, were the B-17s of 384th Bomb Group,
the last USAAF unit to bomb Germany in World War II, and
the first to bomb Soviet forces in World War III.

The blast of cool, wet air felt good on Stimson's face as the
big door slammed open. At the foot of the rickety, metal staircase, he recognized Hap Arnold, the USAAF's commanding
general. Next to him stood General Jimmy Doolittle, the prewar air racing legend who had led the first air attack against
Japan in the dark days of April 1942. Doolittle had then gone
on to command the Eighth Air Force, as it became the largest
component within the USAAF. Based at nearly four dozen airfields spread across southern England, Doolittle's command
had reached the point of being able to send two thousand
B-17s and B-24s into the skies over Germany in a single day.
Even before VE-Day, the Eighth had started to abandon its
wartime bases for its new assignment in the Pacific. Now,
Doolittle was in the final stages of bringing it all back.

"Welcome to Grafton Underwood, Mr. President," Arnold
said, greeting the Commander-in-Chief. "I wish that we could
have arranged a little bit better weather for you."

"I'm sure that you did your best," Truman said with a wink.

"Mr. President, this is Colonel Fish, commander of the
384th Bomb Group here. Do you know General Doolittle?"

"I'm pleased to meet you Colonel Fish, I understand that
your unit has been doing some good work," the President said
to the young Lieutenant Colonel, before turning to the legendary Doolittle. "No, I haven't had the pleasure of meeting
General Doolittle, but General, it is certainly an honor to meet
you now."

Inside the chilly Quonset hut that had been one of the
Grafton Underwood briefing rooms, rows of folding chairs
served as a silent reminder of hundreds of pilots, navigators,
and bombardiers who sat in rapt attention in such rooms all
across England, day in and day out for nearly four years, and
who ultimately brought German industry to a halt. On the wall
was a massive map of central Europe—stretching from the
Bay of Biscay to the Pripyat Marshes—covered with hundreds

of notorious place names that had served as the centerpieces of hundreds of "Target For Today" briefings over the long years before.

Today, there were more targets to discuss. Marshall began the meeting by briefing the airmen on the Chateau Rambuteau summit, on Patton's strategy, and on the unexpected windfall of the Ukrainians. When the Chief of Staff had finished, Arnold and Doolittle took turns laying out the coming strategic air campaign against the Soviet Union. The Eighth Air Force, they announced, was ready to launch a maximum effort with 2,012 B-17s and B-24s the following day. The fact that the next day was the Fourth of July was not lost on the men in the room.

The air officers also noted that the Flying Fortresses and Liberators would soon be augmented by five bombardment groups of the XXI Bomber Command of the Twentieth Air Force, which would be coming in from the Pacific. These were the only groups in the USAAF equipped with the new B-29 Super Fortress. With a payload capacity twice that of the B-17 and B-24, the huge B-29 was also the only bomber in the world that could reach the Soviet industrial heartland from bases in England.

When Truman asked when these powerful weapons would be reaching England, the answer was "within the hour."

Indeed, the first of the behemoths would arrive almost as though it was on cue. As the President and his high-ranking officers reached the runway to reboard the *Sacred Cow,* they could hear a deep rumbling sound in the distance.

"Here they come," Arnold said, pointing off to the west, where a pair of tiny lights was barely visible.

As they watched, the two lights gradually grew into a four-engined airplane. Another set of lights appeared in the distance, and then another. The enormous silver craft touched down in a puff of blue smoke at the end of the runway and rolled past the lines of B-17s. It was a huge airplane, dwarfing the Flying Fortresses. Its lines were cleaner and smoother. Its huge, rounded glass nose made the B-17 look antique by comparison.

As the lead aircraft taxied toward where the President stood, the four throbbing Wright R3350 Twin Cyclones shook the ground with the power of more than eighty thousand horses—far beyond that of any other operational warplane on Earth.

With a series of screams, the engines shut down, one after the other. Even before the huge, black, four-bladed props had spun to a halt, a hatch beneath the nose opened and a heavy-set man with black hair and a sweat-stained shirt dropped out on the runway and started walking toward them. On his shoulders, he wore the three stars of a lieutenant general.

For this man, today was a homecoming of sorts. In 1942, as a colonel, General Curtis Emerson LeMay had commanded the 305th Bomb Group here at Grafton Underwood. During the ensuing years, he'd gone to the Pacific to bomb the criminals of Pearl Harbor into the stone age. Now he was back to take the same punishment to the Comintern's Man of Steel.

About six feet from the line of dignitaries who were still admiring the Superfortress, LeMay paused and snapped to attention to salute the two five-star generals, the Secretary of War, and the Commander-in-Chief.

"Welcome back to Grafton Underwood, General," Arnold smiled, shaking the hand of the unsmiling LeMay. "We're glad to have you."

"Glad to be here, sir. Soon as my guys get a shower and a shave and a good night's sleep, we're ready to take a little Fourth of July fireworks over there to Uncle Joe."

Hotel Seville
22 East 29th Street
New York City
Wednesday, July 4, 1945, 9:47 a.m.

"Call you a cab, ma'am?"
"No thanks, it's a nice day. I think I'll walk."
As she turned up Fifth Avenue, Rosie O'Leary was reminded of the newsreel footage that she'd seen nearly two months ago of New York City celebrating VE-Day. Today, things were much quieter. Flags were flying everywhere, but it was a subdued Fourth of July.

A lot of things had happened in her life since the last time she was in New York—as a college sophomore. Then again, a lot had happened to her since the last time that she'd last set foot in Washington—just a week before. She had met a man who had swept her off her feet in the twinkling of his bright blue eyes. The story that she'd written about that encounter had changed her career. She poured her heart and soul into the article, rewriting portions of it a half-dozen times.

When her "WHAT OUR FLAG SAYS" story reached Rex Simmons at mid-morning Monday, he'd started to scan it at the teletype. Then he decided that he'd better go sit down in his office and close the door. When his assistant editor found him twenty minutes later, there were tears in his eyes.

"Run it. Front page," he said softly as he handed it to his assistant.

Rosie awoke Monday morning Paris time to a dozen telegrams, including one from her mother wanting to know what had happened, and one from Simmons telling her to fly to New York at once. The radio networks wanted her.

When she'd arrived in New York on Tuesday night, she was stunned to discover that "WHAT OUR FLAG SAYS" had been reprinted on the front pages of two of the New York papers. She had phoned Simmons from the hotel; he explained that it had been picked up by the wire services.

As she strolled past the Empire State Building, hung with red, white, and blue bunting for the day, a "WHAT OUR FLAG SAYS" front page was displayed in a window, together with small flags and patriotic posters.

On the phone, the people at the CBS Radio Network had told her that "WHAT OUR FLAG SAYS" was being quoted at Fourth of July celebrations all around the country, and asked her whether she'd heard the song.

"The song?" Just as Simmons had said, there really was a song. It had been recorded and records pressed. The CBS people had an advance copy and promised they'd play it for her when she got to their offices at Rockefeller Center.

By the time that she passed the big library building at Forty-second Street, Rosie could see the seventy dark stone stories of the RCA Building at Rockefeller Center, rising from amid a cluster of smaller buildings up past Forty-ninth Street. As she looked up at it, she realized that for those who followed the Marxist line, the very name of this building represented the darkest bogeymen in the western world—the first family of capitalism.

She glanced at her watch and realized that it was now almost ten thirty. She was going to be late. If she'd taken the cab that the doorman at the Hotel Seville offered, she'd already be there, high up on the fifty-seventh floor, looking out at the world.

There was no warning.

There was just a flash of light, faster than any moving object that Rosie had ever seen.

The explosion erupted amid the lower floors of the great structure. It took a split second for the sound to hit her and then a shower of debris could be heard falling closer to where the explosion had occurred. A huge cloud of dust and what looked like smoke billowed and grew, engulfing all of the base of the great building. The shock wave rumbled beneath her feet like an earthquake. Glass could be heard breaking.

For a moment, there was an unbelievably horrible screeching sound that built to a terrible crescendo and then, abruptly, stopped.

The top, the upper two dozen or so floors of the majestic skyscraper seemed to rise serenely above the maelstrom below, but, as Rosie watched in horror, it began to quiver and vibrate as though being shaken violently by an unseen monster. Stones and bricks and debris were falling like snowflakes, revealing the steel skeleton beneath.

Rosie could hear screams now. People were running everywhere. But still she could not take her eyes off the disaster before her.

Another mass of debris hurtled out from the catastrophe, spilling and splattering all around her. Rosie felt a sharp pain on the side of her head.

World War III had come to America.

PART III

HAMMER
AND SICKLE

★ ★ ★ ★ ★

11

* *

"WE didn't see it coming, and we couldn't have stopped it if we had."

The President of the United States looked at his Secretary of War, who looked at the Secretary of State, who looked back at the young USAAF officer who was the bearer of the sense of hopelessness.

Harry Truman's sleep-deprived face hung like a shroud, with deep, dark bags under his exhausted, bloodshot eyes. He hadn't slept but a few moments since Chateau Rambuteau, more than forty-eight hours ago. The fatigue of the long plane trip made it seem like at least four hundred forty-eight hours. He had expected to come home, make a brief Fourth of July appearance on the balcony overlooking the south lawn, smile, wave, and tumble into bed for ten hours of sleep. Fate had conspired to deny him all of these things.

The President, Secretary Stimson, and General Marshall had been informed of the attack on New York while the *Sacred Cow* was over Labrador. There had been an immediate round of speculation. The general sense was that it may have been an air raid, but Truman had hoped that it was merely a gas line explosion. Marshall had feared a shelling attack by a submarine.

New York Air Traffic Control had shunted all incoming commercial flights away from the tri-state metropolitan area as soon as the explosions had occurred, but as the President's plane entered that air space, he'd requested and received a fighter escort from Mitchel Field on Long Island so that he could take a closer look.

Rockefeller Center and the familiar RCA Building were

heavily damaged. Fires were still burning and black smoke obscured much of the scene.

By the time that the C-54 touched down at Washington's National Airport, damage reports were coming in. These grim details were handed to the President and his entourage as they disembarked. Luckily, it had been a holiday, so there were relatively few people in the office buildings. Nevertheless, the death toll was estimated to be more than a thousand. Over two hundred bodies, mainly of people who had been on the street, had been recovered. Area hospitals were swamped with casualties. All that Stimson could think to say was "It's going to be worse than Pearl Harbor."

They had braved the wall of reporters clustered around the driveway on the north side of the executive mansion, and had staggered into the cabinet room.

Truman's staff brought coffee and the first wave of afternoon "extra" editions of the major newspapers. The papers were unanimous in their assessment that, for the American people, this deadly attack on American soil suddenly made the war against Stalin *very* personal.

The President's secretary brought in a statement on the tragedy that had already been prepared for him. Truman skimmed the words about national solidarity in times of adversity and the American people pulling together. It was short on details but carried the promise that everything possible was being done. The President penciled a couple of changes and told his secretary to make it available to the press.

Truman and Stimson slumped into their usual chairs, craving a hot shower as much as their subconscious craved sleep. Marshall had gone straight to his office at the Pentagon. Stettinius and Forestall were both on their way to the White House. Almost as soon as the other two men took their seats, speculation swirled over exactly what "it" had been. There was a strong sense of disbelief that the cause of the explosion was still unknown to the inner circle of the most powerful men in the land.

When a team arrived from the War Department to provide the initial briefing, Stimson readily admitted "how dumbfounded I am and how dumb this makes me feel."

None of them was prepared for the explanation that was offered by the nervous young major.

"It was a V weapon," he said, conjuring up images of the dreaded V2 missiles that the Germans had dropped on London during the last year of the war. "Actually, there were two, about two minutes apart. One hit Manhattan and the other impacted in the East River. They came so fast, there was nothing that we could do. They were seen on air traffic control radar for half a minute. They were so fast that the radar people thought they were some kind of anomaly. One operator estimated they were going more than a thousand miles an hour."

"I'm not an expert, but my understanding is that V2s have a range of just a few hundred miles," Forestall interjected. "The Germans were barely able to reach London from their bases in the Ruhr. This means that these had to have been launched from . . ."

"Pittsburgh? Rochester? Nova Scotia?" Stimson's head was spinning. "Does it mean that we're under attack from *within* this continent?"

"No, sir," the major smiled hopefully. "We're getting reports that they were also tracked by our radar in France. They were launched from somewhere in Europe."

"Oh my God!" Truman gasped, removing his glasses and covering his face with his hands. "It's Hitler's 'secret weapons,' Stalin's got Hitler's secret weapons."

"I take it that this thing that hit New York was *not* a V2?" Stimson asked.

"That's correct, sir," the young major explained, gesturing with his hands. "The V2 didn't have the range to reach even to Scotland from Germany. But we knew that the Germans were working on a longer-range version at the end of the war. It was a two-stage rocket called A10. Intelligence reports said they planned to hit the Eastern Seaboard with 'em. Apparently the Reds got hold of 'em and they work."

"Apparently," Truman said glumly.

"How can we shoot these down?" Forestall asked.

"We can't," the major said, obviously with more abruptness than anyone in the room hoped for. "Like it says in the Superman pictures. Faster than a speeding bullet. You can't shoot down a bullet. All we can do for the moment is to track 'em in France and telephone the East Coast that one is coming. That's about an hour's warning. That's all we can do."

"You mean that one could hit *this office* and there's no defense?" Truman asked.

The major just nodded.

"That's what worries me," the major continued. "They seem to have solved the guidance problem."

"Meaning they can hit what they aim for," Truman said. The former artilleryman clearly understood the principal.

"With the V2, they couldn't hit the broad side of a barn," the major said. "They couldn't even hit the *farm* with any accuracy. It was guided by a gyroscope that could hit *somewhere* inside of the six hundred or so square miles of London from a range of two hundred miles. That's the best they could do."

"Obviously, somebody has solved that problem, or else this shot today was very, very lucky," Marshall observed.

"That's what really scares me," the major said nervously.

"Me, too," Truman interjected.

"What really scares *me* . . ." Stimson said thoughtfully, "is what happens when . . . if they put this terrible thing together with . . . well, in a word, Klaus Fuchs."

The major glanced at him quizzically, but everyone else in the room knew exactly what he was thinking.

Hradcany Castle
Prague, Czechoslovakia
Wednesday, July 4, 1945, 5:20 p.m.

Nate McKinley had been reading the newspaper when word of the attack on New York had reached Patton's newest Lucky Forward. It wasn't that he had nothing else to do, but when someone handed him a copy of the Fourth of July issue of *Stars & Stripes* with *his* name circled in pencil, he had stopped what he was doing to take a look.

The byline was "Rosemary O'Leary," and the headline read, "WHAT OUR FLAG SAYS." He recalled her having said that she was going to make something of his offhand comment. Apparently she had. He started to read about this noble Sergeant McKinley, whose clear and honorable creed was an allegory for the American GI in Europe—to smite the totalitarian dictators and go home to get on with their lives.

"I'd like to meet this fellow." Nate laughed out loud.

Miss O'Leary had painted an immensely flattering picture of this Sergeant McKinley. He liked the way she wrote. Of course, he liked everything about this girl with the rosewood-colored hair. He wished he'd have another chance to see her.

When Koch wasn't looking, he carefully tore out the small picture of Miss O'Leary that was in the paper, and carefully placed it in his pocket.

Nate's dreamy reverie over the little Celtic goddess that he hardly knew came to an abrupt end as Brigadier General Halley Maddox, the Third Army's operations officer, came into the courtyard to announce that at least one long-range rocket had landed in New York City—on the Fourth of July.

Nate looked around, everyone was momentarily speechless, but he could see it in their eyes. The Reds had attacked their homeland. If it hadn't been before, the war against Stalin was now *personal*.

The O'Leary Home
Diamond Street
San Francisco
Thursday, July 5, 1945, 9:48 a.m.

"Mrs. O'Leary?" The voice on the phone crackled.

"Yes," Bea said, straining to hear. It was obviously a long-distance call and the caller sounded like he was speaking from the inside of a tin can.

"Mrs. O'Leary, this is Rex Simmons at *The Washington Herald*."

"Yes . . . oh yes. You're Rosemary's boss in Washington. She's spoken of you. So nice of you to call. What can I do for you?"

"Mrs. O'Leary . . . I've got . . . I'm afraid I've got some bad news. You know that explosion in New York? That rocket? Well . . . Rose was there. She was at the place where . . . I'm afraid she's . . . Mrs. O'Leary, Rose was killed."

Bea was numb. Her entire body started to shake. Her hand could no longer feel the heavy receiver in her hand.

"Mrs. O'Leary . . . ?"

"Ye-es?" the trembling voice said after a long pause.

"I'm so very, very sorry. We all are. Everybody here at the paper just loved her . . . I don't know what to say."

As the pause seemed to drag on, Simmons figured that he'd better say something.

"Mrs. O'Leary . . . If there's *anything* we can do . . . I mean . . . *Is there* anything that I can do? Please tell me."

After another long pause, the small, trembling voice came back on the line again.

"I'm sorry. I had to sit down. My *son* . . . three years ago in the Pacific. Is there . . . where can I . . . her body?"

"There was a lot of rubble. They're still finding bodies. It'll take time, but I've sent a man up there. We'll stay on top of it and I'll see that it's taken care of. I promise."

"Thank you, Mr. Simmons."

Bea put the receiver down, not realizing until it clunked onto the telephone that she hadn't said "goodbye." Mr. Simmons must have thought her rude, Bea scolded herself.

She looked around the room and the memories of raising three children in this small flat came rushing back. A quarter of a century had passed since little Mike came home from the hospital. Big Mike was completely overwhelmed. He was a father, but he had a son! A little son that carried his name. And then the girls came and the house was full of the noise and hooliganism—and the small triumphs and tragedies of raising kids. There were the skinned knees, two broken legs among the lot, the honor rolls, the first communions and the varsity teams, and finally, the graduations.

Then it was the telegram from the War Department. It came on a morning much like this one. She had sat in this very chair, the very chair where she'd once fed the little ruffian out of a baby bottle. She had sat in this chair and she had methodically called first Big Mike, then Catherine, and then, with the help of the long-distance operator, she'd phoned Rosemary. Now, it would be Rosemary whose voice would never echo in these lonely, lonely rooms again.

Methodically, she picked up the receiver and dialed.

"Hagen's Bakery," the voice said, sounding so much nearer.

"I'd be wantin' to have a word with Mike O'Leary."

"Sure. Jussaminute."

"This's Mike," the familiar voice said cheerfully. Bea wondered what it would be like when there was no longer a Mike to phone with such news. She wondered why she and Mike were cursed with losing their children. It was supposed to be the other way around.

"This's Mike. Who's callin'?"

"It's me. I just got a phone call . . . No other way to say it, but our little Rosemary's *dead*. Killed in that thing in New York City."

Hradcany Castle
Prague, Czechoslovakia
Sunday, July 8, 1945, 8:51 a.m.

Activity at Lucky Forward had picked up considerably as Patton prepared for the attack on Berlin. Since the summit in Paris, the size of the force on the Southern Front had nearly doubled. The Seventh Army was greatly expanded and much of the Fifth Army had relocated from Italy, moving through the Alsace and into Bavaria. Seventh Army would hit Koniev at Frankfurt, while Third Army drove north toward the battered capital of the former Reich.

Patton himself was like a caged beast. He had relished the trappings of the Bohemian monarchs at Hradcany for about forty-eight hours, but now he was anxious to move, anxious to begin the series of moves that he hoped would checkmate Zhukov—as well as Stalin's plan for Europe.

Nate had been briefed on the Fourth of July that they would be on the move within a week. Nobody except those at the very top of the chain of command knew "when," but Nate understood that when "when" came, this jeep had better be ready for a long campaign.

Nate was in the cobblestone courtyard attending to the General's vehicle when he saw Tim Cunningham, the Third Army press officer.

"Hey, sergeant, remember that gal . . . that reporter . . . what's her name? O'Leary," Cunningham asked, walking toward the jeep. "Y'know . . . the one that interviewed you over in Paris? "The one that put you in all the papers back home over the Fourth of July?"

"What about her?" Nate replied. The abrupt mention of the little goddess had taken him by surprise.

"Well, we just got the news reports."

"Yeah . . . and . . . ?"

"Y'know that rocket bomb that hit New York?"

"And . . ." Nate's eyes had glazed over.

"Seems that she was right there," Cunningham said matter-of-factly. "She's was killed."

"She's . . . dead?" Nate whispered.

"Yeah," Cunningham said casually. "Apparently the whole side of a building came down. The death toll is now over two thousand people. That reporter was one of 'em. Damned shame, huh?"

Nate was speechless. Those goddam bastards. The faces of all the friends that he'd lost in two wars came back to him. There was something extra about the guys at Kummersdorf, who got it in cold blood—and now the thought that his gentle little goddess with the dancing freckles and smiling face had died in a pile of falling masonry tore his guts out.

"Are you all right?" He heard Cunningham's voice. It seemed far, far away. He could see the press officer's face, but it was blurry and out of focus. "You look sick."

"Yeah," Nate replied. "Something I ate."

Nate blinked his eyes. He could actually feel tears starting to well up. For him, the war against Stalin had now turned very, *very* personal.

Henry Stimson's Georgetown townhouse
Washington DC
Saturday, July 7, 1945, 11:57 p.m.

The Secretary of War sat at his desk in his bathrobe. He couldn't sleep. He had tried warm milk. He had even tried two fingers of bourbon. He had tried rereading some terribly boring logistics reports. Nothing worked. His mind kept racing back to how Josef Vissarionovich Dzhugashvili Stalin had helped the United States celebrate the Fourth of July.

Every time Stimson closed his eyes he saw that horrible view of New York from the *Sacred Cow*. He recalled the New York City that he'd known for so many years. He recalled when the RCA Building had been constructed. He recalled a time when what had just happened would have been inconceivable. Every time Stimson closed his eyes he saw the blackened destruction and his mind wandered to the images of the newspaper photos. The death toll was worse than Pearl Harbor and it was nearly all civilians.

A second salvo on Friday had been aimed at Boston. They had missed, but only slightly. One had impacted in Boston Harbor and another had killed nineteen people in Quincy. This attack had served to demonstrate that the first attacks were not an anomaly. The Reds could fire at will. It was a repeat of the London blitz in 1940, except that this time, there was nothing that could stop the attackers.

Stimson did know that the Ninth Air Force in Europe was devoting all of its resources to finding the launch sites, but he also knew—better than most—that they were coming up empty. The Eighth Air Force heavy bombers had pounded the suspected rocket factories for two days running, but still a second attack had come.

Stalin had attacked New York and Boston, but Moscow remained untouched. General LeMay's B-29s, which had been earmarked for the first attack on Moscow, had been held back because of weather over the Baltic and northern Russia.

Perhaps more than at any time since Pearl Harbor, the American people were afraid. They were defenseless against the attacks and they were scared. After the New York attack, the people of the Northeast had been numb. After Boston, they panicked. Thousands of people were leaving both cities—and populated areas as far south as Philadelphia. They were going to live with friends in "safe" parts of the country, but nobody could tell them for sure where it was *really* safe.

It was the top of the hour, so Stimson decided to tune in the BBC news on his shortwave radio. He closed the door to his study so that he wouldn't awaken Mabel, and began fiddling with the dials.

As the news began with the familiar peal of Big Ben, Stimson wondered whether it too, was on Stalin's target list.

As if reading Stimson's mind, the top story was a statement from Stalin himself, the first since Patton had decimated his armies in southern Germany.

"Today a new dawn is breaking over all of Europe," Stalin had said in the statement issued in his name. "Today a Red Dawn is breaking over all of Europe. Today, the victorious armies of the Soviet people are on the verge of crushing the last vestiges of capitalism and imperialism in Europe. Soon, the Red flag of the people's emancipation from slavery will fly in every capital of Europe. Soon, the great Eurasian landmass from the shores of the Atlantic to the shores of the Pacific will be governed by the people. Already, the armed forces of the Soviet Union have taken the war across the Atlantic to the homeland of capitalist oppression."

Stimson cringed at the thought of listening to *this* in his own home. He was a former Wall Street attorney. He supposed this made him a capitalist.

The news reader had gone on to other items and Stimson's attention drifted until there was an interruption for a bulletin.

"This just in. It has been announced by the American air forces that approximately two hundred fifty Super Fortress bombers of the Twentieth Air Force have just successfully conducted the first bombing attack on the city of Moscow. This attack occurred at four o'clock this morning, Greenwich Mean Time. The announcement was made by General James Doolittle, who compared it to his own attack on Tokyo, which took place on 18 April in 1942. 'This is just the first of many,' the General is quoted as saying. To repeat, American Super Fortress aircraft have successfully attacked Moscow."

Stimson drained the last drop of bourbon from his glass, shut off his radio and his lamp, and went to bed.

Wilhelmstrasse
Berlin, Germany
Friday, July 13, 1945, 7:16 a.m.

"We're damned near three months late, but by God we're here!" General George Patton said, looking around at the devastated heart of Hitler's Thousand-Year Reich. "It's Friday the thirteenth, and that sonuvabitch Georgie Patton's in Berlin. Not very damned lucky for Joe Stalin . . . We could've been here in April, and we *should've* been here in April."

A long line of American tanks and vehicles were streaming into the city along the broad boulevard named for Germany's last Kaiser. Patton's jeep was in the vanguard.

"It went a lot smoother for us this week than it did for the Russians in April," Nate observed as he drove Patton's jeep north on the broad boulevard at the head of a long column of American vehicles. "It took them two weeks of unbelievable fighting. We've done it in five days."

"With farther to go." Patton grinned. "We had over a hundred miles. They barely had twenty-five. Of course, the Krauts had a year to dig in and get ready. The Russians hardly knew we were coming." The General had begun his Berlin campaign three days earlier than planned, but he'd been ready. He planned to go Wednesday, but Zhukov had resumed his drive toward the West on Sunday, so Patton immediately put his plan into action.

His opening gambit had been to use General Jim Van Fleet's III Corps to envelop the remnants of Tolbukhin's 3rd Ukrainian Front in Dresden. Van Fleet had circled wide onto Tolbukhin's right flank, hitting him from the north instead of the west as he'd expected. With that situation in hand, the Third Army had plowed north and east from Leipzig, cutting through the Russian supply lines and driving into Berlin before General Lyudnikov's 39th Army could organize a coherent defense.

While Third Army was advancing against Berlin, the American Seventh Army was *retreating* from Ivan Koniev's 1st Ukrainian Front near Frankfurt. As Patton had predicted, Koniev's Sunday attack in the Rhineland was timed to begin as Zhukov struck in the North.

Koniev had hoped to encircle Frankfurt, knock Seventh Army out of the war and cut Third Army's supply lines—while other Allied forces were tied up elsewhere. Koniev always felt that Stalin had favored Zhukov over him. This was a chance for Koniev to prove himself.

During the early part of the week, as General Sandy Patch was "retreating" with his Seventh Army, it appeared—especially to Koniev—that the Americans were being routed. Of course, the capricious Patton had no intention of attacking Koniev in a frontal assault with Seventh Army. As Koniev smelled success and pressed his luck, he was actually dashing into a monstrous trap. All of the coordinates for these roads over which Koniev was chasing Patch had been duly plotted as "kill boxes" for the Fifteenth Air Force. Patton, meanwhile, had quietly infiltrated General Truscott's Fifth Army from Italy and Austria north to Erfurt, which Third Army had captured on June 10. Using Erfurt as a back door into Koniev's left flank, Fifth Army punched into Koniev's rear. They overran his supply dumps and attacked him where his best units were *not*. They were overextended toward the south chasing Seventh Army.

After successfully beating the Germans from Moscow to Krakow to Berlin, Koniev was in the fight of his life. He'd laughed at poor Sandy Patch's "retreat." Now he had to withdraw himself and turn his front around 180 degrees. He desperately wanted to move General Katukov's 1st Guards Tank Army to the north to face Truscott, but they were on the opposite side of a pocket and they had to fight their way through Soviet traffic going in the opposite direction.

It wasn't their lucky day—nor was it Koniev's.

Now, on Friday the thirteenth, Patton's Lucky Forward was in Berlin, and at least three days sooner than anyone—even the General himself—had expected.

Patton pointed out a sign that read, "Welcome to Berlin, courtesy of the 10th Armored Division," and grinned broadly.

The XX Corps armored divisions had spearheaded the Third Army's blitzkrieg dash into the capital. General William H.H. Morris's 10th Armored drove straight in from the south through Lichterfelde and Mariendorf to seize the huge airfield at Tempelhof. Meanwhile, the 12th and 9th Armored Divisions had gone west through Potsdam and Wannsee to capture the bridges across the River Havel at Spandau. This effectively cut the Soviet garrison in Berlin off from the bulk of the Red Army, which had moved west to support Zhukov.

The armored divisions acted as shock troops, hitting hard and fast with concentrated firepower. The Russians had not expected Berlin to be attacked so soon—and especially not from the *south*. There were only hastily improvised defensive positions.

Because the overall Soviet battle plan depended on supporting Zhukov's huge offensive toward the west, there was no armor and virtually no artillery with which to counterattack against the Americans.

When most of the enemy resistance around Tempelhof was eliminated, the 10th Armored continued north into the heart of the city, following the same route by which Patton was now having his first look at his new conquest. The 1st Infantry Division then secured the big airport for the waves of C-47 troop carriers that brought in two airborne divisions, the American 101st and the British 6th. Both veterans of the Normandy Invasion thirteen months earlier, they'd flown in from their staging bases—just an hour north in Denmark—to landings that were a great deal more hospitable than what they'd endured in the wee hours of June 6, 1944.

Recalling his last drive down the wide boulevards of a major European capital, Nate found the differences and the similarities striking. Like Paris, Berlin was a vast, sprawling metropolis. They had been on city streets for nearly an hour before they finally reached Tempelhof, and the center of the city was farther yet. Unlike Paris, which was relatively untouched by the war, Berlin was a sea of almost total devastation. The ravages of American bombs and Soviet artillery had made much of it almost unrecognizable as a place where people had ever lived civilized lives. Nate had seen this before in smaller cities across Germany, but in Berlin, it went on for blocks and blocks, for miles and miles.

The people, too, appeared devastated. As they stood along the Wilhelmstrasse to watch the Americans enter their capital, the Berliners stared like manikins with expressionless faces. A few years ago, they had stood here watching Hitler's legions going off to triumph after triumph. Now, in the space of a few weeks, they'd seen Hitler's former capital captured by two conquering armies. No wonder they looked shell-shocked.

Ahead and to the left, Nate could see the Brandenberg Gate, which was about the only recognizable landmark remaining. It was huge and impressive, yet horribly forlorn. The quadriga, the statue of the four-horse chariot that stood atop the gate, was bent and battered. Its two rows of six huge columns looked like tall straight pines that had come through a forest fire. They were charred and blackened, and pocked with hits from every caliber of small-arms fire imaginable. Except for their even spacing, the columns were not readily recognizable as having been carved by human hands.

"Turn here," Patton directed when they had reached the large plaza lay before the gate. "Park as close to it as you can. Remember that arch in Paris? This is the Prussian version. They copied it after the Propylaea in Athens. Napoleon saw it and liked it. Now here we are . . . following him across Europe. Next stop . . . Well, it'll be a *long* road from here to Moscow."

Nate had seen an occasional red flag still hanging here or there since they had reached the center of Berlin, but at the gate, the red had been replaced by the red, white, and blue. There were American and British flags, as well as those of France and Poland.

Allied troops were everywhere—huge crowds of them. They were mostly Americans with a few British paratroopers here or there. Many were perched on tops of tanks to have a better view. As Patton appeared in the square, there were cheers and the occasional rebel yell. Nate saw a small number of Polish uniforms among the officers that were milling around on a sort of platform that was directly ahead of the gate.

As Nate brought the jeep to a stop, all eyes were on Patton. When the General stepped out, the officers snapped to attention and the troops cheered. The large group of photographers who were on hand began to snap pictures. Flash bulbs popped. People in the crowd craned their necks to get a better view.

Patton returned the salutes and plunged into the group of officers, followed by his staff officers. From his vantage point, Nate guessed that there might have been ten thousand people swarming around the huge monument to Prussian militarism to watch the man who had become synonymous with American militarism.

Most people recognized Lieutenant General Walton Walker, the commander of XX Corps, as he stepped up to a microphone, tapped it gently with a gloved hand, took a deep breath, and began to speak.

"I've been with General George Patton through some of the toughest fights that either of us could have ever imagined . . . but I never thought I'd ever be the one who'd have to stand up here before the troops . . . to announce that he's being *replaced* as commanding officer of Third Army."

One immense gasp of disbelief spread across the crowd. There were shouts of "No!" and scattered boos. Those close to the front saw, however, that both Walker and Patton were grinning.

"I've been authorized by the President of the United States to present your new Supreme Allied Commander in Europe . . . and the US Army's newest five-star general."

The pause of disbelief gave way to a single immense ovation as Walker handed Patton the box that Truman had presented two weeks earlier.

"I'd like to dedicate today's victory to a man who couldn't be here with us," Patton said in his squeaky voice as the cheering finally died down. "I'd like to dedicate this day and the conquest of this city to the man whose boots I'm expected to fill. One of General Eisenhower's fondest dreams was a victory parade through the streets of this city."

At the mention of Eisenhower's name, there was a round of cheering and the officers on the platform were seen applauding.

"Circumstances contrived to prevent his wish from being fulfilled. The politicians wouldn't let Ike take this city . . . I'm not supposed to say bad things about the politicians, am I? I apologize in advance . . . I guess I owe this job to a politician . . ."

There was a round of laughter from the crowd and smiles on the faces of the officers. These men were all line officers, so they understood.

"Ike dreamed of a victory parade . . . Dammit, we *all* wanted one. But *we* didn't take Berlin. By prior arrangement, that honor went to Marshal Georgie Zhukov. The only way that Ike could get a parade in this city was to ask that bastard for *permission* to have his victory parade. He asked for permission . . . He never got it. Today, we finally got that American victory parade in Berlin, and I wish Ike could have been here to see it!"

The applause was much, much louder this time.

When it had died down, Patton continued.

"Ike didn't have permission from Marshal Georgie Zhukov . . . and then, today, that impudent sonuvabitch, Georgie Patton *forgot* to ask Georgie Zhukov for permission!"

The applause was practically deafening. Everyone was grinning at the General's sarcasm.

"Now it's *my* turn to decide that Georgie Zhukov does *not* have permission to be in Belgium or Holland or France. He does *not* have permission to be in *Germany!* It's my job . . . your job . . . *our* job . . . to see that he get's that damned message loud and clear!"

The applause was deafening.

The White House
Washington DC
Monday, July 16, 1945, 11:45 a.m.

"The surgery took place this morning . . . Patient did not respond. Diagnosis incomplete, but Dr. Groves hopes to reschedule the operation. Will keep you posted."

The Secretary of War stood in the middle of the President's office reading from a teletype.

"What happened?" Harry Truman asked.

"The weapon failed to detonate," Henry Stimson explained. "They didn't achieve their symmetrical implosion. Groves will try again. Nobody knows when."

"I can hear Admiral Leahy's voice saying 'I told you so' from here," the President said grimly.

"Maybe he's been right," Stimson said, wishing that there was something he could say to put a positive spin on the day's bad news.

"Only a handful of us know what happened in that desert out there today," Stimson continued. "The world didn't change. It'll be the same tomorrow as it was yesterday. For most of the world, nothing happened today in that desert and nothing significant was *supposed* to happen. Maybe, it should . . . maybe it's better just left that way."

"Only a handful of us know what was supposed to happen,"

Truman replied. "And I'm willing to wager that Joe Stalin is . . . or will be . . . one of those who knows that it *didn't* happen."

For a moment, the two men just stood there. The President had his back to Stimson as he stood looking out across the South Lawn toward the Washington Monument on the distant hill beyond. It was another hot and muggy day in Washington, but the dark storm clouds made the scene appear cold and foreboding.

"One wonders what Stalin must be thinking at this moment," Truman continued. "One wonders where *his* scientists are with *their* surgery."

"They never found Fuchs," Stimson said solemnly.

"We'll have to assume the worst, I suppose," Truman said, staring out the window. "What's being done on the other end to stop these dreadful things?"

"The Air Force plastered the area where they think it came from, but they probably use mobile launchers like they did with V2s," Stimson said. "Patton has forces that will be closing in on that part of Germany, but in the best case, it's going to be a couple of weeks. His main focus now, of course, is the coming battle with Zhukov's combined armies. This'll be the most decisive battle in Europe since Normandy."

"Is he ready for it?"

"If anyone *can* be. Say your prayers."

"I say my prayers for the thousands of young men who won't live to see the end of that battle, nor the end of the coming battle with Japan. Three quarters of the one million American casualties that we've suffered in World War II have come since June of last year. They're predicting another two million before the world is finally at peace from both wars."

"It's a sobering thought," Stimson agreed.

"That's why your news from New Mexico is so terribly, terribly disappointing," Truman said. "I suppose every leader in every war has yearned desperately for that single, decisive *something*. Certainly, if you read about Lincoln, you can *feel* his agony. You can read it in his words at Gettysburg. If today's test had been successful, it might have changed history. Stalin would have found out. Just the threat of it might have been enough."

"Unless he has one of his own," Stimson cautioned. "Then you'll have an atomic stalemate . . . unless he feels that he can attack us and survive."

"Survive." The President pondered the word, seeming to turn it over and examine it in his mind. "That's something that nobody in this house has had to think about since Lincoln watched the smoke from the fires across those hills in Virginia."

"We should probably be planning to face that eventuality," Stimson said. "If rockets start falling on Washington, we need a plan to get you and other key leaders to a safe place . . . or at least into a shelter."

"Where *is* a safe place?" Truman asked. "I could get into a car and be most of the way to Harper's Ferry in an hour . . . but what if it missed Washington and hit Harper's Ferry? We don't even know they have the range to hit Washington."

"At the very least, we should get you into a shelter," Stimson said hopefully. "The one across the way at the State Department would protect you from anything but a direct hit."

"That would be ironic, wouldn't it?" Truman said with a half smile.

"What's ironic?"

"If I were to be killed by a direct hit in that bomb shelter. I led one of the nations who beat Hitler, and then it's *me* who dies while cowering . . . in a *bunker*."

12

* *

Combined Soviet Armies Command Post
Nonnenstein Ridge
East of Osnabruck, Germany
Sunday, July 22, 1945, 1:25 p.m.

THREE times decorated as a Hero of the Soviet Union, Marshal of the Soviet Union Georgi Konstantinovich Zhukov commanded the largest geographically contiguous land army in Europe. He repeated this fact in his mind as he stood on a low bluff watching the T34s of General Volsky's 5th Guards Tank Army roll eastward from Osnabruck on the main autobahn that ran between the Dutch border and Berlin.

Zhukov's vast command spread from Koniev's 1st Ukrainian Front in the south to Vasilievsky's 3rd Byelorussian Front in the north and included the 1st and 2nd Byelorussian Front that he and Marshal Rokossovsky has just relocated here to Osnabrock from northern France.

The beefy, forty-eight-year-old marshal was also the supreme commander of *all* Red Army forces. His power was second only to Stalin himself. When the Great Patriotic War had begun with Hitler's invasion—four years and exactly one month earlier—Zhukov had directed the defense of Leningrad, which won him Stalin's favor and an opportunity to organize the defense of Moscow. When this also was successful, he became first deputy commander of Soviet armed forces—and one of the most trusted military advisors to a man who trusted *nobody*—Stalin.

In 1943, Zhukov had planned and directed the encirclement of Germany's Sixth Army at Stalingrad and the great

Soviet victory at Kursk. In 1945, he took personal command of Soviet forces in the final triumph in Berlin.

Two days after the fall of Hitler's capital, Zhukov was summoned to the Kremlin to receive his next assignment. He found Stalin almost giddy with excitement. In previous meetings, the Man of Steel had been a dark and brooding figure. To find him almost effervescent was a change. Zhukov was surprised by Stalin's mood, but absolutely shocked by the ambitious dimensions of his new plan. Stalin explained that the battle-hardened Red Army was now the largest in world history—but with every single day that passed, this inactive behemoth would grow weaker. Now, Stalin had insisted, was the time to conquer the *world*—under the banner of the Comintern, of course.

Stalin must have been planning this for years. He saw it as a natural continuation of the Great Patriotic War. Zhukov realized that simply conquering Europe would stretch the limits of the Red Army—but Stalin insisted that communist uprisings would pave the way. Zhukov also realized that one does not say "no" to Josef Stalin, so he agreed to help him plan the details.

As usual, they did much of their work at night. Stalin was a nocturnal creature, often sleeping until late in the afternoon and rarely hitting his stride before midnight. They would often work alone, with no one else but Commissar Molotov in the room—and he usually sat quietly in the shadows, chainsmoking filterless cigarettes.

When Zhukov had launched the great offensive on May 29, it had gone better than he had any reason to hope. The Americans and British had folded and collapsed like toy soldiers. Koniev had pushed them across the Rhine, while Zhukov and Rokossovsky raced to the French border. Things had gone well. The Red Army had moved so quickly that lead units had outrun their supplies. Many of his troops were complaining of the fever, and he didn't have all the medical niceties with which to treat them. Zhukov had to call a halt. If he'd had the supplies, he could have—*would have*—been in Paris by the middle of June.

This muggy, overcast afternoon, Zhukov had command of more than three million men on the ground, organized into more than thirty field armies, each of them about the size of an Anglo-American corps. He had more than six thousand T34 tanks—many of them with 85 mm guns—and more than a thousand of the new Josef Stalin tanks, some of which mounted 122 mm guns.

Because they now occupied the lush farmlands of Belgium and Holland, the soldiers of the 1st Byelorussian Front and the 2nd Byelorussian Front had been better fed than at any time since the beginning of the Great Patriotic War—but fuel, ammunition, and antibiotics had run dangerously low. Building up the stocks needed for the push into France had been Zhukov's biggest headache. Germany's rail network was in shambles. In fact, thanks to the United States Eighth Air Force, most of it had ceased to exist.

Without the trains, supplies had to move either by truck or by horse-drawn wagon. Without American lend-lease supplies and adequate maintenance, the Soviet armada of Studebaker trucks was rapidly becoming unreliable.

The Americans had achieved air superiority over Europe, so both trucks and wagons were vulnerable from the air, and were forced to operate only at night. The thousand-mile supply line across two defeated nations filled with hostile civilians— Poland as well as Germany—became a nightmare. Zhukov was compelled to divert troops that he'd wanted for the Battle of France to escort duty.

When Patton had scored his unexpected victories over Yeremenko and Tolbukhin, Stalin had been livid. He demanded that Zhukov defeat Patton at once, but Zhukov had insisted they stick to the original plan. Zhukov was certain that, once they resumed the attack on the Northern Front, he and Rokossovsky could take Paris and all of France easily and quickly. After all, Bradley and Montgomery were demoralized and the Red Army was vastly larger than the German Army had been in 1940— when *they* had gotten the job done in a month.

It hadn't been easy, but Zhukov finally managed to convince Stalin that Koniev and Malinovsky could keep Patton in check until France had fallen.

After two postponements, the Battle of France was finally under way on July 8. Zhukov had planned to do here as he had at Berlin: to follow a withering barrage of artillery fire— across a one-hundred-fifty-mile front—with an overwhelming tank attack. The terrain of northwestern France reminded him of the plains of Byelorussia. It was perfect for massed armor, and massed armor was Georgi Zhukov's weapon of choice.

Zhukov would personally command five elite armies, with four more in reserve. Rokossovsky would be to his right flank—the coastline from Ostend to Dunkirk and Calais—with six armies. Marshal Vasilievsky would be right behind with the 2nd and 11th Guards Armies, ready to exploit the opening that would be blasted in the Allied lines.

While Rokossovsky sent the 2nd Shock Army racing through Allied lines toward the Channel ports, Zhukov turned the 1st and 2nd Guards Tank Armies loose on General Courtney Hodges's US First Army at Mons. The Germans had put the British on the run here in 1914 in one of the biggest routs ever suffered by the British Army. Zhukov would move quickly and brutally and do the same.

Zhukov threw his 3rd Shock Army at the Canadian First Army and his 5th Shock at the French First Army at Lille. He had expected the shock troops to drive a wedge between Hodges in the east and the British Eighth Army on the coast. It hadn't worked.

At the end of the first day, Rokossovsky had taken the Channel ports, but the French still held Lille, and Hodges was battering both of Zhukov's prized Guards Tank Armies.

Zhukov had awakened the following day to the incredible—Patton was slicing through his rear, through his vital supply lines. Zhukov had screamed that Patton was insane, but he had quickly realized that Patton was virtually unopposed and Koniev was suddenly under attack from two sides. All of Zhukov's enormous strength was three hundred miles away and pointed in the *wrong direction!*

Where was Malinovsky? Zhukov discovered that Stalin had known about the Ukrainian defection for a week and hadn't informed his field commander. Zhukov was angry—but getting angry at the Man of Steel was pointless.

When Patton rolled into Berlin, it was Stalin's turn to be angry. The whole point of the Great Patriotic War, Stalin explained in a seething wireless message, was to put the Red Army in control of Hitler's capital *forever*. Now, the Americans had snatched it like a crow steals a bauble.

Stalin's directive was simple: Recapture Berlin. *Forget Paris; recapture Berlin.*

Of course, Zhukov knew that Stalin was right—for the wrong reasons, but right. Stalin saw Berlin as his prize. Zhukov saw it as the key to his supply lines. Even with the lines cut, Zhukov estimated that the Red Army had sufficient supplies to finish the Paris campaign. However, he calculated that there would not be sufficient stockpiles to then retake Berlin, *and* the Allies would have had longer to fortify Berlin and to have been resupplied themselves.

It took a week for Zhukov to stabilize his Western Front and to move his elite forces back across Belgium and Holland. With Allied airpower attacking his bridges, the move had also been costly for Zhukov. But he'd done it.

Now, he would smash the impudent Patton with the largest land army in Europe. The Battle of Osnabruck would be the largest battle in European history.

The Soviet vanguard would be Marshal Volsky's 5th Guards Tank Army from Rokossovsky's command. They would take the autobahn route to hit the Americans head on with a mass of armor—a steel hammer—while the balance of the Soviet forces would pivot on their position at Osnabruck and swing like a scythe around the left flank to crush the enemy. Zhukov grinned. It was to be a *hammer and sickle!*

The 1st Guards Tank Army under General Katukov and the 2nd Guards Tank Army commanded by General Bogdanov were already being positioned north and east of Osnabruck in the direction of Belm. They would be the fast-moving, mobile tip of the sickle.

Between Katukov and Volsky would be an array of armor, infantry, and shock troops that was being positioned on the high ground of Nonnenstein Ridge, the range of hills about forty miles north of the Berlin autobahn that ran roughly parallel with the sickle.

General Simonyak's 3rd Shock Army was in place here, and Chuikov's 8th Guards Army was ready, backed by General Perkhorovich's 47th Army. General Berzarin's 5th Shock Army and Belov's 61st Army would be ready to pour through behind Bogdanov. In reserve, Zhukov would have Feduninsky's 2nd

Shock Army ready to go in wherever an opening needed to be exploited.

Overhead, a large fleet of Sturmoviks would be flying from the former Luftwaffe interceptor bases south and west of Enschede in Holland. The Allies hadn't touched these fields, and Zhukov had been assured that their jet fighters didn't have the combat radius to operate this far east of their bases in France. There would probably be American P-51s in the air, but Zhukov could match these with Yaks.

As twilight came, Marshals Rokossovsky and Zhukov stood atop the ridge looking across the gently rolling farmland lying so pastoral and serene. Twice in two months, invading armies had pursued retreating armies across this area. In early April, the United States XIII Corps had chased Germans though here. Two months later, it was the turn of Zhukov himself to oust the Yanks. Both times, the armies sped through, largely sparing this idyllic land the horrors of modern war. Tomorrow would be different.

By the light of a gas lantern, the two marshals studied the maps that showed the swath that would be cut by the sickle. With their artillery on the high ground of the ridge, the Soviets would begin by pounding the distant American positions—some of which were still visible in the fading light. Then, and only then, would the sickle begin to slash.

The tank armies would roll down from the ridge and Berzarin's shock troops would slice into the middle of the American line. They would inflict a deep wound into which Belov's 61st Army would flow. On the Berlin autobahn, the hammer of General Volsky's 5th Guards Tank Army would crush the Americans, capturing both Melle and Bunde.

As he thought of his tanks moving back in the direction of Berlin, Georgi Zhukov counted his blessings. Even if Koniev was taking a beating, and the attack to the West was stalled, Zhukov still commanded the largest contiguous land army in Europe. They were his best and they were at the apogee of their fighting form and they greatly outnumbered the Americans.

Best of all, Zhukov now had a chance to fight a decisive battle against the magnificent Patton, the foremost field commander that the Allies had in Europe. Zhukov had seen "foremost field commanders" before. He had taken on the most magnificent field commanders in the vaunted Wehrmacht. Where were they now? Dead, defeated, or languishing in jail!

Patton was outnumbered, just like Von Paulus at Stalingrad. It had been a terrible blow to German morale when his entire Sixth Army simply disappeared into prison camps. Zhukov could easily imagine what a blow to Allied morale it would be when America's Third Army was crushed—and Patton himself was led through the streets of Moscow *in chains*.

Georgi Zhukov smiled. This was going to make the Man of Steel *very* happy.

Lucky Forward
Southwest of Melle (Between Minden and Osnabruck), Germany
Sunday, July 22, 1945, 4:15 p.m.

"They know you're here," Brigadier General Oscar Koch said, staring at the huge map with Patton and Third Army commander Walton Walker. "They're reinforcing Osnabruck and bringing in whole armies. This looks like it's going to be the place."

The American theater commander had taken over a large, abandoned farmhouse that was on a low hill just south of the autobahn that ran from Osnabruck to Minden and on to Berlin. It was here that he would plan the biggest battle of the war, a war that no one could get used to calling—as the newspapers at home did—World War III.

"If this is where Zhukov wants his showdown, then dammit, let the bastard come get us," Patton said firmly. "I've said it before. The Third Army fighting man is worth twenty of theirs."

Though Third Army was now commanded by his protege, Walton Walker, Patton still thought of it as his army, his teacher's pet among the dozen armies in the multinational coalition that he now commanded at SHAEF. It would be his spearhead in the coming million-man battle against Stalin's teacher's pet. For the moment, Third Army was indeed in the strategic forefront. If Zhukov was to retake Berlin and reopen his supply lines, he would have to pass where Third Army now stood.

Zhukov had underestimated Patton's boldness and left Berlin and his rear lightly defended. Patton had won that round of the fight. He'd outflanked Zhukov. His primary enemy for these past fourteen days, however, was not so much Zhukov's rear guard, but the clock. He'd raced to gobble as much of northern Germany as he could before Zhukov began turning on him with a larger force.

With help from airborne troops and the British Second Army, Patton's blitzkrieg captured Hamburg as planned, but Vasilievsky had reinforced his 38th Army on the Bremen salient as Patton swung south in order to outflank Soviet positions within the city.

General Eichelberger's American Eighth Army had landed in Hamburg on Friday, bringing with it General John R. Hodge's XXIV Corps. They were veterans of the Okinawa fight who had been transferred from General Simon Bolivar Buckner's Tenth Army. Patton had attached this corps to Third Army, while Eighth Army and the British Second moved to encircle Bremen from the north and east.

Patton knew that he would have to face Zhukov with the Third Army sooner or later—and now was that time. He knew that even with Hodge's corps attached, Third Army was outnumbered five to four. It was in Zhukov's interest to strike quickly before Patton could grow stronger.

On Saturday, the Third Army vanguard passed through Minden, which had been burned and abandoned by Vasilievsky's 3rd Byelorussian troops. They'd pulled out to reinforce Osnabruck and wait for Zhukov. Most German civilians who remained in Minden were afraid to go into the streets, but those who remained told horrible stories about the Soviet occupation.

Patton might have reinforced Minden to await Zhukov's attack, but defense was a word that Patton rarely used. To him, the only applicable strategy was *attack*. The decisive battle would occur somewhere in those fifty miles between Minden and Osnabruck with Third Army in motion.

On the autobahn, the Third Army vanguard would be XX Corps, which had already moved into position in the towns of Bunde and Melle. The latter was just twenty miles from Osnabruck. XX Corps was now commanded by General William

H.H. Morris, who moved up from the 10th Armored Division after Walker took over Third Army. Both of the XX Corps armored divisions were fully equipped with the big, fast M26A2 Pershing tanks. These tanks, which could outmaneuver the Russian Stalin tanks, also equipped the armored regiments assigned to two of XX Corps's three infantry outfits, Harry Maloney's 94th Infantry Division and Stanley Reinhart's 65th Infantry Division.

Backing Morris would be two full corps: V Corps, commanded by General Ralph Huebner, with five divisions, including General Clift Andrus's Big Red 1 and General John Pierce's 16th Armored; as well as General Raymond McLain's XIX Corps. Borrowed from Ninth Army, XIX Corps included General I.D. White's 2nd "Hell on Wheels" Armored Division—a unit which had distinguished itself during the 1941 maneuvers when it was commanded by a Major General named George Smith Patton, Jr.

Like Zhukov, Patton had arrayed his forces in the wide, flat fields north of the autobahn. On the right flank of the XX Corps spearhead would be General Leroy Irwin's veteran XII Corps with General Willard Paul's 26th Infantry Division, General Herbert Earnest's 90th Infantry Division and two armored divisions, General Holmes Dagar's 11th and General Hugh Gaffey's 4th Armored Division.

General Jim Van Fleet, whose III Corps approached Minden from Petershagen to the north, would deploy onto the XII Corps right flank without actually passing through Minden. Van Fleet had four infantry divisions, including the newly formed 112th and the mobility of two armored divisions, including General Albert Smith's veteran 14th, which had sizable numbers of M26A2s.

John R. Hodge's XXIV Corps, with Jim Bradley's Okinawa-seasoned 96th "Deadeye" Infantry Division, would form the reserve. To this corps, Patton attached John Leonard's 9th Armored Division, which had been the original Third Army division to equip with M26 tanks.

As the sun, a pale white orb behind the clouds, sank low in the west, more than a million men prepared to do battle across hundreds of square miles of the North German Plain.

In the balance lay the future of Europe.

Lucky Forward
Southwest of Melle, Germany
Monday, July 23, 1945, 6:05 a.m.

The smell of coffee and cigarettes hung in the air and a perceptible electricity was everywhere. There was a pervasive feeling among the scores of men crowded into these rooms that today was the most important of their military careers.

Nate McKinley had been up for nearly an hour before the General had made his appearance just after five, but even then, the rooms on the lower floor of the huge farmhouse had been a hum of activity. Units had been on the move through the night, changing and shifting position according to a carefully choreographed blueprint, so that the Soviets who had observed them at sundown would not be aware of their positions at daybreak.

The Air Force liaison people with the winged shoulder patches and headsets were chattering into their radios and taking notes. Elsewhere, the shoulders of the men working in the room were a crazy quilt of insignia. Every corps and division that would be part of today's operation was represented by someone in direct communication with his home command post. General Walker had positioned his own desk at the center of the largest room with a clear view of a large map spread across one wall.

Crowded into a sitting room at the corner of the building, a G2 team operating on an American frequency that the Russians were known to be monitoring, pretended to represent the various divisions involved in fictitious operations—including a *withdrawal* by XX Corps from their forward position. According to the radio traffic being offered to the Soviets, XX Corps had been ordered by General Walker to withdraw to Minden for "reasons of safety."

From the outside, the farmhouse looked like little more than just a farmhouse. Dressed for the eyes of Russian aircraft overhead, it was not encircled by crowds of vehicles nor the obvious accoutrements of a massive communications center. Patton had picked this building because it was dark-colored and located at the edge of an oak forest—hence hard to notice from the air. The oak trees that were close to the building now had antennas among their branches, and the large barn about a hundred yards away—and barely visible in the fog—held more than a dozen jeeps, including Walker's four-star jeep and Patton's with the ring of five. A nearby creamery had been converted as a large field hospital. Under trees farther away and not visible in the fog was a ring of antiaircraft batteries that would help to protect Lucky Forward from Sturmoviks.

General Otto Weyland, the "air boss" for the operation, would be airborne in a B-17 outfitted as a flying command post. Protected by P-51s flying in rotating shifts out of the old Luftwaffe base near Hamburg, he and General Halley Maddox—Patton's operations officer—would be watching the real battlefield as though it were a map and coordinating operations with Lucky Forward and with the archipelago of Allied air bases that would be involved.

Since Jena, Maddox had developed an extensive radio protocol procedure that completely integrated air and ground operations. Communication was completely meshed, and reaction times faster and more direct.

At the moment, however, Weyland's Flying Fortress remained ground-bound in Hamburg—a deep and opaque fog hung across the North German Plain. It hadn't been so apparent when Nate first got up, but now, as it was becoming more light, the thick grey blanket that hung around Lucky Forward was very obvious. He remembered the thick fog to which Lucky Forward had awakened on the Landgraftenberg on that morning before the Battle of Jena. He hoped that this was a good omen.

Nate knew that the Allies were way ahead of the Russians with radar, and this helped planes flying against other planes, but he also knew that radar was pretty much worthless for helping tanks see where they were going down here on the ground. It was going to be the blind fighting the blind. Somebody had made a joke that if the fog didn't lift, the Reds would end up in Minden and the Yanks in Osnabruck, without either side seeing the other.

In the distance, Nate heard the thundering sound of artillery and glanced at his watch. It was 0630. The games had begun.

The inside of the command post looked like a newsreel that he'd once seen of the trading floor of the New York Stock

Exchange. General Walker had a radio handset on each ear as he looked at the big map on the wall. Blue arrows were being drawn in the direction of Nonnenstein Ridge from the American center. The main ·attack against the ridge had been launched by two divisions of Irwin's XII Corps, the 4th and 11th Armored Divisions.

Nate always felt strange standing around watching during operations like this. All through the winter, when he'd been in the line, he'd been taking the brunt of every battle that the 27th Armored Infantry had gotten into. Now, it seemed as though the only time he *wasn't* working was when there was a battle going on. When Patton was at Lucky Forward, he didn't need to be driven, so the only thing for the driver to do was hurry up and wait.

The change made Nate feel a tinge of guilt. He was a soldier. He'd been trained to fight, not to sit around through the middle of a battle. He thought of the other guys out there in the infantry battalions, creeping through the dense fog, taking fire, returning fire, growing numb and cold and getting hit.

For Nate, it was just hurry up and wait.

Combined Soviet Armies Command Post
Nonnenstein Ridge
East of Osnabruck, Germany
Monday, July 23, 1945, 6:58 a.m.

Marshal Zhukov had gone to sleep with the advantage of the high ground, but had awakened to find it obviated by the dense ground fog. But he wasn't worried. He had a plan—and a damned good one. The Americans gave a great deal of discretion to their individual commanders. As far as Zhukov could see, this would only lead to chaos—especially in the fog.

Soviet armies operated according to carefully orchestrated plans. Everyone knew what to do. If everything went according to the plan and everyone followed orders, there could be no losing a battle. It worked at Kursk and in battle after battle after battle ever since. The present stalemate in the West notwithstanding, Zhukov hadn't lost a fight since the great reversals of fortune in the Great Patriotic War back in 1943.

The Americans started shooting first—an artillery barrage directed at the center of the line in the 47th Army sector. According to reports, it had been accurate, but weak. Of course, it would be met by the answering voice of thousands of Soviet guns and thousands of katyusha rocket launchers.

Now, the thunder of the distant artillery was being drowned out by the thunder of diesel engines as Katukov's 1st Guards Tank Army went down the hill, followed by Bogdanov's 2nd. Ahead of them a Red Army artillery barrage was already crashing down on American positions in the northern end of the battlefront.

The tip of the sickle was in motion.

Somewhere in the middle, Simonyak's 3rd Shock Army would also be in motion—against the American positions around Rodingshausen.

The shock troops would cut the Yanks to ribbons, just as they had the glorious "supermen" of Heinrich Himmler's SS panzer divisions.

Marshal Zhukov had the armies—and he had a plan. It was a damned good one. It would lead to victory.

Lucky Forward
Southwest of Melle, Germany
Monday, July 23, 1945, 7:09 a.m.

"The bastards are trying to outflank us on our right," Patton said, staring at the big map. "Zhukov put his tank armies in the north for an end run around our right flank."

"I'd say its about time to put III Corps into the line," Walker suggested. "If we can stop those tanks up there, we'll have more flexibility in the center."

"That's what we've got them up there for," Patton agreed. "Go for it."

"III Corps is already in action," a young captain interjected. "I've just got word that the 11th Armored is returning heavy enemy fire."

"Good," Patton said. "Now where's my air force?"

Combined Soviet Armies Command Post
Nonnenstein Ridge
East of Osnabruck, Germany
Monday, July 23, 1945, 7:33 a.m.

The deafening barrage that had seemed to go on forever
ended as abruptly as it had begun. Zhukov and Rokossovsky
had just been congratulating themselves on their shock troops
having broken through the American center when it had suddenly started.

It had been a nightmare. Zhukov was stunned. His ears
were still ringing as he began demanding answers. What had
happened? What was the extent of the damage? How could
they do this to me? *Where* was the American artillery that
had done this?

The answer to the latter question lay in the kind of precision
bombing that Eighth Air Force had honed to a fine art—and, of
course, radar bomb sights that ignored the fog like it wasn't
there. The initial barrage of 105 mm howitzer fire from the
American lines had now been supplemented by a downpour of
hundreds of tons of five-hundred pound bombs dropped on the
length of Nonnenstein Ridge.

As for the extent of the damage, that information was coming in piecemeal. The bombs could not, of course, be targeted
with the precision of artillery shells, but when aimed at areas
that contained heavy troop concentrations, they wrought
tremendous havoc.

The deepest wounds were those that Zhukov could see all
around him—a perceptible edginess that hadn't been there an
hour ago.

Lucky Forward
Southwest of Melle, Germany
Monday, July 23, 1945, 7:34 a.m.

"Get me Leroy Irwin," Patton said to the radio operator
with the blue and gold windmill patch of XII Corps. "I need to
talk with your boss."

"General, how much time do you need to get your forces to

the top of Nonnenstein Ridge?" Patton asked when the XII commander came on the line. "I want you to go left and out-flank those sons-of-bitches."

"Ninety minutes oughta be more than enough time, sir."

"All right," Patton said after a short pause. "We can wait another hour."

"Let's go up to the hill and see if we can see anything," Patton said, turning to Walker.

Accompanied by a man with a portable radio and several Third Army staffers, the four- and five-star generals made their way to "the hill," a small rise about fifty yards north of the farmhouse.

The fog had thinned somewhat. The smoke and flames from the center of the line were visible in the distance. Patton squinted through his binoculars at the blurry, barely distinguishable movements of the Soviet forces on the distant ridge.

The Red shock troops had taken a toll on Willard Paul's 26th Infantry Division, but they had played their hand by cutting though this sector. The rest of XII Corps would slip out of their way and outflank them. In an hour, they would be deeply committed in the lower ground and utterly surprised by an attack on their rear *and* on the ridge—or at least that was the plan.

As they stood there, squinting across the valley, the scene was suddenly transformed. Honey-colored sunlight was soaking the landscape before them. They all felt its warmth on their backs. In unison, they turned to see that the sun's fiery orb had finally broken free of the grip of the damp grey blanket.

"Sir," the radio operator said, handing a headset to Patton. "It's General Maddox and General Weyland. They've been airborne for about twenty minutes. Now they can see the battlefield clearly."

"Gentlemen, in half an hour, the whole front will be on fire," Patton said, looking up, staring at the sky. Somewhere up there was a silver B-17, its aluminum glowing golden in the morning sun.

Recalling the moment that the fog had finally lifted over Jena, Nate was still hoping for good omens.

The air was already filled with the sounds of low-flying A-26 bombers.

Combined Soviet Armies Command Post
Nonnenstein Ridge
East of Osnabruck, Germany
Monday, July 23, 1945, 9:42 a.m.

The Allied attack bombers struck without warning the moment that the fog had lifted. Zhukov watched them being hosed by a withering spray of Soviet antiaircraft fire. Tracers ripped the attackers. The sky became a leopard pelt of flak bursts.

The Sturmoviks arrived soon after and had brought the air war home to the Yanks. A handful of the silver and red American Mustangs could be seen chasing the Sturmoviks, but most of the Soviet bombers were finding their targets. High above, streaks of black smoke told the story of aerial victories in the duels between fighters two miles in the sky.

The carnage today would be terrible, but it would pave the way toward ultimate victory. By dealing this decisive blow against Patton, the Allies would be demoralized. Zhukov could turn, smash the Allied armies in the west and deliver Europe to Stalin on a platter.

The landscape was a mass of fire and smoke as far as the eye could see. Through the haze, the marshal could see the Stalin tanks, maneuvering like big green turtles.

As Zhukov had observed before, battles tend to take on a life of their own. They reach a point when, once joined, they become a wild animal, twitching and sliding under their own momentum. The side with the superior plan will then reveal itself. Under the careful and skilled hand of the commander, the animal will strike the winning blow.

The battle joined three hours earlier at the center of the thousand-square-mile valley that lay between Minden and Osnabruck had become two battles. One was being waged at the tip of Zhukov's sickle by his Guards Tank Armies, the other in the center, where Simonyak's shock troops had broken through the line.

It was then that the careful and skilled hand of Georgi Zhukov had released General Berzarin's 5th Shock Army into the center, where a frenzied battle raged near some ponds that lay around Rodingshausen.

Simultaneously, Zhukov had dropped his "hammer." General Volsky's 5th Guards Tank Army now moved on the autobahn. Zhukov had heard from radio intercepts that Patton had pulled his XX Corps back to Minden and the autobahn was clear. With Guards Tank Armies now on both flanks, Zhukov could start to picture a complete envelopment of the American forces in the valley as the shock troops overwhelmed the American center.

Marshal Zhukov would have good news for the Man of Steel.

Lucky Forward
Southwest of Melle, Germany
Monday, July 23, 1945, 10:37 a.m.

"The Russians are in Rodingshausen," Oscar Koch explained, stepping to the huge map.

"I thought XII Corps was in there," Patton said, looking chagrinned.

"They were. Not now. The Red shock troops overwhelmed them and are moving through. Our 90th Division has been clobbered pretty bad. Irwin managed to get Gaffey's 4th Armored upon top of Nonnenstein Ridge, but it's like the parting of the Red Sea. The Russians are putting everything into their flanks. They're trying to outflank *us* on two sides. On the north, the ridge slopes steeply in the direction of the Hase River. Beyond this creek, there's only Dagar's 11th Armored to hold the front."

Nate stepped outside and stared off to the north, where the battle was raging. It seemed to him that there was smoke billowing up from half the horizon and blossoming in dark smudges across half the sky.

He wondered what this scene must be like for the people in that B-17 flying command post. What a spectacle this living map must be. How amazing to be that detached, yet to be seeing and studying the entirety of the battlefield as the battle is going on.

Nate wondered what it must be like for those guys in the 60th Infantry who were just captured at Rodingshausen. He remembered that sickening feeling he'd had last winter in that town in Belgium—he couldn't even remember the name—when he realized that his company was completely surrounded and nearly out of ammo. He had felt that sinking feeling in his gut when all of the guys just looked at each other with the realization they would soon be guests of the Waffen SS. Miraculously, things had gone the other way—but they could easily have not. As much as he had been taught to fear Hitler's SS, the stories that he'd heard about the Soviet shock troops made him cringe.

It was hard to imagine that the Americans could lose today, but if so, how would Patton take it and what would he do to reverse his fortune?

Would this really mark the end to his heretofore successful campaign against the Reds, or would he have done enough damage to them that this war would devolve into another bitter stalemate like the *First* World War?

13

★ ★

With the 487th Fighter Squadron
Somewhere over the Osnabruck Battlefield
Monday, July 23, 1945, 10:38 a.m.

"DOGPATCH Three, this is Dogpatch Leader. I've got bogies at ten o'clock low. Looks like three Yak-7s covering the bombers. Why doncha go on down and kick a little Russkie ass?"

Tex Callaghan was flying Number Three in a four-ship element of blue-nosed 487th Fighter Squadron P-51H Mustangs. He'd gone overseas late in World War II, arriving at the Eighth Air Force base at Bodney in England just after Christmas in 1944—during the Battle of the Bulge. He had his baptism of fire during the Luftwaffe's Operation Bodenplatte offensive on New Year's Day. During that battle, the 487th alone shot down twenty-four Germans. One of the victories belonged to Tex.

By the time that the 487th was forward deployed to Chievres in Belgium on January 27, Tex had three kill marks on his P-51D. He was, as they say, a natural, an excellent fighter pilot with good instincts for air combat. As Luftwaffe activity tailed off, Eighth Air Force fighter jocks found it difficult to find targets, but Tex managed two in February and March. On May 3, during the last mission flown by the 487th, Tex was bounced by a Focke Wulf over Hannover. He managed to roll out of the way, come out on the joker's tail and smoke him for number six.

When the new war started, and Colonel Jim Mayden was ordered to reassemble the 487th. Tex had already been back home in Midland, Texas, for a week and was starting to think about getting a job. When Mayden called, Tex didn't think twice. A lot of the high-time fighter pilots were reluctant to go back, but for many of the newer guys, flying fighters had been the high point of their lives and they were anxious to be back in the saddle.

During June, it had been déjà vu. Tex and the 427th were flying out of Bodney again, and over the same corner of Europe. Only the bad guys were different.

Tex got his first kill of the new war on June 15 over Belgium—not far from where he'd gotten his first during the previous war. He'd added three since. Today, the mission for the 427th was combat air patrol, protecting the fighter bombers working the Osnabruck battlefield.

With the ground fog, the bombers were late showing up, so the Mustangs had stooged around at eleven thousand feet for over half an hour. Now, suddenly, all hell had broken loose. There were planes everywhere.

The element leader spotted a three-ship formation of Yak-9 fighters, so Tex and his wingman wasted no time in taking advantage of this situation. Speed and altitude are great multipliers in air combat and altitude can be turned into speed when diving on a target.

Young fighter pilots tended to hose an enemy with a long burst of tracers, but all the top aces talked about the fast, slashing attack. In and out. Tex had copied this tactic—and it had worked. If you're a good shot, it generally does.

Tex nosed into a steep dive and lined up the big green airplane that was flying lead. When the Yak had filled his gunsight, he opened fire. The .50 caliber slugs from the Mustang's six Brownings ripped into the aft fuselage and the starboard wing root. Tex watched the Russian instinctively break to the left to escape. As his P-51H sliced past the Yak, Tex could see the wing start to buckle as the fighter came apart.

Banking hard and slamming the throttle, Tex pulled back into a climb. His wingman had taken out a second Yak, but the third was on his tail.

Tex tried to hit the third Russian from below, but the enemy fighter broke right. As Tex tried to follow and line up a shot, the Russian accelerated and headed southeast, trying to get lost in the sun. The Yak-9 was no match for a Mustang on speed, but at least that Red pilot had the right idea.

As Tex closed in, the enemy rolled into a dive. Tex tried a deflection shot and missed. The Russian went into some low clouds and was gone.

Tex found himself at eight thousand feet and all alone. He could see the pillars of smoke rising from the battlefield to the north and started to make his way in that direction. He checked his six o'clock and saw the familiar dirty black exhaust smudge of a Klimov engine at full power. A Russian was on his tail—no, *two* Russians—and barrelling in for the kill.

He had seconds to decide whether to outrun them or outfly them. He chose the latter. He counted to two, then fell off on his left wing and kicked the Mustang into a Split S maneuver. He knew that a pilot can turn the tables on an enemy on his tail with a Split S—or at least give him something to think about.

The Mustang was very forgiving in tight turns. Many other planes would pop rivets and even bend metal. At the very least, their controls stiffen. Such was the case with the two Yaks. They raced through the piece of sky where Tex had just been. He was gone.

Tex nosed over and simply fell down onto the top of one of

the Yaks. In a vertical dive, the Mustang quickly picked up the speed that had been lost in the tight turn. Tex found himself in a firing position.

He chewed on the Yak's tail with his Brownings until it came off in a cloud of debris.

Tex rolled out to look for the guy's wingman.

As useful as it can be, the Split S is a notorious guzzler of altitude, and Tex now found his altimeter barely above the numeral "4" The other Yak was probably above him. At last Tex spotted him—a quarter mile away, banking to maneuver onto Tex's tail.

Tex stood the P-51H on its wing to attempt to get inside the enemy's turn. It was a classic Lufbery Circle. Neither pilot was in firing position as long as the other turned with him.

Tex turned, but the Russian turned tighter. The Yak pilot was allowing his altitude to slip. The Russian machines were optimized for lower-level combat. He knew the Mustang had a greater advantage at higher altitudes, and four thousand feet was not exactly high altitude.

He's a tricky bastard, Tex thought. He would just have to out-trick the trickster. He'd have to use the Mustang's power and tighter turning radius to break the stalemate.

As Tex shoved in the stick and tried to pull across the circle of air that separated him from the enemy, he started noticing a lot of low clouds in the way.

The Russian was there, then he wasn't. He'd broken off to make a run for it. He was probably low on fuel. Maybe he was also low on ammo. Tex caught another glimpse of the guy, too far away for a clean shot.

The patches of cloud abruptly gave way to solid cloud. Just as suddenly, Tex was out of the cloud and the Yak was gone. So was the flat terrain over which he'd begun his day of dogfighting. He was in a hilly, almost mountainous country—of course, when you're from Midland, Texas, nearly every place in the world looks mountainous.

Realizing that he'd drifted a long way from where he'd started, he looked at his compass to figure out which way to go. He was at about a thousand feet and headed south, parallel to a narrow, heavily wooded valley.

Tex was just pushing on the stick to reverse course when he saw something that he'd never seen before. Sticking up from the valley less than a mile ahead were what looked like two incredibly huge gray bullets pointed straight into the sky.

What the hell? He started to ask himself. Then he realized. These must be those damned rockets that the Reds had been shooting at New York. They were shooting them off under overcast so that airplanes couldn't see them—except if the airplane happened to be at the right place, the right time, and just a thousand feet off the ground.

In a moment, he was over the two rockets. As he flashed past, he could see people running and the spider webs of thick camouflage netting that probably hid the equipment. There were also billowing white clouds of what looked like steam.

How do you shoot down a rocket? He asked himself as he banked around. The answer, he knew, is that you don't *shoot down* rockets, but you can sure as hell destroy them on the ground.

He lined up the nearest one for a strafing pass. Even though he'd conserved ammo in his two previous encounters, he worried that he wouldn't have enough.

He thumbed the trigger and poured a steady burst at the nearest rocket. The explosive shells were finding their mark, but Tex didn't bother to look as he flashed past and started shooting at the second. He aimed a bit lower this time, hoping that he might hit the damned thing's engine.

Tex passed the second, still unsure that he'd done any damage.

Suddenly, the cold, light grey of the low clouds turned a brilliant yellow, as though reflecting the light of the setting sun. A split second later, a shock wave hit the Mustang with a force that felt to Tex like a midair collision. The P-51H trembled and staggered. After an interminable few seconds of hell, the Mustang was in level flight, as though nothing had happened.

Tex turned the Mustang back toward the scene of the explosion to take a look.

A huge fire was burning in the valley and black smoke was boiling up into the base of the clouds above. Trees a quarter of a mile away were on fire. What an incredibly volatile fuel they must have been using. Tex couldn't tell whether both of the rockets had exploded, or whether the explosion of one had destroyed the other, but they were *both* gone.

Deciding that he just had to share this scene, Tex fired a short burst into the conflagration in order to get the results of his work recorded onto gun camera film for posterity.

As he was winging his way north, high above the clouds, Tex recalled that planes destroyed on the ground were not counted as victories any more, but he wondered if Colonel Mayden would make an exception for *these* things.

Combined Soviet Armies Command Post
Nonnenstein Ridge
East of Osnabruck, Germany
Monday, July 23, 1945, 1:21 p.m.

The intercepts of American radio traffic that Zhukov was being handed from the Americans showed that their resistance was collapsing everywhere. His radio men had been monitoring a radio frequency that seemed to be carrying all of the high priority calls. It might as well have been Shostakovich—it was such music to the marshal's ears.

American battalions were crying for help to the divisions and the divisions were begging the corps commanders. One message had even spoken in oblique terms of a division commander having committed *suicide* on the battlefield.

On the other hand, the reports that Zhukov had been receiving from his own armies since early afternoon were not nearly so encouraging. How, if the Americans were on the verge of collapse, could his own forces be in trouble?

He had thrown in his reserves, but nothing seemed to be moving. On the left, the 1st and 2nd Guards Tank Armies had not advanced since noon. On the right, Volsky's 5th Guards Tank Army had been stopped cold. He was claiming that it had run into XX Corps, but Zhukov *knew* that XX Corps had withdrawn to positions in Minden, fifty kilometers to the rear.

Zhukov was winning, but he was behind schedule. The Americans were beaten, but they refused to withdraw. It was like the German SS. They turned into wild animals, fighting when cornered like crazed beasts—even when it was hopeless.

Oh, well, he'd just have to kill them *all*.

Lucky Forward
Southwest of Melle, Germany
Monday, July 23, 1945, 2:26 p.m.

"Time to move out!" Patton shouted, bursting from the back door of the farmhouse followed by Oscar Koch and a line of staff officers. "The battle's moving west and I want to check in on all the corps level command posts and get a lay of the land before we move into the next phase."

Nate was glad to be on the move again.

As he'd scanned the distant ridge, he'd seen a steady increase in the number of explosions. Bombs and artillery were raking the Reds, but nothing had landed near Melle. Two hours ago, a pack of Sturmoviks came dangerously close, but he hadn't seen an enemy plane in the sky for some time. The thing that continued to strike him was how truly huge the field of battle was. He was sure that none of the GIs out there had any notion of how vast the scale of the battle was. That vision belonged to the men with the maps—or the men high above the battlefield in that B-17.

Seven jeeps left Lucky Forward and drove north to the place where the narrow country road intersected the autobahn on the edge of Melle. The big, four-lane highway was a sea of motion. The two left lanes were crowded with German civilian refugees fleeing from the direction of the battle, although American MPs were trying to keep them confined to the outside lane, so that ambulances and trucks could get past. The two west-bound lanes were choked with military equipment. Here, the MPs were trying to keep the slower-moving tanks and tank recovery vehicles to the right so that trucks and jeeps could take the inside.

As soon as they saw Patton's five-star placard, the MPs immediately stopped traffic in both directions and the General's motorcade turned onto the highway. With a jeep-load of XX Corps MPs in the lead and a pair of M8 Greyhounds falling into line directly behind Patton, they began driving west toward scene of the fighting.

In less than ten minutes, they reached the line of the farthest advance by the Soviet 5th Guards Tank Army during the day. The scene was horrific. T34 and Stalin tanks were everywhere, a few of them on the autobahn, but most in the ditch. Some were blown apart, but others looked unscathed, as though their crews had just parked them, expecting to return. One lay in the ditch, wrapped in huge, snakelike masses of broken tank tread.

While there were fewer, some M26A2s were also among the disabled. Some had inspection crews climbing on them and others were simply parked, looking alone and forlorn.

"Never saw so many knocked-out tanks before," Nate said to the General.

"It's a helluva mess isn't it?" he replied. "Those sons of bitches threw a helluva lot of armor at us here today . . . and a helluva lot of air. Look at that."

Nate looked. A Sturmovik had apparently tried an emergency landing and had run into a T34. Judging by the damage, the plane had probably not been rolling faster than twenty miles an hour. He'd almost made it.

The closer they got to Nonnenstein Ridge, the fresher the battle scene. Destroyed tanks were still burning, or at least smoldering. Nate could see the wounded who were still waiting to be evacuated.

"Turn here," Patton said abruptly as they passed a two-lane paved road leading north.

The General studied his map for a moment and pointed to a small building about a hundred yards away that was surrounded by vehicles.

"That's the XX Corps command post. Let's go get briefed."

Inside, General Morris was standing over his map table looking as Patton strode into the room.

"At ease, General. Damned fine work here today. I'll only take a minute of your time. What's your situation?"

"Hardest fight I've seen since last winter," Morris said. "It was their 5th Guards Tank Army. It was part of Rokossovsky's

command. Tough as shit but we kicked it out of 'em. Couldn't
have done it without the air. Things worked smooth as silk
with the air force today. We called 'em . . . and they were right
there. The Reds are pulling back, but I've got the 10th Armored on their ass. Still plenty of light. I don't think many of
them are going to escape."

"Have you learned much from the prisoners, yet?" General
Koch asked. "I'm trying to get an overview of what kind of
force we're up against."

"We took a lot of prisoners from their 47th Army. I guess
that was one of their cannon fodder outfits. The Guards outfits
fought like hell, but the others just crumpled. They look pretty
underfed. A lot of 'em are really sick, too."

"Don't spoil 'em by givin' 'em too much to eat," Patton
interjected.

"Hodge's XXIV Corps is about a mile north," Patton said
as he looked up from studying his map as they drove away.
"That's those guys that came to us from Tenth Army. A
month ago, they were blastin' the Japs out of their holes over
on Okinawa."

At the XXIV Command Post, several GIs with Thompson
submachine guns and a jeep with a manned .50 caliber machine gun served as perimeter guards. In Third Army, General Patton had been so well known and such an ominous
presence that it had been customary to simply wave him
through any checkpoint at the mere sight of the placard on his
jeep. Here, the motorcade was ordered to halt until one of the
soldiers with a Thompson had walked back to where Nate
and the General were waiting in line and had identified Patton
visually.

"These men in XXIV Corps mean business," Patton said after he'd returned the man's salute and the jeeps were under
way. "I'm impressed."

Inside the perimeter, the guns on all of the jeeps were
manned and pointing outward. At XX Corps, there had been a
large number of prisoners, and they were sitting or standing in
a large, well-guarded holding area. Here at XXIV Corps, the
number of Soviet prisoners was relatively fewer, but they were
all kneeling in long, neat rows, each with his hands tied behind
his back.

Alerted by his sentries, General Hodge came out of his Command Post, saluted Patton smartly, and extended his hand.

"Welcome to XXIV Corps, sir."

"I'm impressed with your security measures, General," Patton said, nodding toward the prisoners.

"These fellows were part of the Red shock troops . . . their 5th Shock Army," Hodge explained. "They're pretty tough sons of bitches."

"Looks like your boys have the situation in hand," Patton observed.

"Well, sir, after a few of those kamikaze banzai charges over on Okinawa, you get to the point where you just don't mess around with people who fancy themselves as tough sons of bitches." Hodge shrugged. "I guess we sort of shocked the shock troops. In Oki we learned the hard way that you don't *take* prisoners. If they go out of their way to surrender, you accommodate 'em. But after you've been ambushed a few times, you don't go out of *your* way. Did you hear what happened over at XII Corps?"

"We heard that 90th Infantry was overrun and the Reds captured a lot of our people," Koch replied.

"That was the Reds' 3rd Shock Army," Hodge explained. "More of these tough SOBs. Apparently, when their advance ran out of steam, a bunch of 'em surrendered to some guys from 26th Infantry. As soon as they got marched to the rear, they overwhelmed the guards, grabbed some weapons, and went on a shooting spree. Massacred a battalion headquarters and killed a lot of people. I saw the Japs do that same thing a couple of times. It ain't nice."

"What happened to the . . . ?" Koch started to ask.

"From what I've heard, they're no longer prisoners," Hodge explained calmly. "As we used to say when the Japs pulled that kind of shit . . . they're with their ancestors."

"Sure as hell better there than *here*," Patton observed.

As the afternoon wore on, Patton methodically visited all of the corps command posts and many of those of the constituent divisions. After passing through the northern edge of the battlefield, where the battle had begun that morning with the 1st and 2nd Tank Armies' attack, they started driving up onto Nonnenstein Ridge. Here, they found Jim Van Fleet's III Corps Command Post located in what had served as the Combined Soviet Armies Command Post earlier in the day.

Binoculars in hand, Patton walked over to the same small bluff where, just a few hours earlier, Zhukov had confidently surveyed his advancing armies.

Temporary Soviet Armies Command Post
Schlosswallhalle
Osnabruck, Germany
Monday, July 23, 1945, 5:08 p.m.

There were some on the 1st Byelorussian Front staff who insisted that Marshal Georgi Zhukov had *not* lost the battle. They were still operating under the illusion of the deliberate misinformation that had been fed to them all day by the unscrupulous American radiomen. Indeed, even Zhukov had only just started to comprehend what had happened.

Despite the setback, Soviet forces still controlled the city and held a large number of Allied prisoners. True, they'd been forced to make a tactical withdrawal from Nonnenstein Ridge, but all of the Tank Army headquarters were still intact. There were plenty of tanks and troops with which to renew the assault on Tuesday morning.

Zhukov could look out the window of the old castle and see the red flags and the Soviet troops. He knew that he still had a formidable force, but he also knew that he'd been badly mauled. He knew that large numbers of his men were ill and feverish and not in their best fighting form.

His knees were still a bit shaky after the wrathful wireless message he'd received from Stalin.

The sickle had failed.

General Bogdanov had explained to Zhukov that he knew there was trouble when he'd heard shooting *behind* him. When he'd taken stock of the situation, he knew that his advance was over. The enemy was at his rear. He had had to turn one of his brigades—and eventually his entire 2nd Guards Tank Army—to the defense. In the heart of the front, where the shock troops punched through and took so many prisoners, the Americans had counterattacked with unexpected ferocity. There was a rumor that the Americans—desperate to defeat the hardened Russian veterans—had created a division in the new XXIV Corps that was comprised entirely of wild Indians from the American West. The bloodthirsty savages had been taken out of their loin cloths and feathers only days before and put into uniform. There were also rumors that these fiends were lifting Soviet *scalps!*

The fact that the Americans appeared on Nonnenstein Ridge came as a surprise to the Soviet commanders, but their reaction was orderly. The Soviet 8th Guards Army was about to descend into the fray, when the American 4th Armored Division materialized on their flank. In spite of the unanticipated turn of events, the Guards formed up and turned to face the Americans. Zhukov had observed this with his own eyes.

Though the Guards were efficient and disciplined in meeting the attack, they soon found themselves under fire from two sides, as elements of both the American III Corps and V Corps were suddenly on the ridge as well.

The Americans seemed to know exactly where to turn. It was as though they had eyes in the sky.

The desperate fight on the ridge lasted for several hours. Ultimately, it had come down to hand-to-hand combat. Casualties on both sides were heavy. At the urging of his staff, Zhukov had retired "temporarily" from his command post on Nonnenstein Ridge and had returned to Osnabruck.

The hammer had also failed.

Marshal Rokossovsky, Zhukov had heard, was with Volsky's 5th Guards Tank Army, when the hammer had attacked. Volsky had moved against the Americans along the autobahn under the impression that they had retired to Minden, but he ran into withering artillery fire and a spirited counterattack at least ten kilometers before he had expected any such thing. He had withdrawn toward Osnabruck.

Outside, the shadows would soon be growing longer and night would fall. Zhukov wondered about a night attack such as he'd used against the Germans in the final offensive against Berlin at the end of April.

He sent orders to Katukov and Bogdanov. The 1st and 2nd Guards Tank Armies should prepare for a predawn assault.

The 4th Armored Division Command Post
Nonnenstein Ridge
East of Osnabruck, Germany
Monday, July 23, 1945, 5:18 p.m.

The battle was not over, but Zhukov had been beaten badly and Patton knew that Zhukov knew this.

"Tomorrow, we'll have to cross another valley and take that damned city," Patton said, speaking to General Walker and several of the corps commanders who'd joined him at the peak of the ridge. "Bring the artillery up to the ridge. I want to bombard the hell out of their defensive line all night long. At dawn, we'll circle north, up by Belm, with III Corps and V Corps. We'll run around the *outside* of the line that we've been blasting all night and hit 'em where they aren't. When they start to shift north, XX Corps moves toward the city from the south."

"Shall we get the other outfits ready to move through the valley at dawn?" Walton Walker asked, as the generals looked west toward Osnabruck, which was barely visible, silhouetted against the late afternoon sun.

"I'd let 'em *think* that we're going to do that . . . but let's outflank 'em and get 'em surrounded. Then we can give them the choice of giving up or . . ."

The General didn't have to finish the sentence.

By now, Patton had pieced together a firsthand look at the state of the battle. From Weyland and Maddox, he learned that an attempted retreat along the autobahn in the direction of Osnabruck had been interrupted by air attack and then overrun by XX Corps. He knew that casualties were severe on both sides, but greater on the Russian side. Huge blocks of sick and exhausted Reds had simply given up. The Americans had bagged the largest number of prisoners since Jena.

From Koch's G2 survey of the prisoners, a picture of the status of Zhukov's armies had started to emerge. Certain units were among the best equipped and most well disciplined in the Red Army. However, *most* of the troops were exhausted veterans, upon whom the fatigue of the battles between the

Vistula and the Oder had taken a toll. Many others were replacements who'd arrived during or after the Battle of Berlin in May. Disease was widespread, if not rampant. Many soldiers had not been on full rations since their units had left the Netherlands.

As the intelligence officers had discovered in their interrogations of captured Russians since Berlin, the NKVD political officers—who were assigned to every Soviet unit down to the company level—were liberally scattered among the prisoners. Most prisoners would not talk to the Americans within earshot of the NKVD commissars or NKVD informants. However, when the prisoners were isolated, they were *eager* to talk. The American G2 had now developed techniques for efficiently weeding out the NKVD. They usually started with the guy in any group that looked to be the best fed. Almost invariably they needed to look no farther.

What they found when the Russians talked was an overwhelming disaffection. The Russian soldiers conscripted to defend the Rodinya against the Nazis had finished their job. They had fought the Great Patriotic War and had danced on Hitler's grave. Now, they were fighting a war they didn't understand. The officers had not explained how conquering France would protect the Rodinya, but the NKVD commissars just insisted that anyone who questioned the party line was a traitor.

Lately, a growing number of the NKVD commissars, not to mention the occasional officer, seemed to be "stepping on land mines." The smile that usually accompanied the telling of such a story suggested that the "land mine" was actually a fragmentation grenade.

The White House
Washington DC
Monday, July 23, 1945, 5:43 p.m.

"I understand that congratulations are in order," Harry Truman said, greeting General Marshall and General Arnold. "The annihilation of that rocket base has a lot of people in the

Northeast breathing easier . . . and what we've done at Osnabruck has a lot of people *everywhere* breathing easier."

"It was better than we could've hoped," Arnold grinned. "We got recon over the site before dark. It looks like they weren't using mobile launchers like the V2 after all. It was just a very well hidden fixed launch site . . . emphasis on *was*."

"At Osnabruck, I'll accept your congratulations on behalf of the boys doing the work," Marshall added. "But the Russians still have a formidable force . . . and tomorrow is another day."

"You're sounding rather pessimistic this afternoon, General," Truman said, pretending to scold Marshall. "I saw your own memo . . . delivered an hour ago . . . shows that your boys did better than even the papers have reported. Not just Patton . . . but what General Patch and General Truscott have managed to do to Koniev in the south."

"There's no doubt, Mr. President, that today represented important victories for us and a great setback for Zhukov," Marshall explained. "But our victory came at great cost, and, theoretically, a renewed effort by Zhukov and Rokossovsky tomorrow could result in the breakthrough that Zhukov is gunning for."

"He can no longer depend on Koniev . . . nor Koniev on him," Arnold pointed out. "Yesterday, there was a vast, interconnected force. Today, it's no longer reasonable to believe that Rokossovsky and Zhukov have any meaningful ability to trade forces with Koniev."

"However, we can't do anything meaningful to launch an offensive against Russia itself as long as Zhukov controls the heart of northern Europe," Marshall replied. "Remember, in 1941, Hitler launched Operation Barbarossa at the end of *June*. They expected to defeat the Soviet Union by autumn. It took them 'til December to reach Moscow. The Russian winter intervened and the Germans never regained the momentum. It's now *July*. When will we be able to begin operations in Russia? Do we want to have an army freezing on the steppes in February? If Zhukov can delay us until 'General Winter' comes into play, Stalin will have until the spring of 1946 to rebuild the Red Army from whatever damage we've been able to inflict this summer."

Lucky Forward
Nonnenstein Ridge
East of Osnabruck, Germany
Tuesday, July 24, 1945, 12:22 a.m.

Nate McKinley was frantically pushing his way through the crowd. He'd seen her face and he was trying to get to her. He couldn't see her anymore. Somewhere, someone shouted, "You'll *never* find her!"

He had to get to her. He had to see her face and have her eyes see him. Somewhere, someone shouted, "You'll never find *her!*"

"The General is asleep," someone shouted.

Nate turned. The crowd had vanished.

"The General is asleep," the voice repeated.

"I think that you'd better wake him," another voice said urgently. "He's going to want to see this."

Nate jerked himself free of his recurring Miss O'Leary dream. The conscious Nate had long ago come to grips with never seeing her again, but his subconscious still pursued a face whose supernatural eyes never met his.

He pulled on his boots, grabbed his helmet and gunbelt and scrambled out of his pup tent.

"What's going on, corporal?" Nate asked the young soldier who was on sentry duty at the perimeter of the Lucky Forward bivouac area.

"The captain here wants to talk to General Patton, but the General has us under orders . . ."

"What is it, Captain?" Nate asked the man with a 4th Armored Division patch on his shoulder. "I'm the General's driver. I can get one of the officers . . ."

"Please do," the captain said impatiently. "I've got General Berzarin down the hill there . . . He wants to surrender."

Within minutes, not only Patton and Koch, but General Walker, General Irwin, and a half-dozen officers were listening to the captain's story.

Finally, Patton ended the discussion by saying, "Bring the sonuvabitch up here and find me an interpreter."

Nate was assigned to accompany the captain and two well-armed sentries back to wherever in the darkness the commander of the 5th Shock Army had approached the lines. In the distance, they could hear the rumble of American artillery cutting loose another barrage against the Soviet forces dug in between the ridge and the city.

The Soviet general was a tall man, almost a head taller than either of the two Soviet officers accompanying him. Nate noticed that, as Patton often did, he was wearing riding boots. The Reds had been relieved of their sidearms, and these were visible on the ground in the moonlight.

The 4th Armored captain picked up the Nagant revolver that seemed to match the empty holster on Berzarin's belt. He snapped the cylinder out, let the cartridges fall on the ground, clicked the cylinder back into place and slipped the gun into his pocket.

Patton was waiting for the Soviet officers as they ducked through the blackout curtain at the entrance of his command tent. Patton, Walker, Irwin, Jim Van Fleet of III Corps, General Koch, and Major Tom Hovalik, the interpreter, rose to their feet to return Berzarin's salute. There were no handshakes.

When the Americans sat back down, Berzarin was offered a chair. Everyone else remained standing. Berzarin's translator stood behind him.

"I understand that you have something for us," Patton said.

Berzarin's man translated; the General looked directly at Patton and said, "Da."

The translator then took a piece of paper out of his pocket and began speaking slowly in English.

"To the Supreme Commander of Allied forces. There is nothing more to conquer. Your victory is complete. You have defeated us. There is nothing more to add to it. Only peace can add to your further honor."

"These are the words of General Berzarin?" General Walker asked.

"No."

"No?"

"No and yes."

"No and yes?"

"They are first the words of Marshal Rokossovsky. General

Berzarin has placed his command under that of Marshal Rokossovsky."

"Marshal Rokossovsky is prepared to surrender all the forces under his command as well?"

"Yes," the translator said, after conferring with Berzarin. "Marshall Rokossovsky will surrender 5th Guards Tank Army, 2nd Shock Army here . . . 31st Army now fighting in Bremen . . . 48th Army now in Netherlands. He will order forces under his command in the West to stop fighting. General Berzarin surrenders 5th Shock Army."

"The 5th Shock Army is under Marshal Zhukov's command, isn't it?" Koch asked.

"It was."

"How does Marshal Zhukov feel about this?" Walker asked.

"We admit defeat. It is time for Marshal Zhukov to admit defeat, but that is his choice."

"Is he prepared to make that decision?"

"We do not know. Marshal Rokossovsky, as a field commander, is doing what he feels is tactically necessary . . . to surrender."

"Does he realize that he's taking a third of the Soviet armies in northern Europe out of action?" Patton asked.

After a long explanation from Berzarin, the translator said, "The situation for all Soviet forces is not so good. We have many troops, but we cannot feed our troops and we are short of ammunition. The morale is bad. Many soldiers are sick. High fevers. Soviet generals cannot explain to troops why we fight Americans in France and Belgium. Only for good of Stalin?"

"Your troops are running out of steam in the West, then?" Koch asked.

"Soviet soldiers do as ordered. They grumble, but do as ordered," the translator explained after a conference with Berzarin. "With the defection of Poles, it is hard . . ."

"What *defection of Poles?*" Koch asked.

"You haven't heard?" The translator smiled. "I am amused to know that sometimes news travels slowly in US Army as in Soviet Army. You will soon know. Kosciuszko Division . . . now

called 1st Polish Army . . . part of Marshal Rokossovsky's 2nd
Byelorussian Front . . . has already surrendered to your Fifteenth Army in Ardennes Mountains. Two hours ago. Marshal
Rokossovsky is informed that they kill all the Russian NKVD
commissars and go over to Americans."

"What is this Kosciuszko Division?" Van Fleet asked.

"It was organized in 1943 by the Red Army . . . from Polish
troops *captured* by the Soviet Army in 1939," Koch replied,
glancing at the translator for a confirming nod. "It's been part of
Rokossovsky's command more or less since then. It was a time
bomb waiting to go off. It's one thing to get the Red Army to
fight in France for *their* motherland, but quite another to get the
Poles to fight in France for the Soviet Union."

The translator explained Koch's comments to Berzarin,
who shrugged and nodded and then said something in
Russian.

"General Berzarin says that the time to fight you is over,"
the translator said. "As you have said. This fight that we are
pursuing is for the greater glory of Stalin and his clique . . .
not for Rodinya. Also practical that we stop now. The Red
Army cannot fight you here and at the same time win in the
West. There is no army left in Rodinya to save us. We are
defeated."

"Your surrender is unconditional?" Patton asked, scarcely
believing his fortune.

"General Berzarin asks that . . . he only wishes to ask . . .
that Soviet officers be not used as slaves in capitalist factories.
He asks that they would prefer a firing squad."

The American generals looked at one another, dumbfounded.

"I think that we can agree to that *one* condition," Patton
smiled.

The translator explained this to Berzarin, whose tensed
shoulders relaxed noticeably. He wiped his forehead with his
sleeve.

"Let's get our technical people to write this up and get
Rokossovsky in here to sign it," Patton said, standing.

Berzarin stood at attention and the 4th Armored captain
handed the Nagant to Berzarin, who, in turn, handed the 7.62
mm weapon to Patton.

Patton, who seemed genuinely moved by the gesture, saluted Berzarin and said simply, "Dismissed."

Temporary Soviet Armies Command Post
Schlosswallhalle
Osnabruck, Germany
Tuesday, July 24, 1945, 5:08 a.m.

There were some on the 1st Byelorussian Front staff who still insisted that Marshal Georgi Zhukov has not lost the Battle of Osnabruck. The Marshal appreciated this loyalty, but the only two men whose opinion mattered—the man in the Kremlin and the man who looked back at him from the shaving mirror this morning—knew otherwise.

The American shelling had stopped at about 0300. Zhukov had slept through the barrage only to awaken to the silence. When he'd gotten the news a short time later that Rokossovsky was surrendering his forces to Patton, Zhukov had been furious. Koniev had been cornered near Wiesbaden, and was being pounded to death—but *he* hadn't given up. An Allied counterattack had begun in the West, but Soviet soldiers still fought bravely there. Why had Rokossovsky gone skulking—like a bitch with her tail between her legs—to the man they called "Blood and Guts?"

Katukov and Bogdanov were supposed to have launched their attacks an hour ago, but Zhukov ordered them to wait. He had to weigh his options. If Rokossovsky was no longer loyal, then Volsky was no longer loyal. This degraded Zhukov's right flank, so he would have to concentrate on his left. He would have to concentrate on what he *had* left.

Zhukov could always depend on Simoyak's shock troops. Wasn't there a captain in the 3rd Shock who had carried around a potato sack filled with the heads of SS officers?

As he sat calculating the reinforcement of his Guards Tank Armies with shock troops for an end run around the north side of the front, there was a knock at the door.

His adjutant reported that General Katukov was there to see him. Katukov had explained that the tank armies had worked all night to repair battle damage and they needed more time. Yes, late in the day, a breakout was possible if air cover could be arranged.

Zhukov sent for Simonyak and was waiting for a reply when he got word that he had a telephone call.

A *telephone call?*

Zhukov had never taken a *telephone call* at the front.

How could it be that any telephone lines were still connected anywhere in Germany?

Overlooking the Oder River
Nine miles north of Guben, Germany
Tuesday, July 24, 1945, 5:09 a.m.

"They won't get fooled again?" Professor Adam Pragier, the minister of information for the Polish Government in Exile, asked Field Marshal Bernard Law Montgomery.

"They won't get fooled again," Montgomery replied confidently as the two men stared across the mist-shrouded bridge in the first light of the dawn. "His Majesty's government will not betray you as the Reds did a year ago at the time of the Warsaw uprising."

The fog that had greeted the previous dawn farther west was present this morning here on the river that marked the eastern edge of the swath of land that the Allies had occupied when they captured Berlin ten days earlier.

Already, there were Polish commandos across the river. They crossed under the cover of fog and darkness to secure the eastern end of the bridge and reconnoiter the roads in the first mile beyond the river. There would be no artillery barrage and little resistance was expected, at least initially. The Russians were spread very thin.

Since his remarks in San Francisco two months earlier, which had been the catalyst for sending Commissar Molotov stomping out of the room, Pragier had become something of a celebrity among the Polish exiles around the world who had seen their country repeatedly raked, raped, sliced, and diced by both the Wehrmacht and the Red Army since 1939.

Today, his mind was on the events of eleven months ago, when Polish resistance fighters, the Home Army under General

Tadeusz "Bor" Komorowski, had risen up against the Nazi oc-
cupiers in Warsaw. They had done so with Zhukov's explicit
promise that the Red Army, parked just outside the city, would
assist them. As both Pragier and Montgomery knew only too
well, Marshal Zhukov had ordered the Red Army to do *nothing*. They allowed the Germans to destroy the people and the
city of Warsaw. General Bor would've been a major obstacle to
Soviet rule in Poland.

When Zhukov moved westward in June, leaving Berlin and
Hamburg less well defended than he should have, he'd done
the same with much of Poland and northeast Germany, relying on NKVD military police and local collaborators to rule
the cities and towns.

Today, just eight days short of the first anniversary of the
Warsaw Uprising, the Polish Army was ready. After four years
of being attached to British units, the Polish divisions that had
fought with the British in Normandy and Italy would be part of
a *Polish* Army—with British units attached. For this operation,
Montgomery had given them the use of two British corps.

Today, after six years without a nation, a Polish army
would reassert itself—not just here in the East, but in the West
as well. Pragier had already received word that General Zyg-
munt Berling's 1st Polish Army had just defected en masse
from Rokossovsky to General Gerow's Fifteenth Army in the
Ardennes. They now wanted to join in the liberation of Poland
from the Soviets.

"We'll see Poznan . . . today?" Pragier asked Montgomery.

"Possibly not today," Montgomery replied. "Possibly not
tomorrow. But this week for sure. By the first anniversary next
Wednesday, Poznan will be free . . . then Wroclaw . . . then
Warsaw."

Lucky Forward
Nonnenstein Ridge
East of Osnabruck, Germany
Tuesday, July 24, 1945, 6:32 a.m.

"Why dontcha just pick up the telephone and call him?"
All the brass abruptly stopped talking and turned to the

impertinent young sergeant who was eavesdropping from the corner of the room in the farmhouse where Marshal Rokossovsky had just signed his surrender. The generals had been debating how to get a message to Marshal Zhukov in Osnabruck, when Nate McKinley made his apparently ludicrous suggestion.

There was a moment of absolute silence during which Nate endured the agony of wishing that he hadn't shot off his mouth. He was about to apologize and blame it all on lack of sleep, when General Koch stood up and walked over to the corner of the room, where an old black telephone sat on an end table.

In the silent room, the erratic buzz of a dial tone could be heard clearly. All of the officers looked at one another. How could it be that any telephone lines were still connected anywhere in Germany?

Patton nodded, and Koch, who spoke German, got hold of an operator who connected him with the Schlosswallhalle in Osnabruck, where Rokossovsky had said Zhukov might have his headquarters.

He put Hovalik on the line, and after about five minutes, he was speaking with the Marshal of the Soviet Union.

"Okay . . . he's agreed to come and parley," Hovalik said as he hung up.

Teutoburgerwald
(An oak forest near the base of Nonnenstein Ridge)
East of Osnabruck, Germany
Tuesday, July 24, 1945, 8:24 a.m.

Unlike the previous day, Tuesday dawned bright and sunny. Birds were singing in the forest and it was almost idyllic. The light filtered down through the trees to cast its fleeting glance on a mat of leaves that had fallen here during the last autumn of the Third Reich.

This tranquil forest was no stranger to battles that had marked turning points of European history. It was here, in the first decade of the first century, that Publius Quinctilius Varus, Rome's governor of Germany "beyond the Rhine," and a

favorite in-law of Emperor Augustus, met his Little Bighorn
in A.D. 9. It was here, though nobody knows *exactly* where, the
German warlord Hermann ambushed and annihilated three Roman legions by forcing them to fight in the forest, an environment utterly unsuited to the weapons and tactics of the Romans,
who demanded an open battlefield on which to maneuver. Just
as the Hunkpapa Lakota warrior, Rain in the Face, cut out Tom
Custer's beating heart at the Little Bighorn in 1876, Hermann
cut off Varus's head.

At that moment, Augustus abandoned any notion of extending his empire "beyond the Rhine." The northeastern
frontier of the Roman Empire was defined from that day.

The irony of a clash of empires on a similar scale returning
to this peaceful forest was not lost on Patton. The Supreme Allied Commander was a great aficionado of Rome's triumphs,
but he was also a student of Rome's defeats.

This morning, as Nate drove him through the Teutoburgerwald on a wagon trail that a romantic might imagine as a one-
time chariot trail, George Patton was confident that it was *he*
who would be on the right side of history in 1945. Of course,
so too was Georgi Zhukov.

Zhukov and three other Soviet officers arrived blindfolded
in a pair of American jeeps. Patton was waiting, along with
General Koch and Major Hovalik. There were also a dozen
others, including a Third Army staff photographer.

The Marshal shook his head as the blindfold was removed. He walked across the carpet of fallen leaves to where
Patton was standing at attention. The broken sunlight reflected off the gold threads of his shoulderboards, making the
scene somewhat theatrical. Nate noticed that he was wearing
the three gold stars of his Hero of the Soviet Union decorations—the equivalent of the United States Congressional
Medal of Honor.

Zhukov stopped about ten feet from Patton and stood at attention. Both men waited for a moment for the other to salute
him first, but neither did. Between these two, neither would.

"Your armies suffered badly yesterday and over the past
few weeks," Patton said at last. Hovalik started to translate,
but one of Zhukov's men stepped forward and took over.

"You're cut off from your source of supply and your troops

are tired . . . and sick," Patton continued. He spoke slowly and deliberately, allowing the translator ample time to digest every word. "I'm suggesting that it's probably time for you to surrender."

Looking directly at Patton and at none of the other officers, Zhukov replied—and then paused, still looking at Patton, to let his translator catch up.

"I have two tank armies that remain loyal to me. Have also shock troops fresh and unbloodied by yesterday's battle. My force is formidable. Also I have information that your armies suffered greatly in yesterday's battle. They fought well, but suffered greatly."

"I agree that your armies are formidable," Patton replied. "But, hell, man, they're falling apart all around you. The armies that you left on your western front are insufficient to stop us there. Even if *I* went away this afternoon . . . you can't reinforce that front with what you have left here."

"I can't discuss my tactical options . . ." the translator replied.

"You don't *have* any," Patton interrupted. "You have heard . . . as I've heard this morning . . . that your boy Koniev surrendered down at Frankfurt. You probably also heard that the Polish people have revolted. The Red Army in Poland can't stop them. And the 1st Polish Army . . . the *Red* Polish Army that was attached to your 1st Byelorussian Front . . . *defected* this morning to General Gerow in Belgium. The whole damned army. You *know* that Malinovsky's army switched sides. You're isolated."

Zhukov's face grew hard and angry. His jaw quivered as he gritted his teeth.

After a long silence, Zhukov spoke. His words were not angry but matter-of-fact.

"Marshal Zhukov proposes a cease-fire," the translator said. "He'll temporarily withdraw most of his forces to east side of Oder River and reopen the discussions that he had previously been unable to have with General Eisenhower about Allied Control Commission in Germany. For your part . . . you will . . ."

"I *will not* do shit!" Patton exploded. "Please tell the Marshal that this phase of the war is over and *he lost*. He doesn't tell *me* what to do. Tell him that there's only one alternative to an unconditional surrender today . . . and he knows what the hell that is. Tell the Marshal that he has until high noon . . . that's 1200 hours . . . to give me his answer, or I'm going to go ahead with Plan B on my own."

Patton had turned to leave even before the translator had finished.

Temporary Soviet Armies Command Post
Schlosswallhalle
Osnabruck, Germany
Tuesday, July 24, 1945, 11:11 a.m.

The red flags still flew. The row of Josef Stalin tanks parked across the street on the grounds of the university were manned by crews anxious to perpetuate the glory of the Soviet Union. Far away in Moscow, their namesake was furious.

In the first decade of the first century, when Publius Quinctilius Varus, the husband of the grandniece of Emperor Augustus, was defeated in these woods, Hermann the German chopped off his head and sent it to Rome. Quinctilius's armies were never seen again. For the remainder of his life, the great Caesar Augustus was seen wandering the halls of his marble palace calling out to no one, "Quinctilius Varus, give me back my legions!"

If today fell to ruin, would the hallways of the Kremlin echo with the sound of the Man of Steel shrieking, "Georgi Konstantinovich, give me back my legions?"

Zhukov knew that *his* potential loss of legions would be on a scale even greater than that which Varus suffered in the service of Augustus. Zhukov also knew that it was far more certain that *his* head would be severed by the Man of Steel than by the American Napoleon.

Today, Marshal of the Soviet Union Georgi Zhukov was feeling alone. He felt as alone as he ever had.

This morning, Zhukov had met the great Patton—with his laughably squeaky voice. He had listened to his angry squeaky demands and had endured his refusal to salute a Marshal of the Soviet Union—a *three-time hero* of the Soviet Union.

As he drove away blindfolded, Zhukov had made his decision. The "squeaker" had to be bluffing. He wouldn't parley if he was not afraid of a fight. Zhukov would attack. He would attack immediately.

These had been Zhukov's thoughts—but they had changed.

On the way back to his own lines from the place where the despicable Yanks had dropped him off, he'd paused to visit his shock troops, to give them a little encouragement before the battle. They had greeted him warmly and with excitement. By chance, he met that model of Soviet manhood—the captain who had carried around a potato sack filled with the heads of SS officers. He had been so glad to see this man and he'd told the shock troops that *these* were the kind of officers that the Rodinya needed—the kind of troops who would crush the Americans.

The captain had wanted to show him something. Happily they had walked into an oak forest—across the carpet of fallen leaves where the shafts of broken sunlight filtered through the tree branches and reflected off the gold threads of the marshal's shoulderboards, again making the scene somewhat theatrical.

Here, amid an armada of buzzing flies, the captain—like a cat proudly showing off a dead mouse—showed Zhukov the captured American soldiers of the 90th Infantry Division. They lay quietly and almost peacefully in the carpet of fallen leaves where the shafts of broken sunlight filtered through the tree branches and made them seem as though they were almost part of the forest itself.

The blood stains that were spattered across the bodies had turned the brown of the fallen leaves that remained, still rotting away from the previous autumn. The olive drab of their uniforms blended nicely with the color of the new, green leaves of this season's growth. The bodies blended so nicely that Zhukov could not tell where the remnants of this mass execution of prisoners ended, and the rest of the forest continued.

Zhukov had been speechless. He knew that *when*—not *if*—Patton saw this, the men of the Third Army and its attached units would exact a terrible vengeance on everything Soviet that crossed their path until there was nothing Soviet left to cross their path.

"Georgi Konstantinovich, give me back my legions!"

Zhukov had found General Simoyak, and he'd instructed to have his surrender notice to the Americans by 1200 hours. Simoyak had protested, but Zhukov replied that this was an order that could not be questioned.

Similar messages had gone out to Katukov and Bogdanov and all the others.

Now, Marshal of the Soviet Union Georgi Zhukov was as alone as he'd been on that first day of December back in 1896 when he'd come into this world. The intervening years passed through his mind and he opened the bottle of vodka and toasted a mighty career.

He was feeling cold and lonely, but the vodka made him feel warm.

There had been his service to the Tsar, and his service to the Revolution in the saddle of a powerful cavalry horse. There had been his successful counteroffensive against Japs in Mongolia in 1939 and Finns the following year. And the Great Patriotic War. No officer had distinguished himself more in the Great Patriotic War.

Zhukov toasted his career. He toasted his triumphs. He toasted each of his Hero of the Soviet Union decorations. After all those toasts, he was getting just a bit sentimental.

Yet those words echoed in his head: "Georgi Konstantinovich, give me back my legions!"

Zhukov had felt cold and lonely, but the vodka had made him feel warm.

Marshal Georgi Zhukov realized as he toasted the man who looked back from the shaving mirror that the three stars of his three Heroes were exactly the same size as the star that was deeply embossed on the grip of his Nagant revolver. He smiled as he looked at all four side by side.

What an interesting coincidence!

He had felt so very cold and lonely. The vodka was making him feel warm, but the gun metal was cool against his temple.

The wind that whispered "Georgi Konstantinovich, give me back my legions," was silent at last.

Marshal of the Soviet Union Georgi Zhukov was as alone today as he'd been on that first day of December back in 1896 when he'd come into this world.

PART IV

THE BUCK
STOPS HERE

★ ★ ★ ★ ★

14

★ ★

On the road
Approximately 20 miles west of Slutzk, Byelorussian Soviet
Socialist Republic
Monday, September 3, 1945, 10:03 a.m.

"WELCOME to the Union of Soviet Socialist Republics . . .
Courtesy of the 4th Armored Division."

Nate McKinley read the sign out loud as General Patton's
jeep bounced along the main road that ran parallel to the
Bialystok-Smolensk-Moscow Highway where General
Vlasov's army was slowly advancing.

General Andrei Andreyevich Vlasov, the enigmatic rene-
gade Russian general—who had been itching to fight Stalin
since 1942—had finally gotten his chance.

Though many in the Allied leadership had distrusted him,
Vlasov and his 1st Russian National Army had just passed
their first test. They had attacked and captured Minsk, the
administrative center of the Byelorussian—*White* Russian—
Soviet Socialist Republic.

Now, a week later, Patton himself had crossed the pre-1939
border of Stalin's Soviet Union. It was as if the late Georgi
Zhukov had lived to lead the 1st Byelorussian Front through
International Falls, Minnesota or Brownsville, Texas—with a
rebel *American* army fighting at his side.

"You know that today is the sixth anniversary of the day that
England and France declared war on the Krauts?" Patton asked
rhetorically. "Stalin just sat out there until they had the Poles
whipped . . . then he took a slice . . . *this* damned slice . . . for
himself. We've just undone six years of evil mischief propa-
gated by the most terrible sonuvabitch to pass this way since
Attila the Hun."

After the victory at Osnabruck, and the almost immediate

collapse of Soviet forces in the West, Patton had spent relatively little time in the field—and he clearly missed being with his frontline troops.

Today he was back, on an inspection tour of his old command, his beloved Third Army. Along with Vlasov's army, his beloved Third was now in the vanguard of the Allied drive into the heartland of the Soviet Union. Spearheaded by the 4th Armored Division, his beloved Third would be the first American army to reach Moscow, *if* everything went according to plan. The plan was unfolding on schedule so far, but that schedule was extraordinarily tight—and Patton knew it. Autumn was already in the air, and winter was close behind.

Above, a formation of about a dozen A-26s, escorted by four P-47s, thundered past, headed for targets up ahead.

"In 1812, Napoleon was in Minsk by the third week of August," the General observed as his motorcade passed a line of 4th Armored Division M26A2s. "In 1941, Guderian was here at almost the same time."

"And Napoleon was in Moscow the second week of September," Nate added. He knew that the General would be reminiscing, so he'd taken some time to bone up on Napoleonic history. He knew that Napoleon's Grand Armee had emerged from the Battle of Borodino on September 7 with Moscow wide open to them, but he also knew that Borodino had exhausted them and put them in an untenable supply situation. September 7 was just four days away. Patton's "Grand Armee" had barely just begun.

There were major differences, but the parallels between 1812 and 1941 were obvious. The soldiers of both the Grand Armee and the Wehrmacht had dashed proudly to the gates of Moscow only to find themselves hungrily wandering the steppes as the snowflakes fell. Now it was the turn of the US Army and its allies. They were still in the "proudly dashing" phase of the operation, but winter would put an end to that.

High above, they could see the contrails of a vast armada of airplanes—probably Berlin-based B-24s—headed out on a run against Smolensk, or possibly even Moscow.

The White House
Washington DC
Tuesday, September 4, 1945, 3:49 p.m.

"Gentlemen, I must say that all of this is very promising," Truman said with a smile as he looked up from the piece of yellow teletype paper that had just been passed around the room by General George Marshall.

Like most of the Washington politicians, Truman had been stunned by the performance of his Supreme Commander in Europe. Pleased, but stunned. At the Warsaw Conference in August, Patton had bullied, cajoled, and organized the armies of *ten* nations into a single fighting force directed at a single purpose on a single front. The Allied Force that had included the United States, Britain, Canada, and France had been joined by the Ukrainians and Poles, as well as Vlasov's 1st National Russian Army. At the conference, Lithuania, Estonia, and Latvia reasserted their independence and offered token support. It was, Secretary of State Edward Stettinius had observed, as though a United Nations Organization had come into being, *without* the United Nations Conference. Even before VE-Day, there hadn't been that many nations cooperating on the ground on a single front. Now that front was being pushed into the Soviet Union.

"George has certainly crossed a Rubicon," Secretary of War Henry Stimson observed.

"Or at least a point of no return," Marshall replied. "I'd be lying if I said I didn't feel a bit of apprehension."

"As Patton himself said so eloquently, that night at Rambuteau, we gotta speak to Uncle Joe in the only language that he understands and respects," Truman reminded them.

"And now we've followed Napoleon and Hitler into the abyss," Marshall said pessimistically. "Nobody has yet marched into the endlessness of Russia and come out unbroken."

"But nobody . . . certainly no military officer . . . understands the ironies of military history better than Patton," Stimson added.

Marshall broke the silence that followed Stimson's remark by suggesting that they move ahead with the situation briefing that had been prepared for the President. The General nodded to a young major, who, in turn, stood up and went to a series of maps that were on easels near the Truman's desk.

Each of the arrows representing an army were color-coded in a distinct hue. Those that were rendered in red were much shorter than they'd been at the previous briefing.

The major described the situation as he traced the tip of his pointer across the maps. Even as Patton and Vlasov were dashing toward Moscow, Montgomery's 21st Army Group had occupied the Baltic states with the cooperation of the locals, and Marshal Bagramyan's 1st Baltic Front had imploded.

On the right flank, American forces had been organized into a new 25th Army Group and were on the move. The Seventh Army was driving toward Lvov, while the Fifth Army and Eighth Army were supporting the Ukrainian thrust toward Kiev, Ukraine's capital.

Overhead, the Ninth Air Force was redeploying to eastern Poland to support 12th Army Group, and the Twelfth Air Force was going into Bucharest to do the same for 25th Army Group. Britain's Royal Air Force Bomber Command was now based at Koenigsberg. The USAAF Eighth Air Force was already operating out of Berlin and Fifteenth was moving to Budapest. Moscow was now getting hit every day—and every night—just as Berlin had been six months before.

LeMay's B-29s had begun flying from a nine-runway base near Jaffa in British Palestine. Sverdlovsk and the factory complexes east of the Urals were under relentless attack.

"Gentlemen," Truman said, sitting back in his chair as the young major concluded his briefing, "can it be said that our greatest threat might come from overconfidence?"

"And General *Winter*," Marshall added. "Stalin's ultimate ally is the weather that can ground our air power, cause engine oil to freeze solid inside our tanks and trucks, and our GIs' fingers to turn lifeless. As someone observed yesterday, autumn is already in the air . . . and winter was close behind."

Heurich's Rooming House
903 16th Street NW
Washington DC
Friday, September 14, 1945, 3:49 a.m.

Rosemary O'Leary felt herself falling. She tried to call out, but failed. She tried to run, but her feet were like anvils. Sweat and tears of frustration were pouring down her cheeks. She was back on Fifth Avenue, reliving that dreadful day. Something sharp hit her head, burning, tearing into her flesh. A horrible, high-pitched, metallic sound seemed to explode in her head. Everything around her was crumbling. Another horrible, high-pitched, metallic sound exploded in her head. A third horrible, high-pitched, metallic sound exploded.

Rosie was in darkness. The only light was the glare of the streetlamp framed by the window of her room. Her face was half buried in a sweat-soaked pillow.

Another high-pitched, metallic sound exploded from the low table near her bed.

"Hello," she said, lifting the receiver from the phone.

"Rosemary? It's Fiona," the voice said excitedly. "Did I wake you?"

"No . . . I'm always up doing my nails at . . . what time is it?"

"Quarter of four."

"What are you doing up at a quarter of four?"

"I thought you'd want to know . . ."

"What should I want to know at a quarter of four?" Rosie scolded.

"I thought you'd want to know that they just bombed Kokura."

"Who bombed . . .? Where's Kokura?"

"It's a city in Japan," Fiona Wells explained. "The American Air Force. Should I ring you back when you're awake?"

"No. I'm awake. You just *woke* me up," Rosie said angrily. "Why did you wake me up to tell me that America bombed someplace in Japan? They do it nearly every day."

"Not like this," Fiona explained. "This was the *Atomic* Bomb. This is the bomb with the power of thousands of tons of TNT. There was a fireball as bright as ten thousand suns. They could see it hundreds of miles away."

As she sat on the edge of her bed, Rosie realized that she'd been awakened *from* a nightmare *to* a nightmare. The Atomic Bomb had been the subject of rumors and whispered innuendos all summer. Apparently, it was real. It was said to be a monster with unparalleled power to destroy. Maybe it would also have the power to end the war—or the *wars*.

As she pondered *that* monster, Rosie O'Leary thought of the inescapable monster within her head, the monster that inhabited her dreams. She looked in the mirror and pushed her hair back, wishing that this jagged scar twisting across her scalp was merely a nightmare.

She had escaped death in the Fourth of July attack, but barely. She had suffered a deep scalp laceration and had lost a great deal of blood. Rosie lay in the rubble for nearly twenty-four hours before her limp body was taken to a hospital. In the meantime, her purse had become entangled with the mangled, lifeless body of another woman who had been identified as Rosie.

Unconscious when she arrived at the hospital, Rosie had been delirious for another two days before she was finally able to tell a nurse who she was. In the confusion that had ensued after the attack, it would be several days before the news of her survival would reach her friends and family.

Rosie had survived, but she had been left with a permanent reminder of the Fourth of July attack. She could comb her hair so that it wasn't visible, but here alone in her room in the muggy dampness of a Washington September, she knew that she could escape neither the monster within her head, nor the horrible disfigurement that had made *her* a monster.

The White House
Washington DC
Tuesday, September 14, 1945, 7:57 a.m.

"It's certainly a good thing for the world that Hitler's crowd . . . or Stalin's . . . didn't discover this weapon *first*," President Harry Truman said as Secretary of War Stimson and Generals Arnold and Marshall took their chairs in his office. "It seems to be the most terrible weapon ever discovered.

Have we stumbled onto the fire and destruction prophesied in the Euphrates Valley . . . after Noah and his ark?"

"The central part of Kokura was flattened," Arnold explained after a long pause. "Sixteen hours later, there were still huge fires burning ten miles from the center of the blast, but the dust cloud had finally started to dissipate."

"I thought they were supposed to drop the bomb on Hiroshima?" Stimson asked.

"Hiroshima was the primary target . . . Kokura was the secondary," Hap Arnold explained. "Major Sweeney reported that the cloud cover at Hiroshima was too dense for the observation planes to get a clear view, so he diverted to Kokura where the weather was clear."

"We'll have to hope that this'll be enough to push the Japanese to accept our demands for unconditional surrender," Truman said.

"This was the gamble when we *started* this exercise," Stimson said. "Now that we've let the genie out of his bottle . . ."

"The press got wind of it in the middle of the night," Truman said. "I was hoping to make an orderly announcement this morning. I had to . . . well, it's a good thing that we had a press release ready to go."

"This is the one where the Japs can expect 'a rain of ruin from the air, the likes of which have never been seen on this earth?' " Arnold interjected.

"That's the one," Truman replied. "Now that we've let the cat out of the bag and we've told the world that we've got Atomic Bombs in production . . . and that we can drop them like raindrops . . . what *is* the status of the Manhattan Project?"

"We have a second bomb out in the Marianas," Arnold answered. "This is the one that's set to go on Monday. The second strike is planned against Hiroshima again, this time with Nagasaki as the alternate in case of cloud cover . . . But those two are the only two that Groves has turned over to us so far. My understanding is that number three is a matter of weeks away, but we don't have to let the Japanese know that. They won't think that we're bluffing after Monday."

"Have we heard anything about how Uncle Joe is taking the news?" Truman asked.

"Radio Moscow calls it a fabrication," Stimson smiled. "Actually, they've had relatively little to say. Just enough to head off rumors, I suppose. Not enough to get their people too worked up."

"To head off rumors that they might be *next*," Arnold grinned.

"And they *will* be," Marshall added. "Sverdlovsk is targeted for November if the third Atomic Bomb isn't needed for Japan."

"One would hope that the first two would be enough to convince Stalin and Hirohito that this war is hopeless," Truman said, glancing at the other men."

"How could they *not* be convinced?" Stimson asked rhetorically.

"How, indeed?" Arnold replied. "Because they're damned fools with a death wish . . . ?"

"Or because they're totalitarian dictators . . . with aspirations of grandeur that come ahead of the lives of their people?" Truman offered.

"Or because . . . especially in Stalin's case," Stimson said thoughtfully, "he knows he's very, very close to having his *own* Atomic Bomb . . . and he can launch a 'rain of ruin' against *us*."

Victor's Italian Ristorante
Connecticut Avenue
Washington DC
Thursday, September 20, 1945, 8:07 p.m.

"Are you sure that your boss didn't put you up to this dinner in order to spy on me?" Rosemary O'Leary said with a wink.

"Not in the least," Stephen Cuthbert said, slicing his veal piccata. "I think that you're a very interesting person . . . I have for a long time . . . I just wanted to get to know you a little better."

"I was just teasing," Rosie said, trying not to blush.

Nothing could have surprised her more when Stephen Cuthbert phoned *The Washington Herald* to ask her out. She'd barely gotten over the humiliation of being jilted by her lover of two years when she met Nathaniel McKinley—and he'd stolen her heart. Since then she'd scrupulously avoided dates.

She had been asked a few times—once even by a rear admiral she met at a reception—but she'd always said "no." When she looked at any potential suitor, there was only one face in her mind. As long as the handsome soldier was in all her dreams, she just didn't feel like dating.

She wondered why she'd said "yes" to Stephen Cuthbert. Maybe she was finally—and unconsciously—moving on. Maybe it was finally time to stop pining for a man she'd barely met. Nathaniel probably wouldn't recognize her on the street.

Cuthbert *was* a nice man. He was a little puffed up—like most diplomats—but he was, as her mother would say, "a nice young man." He was polite and pleasant and seemed sincere.

Stephen expressed a genuine interest in her career and didn't look down on her the way most Washington insiders did with "girl reporters."

They talked about their lives and hopes and dreams, as people usually do on first dates, and each seemed to be enjoying the other's company. Eventually, talk turned, as it often did these days, to the postwar world. As had been the case in the weeks surrounding VE-Day, it now seemed safe to discuss such plans again.

She asked him about the suspended United Nations Conference, and whether it would be back on the table when—or *if*—Stalin was out of the picture. He'd explained the passion that Stettinius still had for the organization. Cuthbert asserted that he shared that passion but was concerned.

"Secretary Stettinius seems to be enamored with the 'Alliance' that was formed at the Warsaw Conference," Cuthbert confided. "He's thinking that the nucleus of the future United Nations might be the military alliance that Patton created."

"It seems to be working," Rosie said.

"As a military alliance maybe, but there's great danger in basing a political and diplomatic association of nations on something that was created by a general . . . especially a general with Patton's power. I heard Patton speaking in Warsaw. He's opposed to the United Nations. Thinks it's a waste of time."

"But wasn't the original United Nations Organization an outgrowth of the alliance against Hitler?"

"Yes, but it was created by politicians and diplomats, and

not dominated by a single, powerful general," Cuthbert asserted. "I'm afraid that he's moved too far into the world of politics."

"Are you one of those who think that Patton will run for President in 1948?" Rosie asked.

"Off the record?" Cuthbert asked, his diplomat's antenna sensing a reporter's question.

"Off the record." Rosie said reluctantly, knowing that if she used the quote she'd have to call Cuthbert an "unnamed State Department official."

"We *assume* that he'll be a candidate," Cuthbert said. "It's well known that General Eisenhower was thinking about a run for the presidency before he died. Popular military figures make attractive candidates . . . but the last time a war hero general of this stature became president, it was Grant . . . and his administration was a disaster."

"And the time before that, it was George Washington," Rosie reminded him. "Unless you include Andrew Jackson . . ."

"The truth is, I'm not so worried about 1948," Cuthbert said, sidestepping slightly. "It's 1946. What really worries me is that all of these comparisons to Napoleon have gone to Patton's head . . . and a lot of people . . . Secretary Stettinius included . . . are enthralled with him. Napoleon became emperor at a time when he was a singularly successful and immensely popular general . . . and he ended up as an immense disaster for France."

"I don't think that's a possibility here," Rosie said. "When Napoleon became emperor, France was leaderless . . . it was run by a committee . . . there was a void begging to be filled."

The conversation continued, with both parties enjoying the spirited discussion on subjects of common interest.

"What do *you* expect to do when the war's finally over?" Rosie asked as they had finished their tiramisu and were waiting for the check.

"I'm planning . . . hoping . . . to make a career of the foreign service," he said. "The State Department has been an exciting place to work these past seven years. I'd planned on staying a year and going back to law school . . . but one year led to two and then the war. You don't quit the State Department in the middle of a world war! What about you . . . are you planning to stay on with the paper?"

"I've always liked journalism," Rosie said, pleased that he continued to show an interest in her career. "I think I'll probably stay as long as they'll let me . . . or until I get a better offer from another paper."

Rosie found herself starting to relax, and starting to like Stephen Cuthbert. When he sat close—but not *too* close—on the cab ride back to her rooming house, it felt natural and comfortable. However, when he sent the cab on its way after they'd reached 903 Sixteenth Street, she began to feel herself growing a bit tense.

It was a cool evening. Autumn was in the air, and winter was close behind. On one hand, Rosie wished that she had a man to hug her—and on the other, she wanted to run away and hide.

"Thank you, Stephen," she said nervously," I really have had a lovely evening."

"It was my pleasure," he said, moving a bit closer.

"I guess it's time to say . . . goodnight," she said, touching his hand.

Suddenly, Rosie felt the tears exploding through her eyes and running down her face, bringing ridiculous little rivulets of mascara across her cheeks. She wanted so badly to share a goodnight kiss with this kind and pleasant young man, but she'd realized that she was totally and desperately in love with a quiet young soldier—who was thousands of miles away, but who did not know that she was alive.

"I'm sorry . . ." he said, abruptly backing away. "Was it something I said? Was it something I did?"

"No . . . please," she sobbed, feeling like a fool and wiping her cheeks with her handkerchief. "It's not you . . . you didn't do anything . . . It's me. *I'm* sorry. I'm getting over something that ended last year. I'm just not ready . . . I'm really sorry. It's been a really swell evening and I'm spoiling it for you."

"No . . . not in the least," he said, showing genuine concern. "I'm just really sorry for whatever it is that's upsetting you."

"It's not *you.*"

"Still . . . I'm really sorry."

"Stephen, you've been an absolute sweetheart," Rosie said, giving him a quick hug. "Thank you for trying to understand me. *I* don't even understand me."

Henry Stimson's Georgetown townhouse
Washington DC
Friday, September 21, 1945, 4:58 p.m.

"Happy birthday, Mr. Secretary," General George Catlett Marshall said, raising a toast to his old friend, Henry Stimson. "What does this make you now, Henry, about forty-nine?"

"Thank you, George," Stimson smiled, touching his glass of scotch to Marshall's tumbler of iced tea. "It's actually the twenty-ninth anniversary of my forty-ninth birthday . . . but in all of my seventy-eight years on the Earth, I cannot remember a better present being delivered on my birthday than the *unconditional* surrender of the Empire of Japan."

"Their little emperor made it official this afternoon," Marshall said. "He made a radio speech . . . the first time that a Japanese emperor's ever spoken to his people."

"The voice of god," Stimson said, shaking his head. "I wonder if they've figured out yet that he's *not* a god."

"They'll have to get used to the idea," Marshall said. "He'll be playing second fiddle to Emperor Doug."

"Is that what they're calling MacArthur now?" Stimson smiled, referring to General Douglas MacArthur.

"That was just something that Leahy said this afternoon when the official press release went out naming him as Supreme Commander of Allied Occupation forces," Marshall nodded. "He's already given Hirohito his first order—demanded a radio station in Tokyo for American use. I'm surprised that the President and Mr. Churchill would allow Hirohito to stay in place at all."

"That was the last sticking point," Stimson replied. "I spoke to Ed Stettinius this afternoon. He phoned . . . of all the days for me to leave early and not be in my office . . ."

"For God's sake, Henry, it's your birthday, after all," Marshall scolded. "After all that you've done . . . you're entitled to leave early on a Friday afternoon when it's your birthday."

"Has there been any comment from Uncle Joe through the diplomatic channels?" Stimson asked.

"Not yet. Not that I've heard," Marshall replied. "Apparently nothing yet on Radio Moscow, although the BBC is carrying the news in their Russian-language shortwave broadcasts. The Chinese are celebrating. Chiang Kai-shek is moving his people into Manchuria. We're expecting him to start moving into Mongolia. Now that the Japanese are gone and the Russians have circled their wagons in the west, Mongolia is just a vacuum.

"What are Patton's plans, now that it's over with Japan?"

"His strategic plan . . . to encircle Moscow and Stalin's wartime capital at Kuybyshev before the end of the year . . . is ahead of schedule," Marshall replied. "Malinovsky is finally in control of the Crimea, so we can go ahead with the invasion at Rostov."

"That'll open up the whole south of Russia," Stimson said, imagining the geography of the region. "Rostov is an all-weather port and the Don River is as wide as the Mississippi for miles upstream."

"It's a flanking maneuver that's destined for the history books," Marshall mused. "It'll force Stalin to divert forces away from defending the Moscow-Smolensk area."

"When MacArthur lands General Krueger's Sixth Army at Vladivostok, that'll further outflank Stalin," Stimson observed. "Assuming they're able to get ashore satisfactorily."

"The first of November is getting a bit late in the year for that operation, so there's no firm commitment to go ahead with that. Even if we have to postpone the invasion until spring, though, Vladivostok will be isolated . . . Okinawa-based B-29s have succeeded in cutting the Trans-Siberian Railway in several places."

"Is there a definite D-Day for the Rostov operation?" Stimson asked.

"It looks like the first of the month," Marshall replied. "Admiral Halsey released Admiral McCain's Task Group 38.1 from the Pacific last month . . . they'll be there with five carriers, a half-dozen cruisers and two battleships. Eighth Army will ship out of Odessa. Two corps from Vlasov's Russian Army will be attached. George thinks that it'll go a lot more smoothly if there are some Russian troops in on the show."

"Certainly from a political point of view." Stimson nodded. "Russians hate to have to fight Russians, especially when Vlasov represents the sort of Russia they were *promised* by the Bolsheviks at the time of the Revolution."

"And which they've been *waiting on* for a quarter of a century." Marshall smiled. "It looks by the number of desertions that we're seeing . . . that they're tired of waiting."

"They're not *all* tired of waiting," Stimson cautioned. "There are still plenty who see Vlasov as 'a puppet of fascism,' and Stalin still has a million-man army. He still has his alliance with 'General Winter,' and the autumn colors have started to appear out on the steppes."

"We're also still waiting for the other shoe to drop with Mr. Fuchs and Stalin's Atomic Bomb," Marshall said soberly. "That's *our* greatest fear."

"I hope and pray that Patton can outrun both General Winter *and* Mr. Fuchs," Stimson replied.

"Happy birthday, Henry," Marshall said, raising his glass and standing to leave.

"Thanks again, George. I'm looking forward to enjoying the *next* one . . . and the few that I have left after that . . . in happy retirement on my porch at Highhold."

"Here's to a peaceful 1946," Marshall said. "Is it too early for us to toast the new year?"

"Not when the toast is to world peace."

Aboard a USAAF C-47 transport
Over the Sea of Azov
Thursday, October 11, 1945, 12:09 p.m.

"What a *damned fine war!*" Patton observed as he looked out the window of the plane at the vast armada of warships below. Escorted by twelve Twelfth Air Force Mustangs, the General's C-47 was the final leg of an inspection tour that was taking them deep into the Caucasus.

This mountainous region west of the Black Sea on Asia's doorstep was vital to the war effort because the Russian port of Rostov-on-Don was the anchor point of Patton's huge flanking maneuver to get behind the Red Army's main line. Beyond this, the Black Sea and Caucasus region was home to a dozen or more of the stateless nationalities whose status as colonies of the Russian tsars had been inherited by the Soviet Union. As Patton had put it: "If I'm going to be fighting this damned war in these people's backyard, I should at least meet them face to face."

"I see the *Intrepid*," General Hap Gay said, pointing to a huge grey slab, the flight deck covered with dark blue airplanes and marked with the numeral "11."

"That one with all the guns must be the *South Dakota*," Nate McKinley said, pointing to a huge battleship whose main turrets were bristling with nine sixteen-inch guns.

"Yep, I see a '57' on her hull," General Oscar Koch said, staring at the big ship through a pair of binoculars. "I didn't know that you'd taken an interest in the Navy."

"Only since the third of September," Nate replied. "I've sort of become a battleship fan . . . especially for one particular ship."

"Oh yeah, that's right . . . you're a Montana boy," Koch laughed.

"We may be a landlocked state, but it was *Montana's* ship that sunk the Japs' biggest battleship," Nate grinned.

"Well, it was certainly a moment for naval history," Patton said, jumping into the conversation. "On her first cruise, the USS *Montana* runs into their super-battleship *Yamato* and puts her under. The last great naval battle of World War II. Decisive battle . . . perfect gunnery."

"Well, I for one am glad that the United States didn't have to go through any more land battles with the Japs," Gay added.

"Of course, if you're looking for history, the *South Dakota* back there made some of her own last week," Koch reminded them.

"The only naval battle that we'll probably see in this damned World War III," Patton laughed. "The last hurrah of the Red Navy's Black Sea Fleet . . . but hardly a fair fight. Those sixteen-inchers on the *South Dakota* were more than a match for the *Sebastopol*. What was her main armament?"

"She had twelve-inch guns. Quite a few . . . maybe a dozen . . . which was fairly respectable," Koch explained. "She was older and slower, but not by much. It was a closer match than you'd think. Both ships had been refitted since the war began. The *Sebastopol* was mauled by the Krauts and repaired . . . the *South Dakota* went home after the Leyte Gulf fight a year ago. Like you said about the *Montana,* General, it all came down to gunnery."

"I see a city coming up, now," Gay said, pointing out the window. "It must be Rostov."

"There she is," Patton said, looking out at the sprawling city covered by a thin layer of brown haze. "Rostov-on-the-Don . . . the 'Gateway to the Caucasus.' Everything that comes out of the Caucasus comes through here . . . everything that comes down the Don River . . . and the Volga, too. This place has a history. Homer wrote about it in the *Iliad* and the *Odyssey.* Both the Greeks and Romans had colonies on the Black Sea. The Turks fought the Persians here. The Mongol hordes swept through here. The Russians have been fighting over the place ever since. First the Tatars and the Cossacks, then the Krauts for the last few years . . . and now us."

"The Russians built the first fort here to protect the mouth of the river from the Don Cossacks," Koch added, as he studied the city with his binoculars. "Biggest fortress in southern Russia . . . . The Russians are *still* fighting the Cossacks."

As the plane circled to land at the seaport city, Nate could look down at the snowcapped mountains of the Caucasus in the distance, and the huge mountains of materiel being unloaded into dumps ashore. He started to count the American liberty ships at anchor down there, but gave up after twenty-four.

Over the past seventy-two hours—as General Patton and his staff had made stops in Warsaw, Kiev, and Odessa—Nate had had a bird's-eye view of the incredible military machine that was being used to defeat the Red Army ahead of the Russian winter.

Since leaving Warsaw, Nate had seen lines of M26A2 tanks and deuce-and-a-half trucks that stretched to the horizon. He had visited airfields with a hundred or more aircraft on the ground, and where takeoffs and landings were occurring constantly. He had watched Patton address several groups of more than six or seven thousand GIs gathered in one place at one time. Now, he'd seen a naval task group so big that nobody in the group had even bothered to mention the seven heavy cruisers that Admiral McCain had brought in from the Pacific.

When the two Wright Cyclones of Patton's C-47 had been shut down and the back door jerked open, Patton led the group down the stairs into the crisp autumn air. The temperature was barely above freezing, but the skies were clear and it was actually quite warm in direct sunlight. Autumn was definitely in the air.

Resplendent in his polished green helmet with its circle of five stars, the Supreme Commander was met by General Robert Eichelberger, a four-star man, who commanded the United States Eighth Army, and by three-star General John Hodge, whose XXIV Corps had been attached to Eichelberger's command since the Battle of Osnabruck two long months before.

"I see that you gentlemen have secured the city," Patton laughed. Of the nearly three dozen aircraft parked at the sprawling airport, only a single forlorn Ilyushin Il-12—a Russian knockoff of the Douglas design in which the General flew—was marked with red stars. The rest all had the white stars and bars of the USAAF, or the blue and gold of the Ukrainian Air Force.

"Compared to Okinawa, this place was a damned cakewalk," Hodge said. "They were sort of stubborn at that big fort across the river, but a few hours of sixteen-inch fire from the battlewagons sort of changed their minds."

"We came ashore south of the city expecting to have to do some pretty tough street fighting," Eichelberger explained. "But by the end of the day, the biggest problem was all these old ladies in babushkas trying to sell the guys this black bread they have here."

"They all think that the damned war is already over," Hodge added. "They hate Stalin and most of 'em are glad to see us."

"It was kind of embarrassing when we finally got here to the airport," Eichelberger laughed. "There was already that big sign over there that says 'Welcome to Rostov . . . Courtesy of the 119th Airborne Division.' They flew in from Odessa and took the place without a shot."

"We've secured the east bank of the Don for about a hundred miles . . . up as far as Tsimlyanskaya," Eichelberger explained. "Vlasov's corps will disembark up there. That way their heavy equipment will be that much closer to Stalingrad."

"I imagine that Stalingrad won't be much of a cakewalk," Patton said, the grin fading from his face.

"No sir," Eichelberger said soberly. "They're not going to let that one go without a fight. Stalin has been pouring reinforcements in there for a month and a half."

"I'm damned glad that it's going to be Vlasov's people," Patton said. "Not because I'm afraid of a fight . . . but because I strongly believe that . . . historically . . . and ironically . . . it ought to be a Russian who takes the Stalin out of *Stalin*grad."

The Offices of *The Washington Herald*
Washington DC
Friday, October 12, 1945, 1:29 p.m.

Rex Simmons felt himself growing old. It wasn't the lines in the face that stared at him from the mirror every morning. It wasn't the aches and pains in his knuckles. A half hour at the keyboard got *them* limbered up.

It was a combination of things. It was the empty apartment and the loneliness that had been greeting him there since Marge left him to go back to Ohio. It was the letdown that a lot of newspaper men were starting to feel now that the war was winding down again—this time probably for the last time. It was the cherry trees, so full of life in the spring, but now nearly bare against the leaden, overcast sky. Autumn was definitely in the air, and winter was close behind. Rex Simmons felt the autumn of middle age and avoided thinking about the winter that was close behind.

Perhaps most of all, it had been watching Rosemary O'Leary grow up before his eyes. He first remembered her around the time of the invasion of Sicily during the summer of '43. She was just one of dozens of little coeds who spent their summer after graduation interning at the paper before going on to their real lives. They were usually a faceless crowd, gone before he could remember their names.

He only remembered Rose—he called her 'Rose' even though her friends all called her 'Rosie'—because she used to bring him his coffee. Getting the managing editor's coffee was a typical intern job. Even for this, he probably would never have noticed her, but for the fact that on the morning of the Sicily action, she'd spilled his coffee completely across the papers he'd spread across the middle of his desk. He had chewed her out with unaccustomed fury, and had come within a hair's breadth of firing her as she frantically tried to clean up the mess.

As much as he tried to dislike her, and forced himself to be sour and overly critical of her, there was something in her smile and her happy, freckled face that got under his thick reptilian skin. He spent a year deliberately giving her harder and more difficult work to do, as though subconsciously aiming to trap her into failure.

She had fought back not only by succeeding, but by *excelling* at the tasks he gave her, until one day, he realized that he'd inadvertently molded her into one of the best people on his staff. He had never intended to do such a thing—certainly not with a *girl*.

Gradually, she had become the daughter he never had. He had watched his Rose blossom at the San Francisco Conference. He'd seen her work praised by reporters at the rival papers. When he thought she'd been killed in New York on the Fourth of July, he'd cried—literally sobbing real tears—for the first time in at least a quarter of a century. When her "WHAT OUR FLAG SAYS" piece had earned a Pulitzer Prize, Rex Simmons knew that he too had wound up with a prize.

He had seen the little girl in ponytail and bobby socks sopping up spilled coffee grow into the assured young woman that he could now see striding confidently across the newsroom toward his office. She had come to *The Washington Herald* as a silly little coed. Now she was a smartly dressed, and actually quite attractive woman. Three years ago, she would have been lucky to have had a date with a fraternity boy. Today, there were rumors of an affair with an admiral, and somebody had seen her at Victor's having dinner with one of Stettinius's aides. For a fleeting moment, Rex Simmons actually wished that he was a few decades younger.

"You wanted to see me, Mr. Simmons?"

"Yeah, I've got a little out-of-town junket that I'd like to send you on," he said, gesturing for her to sit down. "Ever hear of Georgia?"

"Yeah," she said apprehensively. "The Peach State. I had a boyfriend that ended up at Fort Benning. I've never been down there, though."

"I mean the *other* Georgia," he said smugly.

"Oh yeah . . . the one that's one of the Soviet Socialist Republics of the *Union* of Soviet Socialist Republics," Rosie said, knowing that he was playing one of his little games, and turning it back on him by showing off the fruits of her year in exile in his research department. "I've never been there either . . . but it's on the Black Sea and I guess it's warm enough to grow peaches. Most of the people were killed by Mongols six hundred years ago . . . the tsars took it over a hundred years ago. They still have their own language and . . ."

"Okay . . . okay," Simmons said. "I should always know better than to try to be tricky with *you*. Do you know how many people in this country have never heard of the other Georgia?"

"No," she replied, continuing the game that he'd started. "But give me an hour and I can come up with a reasonable estimate of the number."

"The correct number is 'not very damned many,' and that's the point," he said.

"You want me to go over there and find out how many Georgians have never heard of the United States?" Rosie smiled.

"You're getting awfully uppity," he laughed. "It must be Friday. No . . . seriously, the point is that ever since the United States government announced that it was actively backing the rights of the Ukraine and the Baltic states to no longer be Soviet Socialist Republics and get back their independence, all the other Republics want onto the bandwagon."

"I know, it was me who wrote that piece on the hypocrisy

of the Reds *not* freeing all of the Tsar's colonies when the they took over."

"Well, it's not just places like those, and places that you and I have heard of . . . like Georgia . . . and Armenia and Azerbaijan . . ."

"Or the Soviet Socialist Republics out in central Asia like Turkmenskaya and Uzbekskaya . . . to use the Russian versions of the words."

"It's not just those," Simmons said, opening a book that he had on his desk. "There's ones that I bet even you've never heard of. Okay . . . for instance . . . have you heard of Chechnya?"

"No," Rosie said sheepishly, after wracking her brain for a minute.

"Nagorno-Karabakh?"

"No."

"Kabardianno-Balkaria?"

"No."

"Ossetia?"

"I get the point."

"I'm not asking you all this in order to play 'stump the wizard,'" Simmons said. "Even *I* had never heard of these places until I started looking this stuff up. Up 'til a month or so ago, these places didn't matter a whit to Mr. John Q. Public out in Silver Spring or Dubuque, Iowa. Two years ago . . . even two *months* ago . . . you couldn't have found anyone on the street that had heard of the Kazakskayan Soviet Socialist Republic . . . . and *now,* as of this afternoon, Kazak*stan* has been recognized as an independent country by the United States government."

"Yes," Rosie interjected, "I think it's pretty humbling to know that we'll wake up tomorrow morning to have the *ninth* largest country in the world—area-wise—be a place that you and I had never heard of two years ago."

"The world is changing faster than people can keep up with," Rex Simmons said, leaning back in his chair. "It always happens when they have these wars over there. I can remember when there was no Czechoslovakia or Yugoslavia in the world."

"But Czechoslovakia and Yugoslavia had *never* existed,"

Rosie explained. "The interesting thing for me, is that these places we are talking about *used* to exist, but people forgot about them . . . except the people who actually live there. It's like one of those 'mysterious kingdoms of long ago' books that I used to like to read when I was a little girl."

"Now they exist again . . . or they soon will . . . but they're still mysteries," Simmons said. "We could speculate all afternoon about this . . . but that wouldn't really get us anywhere. Our readers need to know what the hell these places are really like. I want you to go over there and take a look. Meet the people. See what they're really like."

"You want *me* to go to the Caucasus?" Rosie asked, taunting him lightheartedly. "You want to send a *girl* on a trip like this?"

"You're the best man that I've got for the job," Simmons said. "Pardon the figure of speech."

"I don't know whether to be honored or insulted by the figure of speech," Rosie laughed. "But I'm honored by the opportunity to do the job."

"You've been overseas before . . . but this won't be like Paris," Simmons cautioned. "This'll be pretty primitive. The Allies have landed in Rostov . . . on the Azov Sea . . . that's right at the edge of the Caucasus . . . you can get a military flight that far. Read everything you can on the Caucasus. Get yourself inoculated for any of those diseases they have over there. Try to be ready to leave by Monday."

"O . . . kay," Rosie said, trying to comprehend the notion of being given the weekend to prepare for a trip to the heart of the unknown. She might as well have been told to leave the next day for the dark side of the moon.

"Oh yeah . . . One more thing," Simmons said as she stood to leave.

"What's that?"

"Please . . . um . . . ah . . . try to take care of yourself out there. I'd really hate to lose you."

15

★ ★

On the road to Kabardianno-Balkaria
Approximately 20 miles east of Tikhoretsk, Russia
Saturday, October 13, 1945, 10:09 a.m.

"Isn't this magnificent?" Patton asked rhetorically, staring across the alpine meadow to the beech forests ablaze with autumn color and at the steep mountains beyond. "Have you ever *seen* anything like this country?"

"Well, sir . . . actually I have," Nate McKinley said as he guided the jeep across a narrow, one-lane bridge on the road that led in a southeasterly direction from Rostov, deep into the Caucasus. "But yes . . . it really *is* a nice view of the mountains . . . enough to make a Montana boy a trifle homesick."

"You don't know how lucky you are, boy," Patton said as he looked at the snow-peaked mountains to the south. "To have had a chance to grow up in a place like that."

"As far as the lay of the land goes . . . this could be somewhere over in Teton County north of Choteau where my dad and I used to go to hunt antelope," Nate said. "I could almost imagine that Great Falls is off over that way."

Shortly before noon, the five armed jeeps that made up Patton's column had reached Naltxik, the main settlement of the Kabardian people. It was not so much a city as a mass of huts, tents, and yurts spread out in a shallow valley, and clustered around several dozen low buildings constructed near the banks of a broad stream that flowed down out of the foothills to the south. Several large herds of horses had been gathered into makeshift corrals around the periphery. Smoke from numerous cooking fires curled into the air.

Even after the relative austerity of Rostov, Naltxik appeared

primitive in the eyes of the Americans. Nevertheless, there was
a sense of electricity in the air that had been absent in Rostov.
There, the Russian residents seemed numb and uncertain about
their newfound deliverance from the Soviet yoke. It had been
the Armenian merchants and Tatar traders, with their hastily established shops and outdoor markets that were bringing the
drab city to life.

Here in Naltxik, there was an excitement and an eagerness
to get on with life. As Patton had pointed out, there was a
fierce independent streak among the people of the Caucasus.
They were clearly relishing their independence.

On the western side of the town were several large olive-
drab tents surrounded by deuce-and-a-halfs, jeeps, and M8
Greyhounds. Among them was a tall pole flying an American
flag.

"That would be General Reinhart's command post," Patton
said, lifting his binoculars to his eyes to check out the divisional field headquarters for the 65th Infantry Division, which
Patton had reassigned to Eighth Army from XX Corps.

As Nate steered the jeep toward the command post, a
large number of people, men in Caucasian garb as well as GI
uniforms, started coming out of the tents. There was some
shouting and finger pointing. Suddenly more people started
appearing from nearby yurts. Quickly, the crowd grew to
several hundred. There were women and small children, as
well as bearded men with bolt-action rifles and turbans. Nate
was finding it hard to maneuver through the crowd. Finally,
he had to stop. The people were milling around and examin-
ing the faces of the GIs in the jeeps as though they were
looking for someone they knew.

Two fierce-looking men closely examined Patton and
broke into smiles as if recognizing an old friend. There were
shouts to the crowd, and before anyone in the jeep could react,
they grabbed the Supreme Commander and started to lift him
out of the jeep.

Nate grabbed for his sidearm. Patton shouted, "Hold your
fire!" as he was dragged from the vehicle.

The men hoisted him on their shoulders and carried him in
the direction of the command post as the crowd began to
chant, "Pah-Tun . . . Pah-Tun . . . Pah-Tun . . ."

The reaction of the people reminded Nate of the reception they'd received in Prague and Warsaw, although none of the Americans could remember Patton ever being lifted onto anyone's shoulders.

When they were finally inside the 65th Division tent, General Reinhart introduced Patton to a pair of gentlemen with long grey beards, who were identified as being Mr. Malqar and Mr. Kebertei, the principal Kabardian elders. They were obviously well past sixty, but their eyes were sharp and they had the hard, muscular hands of men who had worked hard all their lives and were still not strangers to manual labor. Their translator was Ia Azalera, a slender, strikingly beautiful woman in her twenties with long black hair and jet black eyes. She wore a heavily embroidered coat and large silver earrings that tinkled as she moved her head.

Miss Azalera explained, in a vaguely British accent, that Mr. Malqar and his colleague welcomed Patton as *the* liberator that the Kabardian people had been praying for since the nineteenth century. Miss Azalera told Patton that her people saw him as the instrument of the American crusade to free their world of Russian tyranny.

"We are deeply honored to have you in Naltxik," she told the General. "Throughout the town, a feast is being prepared in your honor . . . and the people wish to express their gratitude with gifts . . ."

"Horses," General Reinhart interjected. "It's horses, sir. They want to give you a hundred head of their horses."

"Wait a moment, Miss Azalera," Patton interrupted. "We're quite pleased to join you in a feast . . . but as for gifts . . . I don't want to burden you by taking any of your property . . ."

"But, it's our pleasure," she smiled. "General Reinhart has explained that you are an accomplished horseman."

"Well, I did spend a few years in the cavalry," Patton smiled modestly. "And I played quite a bit of polo back in the days when the US Army had the best damned polo team in the world. Actually, it's Sergeant McKinley here who's the horseman . . . he's a real Western cowboy . . . from Montana."

Miss Azalera smiled approvingly at Nate as she translated Patton's remarks to the elders. They grinned broadly at the news that both Patton and his driver were horsemen. As all Kabardians are horsemen, this was common ground that they could clearly relate to.

From the command post tent, Patton and his staff were taken to a broad plaza in the center of town, where they were directed to what was evidently a place of considerable honor in a tent belonging to Mr. Kebertei. A small lunch was served, but it was clear from the sides of beef that could be seen slowly roasting on fires around Naltxik, that this was merely a precursor to the feast that was planned for after nightfall.

As they were eating, there was a thunder of hooves and a number of Kabardian riders—mostly men, but also several women—galloped into the plaza on horses of the indigenous Kabardian breed. Shaggier and more muscular than the thoroughbreds that Patton was used to from his polo days during the 1930s, they reminded Nate a great deal of the Western quarterhorses that he'd ridden in Montana.

The riders put on a display of horsemanship that the Americans enjoyed immensely. Watching riders dismount and remount at high speed—or seeing a rider leap from the saddle of one horse to that of another at full gallop—is always exciting. Many of the demonstrations reminded Nate of things that he'd seen at rodeos back home, and they reminded him how much he missed being in the saddle.

After nearly an hour, two of the riders approached the Americans with a saddled, but riderless, third horse. The stallion was clearly jumpy and hard to control.

After a brief conversation with the riders, Ia Azalera turned to the Americans to translate. Looking directly at Nate, she explained that the Kabardians wanted to know whether any of the Americans wanted to try their hand at riding an "especially spirited horse," which, it was said, could not be ridden.

Nate shook his head, but, in the back of his mind, he wondered how this Kabardian horse might compare to some of the saddle broncs that he'd ridden during his brief experience with the rodeo circuit during his two summers after high school. After his father had taught him the tricks necessary for breaking a horse to ride, he'd decided to try his hand at bronc riding. He entered a few events, and had done well. However, he'd done just enough bronc riding to learn that it was a bit more punishment to his wrist and shoulders than he wanted.

A smile had come across Ia Azalera's face. As he glanced around, Nate could see that hers was not the only face that was grinning at him.

"Go for it, cowboy," General Oscar Koch said. "Show these folks what you can do."

"It's up to you," Patton laughed. "*I'm* too old for this."

Nate stripped off his jacket and gunbelt, entered the dusty plaza, and walked over to the big animal, who was snorting and pawing the dirt between the two riders. They grinned at him devilishly as he circled slowly, sizing up the horse. He was an attractive animal, mostly black, with some chestnut in his hindquarters. There was an angry, untamed look in his eyes. By the way he tossed his head, Nate could see why he had the reputation he did.

The stallion was saddled, but had no bridle, merely a pair of halters so that the two men could each have control of the horse's head. That was a good start at least. The two halters approximated a bridle. A single halter would have been awkward, because the animal's head could be pulled in only one direction. In bronc riding, you had *no* control over the horse's head at all. So far, so good.

The saddle was not what he was used to, but it was more like a Western saddle than an English saddle. That would be helpful. He remembered the first time he'd ridden an English saddle. It was down in Georgia while he was waiting to go overseas, where he'd gone riding with some local guys. He'd instinctively reached for the saddlehorn when he was mounting the horse and had felt like a fool when there was nothing there to grab. The Kabardian saddle had a wooden structure on it that was like a mirror image of the cantle on the back of the saddle, and the saddle itself was broad and roomy, unlike the English saddle.

Nate approached the horse and patted his withers to get a feel for him. The stallion shivered and jumped to one side. The man who was holding the halter grabbed it closer to the horse's head to better control him. The big stallion side-stepped, bumping into the man's horse.

As he felt the saddle and checked the cinch and stirrups,

Nate talked to the horse, mainly just so that the animal could hear the tone of his voice—calm, but firm.

"Okay big fella . . . I know you like to buck . . . let's give these people a show . . . then we'll get it outa your system."

Moving as quickly and smoothly as he could, Nate grabbed the twin cantles, put his toe in the left stirrup, swung himself into the saddle and grabbed the halter ropes tightly. The man holding the horse's head let go, and Nate was alone with a half ton of rippling muscle.

The suddenness with which the horse exploded upward nearly caught Nate off guard. He wondered what in the world he'd gotten himself into. Equally jarring was the crunch of the horse coming back down. Instantly, Nate found himself on a roller coaster ride as the horse twisted, bounded, leaped, and generally tried to buck him off.

Instinctively, Nate let go with his right hand, but he quickly realized that this was not a rodeo. He *could* use both hands—and he didn't have to spur this beast to earn points. Nor would he be disqualified for losing a stirrup. He just had to stay in the saddle. On the other hand, there would be no eight-second bell, and no pick-up man to rescue him at the end of those eight seconds.

The key to saddle bronc riding is for the rider to maintain a good rhythm, to anticipate and move with the horse. The horse, meanwhile, wants to get rid of the rider and will instinctively buck erratically—this way or that—to separate himself from the rider. An eight-second ride can be like an eternity. Nate was in for a much longer ride.

Everything was a blur. There was no use in trying to look at anything. It was all a matter of feel. Eight seconds came and went. At least it seemed to Nate like eight seconds. Maybe it was just four, or maybe it was sixteen.

He grabbed the ropes as tightly as he could and hung on, waiting for the horse to get tired. A bucking horse will put tremendous energy into the first few bucks, knowing instinctively that most riders can be quickly thrown. After that, it usually becomes a battle of attrition, a matter of testing who will tire first. This horse was different. It had to have been eight seconds twice over and the animal still bucked with an unslackened ferocity.

Just as he was afraid that his wrist was about to be pulled out of joint, Nate felt the horse break into a run. He hunkered down in the saddle and let the stallion run. As first, it seemed as though he was going to want to run through the crowd that ringed the plaza, but Nate pulled him back and forced him into running in laps. He had stopped bucking now, but he ran with incredible energy. Nate was too rummy from the bucking to try to estimate the speed, but he knew he was traveling faster than any horse he'd ridden before.

The horse knew that he was being broken, but he wanted to show his rider that he still had the strength for a full gallop. Finally, the big animal began to slow. Now it was Nate's turn. He kicked the horse, spurring him into a gallop when he obviously didn't want to run.

Nate continued this for several laps of the broad plaza—kicking the horse when he slowed and then reining him in. Finally, Nate felt as though the big beast was understanding him, and understanding the fact that he had, in the lexicon of the bronc rider, "been ridden."

When he was directly opposite the tent where he'd begun this wild ride, Nate pulled on the reins and guided the horse straight across the plaza at a smooth canter. His head was spinning and he was sick to his stomach, but he wanted to make this *look* as easy as possible. His eyes were blurry, but all around him he could hear people shouting and cheering.

The first thing that came into focus after he brought the horse to a halt in front of Mr. Kebertei's tent was the pair of riders that had led this ball of fire and brimstone into the arena. Even though they were heavily tanned, they appeared pale, with expressions on their faces like the proverbial persons who'd seen a ghost. Nate realized that this had been a trick perpetrated for the amusement of these extraordinary riders. The American was supposed to be bucked off by this violent horse that couldn't be ridden. Everyone would have a good laugh at his expense and the show would go on.

The practical joke had backfired.

Nate swung down as nimbly as his shaking legs could manage, handed the ropes back the man nearest him as nonchalantly as possible, gave him a wink, and walked back to where the Americans were laughing and applauding. Sitting in the center like a Roman emperor, Patton was beaming proudly.

"Damned fine show you put on here," the General said. "These people are *very* impressed."

"Thank you, sir," Nate replied, picking up his jacket.

Malqar and Kebertei each said something to Ia Azalera, who turned to Nate to explain: "The elders both wish you to consider riding with us . . . with the Kabardian people . . . in the battles against the Reds. You have ridden magnificently."

"Tell them that I'm very flattered, but I have to stay with my own people," Nate smiled, nodding appreciatively at the two elders.

They spoke with her again, pointing this time to Nate and the horse.

"They wish to make you a gift of this horse," Ia Azalera said. "You deserve such a powerful and spirited animal."

"I'm very tempted . . ." Nate said, admiring the animal he'd just ridden. He knew that after what they'd just been through, there was a powerful mutual respect between the horse and himself.

"Again, I'd have to refuse their generosity. I live ten thousand miles away . . . across a huge ocean. This great horse belongs *here.* I make the gift back to them in the spirit of the friendship between our two peoples and our victory over Stalin and his bandits."

The two men smiled broadly when Ia Azalera completed the translation.

"Oh yeah . . . one more thing," Nate added. "Tell them that if they ever come to my country, I'll take them for a ride they won't forget in *my* mountains."

At this, the two elders lunged toward Nate and embraced him.

"You're turning into a goddam diplomat," Patton grinned.

As the afternoon wore on, there were demonstrations of target shooting involving both rifles and pistols. Targets, mainly empty glass bottles that were in good supply, were being arranged along a low brick wall, with a pile of hay behind it to absorb the slugs after they'd passed through the target area. Small boys dressed in colorful shirts would brave the puddles of broken glass to scamper out after each shooter and replace the bottles that has had been shot away. Thère were also several burlap bags with targets or large *X*s painted on them.

Once again, the Americans were called upon to contribute a contestant. This time, all eyes turned to the General. Patton's marksmanship had earned him a berth on the pentathlon team in the 1912 Olympics. He was still regarded as an extremely good shot. Knowing this as well as anyone, he easily allowed himself to be cajoled out onto the plaza.

Patton stood in the plaza, his arms folded across his chest, while a man named Jatorrizko, who was touted as the top Kabardian marksman, carefully knocked off twelve in a row with his revolver.

The General stepped forward, but gestured to the rear, suggesting that they move back farther. Jatorrizko seemed surprised, but he nodded and Patton led the way, pacing fifteen steps away from the target. The audience, who recognized how truly difficult the shots would be at this distance, watched in rapt attention.

The two ivory-handled revolvers that the General wore on his gun belt were not a matched pair. One was a Smith & Wesson .357 magnum that he'd owned since 1935. The other was a Colt .45 single-action that he'd acquired in 1916, just before he went into Mexico with Blackjack Pershing to chase Pancho Villa. Today, Patton decided to use the magnum.

It was agreed that it would be the best of twelve from the farther distance, with each man reloading once.

The afternoon sun was sinking slowly in the West, and it was getting quite cold, but Patton shed his jacket and doffed his helmet. A silence fell over the crowd as Patton took careful aim.

With steady hand, he squeezed the trigger. There was a pop, but no sound of broken glass. He had missed. There was a murmur in the audience.

Showing no expression, he could be seen to take a deep breath as he raised his arm again.

Pop! The bottle shattered into a thousand slivers of glass.

Again, no emotion was displayed in the eyes, but there was a noticeable sense of relief in the way he took his deep breath.

One after another, the next four bottles exploded and the General stood to one side to a polite round of cheering and applause from the audience.

It was now Jatorrizko's turn. He was a younger man, probably about half Patton's age, and a man who almost certainly used his revolver effectively and often.

The Kabardian marksman took careful aim.

He squeezed his trigger and the first bottle exploded.

Again he aimed. Again a bottle disappeared in a cloud of broken glass.

Patton betrayed no emotion as the man efficiently and methodically emptied his six-shot cylinder and stepped back, leaving six targets destroyed. Again there was a round of applause, this time including some especially wild cheering from a small group who were evidently the Jatorrizko booster club.

The General reloaded and took aim. He knew that he was down by one and he didn't like that.

Pop! The first bottle disintegrated.

Again he aimed.

Pop! The second bottle was gone.

He aimed as though in a trance, as though he was seeing nothing but the gunsight and the bottle.

He squeezed and the bottle was gone.

He didn't bother to lower his arm.

The fourth bottle was gone. Then, at last, the fifth.

General Patton was now one shot away from a perfect second-round score.

A hush fell over the crowd as he aimed. All was quiet except for the snorting of a horse.

Again, he was in a trance.

He squeezed.

Pop! The tinkling sound of broken glass melted into enthusiastic cheering. It wasn't that the people were cheering against Jatorrizko, it was that they enjoyed a good show. Beyond that, Patton had come to them that morning as a myth. They had embraced that myth and now Patton was demonstrating to them how well-founded the myth truly was.

Stalin had *never* come to Naltxik. No Soviet leader had

ever stood in the plaza at Naltxik to demonstrate his personal skill man to man—But Patton *had,* and the Kabardians liked that.

Jatorrizko knew that he could now win only with a perfect score on his second round. Patton could relax now. Jatorrizko was on the spot.

Betraying no emotion, he aimed, fired, and hit the target. Again, he aimed, fired and hit the target.

There was a palpable tension as the tall Kabardian breathed deeply and lined up his third shot.

Again, the bottle exploded, and there was a trace of a smile on Jatorrizko's face as his fan club cheered.

He was relaxed and confident as he squeezed off his fourth shot, but there was a gasp from the crowd as the lane of bottles remained quietly unchanged.

The score was now tied. Everyone knew that Jatorrizko would need two more hits for the match to end in a draw, and that the match was taking place at an extremely difficult distance.

He aimed and fired. There was the clanking of broken glass.

One more to keep the score tied. Once again, he aimed and fired.

Silence. A miss. The American general twice his age had outshot the marksman.

Suddenly, Patton threw his left arm around Jatorrizko's shoulder and held his right hand high in the air. The Kabardian gave the old general a bear hug as the enthusiastic crowd closed in on the two men.

As had occurred earlier, when he'd arrived in the Kabardian capital, the crowd chanted "Pah-Tun . . . Pah-Tun . . . Pah-Tun . . . Pah-Tun . . ."

Patton had succeeded, he'd come as a military leader of considerable reputation, but demonstrated the skill of his own hand man to man, and he'd shown magnanimity in victory. In short, he'd won another ally to the cause. As for the Kabardians, they could now confidently fight the Russians with every ounce of energy, knowing they had looked into the eye of the Allied leader and had liked what they saw.

As the cold October sun dipped toward the horizon, there was nothing left to do but pull the sides of beef off the racks and eat, drink, and be merry.

Patton and the two elders led the procession back to the area near the 65th Infantry Division command post where the feast was to take place. Patton insisted that Jatorrizko join them at the head table. It was a gesture that was typical Patton and it seemed to be winning a lot of points for the cause.

As most of the crowd moved away from the plaza, Nate lingered behind to talk to some of the horsemen about their stock. As with Patton and his pistol, the Kabardians were genuinely pleased to meet one of the mysterious Americans face to face and to have common ground for conversation.

Nate and Ia Azalera, who had been helping to translate his conversation about horses, were starting to follow the crowd, when they were approached by the same two men who'd conned Nate into riding the bucking horse.

"They say if you are an American cowboy, you must also be a good sharpshooter," she explained after they'd said something to her.

Nodding to a line of twelve bottles that the boys had put on the wall after the previous match had concluded, she explained, "They want to see *you* shoot."

"Gee, I dunno," Nate said

"Oh, what the heck," he said after a long pause. "I guess so."

They walked back to the place that Patton had picked for the earlier shooting. Nate took out his .45 automatic. With the sun down, visibility had degraded considerably, but the dozen bottles were clearly visible on the wall.

"Tell them that I'd like to borrow a revolver from one of them," he said as he holstered his Colt. "My automatic isn't very accurate at this distance."

The revolver was a Belgian-designed 7.62 mm Nagant, the type that had been manufactured in the Soviet Union and which was favored by the Red officer corps. For these fellows to have one, Nate knew that there had to be a dead Russian officer somewhere.

Nate felt the gun. His Colt was half again heavier, so he'd have to compensate for the different recoil sensation. It was similar in size than the familiar Smith & Wesson .38, but slightly heavier. He popped the cylinder out and spun the chamber.

"First two shots don't count," he said at last. "I'm going to aim at the bags to get a feel for the sights . . . "Okay?"

They nodded when Ia Azalera had explained his plan.

Nate took careful aim.

Pop! They all saw the bullet hit the open area of one of the targets, considerably wide of the bull's-eye. The two young Kabardians grinned at one another. They had found the American cowboy's weakness.

Nate was amused by these guys. He'd been a wiseass when *he* was twenty. He knew exactly what they were doing. He also knew they had played into one his strengths.

The first shot had shown him exactly how the sight was set—it was off slightly, but not bad. The second shot confirmed what he'd learned with the first. When they didn't see it hit, they assumed the second shot had missed. Nate knew that it had disappeared into a previous hole at the bull's-eye.

He lowered the gun, opened the chamber and inserted the two replacement cartridges that he was handed.

Taking a deep breath, he made an elaborate show of carefully aiming.

The two boys smiled at one another as he lowered his arm and rubbed his eyes.

Ia Azalera had a disillusioned look on her face. She had been quite impressed with the handsome young GI's riding ability and felt disappointed to see him appearing to bungle the challenge from the two young pranksters when it came to shooting.

They watched Nate let his arm drop by his side, relaxed and almost rubbery.

Suddenly, faster than they could follow with their eyes, he jerked it up and pointed at the row of bottles.

Pop!Pop!Pop!Pop!Pop!Pop!

The sixth bottle was a cloud of glass before all the fragments from the first had reached the ground.

The Kabardians, Ia Azalera included, stared in speechless disbelief, as though unable to fully comprehend that the cowboy who'd appeared unable to hit the side of a bag had destroyed six bottles in fewer than six seconds without appearing to aim.

Overcoming the urge to grin, Nate handed the pistol grip back to the young Kabardian, with an understated "Thanks," and gazed back at the target, where the other six bottles still remained.

The man gently took the gun without a word, looking at Nate with a sense of awe and admiration, and then back at the row of bottles as though expecting to see that the absence of the first six bottles was an optical illusion.

Without a warning, Nate suddenly executed his well-practiced quick draw, snatching the .45 from his holster and *shoved*—not really even appearing to *aim*—the automatic toward the target.

Whackwhackwhackwhackwhackwhack!

Again, six bottles seemed to vaporize, but this time, the six rounds seemed to exit the muzzle in a single ripping sound rather than as a series of shots.

Among the cloud of debris in the air, a single green glass bottleneck seemed to float briefly above the others.

Whack!

The bottleneck was transformed into a puff of powdered glass as Nate squeezed off the last shot in the clip.

The three Kabardians looked at Nate in slack-jawed bewilderment as he calmly slammed another seven-shot clip into his Colt and slipped it into its holster. The myth of the American cowboy was alive and well in Kabardianno-Balkaria.

"It's getting dark, and this cowboy's getting hungry," Nate said cheerfully. "Let's eat."

Office of the Secretary of State
State Department Building
Washington DC
Saturday, October 13, 1945, 8:09 p.m.

"You're putting in a little overtime this weekend, Stephen," Secretary of State Edward Stettinius said as he passed through the office where his senior aide was pouring through a pile of papers on his desk.

"Yes, sir," Stephen Cuthbert said, looking up from his work. "With the Armenian and Georgian ambassadors due in to present their credentials next week, there's a great deal of work to catch up on. Saturday afternoon is usually a good time . . . fewer interruptions."

"You're a good man, Stephen," the Secretary said, lowering himself into a nearby chair. "I appreciate the good work that you're doing . . . and here you're on a Saturday night . . . a single fellow like you—and you're burning the midnight oil."

"Well, sir . . . I don't plan to stay quite *that* late. What you brings you into the office on a Saturday night?"

"It's the United Nations Organization. I wanted to pick up some things to work on at home over the weekend."

"I thought the United Nations Organization was on hold?"

"Technically it is . . . but I think it's about time to start the ball rolling again. The Japanese are finished . . . This World War III against the Russians may drag out 'til spring, but it can't last much longer. When it's over, there'll be a void that needs to be filled. I don't want to wait until the last minute. General Patton may wind up starting a United Nations of his own."

"That bothers me a great deal, sir," Cuthbert said.

"What's that?"

"Patton, sir," Cuthbert explained. "This whole idea that Patton is in charge of our foreign policy."

"That was just a joke," Stettinius explained. "I just said that because of the good work that he did . . ."

"I know, sir, the good work that he did in putting together a *military* alliance. What bothers me is that it'll go to his head. The historic precedents . . . Caesar, Napoleon . . . *generals* who become so powerful . . . they become *dictators*."

"You've been reading too many alarmist newspaper columns, Stephen," Stettinius cautioned. "There are those in the press who revile Patton. The man is a professional. You were at Warsaw. You saw him defer the political discussions to the proper authority."

"I also heard his off-the-record comments about the United Nations," Cuthbert reminded his boss.

"Stephen, there are *practical* ways of doing things. This is not to say that the end justifies the means, but that sometimes the end justifies a flexibility in *choosing* the means. Do I wish that we had someone with the political astuteness of an Omar Bradley running that show over there? Absolutely. Do I think that someone like Omar Bradley could have gotten us out of the bind that we were in last summer *militarily?* Absolutely not. Give credit to Patton for the job he's done."

"Well, I certainly agree that his military successes have gone beyond anything that we could have hoped for . . ."

"And thanks to Patton, this war will soon be over. Be thankful. Now, wrap up your work and go home . . . . It's Saturday night."

After the Secretary of State had left the building, Cuthbert sat at his desk brooding. He was so deep in thought that he jumped when the telephone rang. It hadn't rung for hours. That was why he liked working on Saturday afternoons. The switchboards were usually busy Saturday morning, but the traffic typically tapered off in the afternoon as the darkness of the early hours of Sunday morning crept across Europe.

"Secretary's office, Cuthbert speaking."

"Hello . . . I'm calling from Congressman Austin Farmer's office . . . your switchboard said that the Secretary might be in his office."

"He was, but he left about ten minutes ago . . . can I help you . . . I'm Stephen Cuthbert, his senior assistant."

"Dave Williams . . . I'm the Congressman's senior assistant," the man explained. "We just had an all-day session over here and the Congressman asked me to 'get hold of somebody in the Secretary of State's office' and register our concern. I didn't really expect to be able to get through to anybody on a Saturday night . . ."

"Well, you have, Mr. Williams. What's your concern? How can I help the Congressman?" Cuthbert asked reassuringly. No matter how pesky they were, when Congress called, the executive departments had to be on their toes.

"Congressman Farmer is worried that the Supreme Allied Commander may be getting out of hand on diplomatic matters."

"I was under the impression that the Congress was largely in support of the way General Patton is handling the war," Cuthbert said cautiously, trying to conceal his elation at having been found by a kindred spirit.

"Oh, please don't get me wrong. We in the Congress are absolutely supportive of his achievements on the battlefield. What he has done is an immeasurable service to the nation . . .

and the world . . . It's just that we're worried that he's getting just a bit too . . . too much . . ."

"Too much political power for a military man?" Cuthbert interrupted.

"That sums it up," Williams confirmed. "You've heard this concern expressed before, I guess."

"It's not hard to miss this 'concern' if you read the opinion pages in the papers," Cuthbert said. "Some want his power curbed, but others think that he ought to be *running* this government."

"*That's* the opinion that concerns the Congressman . . . and a lot of his . . . our constituents."

"Certainly that's the right of the people . . . to express their concerns in print and to their elected representatives," Cuthbert said.

"Listen, I'm in the middle trying to wrap up here," Williams said. "Could I call you back . . . or . . . better still, could we get together next week . . . maybe grab a bite of lunch or something."

It's always really crazy around here . . . better to talk off-site."

"Yeah . . . I suppose."

"How 'bout Tuesday or Wednesday?"

"Wednesday if we make it after one o'clock," Cuthbert said, scanning his calendar.

"Sounds okay . . . shall we make it one thirty? How 'bout the Capitol Coffee Shop . . . it's about half way."

"Fine, see you then," Cuthbert said, hanging up the phone.

He felt like a conspirator in a Peter Lorre film. He had gotten a tangible message that he was not alone. Cuthbert saw Stettinius as a man growing tired before his eyes. Now he had a pipeline into the halls of power where the other opinion was alive and well.

Naltxik, Kabardianno-Balkaria
Saturday, October 13, 1945, 10:09 p.m.

Lit by enormous bonfires, the feast took on something of a medieval quality. It seemed as though the technology of modern warfare—radar, jet aircraft, intercontinental rockets, and even M26A2 tanks—was as distant and irrelevant as the dark side of the moon. In the firelight, Nate McKinley felt himself transported to the era when soldiers rode horses, fought with spears, and celebrated victories and alliances sitting around huge fires, eating meat off the bone with their bare hands.

While some of the American officers found this spectacle a bit unnerving, General George Smith Patton, Jr. found it very much to his liking. He held court at the center of the festivities, sitting on a rug with the Kabardian elders, Malqar and Kebertei—as well as his new friend, the marksman Jatorrizko.

This was the way that Tiberius and Tammerlane conducted conferences of war. Nate could not imagine, not in a million years, Omar Nelson Bradley fitting into a scene like this. They had presented Patton with a gold-trimmed bridle and had promised to ride north to attack Red Army outposts all the way to Stalingrad and beyond.

What a strange war this war that Patton called "damned fine" had become.

The moon was starting to come up as Nate made his way toward the 65th Infantry motor pool and the bivouac that Patton's entourage had been assigned. He was tired and ready to turn in for the night. The others could allow themselves to be run into the ground by the General's seemingly inexhaustible stamina, but Nate was going to get at least a little rest before Patton ordered reveille at the crack of dawn.

Nate had just paused to admire the clarity of the stars, when he heard a faint tinkling sound behind him.

He turned quickly to see what it was.

It was Ia Azalera moving silently through the cold October night. The only sound was the music of her silver earrings.

"Miss Azalera . . . I barely heard you coming."

"Hello, Sergeant," she said. The Kabardian translator was like a ghost in the moonlight, her long black hair framing her perfect face. "I want to thank you for coming to the Caucasus. It is very important for our people to have a sense of connection to the new world that emerges from this war."

"That was General Patton's idea . . . coming out here," Nate said. "He wanted to meet with your leaders and let them understand how serious the United States is about all the former Soviet Socialist Republics having a chance to be free countries."

"But *we* never had even a chance to become Soviet Socialist Republics," she explained. "Dagestan, Chechnya, Ingushetia, Ossetia, Kabardianno-Balkaria . . . we were never free from Russia itself . . . until now. I hope that we don't have to trade one devil for another this time . . . like we did when the commissars replaced the tsars."

"I don't think so," Nate tried to assure her. "The Russians are going back to Russia."

"Beware of the idea that the Russians are the *only* oppressor in the region," she cautioned. "In Chechnya, they hate the Russians . . . but Kabardians have no wish to be dominated by the Chechnyans when the Russians are gone. The United States has declared the intention to recognize a free Georgia, but what of Ossetia and Abkhazia which are within the border of the Georgian Republic? Will the Ossetians and Abkhazians be free of the *Georgians?*"

"You can be sure that if any American military officer understands the history of the Caucasus and the lay of the land out here, it's going to be General Patton," Nate assured her. He had never heard of Ossetia and Abkhazia, and he hoped that Patton understood the Caucasus as well as he'd just promised Ia Azalera.

"Patton is a great leader who is an inspiration to people everywhere," she said. "Since long ago, there were stories that someday a man such as Patton, a liberator, would come here from elsewhere. The events of this day will be spoken about in these hills and valleys for many, many years to come. Your General Patton has shown himself to be a great warrior king . . . the kind of which traditional songs are sung."

"I'm sure that he'd be flattered to know that," Nate grinned. He imagined that the General would get a good chuckle out of it.

"And he surrounds himself with warriors of exceptional ability," Ia said, looking at Nate in that admiring way that a woman can look at a man and make him nervous. "What I . . . what all of us . . . saw you do today will be told about in stories when you are old and grey and many thousands of miles away."

"I appreciate that very much, Miss Azalera," Nate said modestly. "I doubt it . . . but I appreciate the compliment."

Ia just smiled, the reflection of the moon dancing in her eyes.

"It's getting very cold here," she said, pulling her embroidered coat tight on her shoulders. "Come with me to my tent . . . I want to show you something."

Nate followed almost trancelike, captivated and spellbound by this Kabardian princess and the way she moved though the shadows, the only sound being the tinkling of the hoops of her earrings.

The inside of Ia Azalera's tent was a strange place, like something from the Arabian Nights. Rugs and tapestries hung everywhere, and the aroma was that of perfumes he'd never smelled before. The embers of a charcoal fire glowed in the middle of the room beneath an opening in the roof through which Nate glimpsed several stars. She quickly lit several candles and soon had the fire crackling cheerfully. Nate was invited to recline on a cushion, and Ia sat nearby.

"We've talked about me . . . but what about you?" Nate asked, trying to break the ice. "You didn't learn English with a British accent out here. You've seen a bit of the world yourself."

"Oh yes," she smiled. "I was educated in Britain. My father was one of the favorites . . . picked by the Bolsheviks as one of their appointed leaders in the Caucasus after the Revolution. He could send his children abroad for education . . . and *female* children at that. We thought everything would change after the tsars. There was an optimism . . . I was in London in 1936 when my father was executed by Stalin."

"I'm sorry . . ." Nate offered. "Stalin was a bad guy for a lot more people that we realized when he was one of our allies."

"He killed our leaders and tried to destroy us as a people," she explained. "We read now these stories coming out about what the Nazis did to the Jews and Gypsies in their terrible ovens. Stalin was the same. He killed people . . . mass graves . . . But much worse . . . he tried to kill whole nationalities by erasing their identity as a people. The history of the peoples of the Caucasus has not been written. Stalin tried to destroy our identity by killing those who knew the history and told the stories. New histories . . . false histories . . . were written by the Reds."

"Your father had to go because he knew too much," Nate said.

"Yes," Ia replied. "I was abroad and frightened when it all happened. I was in a daze. I was so confused by this. I had to come back here to begin to learn who I was."

Nate watched her face as she talked. There was such an incredible passion to her beliefs. In her fire and fury, she was not unlike that horse that he'd ridden today. He admired her for this. She was an extraordinary woman.

"All peoples have stories of great heroes who come to deliver them," she continued. "Today, maybe such a story came true. We won't forget it."

It was warm in the tent now, and she'd slipped off her coat. Beneath, her dress was like a gauze curtain, hanging, or rather clinging, about her body. Her bare breasts were all but fully revealed through the faintness of the fabric. They moved seductively as she inched closer to where he was.

She gently and subtly reached inside his jacket and massaged his shoulders. Nate realized that Ia Azalera was one of those women that men talk about around campfires—but rarely ever meet—one of those women who know instinctively how to control a man by giving him everything he wants.

"A warrior such as yourself has an infectious power," she smiled. "You are . . . I'm sure you know . . . a man above men."

"I'm happy to have you believe that," he smiled, reaching out to touch her cheek.

By the light of the flickering candles, she was almost unimaginably beautiful—with her perfect features and her eyes that reflected the flame of the candles and revealed a fire that raged within her. Nate had never seen a woman with hair so long. He had never run his fingers through such fine and beautiful hair. His thumb brushed against her breast as he ran his hand though her fine and beautiful hair—and she smiled softly.

She bent closer and their lips touched slightly. He looked into her eyes. He smelled the fragrance of her skin. He could not believe what was happening. He was being seduced by an exquisite princess. He was not simply alone with her in an Arabian Nights pleasure chamber filled with intoxicating smells that he could not imagine—he was being *seduced*.

She bent closer again and their lips touched. He looked into her eyes and smelled the fragrance of her skin. Their lips met again and he felt as though being transported on a magic carpet. He kissed her back as best he could and felt her tremble in his arms.

"Mmmmm . . . my goodness," she smiled, looking at him longingly as she began undoing the buttons of his shirt.

As she came forward again, leading her kiss with her tongue, Nate closed his eyes and felt a jolt that left him shaking.

Nate opened his eyes to the most beautiful human female on Earth, the smell of her skin still fresh in his nostrils, the taste of her lips still fresh on his tongue. Her perfect face and long dark hair had driven the wild animal within him mad. As she allowed the dress to fall seductively from her shoulders, her flawless breasts emerged. The wild animal within him was slamming itself against the bars of its cage.

Nate paused to catch his breath. Her body was as perfectly proportioned as her face, and it the firelight, it was more than magical. Ia leaned back on the cushion, getting herself comfortable for the next phase of the encounter. She smiled contentedly and she reached out to run her hand gently across his chest. Her expression told him that she had taken as much pleasure from their kisses as he had.

"You *did* say you wanted to show me something," he said as casually as possible.

"Oh yes," she replied seductively. "I confess that I knew about you before you came here, Sergeant McKinley."

"About *me?*"

"Yes . . . you cast a long shadow. When it was said that Patton would come to Naltxik, I knew that you would come . . . I hoped that you would come. I knew . . . everyone knew . . . that you were a warrior of the highest character."

"*How?*" Nate asked. "How did you know all this about me? I'm just a driver."

"You're mocking me with your modesty," Ia said wryly, giving him a long kiss on his stubbled cheek. "Everyone knows you. The world knows you. The world knows you as the great soldier who summarized the promise of the Americans coming to free the people who've been stifled by the dictators. You were the one who gave words to the flag of the United States."

With this, she reached into a leather satchel and pulled out a rumpled, wrinkled copy of the July 4, 1945 overseas edition of *The Washington Herald,* emblazoned with little American flags and the headline "WHAT OUR FLAG SAYS."

Nate stared at the paper, which he'd seen before, and at the picture of himself. His eyes passed over the words—his own, but carefully massaged by the hand of another—and were riveted on a small picture of a face that shown like the sunrise. In this tiny picture, no playful dusting of freckles was visible—but he could see them. There was no hint of the rosewood color in the hair—but he could see it. He knew that she was dead and that he would never see her again—but he could feel her.

Nate looked up at the most beautiful *human* female on Earth, but he felt the infinite beauty of a little Celtic *goddess* who was no longer of this Earth.

Nate was in the place of which most men merely dream.

A *princess* wanted his body.

However, a *goddess* owned his soul.

16

Hotel Rostov
59 Budennovsky Prospect
Rostov-on-Don, Russia
Wednesday, October 17, 1945, 10:09 a.m.

"HERE we are, ma'am," the young lieutenant said helpfully as he helped Rosemary O'Leary down from the back of the deuce-and-a-half. "Sure you don't wanna hand with your luggage?"

"No thanks, I'm fine . . . really," she lied, looking down at her large, heavy suitcase and her GI duffle bag.

As the deuce-and-a-half sped away, her friend waved goodbye, and she gazed around at the broad street and the handful of old cars weaving through crowds of pedestrians who seemed not to notice that they were almost being run down.

Autumn was definitely in the air, and winter seemed close behind.

Two days earlier, she'd been standing at National Airport in Washington, being briefed by Rex Simmons and surrounded by scurrying, well-dressed people who represented the apogee of her idea of Western civilization. In these ensuing forty-eight hours, she'd crossed an ocean and a continent, and had stepped off her airplane at the threshold of Central Asia—in the city known as "the Gates of the Caucasus."

Rosie had stepped into the long line of GIs waiting at the Airport Transportation Desk for rides. It was like waiting for a bus in wartime Washington. When it suddenly occurred to the travel-weary GIs around her in the line that this weary traveler in rumpled khaki was not of their gender, chivalry blossomed and she was quickly swept to the head of the line and placed on the first vehicle headed into the center of the city.

As she gazed from the back of the jerking, jolting truck, she drank in the images of a shabby and architecturally monotonous city. The people were dressed in caftans and colorful head scarves that were *far* from monotonous.

Suddenly, the truck was on a broad boulevard lined with four- and five-story apartment houses that reminded her of Paris. The phrase "Paris-on-the-Don" occurred to her and she scribbled that in her notebook.

"This is Budennovsky," the driver shouted to Rosie from the cab. "Here's that hotel."

The Hotel Rostov was a squarish, six-story building that had been built in the thirties, but was already showing the tawdriness that comes to badly maintained buildings in middle age. Inside, it seemed to have been colonized by Americans. It was strange to see two men in fezes tapping their toes to the sound of "Rum and Coca-Cola" while they swept the lobby.

After relying on the kindness of a stranger to get her luggage up to the third floor, Rosie was at last in her room. She walked to the window and looked out across the city. Smudges of smoke from oven fires were everywhere on the horizon and a brownish haze hung in the air.

Rosie knew that General Patton was coming to Rostov, and she wondered whether *he* would be coming, and whether *he* was still part of the General's entourage now that Patton was the Supreme Commander. She guessed that he probably wasn't. She wanted to see him, but dreaded the rebuff that she knew was inevitable. He embodied greatness, while she was merely a scribbler of newspaper copy. He was monumentally handsome, while she was merely a freckle-faced kid—with a four-inch scar across her head.

The room was quite large, but sparsely furnished. The closet consisted of a tattered curtain hanging over an alcove in the wall.

Outside, she heard the sound of church bells and she stepped to the window again. She imagined the bells ringing across the city in the onion-domed Orthodox churches. She was anxious to get out and see the city. First she had to get cleaned up. One look at the dreadful, stringy-haired reflection

in the old floor-length mirror with the cracked corner told her
that a shower could not be postponed. There was a small sink
in the room, but the shower was down the hall—like her first
rooming house in Washington.

After she'd washed the layers of grime off her body, Rosie
realized that the pile of khaki correspondent's uniform smelled
more like a small animal that had been dead for a week than
anything that she actually wanted to wear. She washed it out as
best she could in the sink and started digging in her huge,
heavy suitcase for something to wear. She discovered that
she'd packed two pairs of boots, five pairs of shoes, but not her
change of uniform. The only one she'd brought on this expedition now hung, sopping wet, on her improvised clothesline.
She looked through the several dresses that she'd remembered
to bring, found the blue one with the little lace collar that
looked warm enough, pulled on a pair of boots, and wrapped
herself in her camel-colored car coat.

She walked up Budennovsky Prospect, her thoughts turning
to what she'd read on the plane about the history of Rostov.
She passed Tatars, whose ancestors had lived here since the
days of the Golden Horde.

There were two Kalmuck girls, who reminded her of Crys-
tal Lum, the Cantonese-American girl who'd been one of
Rosie's best friends during her last year of high school.

There were Ukrainian women with faces and braids that
made them look like Germans. She saw round-faced Russians
in old Red Army tunics stripped of Red Army insignia.

There were Kazaks and Kyrgyzstanis in caps that looked
like turbans, and Tajik and Uzbek women in colorful dresses
and large hoop-shaped earrings. There was even a man leading a pair of two-humped Bactrian camels into a side street.

The markets in the streets offered fruits and vegetables that
she'd not seen before—even in Chinatown in San Francisco.
Meat on skewers sizzled over open charcoal fires.

As she walked, story ideas about her impressions of this
place began to materialize in the back of her mind. She decided to tell her readers about the Caucasus through the eyes
of someone who'd never been to such a place—herself.

The little girl who'd spilled mustard on her dress in the
bleachers at Seals Stadium—while "Jotlin' Joe" tapped the

rawhide across the fence—was now the woman who walked the streets where the Cossack atamans like Stepan Razin and Yemelyan Pugachov led the legendary uprisings which shook Russia centuries before the DiMaggio ancestors had embarked from Naples for the distant sunset.

By now, Rosie was glad that she wasn't wearing her khakis. The only people in khaki were Yanks—and all the Yanks were in khaki. She much preferred the anonymity and wondered whether the Dagestanis and Chechnyans had as much trouble figuring out where this woman in the camel-colored overcoat was from.

Rosie passed a street vendor who was selling the colorful scarves that many of the women her age were wearing here. She couldn't believe that the woman was selling them for five cents in American money, but by the way she grinned when Rosie handed her a nickel, the price was probably vastly inflated beyond what the locals might pay. Those Americans—she probably thought—they'll pay *anything*.

Rosie admired her new purchase. It was colorful, with enough blue that it arguably went with her dress, and a dark red that reminded her a little of her own hair color. It had a curious pattern that she liked. More than this, though, it gave her a sense of fitting into the tapestry of cultures that swirled around her on the street.

From another vendor, she bought two bottles of water—because the sign at the hotel warned against drinking the tap water. From a third street merchant, she took possession of an unusually shaped bottle of something with a mysterious label with words written in Cyrillic and the picture of a dragon. For twenty-two cents, it *had* to be good. Maybe it had a genie in it. At least it would be an amusing gift for her dad.

Back at the hotel, Rosie tried to take a nap, but the lure of the exotic streets outside pulled her back. With her colorful Kabardian scarf around her neck, she walked in the opposite direction as before, this time toward the main theater of Rostov, the Gorky, which the man at the hotel had insisted was the largest in Europe until it was heavily damaged by a German bomb.

As it grew later, and colder, there were fewer people on the street. The food vendors remained, but the other merchants were gone. They had picked up all their wares and seemed to have vanished into the lengthening shadows.

On the street outside the Gorky Theater, a forlorn-looking man in a threadbare topcoat was playing a violin. The piece was from a Russian opera, she thought, but she wasn't sure. Somewhere in the distance, a bell faintly pealed.

As Rosie walked back toward Budennovsky Prospect, she remembered again that General Patton was coming. Would he and his entourage be there when she got back from her walk? Would the face she longed to see more than any other in the world be visible? Secretly, she hoped not. To see *him* again would pull so hard at the strings of her heart that she feared it would break. She knew that the disappointment of never seeing him again would be easier to bear than the disappointment of his passing her with a blank stare when he didn't recognize her.

She was so engrossed in the dilemma playing itself out in her mind, that Rosie was not prepared for the simplicity of what happened next.

She walked through the side door of the hotel, and *there he was!*

He was simply *there,* standing with about a dozen other American soldiers, barely forty feet away. She decided that the best thing to do was simply to turn on her heel, go back into the night, and not cast a glance over her shoulder—but she couldn't move. The sight of him held her spellbound.

He was taller than she had remembered, with his sandy hair slightly disheveled, and a day's grown stubble on his cheeks and chin. She noticed that he now wore the stripes of a master sergeant, and he was the sole enlisted man in a group of officers that included colonels, generals—and, of course, a five-star general.

While the General and his entourage brought an electricity of animation to the lobby, Sergeant McKinley, on his own, brought a sharpness, clarity, and light to this room. This light had the power to warm her, even in the shadows where she hid herself. She glimpsed a hint of a smile as he spoke with one of the officers, as though they were sharing an inside joke.

With a wave of his hand, the General captured everyone's

attention. He gestured eloquently, smiled, saluted, turned, and walked away in the direction of the dining room with several other men. Suddenly, the large group fragmented, with small clusters of men moving in disparate directions. Sergeant McKinley was among the last. He spoke to one of the officers briefly, saluted, and then he was alone.

She froze. She was thirteen again and *so smitten* by a guy that her knees were like Jell-O. As he strode purposefully toward the door, he glanced in her direction, but then he looked away. As she'd expected, he didn't recognize her.

It was over as quickly as it had begun.

Office of the Secretary of State
State Department Building
Washington DC
Wednesday, October 17, 1945, 12:48 p.m.

Stephen Cuthbert flopped down at his desk, glanced at his watch, and grabbed for his calendar.

It had been an exhausting morning with the new ambassador from Georgia. He was a little guy, but a real ball of fire. A year ago, Cuthbert had barely heard of the Georgian Soviet Socialist Republic and probably couldn't have found it on the map. Now it was an independent country and he'd just spent a whole morning learning that there were people called Ossetians and Abkhazians inside Georgia that wanted *their own* independent countries!

It was now American policy for nationalities and nations previously forced into being constituents of the Russian or Soviet empires, were now recognized as free and independent nations—if they wanted to be. Nobody had realized that there were countries within countries—and these *also* wanted to be free.

The State Department found itself walking a delicate line. Georgia was free of the Soviet Union, but the ambassador was now begging for United States aid to help put down the simmering insurrection by the Ossetians and Abkhazians!

Cuthbert had gotten out of the luncheon for the ambassador

by explaining that he had an appointment with a Congressional aide. Cuthbert just couldn't remember what time he was supposed to meet Dave Williams from Congressman Farmer's office. Was it one o'clock or one thirty?

Whew! It was one thirty. He had time to make it to the Capitol Coffee Shop on foot. Cabs were impossible this time of day. As he was looking at the page, he noticed the other notation that he'd scribbled there on Saturday night: "Rosemary."

Oh no! He'd meant to phone Rosemary O'Leary on Monday and he'd just let the day slip away. Was there time? Sure.

He grabbed her card and dialed the number for *The Washington Herald*. Even if she was out to lunch, he'd leave a message. He thought of her smile. Oh, how he missed her smile. He had to see her.

The phone was ringing.

"Newsroom," an impatient male voice said. Newspaper people were always on deadline, always in a big hurry.

"I'm trying to reach Rosemary O'Leary?"

"She's outa town. On assignment in Russia."

"When did she leave?" Cuthbert asked, trying to hide his sudden desperation.

"Over the weekend."

"When'll she be back?"

"I dunno. Try back next week. Gotta go. Bye."

So that was it. The girl reporter—with the smile he didn't realize he missed until she was halfway around the world—was gone. He penciled her name in for the following week, grabbed his coat, and headed out the door.

As usual, the Capitol Coffee Shop was packed. Located about midway between Capitol Hill and the burgeoning cluster of executive department buildings around the White House, this eatery was the crossroads of middle-level power in Washington. Senators and cabinet secretaries never set foot here, but their aides and assistants, the people who actually did the work of government, all did.

It was often said that many of the ideas that became law at the *Capitol* were drafted over a plate of meatloaf at the Capitol *Coffee Shop*.

"You Mr. Cuthbert?"

Stephen turned to face a young man who'd been leaning against the wall near the coat rack.

"Yes, I'm Stephen Cuthbert. Are you Mr. Williams? How could you tell it was me?"

"Black three-piece with pinstripes . . . says State Department. Call me Dave."

"Hi, Dave," Cuthbert said, shaking the hand of this man in the blue plaid sport coat. "You can call me Stephen."

"Lotsa folks up on the Hill are starting to get a little jittery about Patton," he explained when they'd ordered their sandwiches. "Some folks are a *whole lot* jittery. It seems to Congressman Farmer that Patton's in charge of United States foreign policy. At Warsaw, he was running the show. Don't you agree?"

"Yes, I was there and I saw what was happening," Cuthbert admitted, feeling nervous about being cornered into defending something he didn't entirely agree with. "I know that the press likes him. He's colorful. The press likes a colorful character. We fellows in three-piece suits aren't as fun to write about as the more glamorous generals. I *did* see Patton defer the political discussions to the proper authority . . . to the State Department people."

"Did you also hear his remarks about the United Nations Organization?" Williams probed. "I would have thought that Stettinius would've been especially pissed off . . . pardon my language . . . about that."

"I can't really comment on the Secretary's *personal* feelings," Cuthbert sidestepped, nervously watching Williams taking his own debating position, while he took the opposite. "As for Patton, he faces a difficult war and he did get a lot of armies working together."

"If you don't mind me saying, Napoleon was a great general, too. We know what happened with him. We don't want that in *this* country."

"Of course not," Cuthbert shrugged.

"The Congressman just wants the State Department . . . to keep its hands on the authority given to it by the Constitution and the laws . . . and not allow itself to be blindsided . . . and let this man become a threat to *our* government."

Cuthbert nodded. He'd been playing devil's advocate, but

he was glad that he was not the only one who was wary of the devil.

Hotel Rostov
59 Budennovsky Prospect
Rostov-on-Don, Russia
Wednesday, October 17, 1945, 6:49 p.m.

"I still can't get over this one about the Kabardian people writing folk songs about the old man," General Oscar Koch said with a grin. "It's amusing on one level . . . and damned sobering on another."

After a long drive back from Naltxik, Patton's staff was in the hotel lobby mulling over the experiences of the last several days. While they were on the road, Nate had told the General what Ia Azalera had told him—that the Kabardian people felt Patton was a great warrior king about whom traditional songs are sung. Much to Nate's surprise, the news was not met with a guffaw. Patton seemed genuinely moved and had sat silently for some time as if trying to digest his place in their history.

"Gentlemen, you are dismissed," Patton abruptly announced, turning to the group as a whole from the one-on-one conversation that he'd been having with the commander of Eighth Army. "General Eichelberger and I are going to retire to the dining room for a pile of those lamb chops and spuds that people in these parts seem to favor."

It's about time, Nate thought.

There was the usual round of salutes and the General and his group were gone.

Nate had the General's jeep buttoned up for the night, so he'd decided that he'd take a look around the city before he turned in.

As he was walking across the lobby toward the big front doors, he noticed something out of the corner of his eye. A combat infantryman learns to catch things out of the corner of his eye. He notices things, things that are out of place. All of the civilians in the lobby were headed somewhere or doing something. They were busy. The locals were used to Americans, and they didn't stare anymore. Yet, Nate had sensed—sensed more than actually *saw*—someone staring at him from the shadows near the edge of the room.

He glanced quickly. It was a small woman in a long coat, with a scarf around her neck—a scarf like he'd seen the women in Rostov wearing.

As he glanced away, he felt that strange feeling that he'd experienced in Paris—that feeling like an electrical shock that left him a little queasy. He knew that he desperately needed that cold night air.

He was getting that feeling all too often, and he was getting tired of it. There had been the dreams and, even more frightening, there were the times that he was seeing *her* face on people who weren't her. There was that day in Warsaw when he'd followed a poor girl for two blocks before he realized that it wasn't her. This was incredibly embarrassing. And then, there was the night in Naltxik, when Ia Azalera wanted him, and all he could see on the insides of his eyelids were images of Miss O'Leary. Now he was seeing her face on a Russian girl in a hotel in Rostov.

Nate feared he was going mad. He knew for certain that he desperately needed that cold night air.

As he walked more quickly toward the main door of the hotel, he thought about how ridiculous he was for caring so much for someone that had been in and out of his life faster than it took to change the spark plugs on the jeep. Maybe he could find a bar out there that had enough vodka to wash away this feeling.

As much as he tried consciously to prevent it, Nate's neck jerked involuntarily sideways and twisted around. His subconscious was *demanding* that he glance a second time at the small woman with a scarf around her neck like they wear in Rostov.

Rosie O'Leary watched him glance away and continue walking toward the door. Her heart sank, but she was strangely relieved.

Wait.

He had turned.

He was looking at her again.

His expression had changed. It was as though he was trying to recall a vaguely familiar face—then, suddenly the expression changed again. It was terrible—like someone having a bad dream.

"Oh my God . . . Jesus, Mary, and Joseph!" She almost said it out loud.

Nate stopped dead in his tracks. The face. The rosewood-colored hair like liquid jewels. The blinding sheet of light in colors that would make a rainbow jealous.

Nate felt the beads of sweat forming and the hairs standing up on the back of his neck like bristles on a wild pig. So this is what it was like to be shell-shocked? So this was what it was like to loose your mind and see hallucinations?

He was insane.

What had he done to deserve the nightmare of having *her* be the hallucination that taunted him?

He blinked his eyes, but she was still there—the poor little Russian girl in a long coat, with a scarf around her neck like they wear in Rostov.

He knew that he desperately needed that cold night air, but his feet would not obey his conscious mind.

He walked toward her, as though to convince himself that she was not real. He knew that she had to be a figment of his insane imagination, or someone whom his shell-shocked brain had made him think was her. He could already hear himself trying to apologize for frightening some poor little Russian girl.

Much to his horror, the closer he got, the more real this apparition became. The eyes. The little freckles that danced across her face like nymphs.

"Hello, Sergeant McKinley," she smiled nervously.

It was as though Nate had suddenly had his eardrums punched out with an icepick. The only sound in the room was the soft music of her voice, sounding more beautiful and more perfect that he could ever have imagined.

"Are you all right?" she asked, a little furrow tracing its way across her forehead. "You look like you've seen a ghost."

"Yeaaaaah . . ." Nate tried to speak, but the inside of his mouth was so dry that he couldn't.

"Yeaaaah . . . I *am* seeing a ghost. Right? You . . . you're . . . I heard you were . . . dead."

"I'm sorry," he said. "I'm . . . you look so much like

somebody I knew who was killed. Please let me apologize for scaring you . . . I don't mean any harm."

"Sergeant McKinley . . . It's me . . . Rosemary O'Leary."

"Oh my God."

After a pause that seemed so long that he could not calculate the duration, he finally explained: "I heard you were . . . dead."

"Oh!" She blushed, a smile coming across her supernaturally beautiful face in another blinding flash. "I *was* 'dead,' sort of . . . for two days . . . I mean . . . I was missing. In New York. I was there when it happened. They couldn't find me. I was actually at the hospital, but there was so much confusion. I didn't know I was lost until they found me . . . *I* knew where I was."

"I'm so glad . . . you're all right," Nate said, wishing that he could reach out and hug her, and feeling ridiculous for the way he was behaving. "I'm really sorry for acting like a dunce. I had heard that you were . . . well . . . you know."

"Oh, you should have seen my poor mother. She actually fainted dead away when I phoned."

"I'm so glad you're all right," Nate stammered again. It was the only thing that he could think of to say.

"So I guess you *did* remember me from Paris?" she said, biting her tongue and realizing that she was really pushing her luck—and probably pushing him farther away.

"Oh . . . yeah . . ." he said, wishing he could find the words to tell her that he'd thought of her—and dreamed about her—constantly since the day he'd met her. For the longest time, the words wouldn't come. He couldn't speak and he couldn't think. He could only feel the tidal waves of emotion that came with every beat of his heart.

"So . . . what are you doing here in this out of the way corner of the world?" he asked, trying nervously to fill the awkward silence.

"Working on a story about what's going to happen with all of these smaller countries that are part of the Soviet Union that nobody in the United States has ever heard of," Rosie said, happy to be able to talk about something that wasn't making her blush. "It's a really fascinating part of the world. When I was a little girl in school there was just this big place called 'Russia.' Maybe some people had heard of the Ukraine or Armenia, but who knew anything about Azerbaijan, or Uzbekskaya, or Kazakskaya, or Turkmenskaya . . . not to mention Kabardianno-Balkaria or Chechnya?"

She found herself jabbering, but could not imagine that she was making any sense.

"Yeah, I know exactly what you mean," Nate said. "I've been out in the Caucasus all week, most of the time in Kabardianno-Balkaria. I've learned more than I ever imagined."

"I'd like to hear about that," she said, biting her tongue for being so pushy. "I mean . . . I just got here and I'm not really up on what's going on . . . still learning my way around . . . still learning more than I ever imagined."

"Um . . . I was just on my way out to take a little bit of a look around the town," he stammered. "If you're not busy with something else . . . Ya wanna come with me?"

"Oh . . ." Rosie answered. She was screaming "yes!" on the inside—while trying her damnedest to appear aloof and not pushy on the outside. "I guess . . . I really don't have anything else. Yeah, I'd like to."

Nate's heart soared. Five minutes ago, Miss O'Leary had been just a dream and a memory. She had been a goddess no longer of this world—or a heavenly angel that he would never see again. Now she was at his side. He was nervous as hell. He felt like he'd grabbed hold of a runaway truck.

"Nice scarf," he said as he held the door for her. It had been so long, but he was remembering the rudiments of being a gentleman—and he knew that women always like compliments about what they're wearing. It *was*, in fact, a nice scarf. It was colorful and it reminded him of this place, this exotic place. It was something that one might expect a goddess to wear.

"Thank you," she blushed. He had noticed her scarf! She would keep it forever as a reminder of this precious moment with her soldier. "I bought it here this morning. I kinda liked the colors."

"The rosewood color . . . um . . . kind of goes with your hair," he said, suddenly realizing what a fool he was. First of all, he didn't know one thing about what went with what color, and, second, you don't compliment a woman's hair five minutes into a conversation.

Rosie was speechless. He had noticed her hair. Was he

toying with her? Was he making fun of her? Had he seen it? Had he seen the scar?

"Um . . . yeah, these local things are pretty nifty. I was talking to General Koch. He's the General's G2. He suggested that I oughta get one of those Cossack blankets to take home to my mom. I thought that was a good idea. She'd get a kick out of it. Dontcha think?"

"Yes, I think she would love to have you bring her something from out here," Rosie smiled, looking up at the kindly face of this soldier. His mother! What an amazing, gentle man. He's fighting a war in the middle of nowhere and he wants to take a memento home to *his mom!*

"You might also want to take back something nice for your girlfriend," Rosie added. The words had slipped out before she saw them coming. She wished that she could reel them back in, but they were out there. She wished that she could press herself into one of the cracks between the cobblestones underfoot and disappear forever.

"Oh, I think my girlfriend back home *has* a 'something nice' already," he said, betraying more vexation than he wanted to. "She's got the arm of a gentleman with a Navy lieutenant's stripes on the sleeve. I don't think that she'll ever be wanting anything else from me."

Her soldier had been jilted? Who could do such a thing to this man in whom Rosie saw only infinite, boundless goodness?

"Guess things like that happen in wartime." She shrugged, ecstatic that he was unattached and eager to explain to him in as roundabout a way as possible that she too, was alone. "My last boyfriend. It was kinda serious. I was—this sounds sort of stupid—I was wondering why my letters started coming back 'return to sender.' Found out that he was shacking up with a little southern belle down in Georgia."

Was this guy a madman? Who could turn his back on a goddess of supernatural beauty?

"Makes you wonder where we'll all end up when this damned war is finally over," Nate said, part philosophically and part with a sense of sadness. "There I go again. Just like last time. I mean the *darned* war."

"Dammit, Sergeant McKinley, stop treating me like a little

prude," she teased, hitting his arm lightly with her shoulder. "I've heard practically every word that you boys toss around in your bivouacs. And . . . it *is* a *damned* war."

"You're right, Miss O'Leary. It is."

She was going to tell him to call her "Rosie," but she decided that she kind of liked the way he said "Miss O'Leary." It was kind of sexy.

The ice seemed to have broken somewhat, though each resisted the urge to take the other's arm, still not absolutely certain where things were—and where they were headed.

They walked together down Budennovsky Prospect, with its big apartment blocks from tsarist times, generally oblivious to the people in native costume and the American GIs, who were merely the latest in a long series of strangers in this strange land.

"You were going to tell me abut the Caucasus, Sergeant McKinley," Rosie said, grasping for something neutral to talk about.

"Beautiful country," he started to explain. "Reminds me of the front range of the Rockies up in Montana. The people live pretty close to the land. They're really very good with horses. That reminds me of Montana, too. They all hate the Russians. They've been part of the Russian Empire, either the tsars or the Reds, for centuries. They're really anxious to be free. Stalin's been very cruel . . . but I guess *that's* not news any more."

"No, that's getting to be a very familiar theme," Rosie said. She wasn't really thinking about Stalin.

"Like you said back at the hotel, there are a lot of groups of people out there . . . you can't really even call them countries except for a few . . . who want to get Stalin off their backs. I knew that going in—as you do—but what surprised me is how much they don't trust *each other*."

"I guess I really hadn't thought of that," Rosie admitted.

"You'd think they'd just chase out the commissars and be fine. But they've been so long without borders between these small places . . ."

"That they don't know where the borders will be," Rosie interrupted.

"Now you got the idea," Nate grinned. "You got your first

lesson in the Caucasus from an old Caucasus hand who's spent, oh, the better part of a week out there."

Rosie giggled slightly. Not only was he unbelievably strong and handsome—and kind to his mother—but he was amusing, and he seemed to understand the essence of the project she was working on better that she herself had just a week ago.

They walked and talked, gradually feeling more and more relaxed with one another, but still on guard, still trying to be polite. Each was overjoyed to be with the other, but still cautious and uncertain whether the feeling was reciprocal.

They finally had reached a place where they could look out and see the inky darkness of the River Don, with the lifeless shadows of barges and the weak red lights aboard the naval vessels that were blacked out in anticipation of a possible air attack.

It was cold, but the air was clear. There were only a handful of streetlights working, so it was possible to see the stars. Out on the horizon beyond the river, there was the glow of an impending moonrise.

"Wish I'd remembered my gloves," Rosie said, rubbing her hands together and then wishing she hadn't been so damned obvious.

"Here, let me . . ." he said, falling helplessly into her little trap. As he held her tiny hands in his big, clumsy mitts, he was struck by how delicate and perfect they were.

Suddenly, he felt her thumbs close onto the tops of his hands. They were much stronger than he'd expected. Why was she squeezing his hands? Could it possibly be that *she* was attracted to *him?*

"Your hands are so big and warm," she smiled, tilting her head slightly.

Nate's mouth went dry and he felt dizzy. What could he do? What could he say? What indeed? He was looking into the most beautiful face in the world—the one that radiated light from all corners of the universe.

"Well . . . you sure have the most wonderful smile . . ."

He felt her move closer and he felt his hands start to touch her arms.

"You sure have the most wonderful smile that I ever saw. I have thought about that smile so much since . . . I'm so glad that you weren't killed . . . I'm so glad I had a chance to see you again."

"You are such a sweet man . . ." she said, realizing that this sounded too much like a brush-off. "No. You *are* such a sweet and wonderful man. You're so . . . I felt two inches tall when I first met you. I mean . . . you were a hero . . . I felt so insignificant around you. But you were so kind to me. I'm so glad that *I* got to see you again. I'm so lucky . . ."

She felt his arms around her—so powerful but so gentle. She looked up at his calm face with its chiseled lines.

She closed her eyes and felt his lips touch hers.

Suddenly, she was in heaven.

Nate was startled by the softness of her face . . . and by the scent of her face. It smelled like those kinds of soaps that women always seem to have—not the kind that you have around to clean your hands or anything practical, but which women have for some mysterious and exciting reason that no man can understand.

He started to lift his head, but he felt her hands suddenly react by squeezing his arms more tightly. He tasted an eagerness and passion in her lips that he'd never imagined.

As abruptly as it had begun, it was over. He found himself looking down into her face as the moon rose over the distant ridgeline. To him, it was the most beautiful sight that he'd ever experienced.

He had seen the reflection of the moon dancing in Ia Azalera's eyes, but Rosemary O'Leary's face reflected the moonlight as though it was another celestial body of equal brilliance and greater magnificence. Her smile was one of blushing innocence, but at the same time, there was a touch of mischievousness in the twinkle of her eye. There was no doubt now of her divinity. She *was* a goddess.

"Well, it sure is a lucky coincidence that you showed up here," he said, feeling the lameness of his choice of words. "I'm sure glad that you're okay."

"Did you ever think that things happen for a purpose?" she asked.

"Sometimes . . . I suppose," he admitted. "But when too many innocent people get hurt, it makes you wonder. I'm so glad that *you're* okay . . . but I guess that there were a lot of other people . . . and the people who care about them."

Rosie blushed slightly, inwardly ecstatic at his implication that he cared about her.

"What exactly happened over there?"

"There's not much to tell, really," she shrugged. "I guess I'm not being a good reporter. We're supposed to observe. I really don't remember much. I was walking down the street . . . late for an appointment . . . this building started to explode. I woke up days later in a hospital ward. Nobody knew who I was. My purse got mixed up with another girl. Her face was . . . Anyway . . . for four days, they thought she was me. I don't know whether they ever figured out who *she* really was. I still have nightmares sometimes."

"You were hit?" he asked, feeling ridiculous for being surprised that the woman whom he thought was dead had been hurt.

"Just a scratch," she said, pushing her hair back to reveal the scar on the side of her head.

The scar was well hidden by her hair, but when revealed, it was an ugly thing—about four inches long and silvery, not pink, in the moonlight. Without thinking, Nate bent down and gently kissed her injury, instinctively pulling her closer as though to protect her from all future harm.

As the powerful, yet gentle knight held her, Rosie realized that though she was in a strange land, half a world from home, she'd never felt safer. She also felt as though his kiss had somehow cured her of the horrible psychological grip that the scar had on her.

They walked for what seemed like hours, talking, telling childhood stories and laughing at one another's various trivial predicaments.

Night had fallen over the city like a sigh of relief. It was a clear purple night and you could almost hear the stars. They passed the little cafes and gambling dens that dotted the boulevards and side streets of the city. The nocturnal version of the city she'd seen in daylight seemed even more exotic, and almost dangerous in a tantalizing way. For Nate, the goddess with the unimaginable radiance was part of the mystery of this ethereal scene, and as such, more inaccessible, and simultaneously more desirable.

He had asked her whether she was hungry. She lied that she was, because she'd figured that *he* was. In fact, food was the farthest thought from her mind. They had bought some of the skewered meat that was being sold on the street corners and had laughed and giggled like kids as they ate it with their fingers.

Rosie and Nate walked quietly amid the surreal light of the cafes and the orange glow of occasional street fires that cast a wild, unnatural illumination on the faces of the people that sat in doorways talking, or rushing about on the street.

Rosie was amazed by the depth of his knowledge of this part of the world and of its people, but he just tossed it off as having been a fly on the wall at a lot of places where General Patton had been.

Finally, they were back on Budenovsky Prospect, with its big buildings, and the Hotel Rostov.

Except for a single desk clerk who was engrossed in reading a newspaper, they were alone in the vast lobby. Rosie felt small, but she'd not felt so far from being alone in years.

"You're staying here?" she asked, almost hopefully.

"Yes, ma'am," he said. "The staff took over the whole fifth floor. And you too, I guess?"

"Yeah," she shrugged nervously. "I guess it's the only place in town."

"Well," he said self-consciously.

"Well," she said, half teasing.

"Well . . . I guess it's good night, then. I'm really glad to have seen you again . . . You don't know how glad."

"The feeling is very much a mutual one, Sergeant . . . very, very much. I had a very nice time tonight . . . being with . . . talking with you."

Sensing the awkwardness that he seemed to be feeling, she reached out and gripped his hand in a firm handshake. His hand felt huge and mighty, but his handshake was so tender. She found his shyness so terribly appealing.

He began to walk away, as though he was in a daze.

"Oh, there's no elevator," she said. "I'll walk with you as far as the third floor. I'm on the third."

When he turned, he was smiling like a little boy whose mother had allowed him to stay up a half hour past bedtime. A few hours ago, the very sight of this warrior—in her fantasy world he was *her* warrior—had absolutely petrified her. Now, she'd become so relaxed in his presence that she almost dared to feel at home with him.

The staircase was wide and open, as though designed for a palace, rather than a Soviet hotel. With his long legs, Sergeant McKinley was able to climb with smooth, easy strides, but he was deliberately climbing slowly.

"I wish we were going to be around for a few days," he said, a hint of sadness in his voice. "I'd really like to spend some more time with you."

"I would like that very much," she said. "But we seem to keep coming up with these chance meetings. We may see one another again."

"Can I write to you in care of *The Washington Herald?*"

"Absolutely," she said, the small voices inside her head had risen in a standing ovation. "Here, let me give you my card."

She handed him her business card and he studied it carefully. Secretly, he was ecstatic to have this tiny artifact of her, something that would allow him not only to remember her, but to communicate with her.

As he reached for his wallet, she glanced around and discovered that their climb had finally taken them to the third-floor landing.

"Well . . . I guess this is the third floor," she said.

"Yep . . . guess so," he said.

He looked up to take in the long hallway of the third floor just as he opened his wallet. A small scrap of yellow, almost brown, paper flew out. Caught by a small gust of wind it fluttered out of his grasp. Like a tiny bird, it drifted in a wide arc, darting behind Rosie and landing near her feet. They both bent to pick it up, but she was much closer and her hand reached it before he'd scarcely had a chance to react.

She turned the small square of newsprint over in her hand and found herself staring—at herself.

It was *The Washington Herald*'s stock portrait photo of Rosemary O'Leary. She was taken completely off guard. Her jaw dropped slightly, and she glanced at him. He was blushing and hesitantly reaching toward it. He had a picture of *her* in his wallet!

She wanted so desperately to hug him again, but she held back. Maybe it was his shyness. Maybe it was her fear of the unknown. Rosie had been in situations like this with men before, but she'd never been in a situation like this where she cared so much about saying or doing the right thing.

As she handed his little clipping back to him, Nate felt mortified. He felt as though he'd been caught invading her privacy. How was she reacting to the discovery that he carried her picture in his wallet? He couldn't tell. Her expression was one of bewilderment.

"Well . . . I guess it's . . . it's the third floor," he said nervously.

"Well . . . I guess this is my stop," she said, smiling. She was not sure whether to grab him, or shake his hand.

Nervously, he reached out to give her a hug. She squeezed him politely, wanting to hang on for dear life. They looked at one another, neither looking at the expression, only the eyes. He leaned down and kissed her. It was a deep and passionate kiss, but it was over almost as quickly as it had started.

"Well . . . I guess it's . . . good night. Good night, Miss O'Leary."

"Good night, Sergeant McKinley," she smiled.

He smiled, let go of her hands, and turned and started up the next staircase. As she watched his powerful legs moving inextricably away from her, Rosie's heart was pounding fiercely.

He had taken two steps, then three. She tried to speak, but her caution would not allow it.

He took a fifth and sixth step. She had almost overcome the caution, but the inside of her mouth was dry to the point of brittleness.

He took an eighth, or was it the ninth step.

It was almost too late!

"Sergeant McKinley," she heard herself say in a raspy voice. "Do you want to come to my room and have a drink . . . I bought a bottle of this stuff they have here."

For Nate, it was like an angel calling him to say that his place in heaven was open now. It was like someone had turned flood lights on in the dimly lit corridor.

He turned and looked down at her. She looked so small

down at the bottom of the staircase in her tan wool coat, with her boots set apart. But she looked so radiant and so beautiful with her long hair the color of rosewood and that scarf like the women wear here in this exotic place.

She was smiling with her whole face.

They walked without speaking down the musty hallway, which was illuminated by two bare lightbulbs. There had been four others, but they'd burned out.

At last, they reached her door and she pulled the big clanking key out of her purse.

Inside, the window was open slightly, so the air was cool and fresh. She turned on the one electric light in the room and slipped off her coat.

"Can I take your coat?" She smiled politely.

"Um . . . sure."

She hung his next to her own on a set of hooks behind the door.

"Make yourself comfortable," Rosie said casually. "It really isn't much . . . but it's 'home,' courtesy of *The Washington Herald* . . . for a few days."

Nate lowered himself into one of the rickety chairs and watched as she took out a bottle of something and stared at the label, which was written entirely in the Russian Cyrillic alphabet.

As she scrutinized the bottle, he looked at her. The blue dress with the little lace collar that she was wearing flattered her figure perfectly. The long, full skirt, which hung almost to the tops of her boots, made her movements a symphony of motion. She was more beautiful than he'd imagined.

"I'm sorry, Sergeant, I really don't know what this is." With a little pout to her lips and an arched eyebrow, her expression was one of bemused bewilderment. "I really just bought it for the label, and . . ."

"That's fine, I see you've got some of that bottled water. That'll be fine for me."

"Are you sure?"

"Yes, ma'am, absolutely."

She loved the way that he called her "ma'am." But she was finding that there was nothing that she did *not* love about *her* warrior.

She unscrewed the cap and handed him a bottle of water and took one for herself. The wetness felt so good on her dry throat.

He watched her drink from the bottle like a teenager with a bottle of Coke. She was as much nymph as goddess, but absolutely supernatural. He reckoned that if this is what it felt like to have a spell cast on you—to be bewitched by an etherial being—then it was just fine with him.

She was looking at him now, and smiling again with her whole face. The soft light from the low-wattage incandescent lamp made her hair look absolutely sublime.

He remembered how wonderful she'd looked in Paris, sitting opposite him in her baggy khaki correspondent's uniform. He remembered how it had accented her hips and all but camouflaged her breasts. The blue dress magnified the wonder of her appearance a thousandfold. The soft blue belt molded the contour of her waist perfectly, and the shapes of her breasts were perfectly suggested in the folds of the garment as she moved. As she sat and crossed her legs, a flicker of her slip was visible as the hem of the skirt pulled back to reveal her right knee. She was the most beautiful creature in the universe.

Back in Naltxik, Ia Azalera might very well be the most beautiful human female on Earth, but Nate had been bewitched—bewitched by a *goddess* whose beauty was not of the earth, but of the moon and stars. He had been bewitched by a little Celtic goddess—who was now *with him* on this Earth.

They talked for a while as though trying to recapture the magic of their stroll outside, but there was the strange awkwardness of something unfinished hanging over their conversation.

At last, Nate stood up slowly.

"Well, I guess I'd better run along now and let you get some rest," he said, trying not to appear nervous.

Without speaking, she also stood. He watched a smile crease her face. With a slow and fluid motion she moved toward him. She put the palms of her hands on his shoulders and slowly slid them behind his neck. Closing her eyes, she gently pulled his face toward hers and kissed him on the lips. The synapses in his brain exploded. His dry throat did not crack; it splintered.

Without letting go of him, she leaned back and smiled broadly, tossing her head slightly to one side. A ripple of motion coursed through her long rosewood-colored hair.

Her kiss was longer the second time. He felt her tongue lightly brush his lips, and savored the feel of her hair against his cheeks. The aroma of her body swept over him. Her small hands were kneading his shoulders and his were exploring her body through the folds and fabric of her dress.

He felt her tugging to untie his tie and he reached up to help her. She pulled the tie away from his neck and kissed the top of his chest.

"Can you undo the back of my dress?" she asked innocently as she turned and pulled her long hair away from her back.

Of course he could . . . or at least of course he *wanted to*. He lifted a trembling hand and grasped the first tiny button. One by one, he unfastened them, each one a step toward revealing another two inches of the smooth whiteness of Rosie O'Leary's back. He tried to remind himself that this was *not* a dream, but then again, maybe it really *was* a dream.

With a quick twist of her body, the blue dress with the little lace collar that had defined her form through the evening slumped lifelessly from her shoulders. He could see her breasts clearly now, looking so smooth and so full. Her colorful scarf with the intricate patterns hung beside them, casting amazing shadows that made the shape of her body seem at one with those patterns.

He felt an instinctive embarrassment when her eyes caught him looking down at her.

"Are you nervous?" she asked with a smile, looking up at him with her beautiful, radiant face.

"Yep," he readily admitted, feeling like a dunce again. "And you?"

"Incredibly . . ." she said, hugging him.

With Ia Azalera, he'd not felt nervous, even though he probably should have, but with Miss O'Leary, his head spun too fast to think.

Abruptly, and as though intended to break the tension, the lamp suddenly went out.

"What's that?" Nate said with a start, his combat infantry-man's instincts surging to the fore.

"That's eleven o'clock," Rosie said, almost giggling. "They shut off the electricity at eleven o'clock every night. You're stuck with me here in the dark."

Stuck with Rosemary O'Leary in the dark! *Stuck* with Rosemary O'Leary in the dark!

"No place better to be stuck," he said, kissing her again. "No place better in this world to be *anything*."

In the half-light of reflected moonlight, he watched her care-fully remove her scarf and place it on the table near the lamp. Images and sensations—and articles of clothing—seemed to come and go in abstract fragments, like the curious patterns on her scarf, like different colored pieces of broken glass being tumbled together in a kaleidoscope.

Nate found himself on the edge of the bed, pulling off his boots.

He glanced up at her standing, completely naked, by the window—his little Celtic goddess—in the transparent, silvery moonlight. She was not so much illuminated by the moonlight as she was *of* the moonlight. Her beauty was beyond sublime. He marveled at the perfect contours and perfect proportions of her shoulders and of her breasts. He marveled at the profile of her face as she looked out the window with that boundless curiosity that was so much a part of her magic.

Somewhere in the distance, somewhere in the night, there was the faint sound of a bell being rung. For a brief moment, she seemed to be straining to listen to the tolling of the bell as though it was conveying a secret message to her.

She turned and smiled at him as he leaned back on the bed, watching her in the moonlight.

"What is it?" she asked, innocently covering her breasts with her arm.

"What's what?"

"You were looking at me . . ."

"What's the wonder in that?" he asked, almost laughing. "You're the most beautiful . . . You're so, so beautiful."

She smiled and seemed to relax slightly.

"Know what . . . you know what the most beautiful thing is about you?"

"No, Sergeant McKinley," she smiled, tipping her head slightly like a little bird listening to the song of her mate. "What's the most beautiful thing about me?"

"It's your smile. It just lights up the room . . . Your smile . . . it lights up the whole world as far as I'm concerned. Do you know that you smile with your whole face?"

Even in the cold moonlight, he could see her blushing a little bit.

"Do you know why I'm smiling right now . . . Sergeant McKinley?"

"No . . . Miss O'Leary . . ."

"It's because I'm so happy . . . Are you . . . are *you* happy?"

"Unimaginably . . . Miss O'Leary. I'm unimaginably happy to be here with you."

It was true. His joy was beyond anything imaginable.

She kneeled on the edge of the bed, leaned forward and put her small hands on his powerful shoulders. As she bent down to kiss him, the tiny cross that she wore on a chain around her neck tinkled on the metal of his dog tags.

He liked the way her thighs felt, squeezing his. He liked the way that her breasts felt as they touched his bare chest. He liked the way her hair felt as it brushed his cheeks when she bent down to kiss him. And he liked the way her kiss felt.

She kissed him deeply, pulled back, pecked his lips lightly and then sat up, her knees on either side of his torso. He was absolutely stunned by how she looked. It was as though her beauty expanded supernaturally with every moment.

The moonlight shimmered on her body.

She was one with the moonlight.

He was crossing the point where matter and energy become spirit—and where time has no meaning.

"You know what?" she asked playfully, beginning to run her hands though the mat of hair on his chest.

"What?"

"Sergeant McKinley . . . do you know what I'm going to do?"

"No."

"I'm going to make *you* as happy as *I* feel right at this moment."

17

★ ★

Henry Stimson's Georgetown townhouse
Washington DC
Monday, October 29, 1945, 6:21 p.m.

"IT'S not too late in the day . . . would you care to come in for a cup of something to warm you up?" The Secretary of War asked the Chief of Staff of the US Army, as their car pulled over to the curb in front of Henry Stimson's home.

"In my case, that would be a cup of coffee, rather than a tumbler of that which seems to be poured in abundance every evening around this town," General George Marshall grinned.

"I think that Mrs. Stimson may have a pot of that on the stove."

Marshall instructed his driver to come back in one hour, and the two men went inside the modest, red brick row house. Through their years in Washington, Mabel Stimson had typically greeted her husband around half past six, but over the past few weeks, the Secretary of War had taken to coming home before six, and she routinely had a pot of warm coffee waiting. Henry Stimson usually helped himself, but this evening, his wife played hostess, serving the two men in the living room. Marshall was invited to stay for dinner, but he begged off.

"The press seems to be consumed with our Supreme Commander," said Marshall, nodding to a copy of *The Washington Herald* that was lying on the coffee table.

"Our friend, George . . . and his imperial aspirations," Stimson said. "This'll blow over like so many things in this town. It sells papers for a while, then the people find something else to worry about."

"And *that* blows over, too." Marshall shrugged.

"Could I share something with you in strictest confidence?" Stimson said at last.

"Of course . . . always."

"The President is deeply concerned about this," Stimson confided. "He's told me that he's worried about all this Patton business in the press. He's more worried than he's let on. He didn't even want to discuss it with me at the White House."

"Really?"

"Last week, I went to the White House for a routine briefing. He met me at the door . . . wanted to go for a drive in the country. We went to Mount Vernon . . . where we walked and talked . . ."

"The home of the one American general who *could have* become an imperial president . . ." Marshall interrupted.

"And who chose the other path," Stimson reminded him. "Washington deliberately rejected the notion . . . he had to fight *not* to be crowned king! Who else in history . . . ?"

"Is Truman seriously worried about the government being *overthrown?*" Marshall asked. "Or is he merely concerned about the midterm elections a year from now?"

"Having the Republicans gain in Congress—even take *control* of Congress for the first time since 1930—is a real possibility in 1946. Of course, losing control of Congress is trivial when compared to Truman's concern over a possible subversion of the Constitution."

"And this is what Truman really . . . *truly* fears?" Marshall asked with disbelief.

"He reads the same newspapers as everyone else," Stimson shrugged, sidestepping the question.

"But where is there any concrete indication that Patton is planning to overthrow the government?" Marshall asked rhetorically. "I read the same papers. So far it seems to be *staying* in the papers."

"That's what *I* told the President," Stimson said.

"We still have a war to fight . . . George has a war to fight," Marshall reminded his old friend. "Despite what they're saying in the press, I think that Patton's eyes are on the job that he has . . . and the difficult obstacle that he has ahead of him."

"The winter."

"The winter," Marshall agreed. "This week, it will be November, and the cold winds will soon be howling, relentlessly and unpredictably, out of Siberia."

"Even on a cold day in Washington, I know that it's easy to minimize the fact that fighting a war on the steppes of Russia in the dead of winter is a horribly difficult task," Stimson said.

"By this time in 1812, Napoleon had been *in Moscow* for nearly two months. Plenty of time to prepare for winter?" Marshall asked.

"He lost it all," Stimson said soberly.

"He lost the greatest army that had been assembled in Europe for centuries . . . and he lost it all to General Winter."

"And history could repeat itself."

"Tell that to President Truman the next time that he voices a concern about the unpredictable winds of Washington politics," Marshall said. "Remind him of the unpredictable winds of *Mother Russia.*"

Naltxik, Kabardianno-Balkaria
Wednesday, October 31, 1945, 2:44 p.m.

"When General Patton came here, we were uncertain of what to expect," the Kabardian translator explained to the corespondent from *The Washington Herald.*

"We had heard the stories, too grandiose to be true. We met General Patton. Now we *know* they're true. There was a contest with the man named Jatorrizko, the Kabardian marksman. Patton himself engaged in the contest. A general with so much skill and assurance when standing alone gave us great confidence in the man. The people of this region admire such a man."

Rosemary O'Leary had arrived in Naltxik eighteen days after Patton had visited—and eighteen days after Patton had apparently made a tremendous impression.

For more than two weeks, Rosie had traveled through the Caucasus, hitching rides with Eighth Army units, meeting people, and gaining a perspective on the future of what had been Stalin's great southern empire. Naltxik was her last stop before returning to Rostov and the flight back to the United States.

Everywhere she'd gone in the Caucasus, people talked of Patton. They told amazing stories about Patton and his shooting skills—and what that had demonstrated about the character of the man.

The translator, a woman called Ia Azalera, was about her own age, obviously Western-educated, extremely articulate, and held in high regard by a culture where women still were second class. In fact, she appeared to be treated as a princess.

Even as she spoke of the charisma that her people saw in the American general, Ia Azalera exuded a charisma of her own. Her political status was in part because of the position among the people that was once held by her late father, but she herself possessed a wit and wisdom that gave her a role and a respect that was enjoyed by few Kabardian men. With her finely formed features, her dark eyes and long black hair, she seemed to hold the men of Naltxik in a sort of trance.

The two women talked for more than an hour, with Ia describing how the Soviet Union had used murder, including that of her own father, to stamp out the aspirations of nationalities throughout the Caucasus. In the course of the conversation, Ia mentioned to Rosie that she'd read "WHAT OUR FLAG SAYS," and had even saved the clipping. She explained that people in the Caucasus had been inspired by what it said about the United States and its intentions in the postwar world.

"My article . . . really?" Rosie said. "I'm flattered."

"Your words were quite moving," Ia replied. "They spoke to many people in many places . . . not just here . . . more, probably, than you realize."

"The words were mine, but the phrase, the idea, came from . . ."

"The American sergeant . . . McKinley," Ia Azalera interrupted.

"Exactly," Rosie nodded. "His insight was very powerful . . . but it's all that much more important because it's the insight of a man who has fought the troops of both Hitler *and* Stalin with his own hands."

"He's a great warrior," Ia smiled. "If *he* represents the skill and character of the American soldiers, your armies are truly the greatest in the world. I know. I've met him."

"Really?" Rosie was taken aback momentarily, but of course, Nate *had* said that he'd been in the Caucasus with Patton, and he too had described the shooting contest.

"Oh yes," Ia laughed. "The demonstrations of McKinley's skill were as impressive to our warriors as General Patton's were to our leaders. It began as a prank. A horse was presented for an American to demonstrate his skill of horsemanship. It was a spirited horse, a wild and vicious animal that no man had ever ridden."

"And they put Sergeant McKinley on this horse?" Rosie asked. He had not told her about this.

"Yes. The horse fought violently, but McKinley fought back. When he finished, the horse was tamed. Horses are second nature to Kabardians. For him to do what we cannot do earns great respect."

"He impressed me as a good and competent soldier," Rosie smiled, trying to conceal any hint of her special interest in Sergeant McKinley.

"He a skilled warrior, and he is a man that a woman would find desirable as well," Ia Azalera smiled with that sort of smile that a woman smiles to another woman, and which requires no further explanation.

"I suppose . . ." Rosie said, blushing slightly.

"I think you know what I mean," Ia Azalera continued.

"Yes, I do," Rosie smiled weakly.

"I thought you might. I sought him out later . . . to talk . . . in my tent . . . and, for a moment, he even lay on my bed."

"He lay in your bed?" Rosie gasped. Usually a shared confidence between women about a man gets a knowing nod, not a surge of jealousy. She pictured Nate in the bed of this princess and she wanted to scream.

"For a moment," Ia Azalera nodded, apparently not sensing the depth of Rosie's envy. "I tasted his lips, and, in that way, I had a small experience of his sorcery . . . but he went away."

"He went away? I don't understand."

"I'm not used to having men refuse me . . . . I don't mean to say that in a haughty way."

"I understand," Rosie nodded. She could see that this ravishing princess was the sort that was never turned down by men.

"But he left me . . . he went away. He left my bed without lying in it. He spoke of a goddess who owned his heart."

"A what?"

"He called her a goddess. He said that his heart was owned by a woman who was now *dead*. She *still* owns his heart. For a woman to have such power over a man, she must truly be as he described . . . a goddess."

Office of the Secretary of State
State Department Building
Washington DC
Tuesday, November 6, 1945, 11:40 a.m.

"Mr. Secretary, I got another call from Congressman Farmer's aide," Stephen Cuthbert explained to Edward Stettinius. "This latest article in *The Washington Herald* has them really steamed up on the Hill."

"And, I see that it's under the byline of our friend, Miss O'Leary," the Secretary observed. "Seems that she's been to Russia . . . and she's been speaking to the people."

"The way she writes, Patton's being received like a conquering warlord."

"But he's doing so under the flag of the United States," Stettinius cautioned. "You're making it sound like he's building an empire for *himself* out there."

"They're still nervous about it up on the Hill."

"What do they want us to do?" Stettinius asked.

"He wants the State Department to issue a statement, or . . ."

"Or what?"

"He said that Congressman Farmer will . . . he'll get Congress itself involved . . . he wants Truman to fire Patton."

"That would seriously undermine the war effort," Stettinius said. "It would seriously damage the morale of our fighting men at a critical moment . . . with the winter coming very, very soon. I'm surprised they're not up to their axles in snow already. President Truman has every confidence in his leadership ability."

"I understand that sir, but . . ."

"Stephen, if he calls again . . . tell Congressman Farmer's aide what I just told you."

Moskvoretsky Bridge
Moscow, Russia
Sunday, November 11, 1945, 11:02 a.m.

"It sounds like they've got all the church bells in Moscow ringing to celebrate your birthday, General," Oscar Koch said from the back seat of the jeep as they crossed the Moscow River. The air was filled with the sound of brass hitting brass— all across the city. Ahead, the steeples of St. Basil's Cathedral, Moscow's signature landmark since tsarist times, were clearly visible.

"It's the eleventh hour of the eleventh day of the eleventh month . . ." Patton observed.

"The hour the guns fell silent in the *First* World War," Nate added, having heard the famous phrase every year around Armistice Day from his uncle who'd been in France on that fateful morning when World War I ended.

"But the guns are not quite silent in this way . . . yet," Patton cautioned. "There's still gonna be a helluva fight down in Kuybyshev."

After the terrible carnage of World War I, the end had come in November 1918 with more of a whimper than a bang. The same had been true with the fall of Moscow in 1945. It had all started with the bells. On Thursday morning, Muscovites awoke to the distant, lonely sound of the bells at St. Danilov's Orthodox Church on the south side of central Moscow.

As the sun rose, the lonely belfry at St. Danilov's was joined by the sounds of bells from other corners of the city. Within an hour, the streets had been filled with people. Strangely, there were no police anywhere in sight, no NKVD, no city police. The Red Army troops that had been parading everywhere on Wednesday for the twenty-eighth anniversary of the Bolshevik Revolution were *gone*.

People told of having heard the tanks and trucks during the

middle of the night. Stories circulated, rumors spread, and crowds gathered. By noon, the crowd in Lubyanka Square had discovered that the NKVD Headquarters had been abandoned. The crowds entered the building, cautious at first, and then with the rage of revenge—revenge for Stalin's two-decade reign of terror against his own people.

Inside, they discovered that the cobblestones in Lubyanka Prison were awash with the blood of 143 prisoners, all hacked to death and left behind. Among them were the bodies of the sixteen Polish resistance leaders whose presence in this prison had helped to push the world to fight the war that was being called World War III.

By afternoon, the red banners, still hanging on every lamp post since the somber parades of November 7, were starting to come down. The word had reached General Vlasov at his headquarters east of Smolensk. It was over. The city was his for the taking.

Nate had been with Patton, who was visiting Walton Walker's Third Army headquarters at Bryansk when the news came in late on Thursday. It was a whimper, not a bang. There would be no Battle of Moscow as the snows came in 1945—as there had been in 1941. As with Napoleon in 1812, the battles were over, the city lay open. By Friday morning, the whole world knew that Stalin had withdrawn from Moscow to make his final stand at his wartime capital in Kuybyshev, five hundred miles to the east.

By Friday night, Vlasov was in Moscow, welcomed by war-weary Muscovites who clearly understood the irony of their city being "conquered" by the man who'd helped save it from the Nazis four years before.

As Patton had promised months earlier, Third Army would be the first American army to enter Moscow. Units of the British Second and American First would be close behind, entering from the north as Third Army came in from the south through Chertanovo.

As though tweaking irony once again, General Winter had intervened with a snowstorm on Saturday to delay the American arrival one day—to the birthday of his rival, General Patton.

By dawn on Sunday, the snow had melted from the roads, but there were still drifts in the shaded places as Third Army traveled the last thirty kilometers to enter the city that Hitler's legions coveted but never conquered.

There were a few flakes of snow in the air as Patton's motorcade pulled into Red Square, but it was still warm enough that they weren't sticking to the ground.

With the imposing wall of the Kremlin looming to their left, Nate brought the five-star jeep to a halt in the center of the sprawling, cobblestoned square. There were relatively few civilians to be seen, but a large number of Russian troops and American GIs were present. There was a line of 12th Armored Division M26A2s parked near a line of T34s whose red stars had been painted over with the white, blue, and red squares of the new Russian flag.

At the command post that had been set up near the entrance to St. Basil's, Nate recognized General Vlasov, along with his senior generals, Trukhin and Boyarski. Along with Third Army boss General Walton Walker, were General Rod Allen of the 12th Armored and General Wild Bill Donovan. The tall and gangly Vlasov, who never smiled, had a relaxed expression on his face, and General Boyarski was joking with Allen through a translator.

Vlasov and Patton exchanged salutes, followed by the customary Russian bear hug. This was obviously an emotional moment for two tenacious soldiers who each recognized that they would not be standing here in Red Square were it not for the other.

"Please tell the General that I congratulate him on his return to Moscow," Patton said to Madame Posdnyakov, Vlasov's personal translator.

After a brief round of congratulations and counter-congratulations, General Boyarski produced a bottle of vodka and a Third Army photographer memorialized the image of Vlasov and Patton raising their glasses with the Kremlin wall in the background.

Donovan waited for the conclusion of Madame Posdnyakov's translation of Vlasov's toast to pull Patton aside.

"General, we have a situation," the Office of Strategic Services boss explained, nodding toward the Kremlin.

"What's that?" Patton asked, looking at the great walled complex.

"He's still inside," Vlasov's people have him surrounded. "He wants to talk to you."

"Who's inside?"

"Molotov. Commissar Vyacheslav Molotov."

"What?" Patton said shaking his head. "I thought all those bastards left town Wednesday night."

"That's what we'd been led to believe, but *he's* here."

"Have you talked to him?"

"No, but one of my guys who speaks Russian has," Donovan explained. "Molotov says he wants to talk to *you*. Vlasov wanted to take a T34 in there and blast him out, but he finally agreed to wait for you."

"How the hell . . . ?"

"I had one of my teams coming in here with Vlasov on Friday. We knew that the civilians ransacked the NKVD headquarters and started a lot of fires. I wanted to secure the place and preserve as many of the records and paperwork as possible. Ditto with the Kremlin. Since it's a fortress, the civilians didn't get in here. I convinced Vlasov that we should take the Kremlin pretty methodically and make sure that nothing got destroyed. In the course of that . . . we discovered pockets of Reds in there . . . mainly in the office building on the far side."

"What the hell? Are they set to go down shooting?"

"No. The fact is, they wanted to surrender to *us* and *not* Vlasov's people. They're scared to death. We worked that out with our Russian friends and the whole place is secure now . . . except the floor of the building where Molotov is."

Working through interpreters, Patton and Vlasov agreed that Patton and Donovan would go in and talk with Molotov.

As they drove through the Kremlin's Kutafya Tower Gate, Nate had been expecting architecture that was in keeping with the hulking, utilitarian, Stalinist style that he'd seen elsewhere in Moscow and in the many other Russian cities through which he'd driven. Instead, the inner sanctum of communism was like a precious little jewel box. There were looming, severe office blocks, but the Americans' attention was taken with the delicate and showy medieval religious buildings that had obviously been kept up at great expense.

"We must be getting soft, Bill," Patton said to Donovan as they climbed out of the jeep.

"What do you mean, General?"

"Look at this damned place," Patton said, gesturing broadly. "Berlin got blown to holy hell. The fucking Kremlin is still intact. Hitler killed himself . . . and his goddam *dog* . . . to keep from getting captured by the damned Russians. Now, here we're in Moscow . . . and this sonuvabitch Molotov thinks he can *talk* his way out of this. Bill, we're just too damned soft on these bastards."

"Hitler also shot his wife," Donovan added.

"*And* his goddam *dog,*" Patton insisted.

Accompanied by Major Tom Hovalik, the translator, and four GIs with Thompsons, Patton and Donovan strode into the Kremlin office building where Stalin had once maintained his own office. Nate brought up the rear with the shotgun from the jeep.

Inside, the building was cold and gloomy. The electricity had been cut off and the heat had been off for some time. The shivering GIs who held the lower floors grinned and saluted as they recognized Patton.

Slowly, the group made its way up the main staircase, pausing to gawk at the large portraits of Soviet leaders that still hung everywhere. About half of the portraits were of the same subject—the Man of Steel, whose eyes were always eerily cold and brooding.

When they reached the top floor, there were three men in ill-fitting black suits standing nervously opposite a half-dozen tough-looking GIs. The Americans were especially happy to see Patton, who greeted them gregariously as Hovalik spoke to the men in black.

"They say that Molotov's in that room," he said, pointing to a large door at the end of the hall.

"Let's get this the hell over with," Patton growled.

With the men in black scampering ahead and Nate now in the lead with his trench cleaner, they walked down the marble hallway toward their rendezvous with the Soviet Union's penultimate leader.

The inside of the room was damp and stuffy. The air was blue with cigarette smoke. Between the windows that overlooked the street, Molotov was seated at a large desk beneath a gold-painted plaster casting of the hammer-and-sickle emblem of the Union of Soviet Socialist Republics.

"The Commissar wishes to . . ." one of the men in black started to say.

"Never mind, I will speak," Molotov interrupted. "I wish to congratulate you on delivering this *temporary* setback to the Soviet Union and the workers of the world. You are here because of the crippling blows dealt to the armies of the Soviet Union by the fascists, while your capitalist bosses delayed the second front for two years."

"That's bullshit and you know it," Patton said calmly. "The first thing that you bastards did after we invaded in Normandy was to attack *Finland*."

The Commissar looked startled, obviously unaccustomed to being spoken to disrespectfully—especially by someone with a mastery of historical facts.

"Let me remind you that when the Soviet Union was invaded by more than two hundred fascist divisions . . . the Red Army fought heroically . . . and the workers, men and women, fought heroically. Seven of ten fascist troops were fighting the Red Army. When we intervened in May, you were already restoring the fascists to power . . ."

"This was your excuse to launch an invasion of France and the low countries, then to attack the United States with rockets?" Donovan asked.

"The international working class led by the Soviet Union crushed fascism in the Second World War," Molotov said impatiently. "This victory is one of the greatest achievements of the working class . . . led by the Red Army . . . but the job was not finished. Our armies undertook the supreme sacrifice to rid Europe and the world of the fascist and capitalist masters once and for all."

"Didn't work, did it?" Patton smirked. "Have you been out on the streets of Moscow lately? The *workers* don't seem to be missing your goddam regime very much."

Molotov simply pouted as he lit another cigarette.

"I think we've heard enough bullshit for one day . . ." Patton said, starting to get up.

"Wait," Molotov interrupted. "I have a proposal . . . I'm not an unreasonable man."

"You could have fooled us," Donovan smiled.

"Can we talk alone?" Molotov asked nodding toward Patton and Donovan. "Just the three of us?"

The two American officers looked at one another. Donovan nodded and Patton looked around the room.

"Okay, I want men outside both of the doors," Patton said. "Nobody comes in."

When the GIs and the men in black had left the room, Patton and Donovan seated themselves in opposite corners of Molotov's office, so that if Molotov pulled a gun, the best he could do would be to hit just one of them.

"General Patton, you are, today, the most powerful military man in Europe," Molotov said, leaning back in his huge chair. "They are comparing you to Napoleon. You have an empire greater than any Europe has seen since Roman times. You have Atomic Bombs. You could rule the world. I sense by your demeanor that you would be pleased by such a turn of events. I can help you."

Patton and Donovan exchanged incredulous glances, but even Patton remained silent as Molotov spun his fantastic scheme.

"The International Communist Revolution is inevitable. Marx said so. We all know that it is true. Only a matter of time. All correct-thinking people know this. With or without the Red Army, the workers of the world will arise and throw off their chains. Frankly, it was your victories in June that intimidated the workers of France. We know your popularity in the United States. You could take control of the American government. With no one to challenge us, the workers would revolt everywhere. *We* could rule the world!"

"What do you mean *we?*" Donovan asked, shaking his head in disbelief.

"You have two choices, General," Molotov said, leaning forward across the ornate desk. "You can *ignore* the inevitability of a universal workers' revolution . . . or you can *accept* it. You can be with us or against us."

"You're outa your goddam mind . . ." Patton said, standing up.

"It's actually quite interesting," Donovan said, gesturing for the General to remain seated. "I think that perhaps on second thought, General Patton would like to hear a little more about what exactly you're proposing."

Patton glanced at Donovan as though he was insane.

"I thought that cooler heads would prevail," Molotov said with a sly smile. "My dear General Patton, I understand your wishes to rule the world. I can help. I am your key . . . The Red Army may have crumbled, but we still have a network of agents in France . . . and England . . . and in the United States. They can help. With your popularity in the United States . . . and an appropriately timed series of workers' revolts . . . strikes . . . we can take control there easily."

"How can we make contact with these people in the United States?" Donovan asked innocently.

"Just a moment," Molotov said with a grin. "I am not a fool. I have been at the arm of the master of suspicion for too long to trust you so easily. No, I will have several conditions to be met. Then, I will put my forces at the disposal of our common objective. First, I wish to be guaranteed safe transit, for myself and my staff, out of Moscow . . . and I do not mean to join the fools at Kuybyshev . . . I have a home near Zurich. Second, I wish to have fifty million United States dollars to be wired to a Swiss bank account whose number I shall give you. *Then* I will make the necessary arrangements."

"That's rather a lot of money," Donovan said.

"Don't play games with me, General Donovan," Molotov cautioned. "I know that your friends on Wall Street can get it for you . . . for the right reasons . . . and I think that control of the world is clearly the right reason . . . Don't *you?*"

"Assuming that we went ahead with this business venture . . . what guarantee would *you* have that we wouldn't come after you in Switzerland?" Patton asked.

"Oh General," Molotov cooed. "You're a capitalist, you understand the importance of Swiss sovereignty. You need their banks. We all need their banks. And one more thing . . .

A moment ago, I made a point of watching your expression when I was reminding you that you have Atomic Bombs. But, as you may know, you are not the *only* one in this room with Atomic Bombs."

Molotov paused briefly for effect and then looked Patton squarely in the eye.

"Happy birthday, General." He smiled. "I'm looking forward to doing business with you."

The White House
Washington DC
Tuesday, November 12, 1945, 3:02 p.m.

"Harry, we gotta talk," Congressman Austin Farmer said as he was ushered into the President's office. Visitors usually weren't so familiar as to assume a first-name basis with the President of the United States, but Austin Kenmore Farmer was not just anyone. He and Harry Truman went back a few years, back to the days when they were still wet-behind-the-ears Midwestern boys, new to the strange and arcane world of Capitol Hill.

"I'm always happy to see you, Austin," the President smiled.

"Harry, we all thought this damned thing would go on through the winter. You yourself said that Patton wasn't anything to be worried about until spring."

"All morning, there's been celebrating and church bells ringing," the President observed. "Our armies are in Moscow. There's cause for celebration . . . and you're worried about Patton?"

"Tell me that you're *not* worried about Patton," Farmer replied.

"To the extent that you are? No. I'm not."

"Julius Caesar crossed the . . ."

"Congressman, you have no idea how many times the word 'Rubicon' has been used and discussed in this room over the past few weeks," Truman interrupted. "And you don't know how many times this analogy has played out in my mind."

"I'm glad to know that we're on the same page," Farmer

said, adjusting his immense bulk in the chair. "Wouldja like a cigar?"

"No . . . thank you," the President replied, contemplating the potential lingering effects of the Congressman's stogie on the room.

"You wouldn't mind if I got right to the point, wouldja, Harry?"

"Austin, I'd be disappointed if you *didn't*."

"There's a bunch of us up on the Hill . . . lotta your old pals among us. We don't like the sound of what we're hearing in the papers about Patton," Farmer explained. "Haven't for months. Haven't for years, really. The sonuvabitch shoots off his face too much. I think it's gettin' to be high time you canned his ass before we have ourselves one of those good old-fashioned Constitutional crises."

"In case you didn't notice, Austin, the United States is at war and General Patton is the Supreme Commander of our troops in the field," Truman replied. "And he'd been doing a pretty good job . . . a *damned fine job* in fact."

"He's a sonuvabitch, Harry."

"He is, Austin. But he's *our* sonuvabitch and he's got *their* sonuvabitch cornered in Kuybyshev."

"He wants your job."

"I've read that in the papers, but I've yet to hear anything from his lips to that effect. The moment that I do, you can be damned sure that I'll be taking steps to 'can his ass,' as you say. Until then, he's our sonuvabitch, I'm his Commander-in-Chief, and the buck stops with me."

"A lot of us up on the Hill . . ."

"I know, but I'm not going to can the ass of a general who's leading our troops against the enemy and doing it successfully . . . no matter what the papers say . . . no matter what *you* say . . . until I'm damned sure that it's the prudent thing to do."

"Harry, the *President* wouldn't have let things get out of control like this."

"Austin . . . *I'm* the President!" Truman said angrily, not certain whether Farmer's slip-of-the-tongue reference to Roosevelt was deliberate or not.

"You know what I mean."

"You know what *I* mean, Austin."

Office of the Secretary of State
State Department Building
Washington DC
Wednesday, November 28, 1945, p.m.

"This is a great honor, Mr. Secretary," Stephen Cuthbert said.

"You're the man for the job," Edward Stettinius said. "You met General Vlasov at Warsaw, and you've done some great work with the Georgians. It's high time that you went over to Russia and got a good look at things close at hand yourself."

This was a proud moment in Cuthbert's career—a promotion to Undersecretary of State and an assignment as Stettinius's personal eyes and ears on a fact-finding mission to the former Soviet Union. He felt like a kid who'd just made the varsity.

"I'm really depending on you, Stephen," the white-haired Secretary of State said, leaning back in his chair. "Things are very fluid over there. I need to know what's going on. I want you to call on Vlasov in Moscow, but you also need to go down to Kuybyshev. The battle down there will be the climax, the last stand of the Soviet Union."

"Kuybyshev will be *Patton's* big show," Cuthbert said, knowing that the eyes of the world were watching what promised to be the General's final campaign.

"When the war is over, then it'll be our job, but for now it *is* his 'show,' as you put it. When the fighting is over, the military men will be replaced by the diplomats, men like you. For the moment, though, your job is to learn from him. I know that you're suspicious of his motives, but remember this, he had to do his job before we can start to do ours."

"You can count on me to do *my* job, sir," Cuthbert said. He was not convinced that Patton would allow himself to be shunted to one side by civilians after he achieved such a glorious victory.

"I know, Stephen, you will," Stettinius said with a fatherly tone, responding as much to what he knew Cuthbert was thinking as what he'd said. "And one more thing, when you're dealing with Patton."

"Yes?"

"You're a diplomat. Be *diplomatic*."

Cuthbert nodded thoughtfully.

Lucky Forward
Kuybyshev, Russia
Saturday, December 1, 1945, 12:28 p.m.

The weather had been chilly, but so far, there had been relatively little snow on the steppes of central Russia. General Winter, which had been Stalin's decisive ally in 1941, was uncharacteristically generous to Stalin's enemies in 1945.

In the distance, they could clearly see the silvery lines of Russia's signature river, the great Volga—which snaked in a great, wide arc through Kuybyshev—and the smaller Samara River that flowed through the eastern part of the city. Pillars of smoke could be seen everywhere, and in the distance, there were orange flashes of artillery explosions.

The air was filled with buzzing and growling aircraft engines, as clouds of A-20 Invaders and P-47 Jugs streaked in to slam segments of the fortified city with bombs and rockets.

The assault on Moscow, had it been necessary, would have been largely in the hands of Vlasov's army, just as the Polish army had spearheaded the drive on Warsaw. However, with Kuybyshev, the attackers were the veterans of Normandy, the Ardennes, and Okinawa.

Patton's favorite, the Third Army, had crossed the Volga at Kazan in order to push into Kuybyshev from the north in conjunction with the Ninth Army. The American First Army and the British Second Army had driven into the portion of the city west of the Volga, while the American Fifth and Eighth Armies advanced on Kuybyshev from the south side of the Samara.

The US Army, molded by four years of war into a vast and powerful fighting machine, was made all that more formidable by something that neither Napoleon nor Hitler could have imagined. The secret weapon that had made this day possible was not the Atomic Bomb, whose threatened use had broken Japan's will to fight, but an efficient and responsive logistical network that had given Patton's legions an unlimited supply of fuel, ammunition, and Spam. The supply network now stretched from Koenigsberg to Moscow, and from Moscow to Kuybyshev. It defied Washington bureaucrats and the Russian winter to operate with clocklike precision. It was a wonder of modern warfare that assured the very victory that would render it unnecessary.

For their part, the Red Army divisions had dug in for another Stalingrad. They had been prepared to give the Allies the sort of house-to-house fight that had crippled the Germans at that other citadel city on the banks of the Rodinya's mother of rivers.

Marshal Semyon Konstantinovich Timoshenko was in the battle of his career. Deep down inside, he knew that it was his last battle, but it was, he hoped, a battle in which the long memory of history would recall him as a gallant, if not victorious, officer.

A hero of the Russo-Finnish War in 1940, he'd led the armies that recaptured Rostov from the Germans in 1941. He had, along with Andrei Vlasov, helped save Moscow. When Vlasov turned on Stalin, Timoshenko remained slavishly loyal. It was to Timoshenko whom the Man of Steel turned when the legendary Georgi Zhukov lost the cream of the Red Army at Osnabruck.

The end had finally come, but Timoshenko was going to make sure that the Soviet Union would end with a bang and not a whimper. The Man of Steel would be proud. When the battle had been joined a fortnight earlier, with the American tanks probing the city's outer defenses, it had seemed as though the Allies expected an easy victory, but Timoshenko had greeted them with withering cannon fire and they fled. For days, an artillery duel had ensued, with the tenacious Yanks biting off sections of Kuybyshev like a dog eating a biscuit.

On Saturday morning, the first day of sunshine in more than a week, it seemed as though the Soviet will had collapsed. Large numbers of hungry, sick, and exhausted pawns of the Red Army had started drifting through the lines. By afternoon, the trickle became a deluge. The number of prisoners swelled, and resistance was reduced to a few isolated pockets.

"It's been a *damned fine war,*" Patton said, taking a last look through his binoculars at the scene that spread before them.

"It'll be a relief to go home knowing that we *finished* the job this time," Nate added.

"We've done our job," Patton said emphatically. "Now we can hand the politicians what's left and let *them* sort it out."

As Patton approached the main tent, reporters started streaming toward him. They had started to arrive that morning, sensing the impending finale. Poor Tim Cunningham was like a sheep dog, running around and trying to keep them in line. Nate looked in vain for a certain female face among them, but she wasn't there.

"What are your plans for Russia and the Reds when this is over?" one of them shouted.

"That's a question for the politicians," Patton shouted. "I catch the fish and they cook 'em."

"When do you expect to catch Stalin himself?"

"If I knew, I'd become a fortune-teller."

He tossed off the usual replies to the usual sorts of questions, finally summing it up with a wave of his hand: "I have no more comment until the job's done."

When they reached the tent, there were other strangers present. The General's comment about everybody wanting to be in on the action was certainly apt, although it struck Nate as a bit opportunistic. After the years of war, people were coming out of the woodwork to watch the last battle as though it were a spectator sport.

It was sort of like First Bull Run in 1861, when everybody streamed out of Washington on a warm July morning to watch the battle as picnic entertainment. They had expected to be entertained by the opening and final battle in an almost comic-opera war. Instead, the battle at Manassas, Virginia was just the unbelievably bloody opening to four years of the most savage war ever fought in the Western Hemisphere.

Kuybyshev today would probably not be like Manassas, but the zealous overconfidence could not but help those with any sense of historic irony feel just a trifle uneasy. For those who had any sense of Stalin's lust for an Atomic Bomb—and only Patton and Oscar Koch knew of this—a final battle with a cornered foe had to be especially troubling. However, if the Supreme Commander was at all uneasy, he showed no hint of it. His mood was decidedly optimistic.

As Patton left the reporters outside and strode into the command tent, Hap Gay was talking to a trio of Asiatic men in baggy, collarless suits.

"Sir, I have some gentlemen here who'd like to meet you," Gay said, motioning for his boss.

"General, this is the Chinese delegation from Yenan," he explained. "They've been traveling overland for weeks, and they're very anxious to meet you. This is General Lin Piao, Mr. Chou En-lai, and Mr. Mao Tse-tung . . . They're all vets of the fight against the Japs."

The man called Mao said something to a translator, who told Patton that they had followed his campaigns with great interest and were deeply honored to meet him.

"Tell them that it's *my* pleasure," Patton said, shaking their hands.

"They say that it's their fortune to meet you," the translator continued. "They hope never to have to face you on a battlefield."

"Tell them I hope not, too." Patton smiled.

As though working a receiving line, Patton shook hands with a large number of people who had lined up to greet him. Finally, he worked his way to a slender young fellow, whom Nate recognized from having seen him at the Warsaw Conference.

"Sir, I'm Undersecretary of State Stephen Cuthbert," he explained. "I'm Secretary Stettinius's personal representative over here. I'm in Russia on a fact-finding mission."

"Are you finding all the facts you need?" Patton grinned.

"I'm certainly impressed with the efficiency of your operation, General."

"We've had a lotta practice," the General replied. "It's been a helluva long way from Normandy to Kuybyshev. We've learned how to do a job . . . and we do it a helluva lot better than the other guy."

"Your comment outside . . . about you catching the fish and the politicians cooking them . . . I'm intrigued by that."

"That's the way our system works," Patton told Cuthbert. "It's the job of the politicians to pick the fight and clean up after it. It's a soldier's job to do the fighting . . . that's the ugly job we're trained to do. It's the soldiers who are trained to beat the shit out of the enemy until he stops fighting. We've very nearly done that. Then it's up to the politicians to sort out the mess that's left over."

"Secretary Stettinius—and the department—have absolute confidence in the way that you're catching them . . . and we look forward to the opportunity to cook them," Cuthbert said nervously, trying to be diplomatic.

"Good man!" Patton said, slapping Cuthbert on the back. "You wanna go into town and find some facts? Sergeant McKinley, requisition a jeep and take Mr. Cuthbert on a fact-finding trip into the First Division sector in Kuybyshev."

"What sort of facts are you looking for?" Nate asked, making small talk as they cruised toward the First Infantry Division checkpoint on the outskirts of the city. Nate's old friend, Johnny Rotelli, and another GI were riding shotgun in a second jeep. After what had happened to Nate in Jena, the General didn't send anyone anywhere alone, no matter how routine it seemed.

"The political situation seems to be changing constantly out here. The Secretary wants me to look around . . . get a firsthand impression. In order to make postwar policy, you sort of have to take it all in with your own eyes and ears," Cuthbert said.

As the two jeeps passed through the outskirts of Kuybyshev, tangles of barbed wire and damaged T34s were everywhere. Small groups of GIs guarded large numbers of prisoners in various states of dress. Most had overcoats, but some were wrapped in GI blankets. Nearly all had boots, but a few of the Red Army POWs simply had their feet and ankles wrapped in cloth.

The weather was noticeably cold. Cuthbert's ears stung. He wished he'd taken the silly-looking cap with ear flaps offered to him at Patton's headquarters. There was about a foot of hard, crusty snow on the ground, but the roads were bare and generally dry.

When they reached the 1 Infantry Division command post,

Nate introduced Cuthbert to the officers and explained why Patton sent them. They gave Cuthbert a fast briefing and explained that the area of the city ahead of them had been cleared that morning. Most of the fighting was now on the other side of the Samara River in the Eighth Army's sector.

"It's probably safe if you wanna take a closer look," the major in charge explained. "Just watch out for snipers."

"It's up to you," Nate said, looking at Cuthbert.

"I suppose," the Undersecretary replied uneasily, not wanting to appear cowardly around all these battle-hardened fighting men who were about his age. "I'm here to find facts . . . I suppose I might as well see where the front was this morning."

They left the command post area and turned onto a long, broad street lined with featureless, grey buildings. Everything on the street seemed to have been designed by an architect with no imagination, built to the same set of blueprints. At least the street was wide. It was also quiet—although the sound of artillery and occasional small-arms fire could be heard about a quarter of a mile ahead.

"Nice cars," Nate said, nodding to an abandoned 1937 Cadillac Fleetwood parked at the curb. Despite piles of rubble and a burned-out Stalin tank nearby, the car looked to be in good condition except for a thin coat of dust.

"This was the Soviet wartime capital," Cuthbert observed. "I guess the Communist Party elite lived pretty high on the hog down here. This city was *designed* for them. Apparently Stalin was hoping to get through the winter here. He didn't have the weather on his side like he did in '41, though."

"He also didn't envision such a well-equipped foe," Cuthbert replied, looking at the M26A2 tanks and the well-armed GIs. He'd never been this close to military hardware on a battlefront before. The luck of the draw of his State Department job had kept his draft board at bay. Stephen Cuthbert had never worn a uniform. That separated him from the vast majority of the men in the generation of which he and Sergeant McKinley were members. This made him feel lucky *most* of the time. Out here, surrounded by men his age who'd spent much of the past year or two in trenches, he felt a touch of chagrin.

"I think we'd probably better turn around," Nate said after

a while. "The Major said to watch out for snipers and it's starting to feel a little too quiet."

Nate's instinct had been correct. Just as the two jeeps were starting to circle into a wide U-turn, they heard the *ping . . . ping* of sniper fire.

"Hang on!" Nate shouted as he pointed the hood of the jeep toward a side street and floored it.

They had just passed into the shadow of the narrow alley when they felt the bone-jarring crash of the vehicle hitting a shell crater that was partially obscured by a pile of debris. Cuthbert was barely able to hang on as Nate fought to control the skidding Willys.

There was the screeching sound of tearing metal and the stench of burning rubber. The jeep came to a halt pointed back in the direction from which it had come.

Ping . . . ping!

"Get down," Nate screamed, grabbing the sleeve of Cuthbert's overcoat and dragging him out of the jeep into the relative safety of a pile of cinder blocks.

"Damned axle is bent," Nate said, nodding toward the jeep. "I could feel it."

"Looks like the other jeep was hit," Cuthbert said in a quavering voice, his gaze cast back toward the main street.

The other jeep had been hit by a volley of sniper fire that shattered the windshield. Steam was pouring from the radiator. He saw Rotelli and the other man huddled on the ground near the mouth of the narrow side street. He also saw blood on the ground.

"How bad are you hit?" Nate called.

"Bob took one in the thigh!" Rotelli shouted. "I'm wrappin' it with a tourniquet now. Can you see where the bastards are?"

"Not yet. They're probably in a coupla places. Probably got the whole intersection covered. They let the tanks pass . . . guess we looked like easy pickings."

"What happened?" Cuthbert asked helplessly. "There are American tanks just a few blocks ahead and behind. What can we do? Are we gonna be all right?"

"We can't call for help . . . the radio's in the other jeep," Nate said in a matter-of-fact tone. "But you're right. There *are* friendlies everywhere. Somebody will come along . . . Soon. I hope."

Nate scanned the building that loomed above them, looking for any hint of movement. He was not disappointed. High up on the third floor, he saw the flicker of a sleeve and the unmistakable profile of a rifle barrel. Somebody was trying to line up a shot at the other two men, and finding the angle a trifle difficult.

In an instant, Nate had pulled off his overcoat and was aiming his Colt automatic at the figure in the window. He saw the arm and the wiggling barrel. He waited, knowing that the sniper would have to lean out to take aim at the other guys from that angle.

There was a flash of a pink cheek and then the head came into view. He didn't wait. He squeezed the trigger, saw the head jerk slightly and the arm fall limp. He kept his eye on the window, ignoring the rifle as it plummeted three stories to the street below.

A second face appeared at the window and Nate fired again. There was a brief expression of surprise and the second head fell back lifelessly.

"You get him?" Rotelli shouted.

"Got *two*."

"Damned Montana cowboys," Rotelli complained in a parody of his own South Philly accent. "You hicks make us all look bad."

"How's Bob?"

"He'll be okay if we can get him to an aid station."

"Can you get to your radio?"

"It was hit."

"Cover me."

"Whatcha gonna do?"

"I wish I knew."

Nate stood up and cautiously scanned the possible vantage points for snipers. He couldn't believe his luck. He'd survived a situation like this at Jena in the *first* major battle of World War III only to wind up doing it again in what Patton had that morning decreed as the *last* battle of World War III.

Nate made his way across the street and back to the mouth of the alley where Bob and Johnny were crouched.

"How ya doin', Bob?" Nate asked.

"Hurts like hell, but I'm all right."

Nate stepped around the corner, counted to two and jumped back, just as bullets started to fly.

"I think we're safe in the alley, but not on the main street," Nate explained.

"No shit?" Rotelli replied, suggesting that Nate's diagnosis was pretty obvious.

"Let's get Bob out of the weather and wait for the good guys. Shouldn't be long."

The two GIs hoisted the wounded man's arms onto their shoulders and began moving him down the alley and away from the main street, which was still covered by the snipers. With Cuthbert lending a hand, they made their way toward an open door in a building near a place where the alley intersected the fork of another, narrower alley.

Just as they reached their destination, there was a scraping sound and the men turned to find themselves face to face with three Red Army soldiers and an equal number of officers.

Nate's heart sank. He remembered Patton's stated goal of being killed gloriously in the last battle of the last war, but he'd never envisioned such a fate for himself. The Yanks had two submachine guns pointed at them. If he hadn't had Bob's arm on his shoulder, Nate was sure that he could get his gun out, but the overall situation was hopeless. They could try to surrender, but the Red Army in Kuybyshev—especially at this stage of the war—had no incentive for taking prisoners.

The two sides stared at one another for what seemed like several minutes. Finally, two of the officers started to argue with one another.

"Whaddya 'spose we oughta do?" Rotelli asked.

"Whatever they *tell us* to do," Nate replied.

"Are we going to be shot?" Cuthbert asked. He was wishing that the State Department had given him a bit more language training so that he could figure out what the Russians were arguing about.

Finally, the argument between the two officers was resolved. The prevailing man gestured for them to walk up one of the narrow alleys that led from the fork.

"Are they going to shoot us?" Cuthbert asked again.

"Stop asking that," Nate insisted. "The longer we go without being shot, the better, but I don't know what the hell they're gonna do with us."

With Bob obviously wincing in great agony, they were ushered through a nondescript exterior door and into a small room, where one of the officers lifted a trap door. They peered down a long shaft with a metal ladder bolted to one side.

"There's no way that I'm gonna be able to climb down *there,*" Bob said, with a panicked look on his face.

Nate and Johnny carefully lowered the wounded man to the floor and Nate made it clear by pointing at the injury and the trap door, that taking Bob into this hole was impossible.

The two Red officers who had argued before argued again. At last, a decision was reached and it was indicated that Nate was to go with two of the Red officers into the hole, while everyone else remained in the room.

"What do they want?" Rotelli asked.

"How the hell do I know . . . you know about as much Russian as I do. But, in case you haven't noticed . . . you and I still have our sidearms."

"That's weird."

It was true. Even though they seemed to have been taken prisoner, they hadn't been disarmed. It would have been extremely difficult and probably fatal to have attempted an escape, but for them not to have been disarmed was, as Rotelli's said, "weird."

"Don't try anything 'til I get back," Nate said, as he started down the ladder.

"*If* you get back," Rotelli replied.

The ladder led to a low, poorly lit tunnel that Nate guessed must be part of a network of bomb shelters that had been built when the city was being constructed. Most of the Russians were able to walk without stooping, but Nate had to lean down to move through the tunnel. Several times he hit his helmet on a bolt or some such thing that was protruding from the ceiling.

It was warmer down here than it had been outside, but damp and musty. The odor reminded Nate of a locker room after football practice.

Finally, they reached a wider area, where Nate was led through a door into a room where a group of people in Red Army uniforms seemed to be waiting for them.

A heavy-set woman with an exhausted-looking face and captain's shoulder boards on her uniform stepped up to him and announced that she spoke English.

"Am I . . . are we . . . being taken prisoner?" Nate asked.

The woman looked confused.

"They not *explain?*" she asked.

"Nobody explained anything. My unit was captured . . ." Nate started to explain.

"No," the woman interrupted. "You are not captured. Other way around. These men were ordered to find Americans for *him* to surrender to."

"Him?" Now it was Nate's turn to be confused.

She abruptly took Nate through another door into another room.

As the heavy metal door closed, Nate found that he and the woman were in a large room that smelled of stale cigarette smoke. It was lit only by a desk lamp perched on a large metal desk, behind which sat a man with a sad, hollow-cheeked face and the insignia of a marshal of the Soviet Union. Nate recognized Semyon Timoshenko from pictures that he'd seen in magazines.

The Marshal stood stiffly and scrutinized Nate for a moment. He said something to the woman and she explained that the Marshal wished to surrender. He had sent a patrol to find an officer for him to surrender to and they brought him a *non-com.*

"This will have to do," she said with a shrug.

The light made Timoshenko's face look strange and mask-like. Nate felt like he was in a movie as the officer saluted him. Officers don't salute non-coms, but apparently they do when they're ready to give up. If Rotelli could only see what was going on down here!

"Ask him whether he's surrendering the whole city?" Nate asked.

After a moment, the woman explained that Nate was being asked to accept the surrender of the entire Red Army, or what was left of it. Through his interpreter, Timoshenko explained that he felt that the war was over and to prolong things was a useless waste of lives.

"He wants not to be remembered by history like Hitler,"

she said. "No fighting and wasting lives in last stand for hopeless cause . . . turn city to ashes . . . spill more blood . . . for
nothing."

After he'd gotten over the initial shock of what was happening to him in this movie set of a place, Nate had the presence of mind to ask where Stalin was.

The woman answered that they had been out of touch with
Stalin for two days and that the bunker that he'd been using
took a direct hit from a thousand-pound bomb dropped by a
four-engine bomber. Then she insisted that Timoshenko had
"all authority" to surrender.

Documents were produced that had been carefully hand-
lettered in both Russian and English. Nate guessed from the
expression on her face that the captain had lettered them herself.

Nate took the chair that was offered and carefully read the
English side. It was amazingly simple and straightforward. It
directly paralleled what Timoshenko had just said. Timoshenko himself would sign for the Armed Forces of the Union
of Soviet Socialist Republics. He wanted to give up in accordance with the principles of the Geneva Convention. He
would surrender everything to "a Representative of the Allied
Armies."

Nate was it.

He asked the translator whether Timoshenko was in contact with all his forces and whether he could call for an immediate cease-fire as soon and Nate signed the papers. She
nodded that this was possible. He could make a broadcast that
would reach all the forces in and around Kuybyshev that were
still holding out. Thinking of Bob, Nate then asked whether
there was a vehicle available to take the Americans to Allied
lines immediately, so that the wounded man could get to an
aid station. Again, there was a nod to the affirmative.

Nate took a pen, and looked at the paper. Even though this
all seemed like a scene from a movie, he was starting to feel
the weight of the responsibility. He thought of the men. He
needed to act quickly for Bob's sake, but he recalled that there
was an Undersecretary of State upstairs.

"Just one more thing," Nate told the translator. "There's a

civilian upstairs who was with my outfit. I'd like to have him take a quick look at this. Could you have him sent down?"

When the Soviet soldier came up the ladder and gestured for him to come down into hole, Cuthbert panicked. He imagined a terrible dungeon where he'd be interrogated. He thought about what Patton had said about soldiers and their being trained for the ugliness of the battlefield. Cuthbert realized that, as a civilian diplomat, he'd never been trained to resist torture.

As he was led through the damp, smelly tunnel, Cuthbert remembered his comfortable office, his spacious Alexandria apartment, his draft deferment, and the comfortable life that he had led in Washington. He reflected on the hundreds of thousands of men of his generation who had fought hard and had been taken prisoner in these two world wars, and the savage hell they'd had to endure in prison camps.

Now it was his turn. What was in store? How would he survive?

Stephen Cuthbert could not believe his eyes. He had expected to be led into a torture chamber, but instead he was in a room where Sergeant McKinley was sitting at a desk drinking vodka with Marshal Semyon Timoshenko.

He had to be hallucinating.

"Since you're the diplomat, I'd like to have you take a look at this," Nate explained, handing him the paper. "Do you think it's legal?"

Cuthbert studied the paper, reading and rereading the simple paragraph and counting the words written in Russian to get some idea that it was the same text as on the English side.

"Yeah, it's legal," Cuthbert said, finally handing it back. "I guess the Marshal has the authority. If he wants to surrender, he has the right to do it."

"You're the diplomat," Nate said. "Do you think that it oughta be you who signs it?"

"No," Cuthbert said. "It says 'a Representative of the Allied Armies.' That's *you* . . . not me."

In that instant, Cuthbert was discovering that he had it in him to be diplomatic.

"*You* catch 'em, Sergeant." He smiled. "Then *we'll* cook 'em."

The Offices of *The Washington Herald*
Washington DC
Monday, December 3, 1945, 2:34 p.m.

"You know Stephen Cuthbert, dontcha, Rose?"

Rex Simmons's question was more of a statement than a question. There were few secrets in Washington.

"Yes, Rex, I *do* know Stephen Cuthbert."

"I thought you did," Simmons said with a wink, expecting Rosemary O'Leary to blush slightly, which she did not. "Good . . . right. When you get to Moscow, I want you to make arrangements with his office to get transportation to wherever Patton is. Cuthbert's the top State Department man in Moscow, until they get an ambassador over there. He's kind of a hero after the Timoshenko affair."

"I hear it *wasn't* him who actually accepted Timoshenko's surrender," Rosie reminded her boss.

"No, it wasn't," Simmons agreed. "It was actually that driver, that sergeant whom you interviewed for 'WHAT OUR FLAG SAYS.' He was the one, but Cuthbert was the senior State Department official at the scene."

She had been astounded when Fiona Wells phoned in the middle of the night Saturday to tell her, in so many words, that "The whole Red Army just surrendered to *your* boyfriend."

The news that Timoshenko had just surrendered the last remnants of the Red Army to *her* Sergeant McKinley had been incredible. Not only was the war over, but he had been there. It was only right, she thought. He wad witnessed the horrible beginning at Kummersdorf—and now, it had been him to whom Timoshenko had handed an old Imperial Army-issue cavalry saber. What had Timoshenko thought when he'd discovered this simple twist of fate?

The excitement of the end of the war had been overpowering. All day Sunday, as details poured into Washington, people had been flooding into the streets to celebrate. The bars were ordered closed at six o'clock that evening, but the enthusiasm was undampened. President Truman had declared Sunday as the "official" VS-Day, but many people insisted on continuing the festivities on Monday.

Already, VS-Day, which was supposed to stand for "Victory

over the Soviets," was being called "Victory over Stalin." The Man of Steel's body had not yet been found, but FBI forensics experts had been dispatched to sift through bombed-out bunkers. Prisoners were being carefully scrutinized.

A formal surrender had taken place Sunday evening in Kuybyshev. Patton had invited the representatives of the armies of Britain, Canada, Poland, and France to add their signatures, but he allowed his driver's to remain on the document—ahead of his own.

Rosie was in the newsroom before dawn on Monday when the wire photo of the document came through. It made the hairs on the back of her neck stand on end to recognize the same scrawled signature that she had on love letters carefully secreted in her dresser drawer. She had recognized his face in the wire photos of the ceremony, and she made sure that the accompanying article that ran in Monday's paper recognized him as well.

Now, she was on her way to Moscow—her second trip to Russia in less than two months, her third trip abroad in half a year. The little girl from Noe Valley was now the world traveler. There would be a lot to talk about around the Christmas dinner table this year.

"Remember, the main thing is to get a statement from Patton himself on his own political future," Simmons instructed. "Now that the Red Army has surrendered, that's the one thing that everybody wants to know. There are all sorts of rumors . . . but he won't talk to reporters."

"You think that I might be able to use my feminine charm on him?" Rosie laughed, slowly crossing her long, well-shaped legs in a deliberate parody of a movie starlet.

"I think that you might be able to use your usual dogged determination and your usual *common sense*," Rex Simmons replied with a disgusted shake of his head. "Not to mention your unfathomable good luck. You might also get something from this sergeant who always seems to be in the right place at the right time."

"I hope to." Rosie smiled. "I do hope to."

18

★ ★

Schloss Adler
Rupperswil, Switzerland
Friday, December 7, 1945, 10:23 a.m.

"THANK you for coming, Comrade Donovan," the short, solidly built man with a close-cropped mustache and small wire-rimmed glasses said as he glanced up from the comfortable chair in which he was sitting.

Outside the big window, it was snowing. Large delicate flakes were dusting the pines and turning the landscape overlooking the Zurichsee into a winter wonderland. A cheerful fire crackled in the old stone fireplace.

"I have a special toast today," Vyacheslav Mikhailovich Skriabin Molotov said, rising to shake hands with the stocky man with the ruddy complexion. "This is in honor and tribute to the fourth anniversary of the tragedy at Pearl Harbor . . . that your people turned into glorious victory."

"Your 'private stock' of vodka?" General William J. "Wild Bill" Donovan laughed as his host walked to the liquor cabinet in the corner of the room.

"Fuck the vodka," Molotov said emphatically. "This is eighteen-year-old single malt from the Highlands. My friend, Kim Philby, brought it last week when he visited from London. He said 'save for a special occasion.' *This* is a special occasion . . . wouldn't you say?"

"You've seen the reports," Donovan smiled. "The plan is coming together nicely."

"Yes . . . I have seen these reports," the former Foreign Commissar of the Soviet Union said as he poured the precious amber liquid. "As I recall . . . you take your whiskey straight up?"

"Yes, comrade, that's just fine."

"May I toast you . . . and the brave workers of America?"

"Cheers," Donovan said. "Here's to no more Pearl Harbors."

Molotov slugged his whiskey down and poured another, as Donovan merely sipped his drink.

"You're not drinking with me, comrade," Molotov chuckled.

"I'm sipping," Donovan said. "At home, we call single malt *sipping* whiskey. Here's to the postwar world."

"A world free of fascists."

"Dr. Vojoknia, would you care to have a drink with us?" Molotov said, shouting in the direction of the main part of the house.

A large, jolly-looking woman with short, blonde hair appeared at the door.

"You know Dr. Vojoknia, don't you?" Molotov smiled as he poured the woman a glass of scotch and added two ice cubes. "She's been with me for many years."

"Yes," Donovan nodded, shaking the woman's hand. "We've met. Doctor, we were just toasting the postwar world."

"A world free of fascists," Molotov insisted.

"To a postwar world free of fascists and totalitarians of every stripe," the doctor smiled, raising her glass.

They clicked their glasses and Molotov downed another finger of malted magic.

"You'd better get your coat, comrade," Donovan said as Molotov was pouring another drink. "It's time to leave."

"Leave?" Molotov said with a confused expression. "I'm not going anywhere. My masseuse is driving up from Zurich this afternoon . . ."

"You'll just have to disappoint her," Donovan smiled. "Maybe Dr. Vojoknia can convey your regrets?"

"Regrets? I don't understand."

"You and I have an appointment in Wiesbaden," Donovan said, standing up.

"What . . . appointment?" Molotov demanded. "What's this about? Is this some kind of a joke?"

"No joke," the American said. "Allied War Criminal Processing Center . . . I'm afraid that I'm going to have to place you under arrest, comrade."

"Arrest?" Molotov said, glancing nervously toward Dr. Lidiya Vojoknia, who just continued to smile. "We had a deal . . . . You can't do this. You *need* me."

"We did . . . now we don't."

"Fuck you . . . I have secrets that you need," Molotov insisted. "Without me, you can't . . ."

"You *did* . . . We *can*," Donovan asserted. "Remember the World War against the Nazis that the Red Army won single-handedly? There was that insignificant ally of yours that had a facility at a place called Bletchley Park?"

"The code-breaking machine?"

"Yes, comrade, the Colossus. It's the artificial brain that we've built at Bletchley Park. Actually, it's now the Colossus Mark *Two*. Much faster than that old clunker that broke the German Ultra Code. You and your people should have been using more imaginative codes these past few weeks. We had no idea that we'd be able to crack your organization so quickly."

"You're forgetting that I have an insurance policy," Molotov said smugly, jerking away from the Office of Strategic Services chief, who had reached for his arm.

"What's that?"

"You're forgetting the Atomic Bomb . . . you're not the *only* ones . . ."

"You're bluffing," Donovan said with a relaxed smile. "We know that when you sold out to us, you didn't cut Uncle Joe in on the deal. We know that *he* still has the Atomic Bomb team with *him* . . . and *you* don't."

"How . . . ?"

"We broke your codes. We know everything."

"You can't take me out of Switzerland," Molotov insisted, backing away from the American. "Swiss sovereignty. I'm a Swiss resident. You can't arrest me here . . . it's kidnapping!"

"What's a little kidnapping among friends?" Donovan laughed. "Your NKVD dragged ten million people out of their homes in the dead of night . . . surely you're no stranger to a little bit of kidnapping?"

"But you can't do it *here!*" Molotov insisted in a quavering voice. "You can't just drag Vyacheslav Mikhailovich Skriabin Molotov out of his home like he was some politically incorrect diversionist."

"We aren't," Donovan replied simply. "Dr. Vojoknia, would you ask Comrade Molotov to come here for a moment, please."

"What's this all about?" Molotov asked nervously as Lidiya Vojoknia reappeared in the doorway, accompanied by a short, solidly built man with a close-cropped mustache and small wire-rimmed glasses.

Molotov stared at him incredulously. It was like looking into a mirror. The man was apparently about ten years younger, but aside from that, they could have been identical twins.

"Comrade Molotov, would you care for a cocktail?" Donovan asked the short, solidly built man with the close-cropped mustache and small wire-rimmed glasses. The man who could have been a twin just shook his head, and he and Lidiya Vojoknia smiled quietly as Donovan put his hand on Molotov's shoulder.

When Molotov had been bundled into a waiting Mercedes, Donovan paused for a moment. The snow had stopped and a shaft of sunlight was shining down onto the lake. The snow-capped mountains were visible in the distance and the landscape looked so peaceful under a soft blanket of newly fallen snow. It was turning out to be a very beautiful day for a drive.

Glancing up at the smiling man with the close-cropped mustache and small wire-rimmed glasses who was standing at the top of the stairs, Donovan said with a wave, "Have a nice massage, comrade."

Eighth Army Command Post
60 miles southwest of Kuybyshev, Russia
Friday, December 7, 1945, 12:34 p.m.

"I see that you're wearing that same scarf . . . the one that you bought in Rostov," Nate McKinley observed when he had a moment alone to speak with the young reporter from *The Washington Herald*.

Just two hours ago, a small gaggle of reporters had flown in from Moscow to visit the Eighth Army command post. When Nate recognized the small, familiar, *glorious* face smiling at him from the collar of a heavy fur coat, he felt as though he'd been struck by lightning again.

It was an exhilarating moment for both the journalist and the sergeant. Though they would both have preferred to be back in the room at Rostov where their passion had been first consummated, the opportunity to have their boots crunching in the same patch of dry, crusty snow brought a shared gladness that was far better than any third choice of a place to be.

"It's my *lucky* scarf," Rosemary O'Leary said with a wink. "The first time I wore it . . . I had some especially good luck."

"I thought that was *me* who had the good luck that time," Nate said with a grin.

"Yes, you as well, I suppose," Rosie admitted with a coy smile.

"Maybe it'll bring you some good luck today," Nate added.

"Well, certainly on the *professional* side, my getting an invitation to tag along on this patrol that General Patton is leading was a stroke of genuine good fortune."

She had just talked her way into being allowed to accompany the Supreme Allied Commander as he conducted a field reconnaissance across the steppes south of the city that had served as the last capital of the Union of Soviet Socialist Republics.

"I think that it was an equal measure of you bullying poor Tim Cunningham," Nate said, recalling how she'd refused to take no for an answer from the SHAEF press officer. "But the General *does* like to show off after a battle."

"After a *war*," Rosie corrected. "After Kuybyshev, it's over."

"They still haven't found Joe Stalin yet," Nate cautioned.

Their conversation explored the rumors of Stalin's whereabouts and turned to reflections on what two young Americans had seen of this distant part of the world.

"You know what I regret most about my work out here over the past couple of months?" she asked rhetorically—wanting to add that her biggest regret at the moment was not having Nate alone in a yurt for an hour.

"What's that?"

"That I didn't bring a camera with me out here," she said. "There's just so much that I wish I'd taken pictures of."

"It's kinda late . . . but better late than never," Nate said. "You're welcome to borrow my Leica . . . I've got it in the tent. It's even got a roll of film in it. I promised it to my kid brother . . . said I'd bring him a souvenir. But you're welcome to use it in the meantime."

"The *famous* Leica . . . the one you used for the Kummersdorf pictures?" Rosie gasped anxiously. "I couldn't . . . really."

"Why not? I'd sure rather have you getting some use out of it instead of it laying in the bottom of my duffel bag."

"Thanks . . . I appreciate this very much," Rosie said gratefully, adding with a wink, "Maybe I can also get a picture of Patton's driver while we're out on this patrol . . . something for *my* wallet."

The "patrol" that Patton was leading was more just an excuse to get out of camp. He was bored with inaction, and he wanted simply wanted to go for a drive. The talk around the map table in the big green command tent was no longer of tactics or maneuver, of coming battles or outsmarting a wiley foe. It was talk of demobilization and dismantlement—and this depressed the warrior in Patton in December as it had it May.

The General wanted a diversion. He wanted to get out to have a look at the lay of the land through which Ghengis Khan had led his Golden Horde in the thirteenth century—and where Ivan the Terrible had butchered the Khan's Tatar descendants two centuries later.

As he drove the Willys across the sprawling, open country, Nate was struck by how little in the landscape that there was to see. Elsewhere, when the General had deviated onto one of his historical discourses, there had been a castle, or the ruins of a fortification, or even a terrain feature to look at. Out here, there was nothing. In Western Russia and Byelorussia, The land reminded him of North Dakota. Out here, it looked more like the North Atlantic Ocean had appeared from the deck of the troopship last December—not flat like a pane of glass, but hypnotically undulating.

At least he had Patton in his jeep. On long, otherwise uneventful drives, the General was always interesting company. Colonel Maxwell of 125th Infantry Division, who was in the second jeep today, was not so lucky. Because of the cold weather, the jeeps were enclosed, and the people in them couldn't carry on a conversation between vehicles as they often did when traveling in open jeeps.

Rosie had climbed into the back seat of Patton's jeep next to Sergeant Cooke, the radioman. She was carrying on the bulk of the day's dialogue with Patton.

The catalyst for the conversation had been the fact of the day being the fourth anniversary of Pearl Harbor. Patton, as usual, had plenty to say, and Rosie was frantically scribbling in her notebook. As often happened with Patton, though, talk turned to the military history of the region through which they were driving.

"No foreign invader has ever reached this point from the West in the past thousand years," Patton explained, being the only one in the jeep who found this great void interesting.

"Guderian's Second Panzer Army got close, though," Patton continued. "They'd crossed the Don and were out here south-west of Moscow. His tanks would have outflanked Moscow if it hadn't been for the weather. General Winter sure as hell inter-vened. That was was also four years ago . . . the same weekend that the Japs bombed Pearl Harbor. If Guderian had had weather conditions like *today*, we'd be fighting the Krauts right now and not the Russians. This would be perfect for armor. Ground frozen solid, no mud, good visibility."

"General Winter seems to have cut you a bit more slack," Rosie remarked.

"But he's a crafty old bastard." Patton nodded. "He played Napoleon and Hitler the same way . . . he let them *see* Moscow, and then he went for the jugular. He suckered them and did his worst damage while they were in retreat."

"Why is it that General Winter seems to favor the Rus-sians?" Rosie asked, knowing that Patton would understand the allegorical dimension of her reference.

"They understand him," Patton said. "They've lived with him. They know him. They respect him. You can't underesti-mate him. We've been damned lucky . . . so far."

Nate looked around. The General was right. It dipped well below zero at night, but there had been very little snow so far this winter. There were snowbanks where the drifts had been, but for the most part, he was driving on bare ground. It was cold, too cold to be outside without gloves, but not so cold that the vehicles wouldn't run.

"General, you seem to have an immense depth of knowledge

of this place," Rosie said, buttering up her quarry before slipping in the knife. "Do you think you'll be tapped for another military governorship out here when this is over . . . like you did in Bavaria?"

Nate winced. He'd told his little goddess how to bait the warlord and now she was doing it.

"I sure as hell hope not," Patton said emphatically. "I sure didn't know what I was letting myself in for when I let them put me into that job in Bavaria. You're a goddam politician in a job like that. I'm *not* a goddam politician. If I had any doubts, *that* experience sure as hell disabused me of doubt. A soldier should lead soldiers on a field of combat . . . not hire and fire goddam dogcatchers.

"I don't know what to say about those dimwits back home that think I want to take over the government," Patton continued. "I have no stomach for that crap. It's like a joke. Haven't these jokers read history? Don't they know what happened when Julius Caesar did this . . . when Napoleon did it? 'Et tu Brute?' I wouldn't trade places with a Caesar if you *paid* me. He should've stayed where he belonged. As I said to the troops before Normandy . . . and again when we took Berlin . . . I have my job because I have the confidence of the President of the United States. I desire his *confidence,* but I do *not* desire his *job.* I wouldn't mind George Marshall's job when he's ready to hang up his spurs, but I sure as hell do *not* covet Harry Truman's."

Patton paused for a moment, as though waiting for his emphasis to resonate.

"Truman's got that little sign that says 'The Buck Stops Here' on his desk," Patton continued. "Everybody can pass the buck to him. I sure as hell wouldn't want all those bucks passed to *me* . . . and, Miss O'Leary, you can damned well quote me on that!"

Nate glanced in the rearview mirror at Rosie taking notes in the back seat. He could tell by the satisfied expression on her face that she'd gotten what she wanted. Her story was probably already half written.

As the afternoon had worn on, it had started to get colder. The occasional snowflakes in the air were now more than occasional.

It was Nate who sounded the alarm.

"Looks like we're getting a bit of a snow squall here," he observed. "I suggest that we call it a day and head back."

The second jeep followed Nate as he made a broad U-turn and started back toward the Eighth Army command post. He picked a more direct route, hoping to get back in less than the three hours they'd been driving. Sergeant Cooke contacted Eighth Army, explained the situation, and was told that it was snowing back there as well.

"It's General Winter," Patton laughed. "The sonuvabitch heard me coming."

Within twenty minutes, the snow was falling heavily. Visibility had been reduced to twenty or thirty yards, and the wind had started to blow.

"We've got us a blizzard," Nate explained matter-of-factly.

"I would have guessed as much," Rosie said, trying not to betray any of the sense of the nervousness that she was feeling.

Nate stopped the jeep and stepped out. The other jeep followed suit. Colonel Maxwell got out and came forward.

"Why are you stopping?" he asked.

"Can't see where we're going through the windshield," Nate explained, glancing at the compass that he carried in his pocket. "I need to take a look around . . . get my bearings."

For a moment, the snowfall slackened, and they could glimpse the dramatically transformed landscape around them. If it had not been for the temperature—which hovered around zero degrees—the scene could well have been that of the middle of a desert. The layer of wind-blown snow had turned the gently rolling hills into what looked like sand dunes.

"We could knock on the neighbor's door and ask to come in to get warmed up," Rosie said, staring into the distance.

"What?" Patton asked.

"Look," she said, pointing to a ridge about a half-mile away.

They waited for a moment for the blowing snow to let up slightly, and they too saw what she'd glimpsed. In the distance, a long, low building could barely be seen hugging the ridgeline—like a cat waiting to pounce.

"Do you suppose anybody's home up there?" Maxwell asked.

"If there is, its the Reds," Patton said. "There're still a few units that haven't been rounded up yet. Can't be Vlasov's people. They aren't this far south yet."

"It looks deserted," Nate said, studying the building through his binoculars. "What do you suppose it is?"

"I can't really tell," Patton said, training his own field glasses on the structure. "It's too big and well built for a farmhouse . . . but it has several windows, so it's probably not an ammo storage bunker or a fort."

"It's strange that a building like that is so far out here away from everything else," Maxwell observed. "And it doesn't have any kind of fence around it."

"It's almost certainly abandoned," Patton said. "And Miss O'Leary's right. It *would* be a good place for us to wait until it stops snowing. Radio Eighth Army and tell 'em what we're doing."

"It must have been important," Maxwell theorized. "There's no sign of power poles or overhead lines, so they must have gone to the trouble of running their electricity out here underground."

"Or they blew down or fell down and nobody bothered to replace 'em," Patton said.

Rosie shivered, as much from the excitement of their finding something unknown but important as from the freezing cold.

"You all right, Miss O'Leary?" Patton grinned. "It isn't getting too cold for you out here, is it?"

"Not in the least," she lied. "I'm just fine."

Aside from Nate, who was used to cold weather from his years in Montana, and Patton, who seemed generally impervious to ambient temperature extremes, everyone in the small group was chilled to the bone.

"I think that we're just wasting a helluva lot of our time talking," Patton said enthusiastically. "Let's get on up there and look it over. How deep to you suppose the snow is down there in that gully?"

"It's hard to tell from here," Nate replied. "I think that we should circle left . . . or right . . . and not go through the deep part. I can see some grass sticking through the snow over there, so it's probably not so deep. Either way, it dips down. Most of the last hundred yards, you're below the angle of sight from the building. That means, if anybody's there, we could get really close before they could see us."

"If there is, we'd better be ready for a fight," Patton said with a certain amount of enthusiasm for the notion of being on the threshold of an unexpected battle. "Just in case."

Following Nate's plan, Patton ordered Maxwell to circle right, and Nate to go left. They'd leave the jeeps in the shallow places out of sight of the building, and approach on foot.

"We should probably get going," Nate urged. "It's snowing just enough to keep us hard to see from up there. If it lets up any, they'll have a better chance of spotting us . . . but if it starts coming down harder . . . we could have a whiteout, and we wouldn't even see our hands in front of our faces."

Rosie smiled, but she was suddenly starting to get very frightened. The idea of being blind, lost, and cold was not particularly appealing, but the thought of freezing to death while blind and lost was fearsome.

"At least, with the wind blowing out of the east as strong as it is, they can't have heard our jeep motors . . . yet," he smiled.

When they reached a point about a football field's length from the building, Nate stopped the jeep.

"Let's walk from here," he said.

As Patton dutifully stepped out of the jeep, Rosie thought it somewhat amusing that—even with a five-star general present—it was Nate who now seemed to be in charge.

She said a quick prayer, begging God for a warm fire, but also, at the same time, thanking the Blessed Mother and her Son for a man like Nate McKinley, who seemed to know exactly what to do.

"Miss O'Leary, I think it would probably be best for you to wait here until . . ." Patton started to say, a chivalrous tone in his voice.

"No, General," she replied. "With all due respect, I have a job to do out here . . . and that job is to report on whatever happens up there. Besides . . . you boys might decide that it's too nice and warm by the big, blazing fire to bother and come back to escort the lady up the hill."

Nate froze. Not from the cold, but from the sight of the first person he'd ever seen defy one of General George Patton's orders.

"Dammit, young lady," Patton laughed. "You have more balls . . . pardon the expression . . . than a lot of men I've met in this war."

Nate looked at his little Celtic goddess, standing there with wisps of that hair the color of fine rosewood blowing across her face, with snowflakes landing amid the freckles on her cheeks. She was at least a head shorter than everyone else, but her presence dominated the scene. Her eyes were, of course, the most beautiful ever created, but this afternoon, they were firm and defiant. If she was afraid, there was no sense of fear in her eyes. Patton could clearly see that, too. Nate could tell that the General admired the plucky little redhead in the fur coat.

They made their way slowly up the ridge, the three men walking abreast twenty yards apart, Nate on the right, Patton on the left, and Cooke in the middle with the Thompson sub-machine gun. Rosie followed Cooke, staying about twenty yards behind. When they were forty yards from the building, the air started to clear. There was still a low overcast, but the snow had practically stopped falling. They were on the building's blind side. There were no windows visible, just a long wall with an arched doorway near the center.

With the improved visibility, Nate could see someone from Maxwell's patrol in the distance on the far side of the building. He waved slightly and Nate returned the greeting.

Nate glanced at Patton, who gestured to Nate to tell the men on the other side to wait, while they approached the blind wall. Patton then turned back toward Rosie and gave her a gesture that said, "Don't come any farther and don't argue."

Rosie didn't. She just crouched down in a position where she could see what was going on, but where she would present as small a target as possible if the shooting started. As she was squirming to get situated, something jabbed her in the side. It was Nate's Leica.

She reached under her coat and took out the camera. It still had most of a roll of film in it.

Why not?

As the snow had stopped, it had become quite a bit lighter, so she rotated the aperture to f8 and set the speed at 250. Her heart was pounding as she squinted through the viewfinder and tried to steady the camera. She thought about Nate, and about that horrible morning at Kummersdorf—and what he had seen through this same round glass.

Rosie focused on Nate, crouching, but moving slowly forward. She focused on Cooke, training his Thompson on the arched doorway as he inched closer to the building. Patton had shed his overcoat, apparently so as not to have it interfere with his ability to use his arm to aim his guns.

For the past three years, as Rosie had become aware of General George Smith Patton as a public figure and had watched his public image grow into a public myth, one of the more colorful aspects of this mythic hero had been the pair of ivory-handled revolvers that he always carried. "Just for show," people had said.

Rosie held her breath and squeezed off a photograph of Patton advancing toward the building, one of the pistols held high. To her relief, none of the men heard the *clunk* of the shutter.

It was a pretty damned strange sight, Nate thought to himself. For all of the months that he'd been in combat, he had almost never seen an officer above the rank of captain in an actual firefight. When enlisted men got together, they always groused about the officers' knack for avoiding any real fighting.

Today, thanks to a devious trick played by General Winter, here was a general—and not just *any* general—poised for a fight.

They had closed in to about fifteen yards, when, suddenly, the door in the archway burst open. In a split second, five armed men were out the door. It occurred to him that the men had probably seen Maxwell's party on the other side and had decided to slip out the back door to outflank them. Foolishly, the Russians hadn't bothered to look to see whether *they* had been outflanked.

Nate squeezed the trigger of his .45 and watched a man go down. Patton got another one, and the fusillade from Cooke's Thompson chewed its way through the others.

The radioman was sprinting toward the doorway now. There was blood all over the snow. Pools of bright, red blood.

In the distance, Nate could hear the pop of small-arms fire and the deep, dull bass thunder of automatic weapons.

There is something about the daylight on cold winter afternoons—when the sun is buried behind impenetrable layers of overcast—that drains the color away, rendering everything in either black or white.

Today was such a day. Everything had turned black and white. Everything, that is, except the pools of sticky blood that lay congealing on the frozen ground.

Rosie had watched in horror as the Russians bolted from the door. It happened faster than she could have imagined. The noise of the gunfire was deafening. The sight of the blood was almost unreal.

Then there was another Russian, up on the parapet above the roof line, like a black raven on a wire.

He was a big man, with his epaulets defining the squareness of his massive shoulders.

His eyes on the prism within the Leica were eerily cold and brooding—just as they had been in those oversize lithographs of the Man of Steel that she remembered from that night on the *Smolnie*.

His broad, full mustache, flecked with grey, looked so vivid and real—and close—as she watched him in the viewfinder.

Josef Vissarionovich Dzhugashvili Stalin, Supreme Commander-in-Chief and Marshal of the Soviet Union, had ruled a land so vast that it spanned a dozen time zones. The boy from Georgia whom nobody liked or trusted, had once longed for the love he'd never known. But for as long as he could consciously remember, he hadn't cared about being loved.

The demons screamed within his head. He wanted only to be feared. The boy whom nobody loved had molded himself into the Man of Steel whom *everyone feared*—and *no one loved*.

The Man of Steel killed his enemies and he killed his friends. He killed each and every one with equal ruthlessness. He had inherited a sprawling and unmanageable empire from a naive and inbred family and had turned it into a police state the likes of which the world had never seen. He inherited an improbable revolution from a naive and inbred gang of anarchists and had turned it into a global subterfuge that shook the nations of the world. Yet still the demons within him screamed.

Rosie screamed. "Above you!"

Nobody had seemed to see the raven.

"Above you!" Rosie screamed again.

Nate had seen. Nate had heard.

Nate had drawn a bead on that huge, square head with the dark and drooping eyes and the drooping mustache. He squeezed the trigger and felt the hollow click of an empty chamber. Nate would not be able to reload fast enough to get off the next shot.

But it was not Nate who was in the sights of the Webley .38 in the hand of the Man of Steel.

It had come to the showdown between the Man of Steel and his ultimate foe, the Napoleon of the age, whose dogged determination had outflanked the Man of Steel and who had destroyed his dreams.

Just as George Smith Patton, Sr. had died a hero's death at Fredericksburg, George Smith Patton, Jr. had wished that he too would die in battle, struck down, as he had liked to say, "By the last bullet of the last battle of the last war."

Patton's cold, blue-grey eyes caught Nate's and he knew immediately what was happening.

Two of the most powerful men in the world were now face to face.

It happened in the twinkling of a blue-grey eye. The hand was steady, the arm was strong. The finger was the same finger that had squeezed the trigger in the Pentathlon of the 1912 Stockholm Olympiad. The finger was the finger that had squeezed the trigger that made a man into a myth at Naltxik in 1945.

The *same* finger was on the *same* trigger of the *same* ivory-handled Colt Model 1873 .45 caliber revolver that had won that dual with General Julio Cardenas—the butcher of Columbus, New Mexico—on that hot and dusty May day in 1916.

The Man of Steel pulled the trigger of the Webley and felt it buck in his hand.

At the same time, he felt the sudden pain as a fist of lead chased the leather-winged demons through his brain.

At last, there was quiet.

The demons were mute, their screams replaced by a vast, eerie, peaceful quiet.

EPILOGUE

★ ★

The White House
Washington DC
Wednesday, December 12, 1945, 11:57 p.m.

"THE buck has stopped," Harry Truman said. "The buck finally stopped . . . right *here*."

The President pointed to a copy of the December 10 issue of *LIFE* magazine.

"Those pictures say it all," Henry Stimson agreed. There were nods all around the room as the great men looked at the photograph taken by the young woman from San Francisco with an old Leica traded for a candy bar.

General George Patton was frozen in time, standing as though at attention, his signature riding boots placed two feet apart. He was looking up, his extended arm holding a pistol. Above him, a hulking, clearly recognizable figure had just started to tip forward, an angry but horrified expression on his face. His hand had just lost its grip on a revolver, which was clearly silhouetted against the whiteness of the sky.

Though few people in the world beyond the President's office would ever know it, there was further reason for celebration in the picture. It had been discovered that the roof from which the Man of Steel was falling covered an immense, mainly subterranean research center—the Soviet Union's supersecret atomic weapons research center.

The young woman from San Francisco who'd changed America's image of itself with the words of a Fourth of July feature article had taken a picture worth a hundred thousand words that summarized the end of World War III in such a way that no words were necessary.

Rodinya Hotel
Moscow, Russia
Friday, December 21, 1945, 8:41 a.m.

"Why aren't you driving the General this morning?" Rosemary O'Leary asked.

"Oh, he's gone out to do some pheasant shooting with
General Gay this morning," Nate McKinley replied. "They're
meeting some of the Russians out at somebody's dacha south
of here. I get to spend the day making sure that everything's
packed up for his flight out tomorrow. He's going home for
Christmas . . . maybe for good."

"Going home to a hero's welcome," Rosie observed.

"Yep," Nate confirmed. "A ticker-tape parade up Broadway on Christmas Eve."

"And you're going, too?"

"Somebody's got to drive that old jeep up Broadway." Nate
grinned.

"That'll be an experience to remember," Rosie added.

An air of sadness had fallen over the pair as they stared
into one another's eyes in the lobby of the bustling hotel that
served as the billets for the Allied command staff—as well as
the burgeoning Western press corps. They had been thrust together briefly—all *too* briefly—and they both craved the
other's company. However, they both knew that such longing
was in vain.

Nate's duty with the General, and his time before he could
get a discharge, would last for months. Rosie knew that the
Air Transport Command plane leaving that morning was her
last chance for a ride to Washington that would connect with a
flight that would get her to San Francisco for her first Christmas at home since before the war. They hoped that they'd
cross paths again in America—they *longed* for it.

For the moment, though, they were together. They stood
awkwardly, oblivious to the crowds of people, mainly Americans.

They didn't even notice the man in the blue plaid jacket
who was watching them from the corner of the room.

"Well, I guess this is goodbye," Rosie said awkwardly, nodding to the truck parked at the curb beyond the big, heavily

smudged glass doors of the Rodinya's main entrance. "That's my ride to the airport out there . . . I see the other folks already getting aboard."

"Well, I'd rather say 'see you later' than 'goodbye,' " Nate said, squeezing her hands.

"Oh God . . . how I hope you will," she said, feeling tears welling up in the backs of her eyes. "I love you . . . so much."

"Me too," Nate said, the full depth of meaning obvious in his exaggerated understatement.

"The General will be having a parade in Washington and he'll need a driver . . . and I'll finally be getting my discharge in a couple of months."

"What are your plans then?" Rosie asked.

"Well," he winked, "I got that telegram from that oil man down in Texas that offered me a couple grand for the camera that took the Kummersdorf pictures . . . as well as the Stalin pictures. He thinks it's going to be a collector's item. A fellow can do quite a lot with a couple grand."

"I thought you promised the camera to your kid brother?"

"I can buy him a better one," Nate smiled.

As he hugged her again, someone across the crowded room shouted, "Hey O'Leary, make it snappy, the truck's ready to leave!"

Rosie lingered a moment, kissing him as passionately as she dared in the room crowded with people. At last she stepped away, wiped her eyes and said, "Well . . . goodbye . . . for now . . . I mean . . . see you later . . ."

"Have a safe trip," he said. "I'll see you . . ."

"Oh . . . wait," she gasped. "I almost forgot to give you these."

She dug into her purse and pulled out a rumpled, well-worn envelope with a San Francisco postmark addressed to her. She handed it to him, blew a kiss, turned and ran for the door.

Nate watched the truck pull away and disappear out of sight before he looked at envelope.

He folded it open. Out dropped a pair of cardboard rectangles—two season tickets for the 1946 San Francisco Seals baseball team.

On the road south of Moscow
20 miles southeast of Orekhovo-Borisovo, Russia
Friday, December 21, 1945, 11:34 a.m.

"Hap, I'm damned glad that we're getting the hell out of
this country tomorrow," General George Smith Patton, Jr. said
as he looked out the window at an ox cart moving ponderously
in the opposite direction.

"Why?" General Hobart R. Gay asked. "I think we've
found the Russians a lot more hospitable than the Krauts were
after we beat *them*."

"It's not that," Patton replied. "It's that I can see nothing
but trouble here in this place . . . and *none* of it's *our* kinda
trouble. Russia's gonna have convulsions that you can't imagine when all these people break off and want to start their own
countries."

"You're predicting a civil war, then?" Gay asked.

"A *dozen* civil wars," Patton said with a shake of his head.
"The Armenians hate the Azerbaijanis who hate the Georgians. Everybody hates the Russians except the *White* Russians. It's not our fight anymore. It's time for the soldiers to go
home and time for the politicians to try to put this place back
together. I don't want any part of what we had to endure down
there in Bavaria after the last war. This has been a *damned fine
war,* and I'm damned glad that we're leaving the aftermath to
the politicians."

It was a cold, clear morning. The temperature was still below zero, but the sky was blue and absolutely devoid of
clouds—a perfect day for hunting.

The Supreme Commander and his Chief of Staff were
traveling in the spacious back seat of a 1939 Model 75 Cadillac limousine that Patton had used occasionally in Bavaria
during the brief interlude between VE-Day and World War III.
A SHAEF motor pool driver was at the wheel, and a SHAEF
motor pool jeep followed with the shotguns that he and Gay
would be using for the day's outing with General Boyarski
and General Trukhin.

The driver slowed as they passed a huge supply dump. The
road was becoming heavily congested with trucks coming and
going, hauling away everything that wasn't being turned over

to General Vlasov's army. In among the mountains of supplies that had not been necessary for the assault on Moscow were dumps containing the detritus of the costly war.

"Look at all these vehicles," Patton said, leaning forward in his seat to point out a row of burned-out passenger cars and lend-lease Studebaker trucks. "I don't think I'll ever get used to the terrible waste of modern war. Do you suppose bastards like Hitler and Stalin who decide to start conquering the world ever stop to think what they're doing?"

Gay glanced where Patton was pointing, and the driver instinctively looked to see for himself.

When the driver looked back, he was no longer looking at the road, but at the broadside of a deuce-and-a-half with a Signal Corps insignia ahead of the white star on the door.

He slammed on the brakes and the Cadillac swerved.

It was too late. The limousine's radiator crunched into the front fender of the GMC, bringing the car from twenty-five miles an hour to zero instantly.

Inside the roomy back seat, Hap Gay felt himself flying forward. He had been sitting back in the seat, and was able to catch himself before he fell all the way.

His boss, however, had lost his balance. Gay watched helplessly as Patton was thrown suddenly forward from his precarious perch on the leading edge of the seat.

There was a terrible *crack* as the Supreme Commander's body smashed into the partition between the rear compartment and the front seat.

Patton looked back at Gay and started to speak:

"This is a helluva way to . . ."

ABOUT THE AUTHOR

Bill Yenne is the San Francisco-based author of more than three dozen nonfiction books, primarily on historical topics. This is his second novel. Among his nonfiction works are *Secret Weapons of World War II; Aces: True Stories of Victory and Valor in the Skies of World War II;* and *SAC: A Primer of Modern Strategic Air Power.* Of the latter, Major Michael Perini wrote in *Air Force Magazine,* "This book deserves a place in the stacks of serious military libraries." Mr. Yenne was also a contributor and aviation consultant to *The Simon & Schuster D-Day Encyclopedia,* and he worked with the legendary US Air Force commander, General Curtis LeMay, to produce *Superfortress: The B-29 and American Airpower in World War II,* which *Publisher's Weekly* described as "an eloquent tribute."

In 1945, Mr. Yenne's mother happened to be present for General George Patton's funeral in Heidelberg, Germany.

True stories of victory and valor
in the skies over World War II by

William Yenne

ACES

0-425-17699-1

During World War II, tens of thousands of
aircraft engaged in deadly dogfights across the
globe, and hundreds of pilots became "aces"
after claiming five or more enemy planes.
These are their stories.

Also available:

THE SECRET WEAPONS OF
WORLD WAR II

0-425-18992-9

Available wherever books are sold or at
www.penguin.com